A MOTHER'S SHAME

ROSIE CLARKE

B

First published in Great Britain in 2022 by Boldwood Books Ltd.

Copyright © Rosie Clarke, 2022

Cover Design by Colin Thomas

Cover Photography: Colin Thomas

A CIP catalogue record for this book is available from the British Library.

Paperback ISBN 978-1-80162-165-6

Large Print ISBN 978-1-80162-164-9

Hardback ISBN 978-1-80162-163-2

Ebook ISBN 978-1-80162-166-3

Kindle ISBN 978-1-80162-167-0

Audio CD ISBN 978-1-80162-158-8

MP3 CD ISBN 978-1-80162-159-5

Digital audio download ISBN 978-1-80162-161-8

Boldwood Books Ltd
23 Bowerdean Street
London SW6 3TN
www.boldwoodbooks.com

PROLOGUE

The moon shone full on the water, mysterious and compelling, drawing me to the side of the bridge. I peered over the edge at the golden pool that seemed to mesmerise me, cutting through the apathy and the muted haze of grief clogging my mind. By day the river appeared brown, sluggish, polluted by oil from the ships in the docks, and by the debris that swirled relentlessly in little circles—on and on, always present, like the ache that gnawed at my heart. Tonight, there was a golden glow, warm and deep, tugging at my senses. I felt that if I could fall into the reflected moonlight, I would be able to let go of all the memories. There would be no pain, no feelings of regret. I could drift down into that shining pool and my body would dissolve, become part of the light I found so inviting.

It would be the best way to end it, this life that had no meaning, no joy. If I could cry the agony inside me might ease, but my tears had long since dried. Now there was only emptiness and the nagging ache that would not let me rest. I should end it instantly, fall into the moonlight and let the water take me. I could almost feel myself drifting in a warm haze, dissolving, and becoming a part of the light. I moved forward, intent on climbing the wrought iron structure of the railings so that I could take that final jump into oblivion.

'Now that's a foolish notion, lass. What do you want to do something like that for?'

I became aware of the man standing at my side. He wore the uniform of the Sally Army and he was trying to be kind, but he did not understand. Panic swept over me. He would stop me reaching that golden glow, force me to return to a world where the pain was too hard to bear. I tried frantically to scramble up the iron structure so that I could leap into the reflected moonlight, but his strong hands held me back. I screamed at him, desperate to escape, but he hung on despite my struggles.

'Leave me alone! It's the best thing. I want to be with them...'

'Nay, lass. You don't know what you're saying. Whatever is wrong, it can't be that bad. You're too young to die in that filthy river. Do you want to be eaten by rats?'

His words broke through the mists in my head. I stared at him, half dazed, hardly understanding. 'I wanted to drown in the moonlight, become part of the light.'

'Drowning isn't like going to sleep. You'll be swept down river by the tide and caught in the reeds. As your body decays the rats will come and tear at your flesh. When they fish you out of the water your face will be half gone, your eyes just empty sockets—'

'Stop!' How could he know that I had always feared rats? Suddenly I was sobbing; heavy, dry sobs that wracked my body but gave me no relief. 'You don't know... you don't know what I've done. I deserve to die...' I grabbed at him wildly, tugging at his coat as if somehow it was his fault for saving me. 'I should be dead.'

'Nay, lass, I doubt you deserve to die in the river.' He smiled at me; a gentle, sweet smile that wrenched at my heart because it reminded me of another person's smile. 'Why don't I take you to the café for a cup of tea and a bun? You can tell me all about it if you like.'

'Tell you?' My mind reeled as I tried to remember, the pictures misshapen and changing like the pieces in a kaleidoscope I had once won at a church fete. 'I wouldn't know where to begin.'

'Why not start at the beginning?'

His fingers gripped my arm firmly. I felt the pressure of his hand guiding me away from the river. I wanted to break free and run back to the moonlight. I did not want to tell my story. I wanted to let go, forget. I wanted the forgiveness of death...but already I was remembering. The pictures were crowding in on me, settling in my mind, making me remember the things I had tried so hard to forget.

'I suppose,' I said and the words were forced from me. I could not stop them tumbling out now that I had begun. 'I suppose it began that November night in 1925 when I was still young but not innocent. I doubt that I was ever truly that.'

1

'Bugger orf!' my mother's shrill voice cried. 'I've had enough, do yer hear me? I'm sick of yer comin' home stinkin' of the drink and...' Her words were halted abruptly by the sounds of furniture crashing and one piercing scream.

Standing at the top of the stairs, I listened to the wild sobbing that followed. There was nothing I could do. I knew what had happened below. In the morning Ma's face and arms would be covered in bruises.

Why did she put up with it? He was a bully and a drunkard and she should send him packing. She should have done it long ago. If a man treated me that way I would leave him—better still, I would kill him!

Pa was leaving the kitchen. The sound of his heavy tread sent trickles of ice down my spine and I scuttled back to the bedroom. If he were only half drunk, he would use his fists on me, but if he were maudlin, he would put his arms about me. The last time he'd caught me unawares, he had pawed at my breasts and tried to kiss and fondle me.

Quickly locking the bedroom door, I stood with my back to it, sickness rising in my throat as he rattled the door handle.

'Maggie...Maggie darlin, let yer pa in fer a minute.'

I held my breath, praying he would go away, but he continued to bang at the door. Hearing a whimper from the bed, I realised his noise had woken my brother.

'Hush love.' I put a finger to my lips. If Pa heard us talking, he would keep tugging at the door handle. Robin pulled back the bedcovers and I crept in beside my little brother. 'He'll go away in a minute.'

'Is he drunk again, Maggie? Don't let him come in, please!'

'He won't.' Robin's hair smelled clean and fresh. I had washed him myself before putting him to bed. Ma no longer bothered about things like that; she was too worn down by worry and grief. I was determined that Robin should not be neglected. He was never quite well and, at nearly eight years old, too thin and slight for his age, always coughing. 'I shan't let him hurt you.'

'Damn you, Maggie! Open this door, you slut!' Pa rattled the handle. 'You wait 'till I get hold of yer!'

The door shuddered as he put his shoulder to it, but the lock was stout and it held. After a few moments we heard his heavy footsteps moving on down the landing.

'I hate him,' Robin wept as I held him to me. 'I hate him...'

'So do I. Don't cry, Robin. Go back to sleep love. He will sleep it off and you'll be at school before he comes down in the morning.'

'Why don't Ma send him away?'

'I wish she would, but I'm not sure he would go. He knows where his bread's buttered. He would be on the streets if she turned him out.'

'I wish he would die.'

I held Robin's thin body against me, kissing the top of his head.

'Go to sleep, love. You've got a spelling test at school tomorrow, and I mustn't be late for work or I'll get the push.'

* * *

It was nearly six o'clock when I was allowed to leave my job at the bakery the following evening. When Mr Shirley finally got the lock on the door, he asked me to wash the shelves ready for the next morning.

'I know it isn't strictly your job,' he said. 'But the woman who cleans is going to be late in the morning and those shelves need a wash.'

It didn't matter how hard you tried to keep things clean, the dust and dirt blew in off the streets of London, and people would leave the door open as they gossiped on their way in or out.

It was already dark when I emerged into the chill of a late autumn evening that dark November day. Shivering, I walked through the narrow, grimy lanes of the London docklands. In the Queen Victoria public house, I heard someone playing what I knew was jazz on the piano. Sung with a broad cockney accent, it sounded like fun.

'Maggie! Maggie Bailey, wait up a minute!'

The young man who had called to me lived just two streets away from the terraced house where I'd been born sixteen years before. Duncan was nineteen and worked on the docks like Pa and most of the men round here.

'I can't stop. They kept me late tonight and Ma will be waiting.'

'I'm going your way. I've got to meet someone to talk about a job.'

He was tall and lanky, dark-haired with a gentle smile and soft eyes. His trousers were really wide in the fashion that people called Oxford Bags, which had come in a couple of years previously. They looked odd on him, but as he was wearing them for work, he had probably bought them second-hand, like most of us did in the lanes. It was 1925 and the country was still recovering from the terrible war that had killed thousands of men.

'I thought you worked on the docks?'

'That was only temporary. I'm going to train as a ship's carpenter.'

'You're going to be a sailor?'

'I want to build ships, Maggie. It is what I've always wanted, but there's no work round here and it means going away for a few years, but that is better than staying here and standing in line on the docks every day.'

'Where are you going? Tilbury?'

'They had no vacancies. I've got to go right away, to a place on the east coast called Yarmouth. It is a private boat builder and I'll be working on mostly fishing boats until I've got my papers but one day I'll have my own boatyard.'

His voice rang with pride, and that made me smile.

'If you want it enough, Duncan, I am sure you will. I shall miss seeing you around, though.'

'I'll miss talking to you, Maggie but this is what I have to do if I'm going to get somewhere in life.'

'You must be clever too or you wouldn't think of doing something like that.'

'Oh, I'm not clever, but I'm good with my hands.'

We had reached my house. I stopped, lingering for a moment.

'I've got to go. Ma will be waiting for me.'

He nodded, looking hesitant, as if there was something more he wanted to say, but the words didn't come.

I ran the last few steps to our house. The outside of it looked grimy, as did all the other houses in the lane, but at least the lace curtains were clean. Ma was always saying as how she wanted some new ones, but there was never enough money for extras, and there never would be while Michael Bailey drank most of his money away.

My mother came out into the parlour as I took off my coat, hanging it on an old-fashioned stand just inside the door. There were no halls in these back-to-back houses, just a front parlour, a kitchen and a scullery, with three bedrooms over and an outside toilet.

'Where have you been until this time? If you've been talking to boys I'll have your hide, my girl! You're too young for courting. I've told you before, I won't have it. Do you hear me?'

'I did talk to Duncan Coulson as we walked here, but I didn't stop to gossip or mess around, Ma. I was kept late at the shop.'

'They've no right to keep you over your time. I hope there will be extra money in your wage packet tomorrow.' Her face was badly bruised, her body stooped as if she were so much older than her years.

'I shouldn't think so. What's for tea, Ma? I'm hungry.'

'Did you bring some bread home?'

'Yes, and there's a stale bun for Robin that you can toast for his supper if you like. Where is he?'

'Out in the yard. He can have the bun for his breakfast. As for you, you can have the same as your brother—a bit of toast and dripping.'

'Oh, Ma...isn't there anything else?'

'I've got a scrap of bacon but that's for your pa's supper...when he gets here.' Ma looked at the clock on the kitchen mantle. 'I thought he would be back by now. It's Friday and he gets paid for the week. He promised he would come straight home with the money tonight. I owe for last week's rent.'

'You'll have my wages tomorrow, Ma. What have you had to eat today?' She shook her head impatiently. 'You've got to eat, Ma! I've got a shilling saved towards my new coat. If I fetch some eggs from the corner shop, will you have something for yourself?'

'I'm not hungry. I'll have a bit of toast if you'll make it, and some dripping same as you. Keep your money, Maggie, or you will never save enough for that coat.'

'The coat doesn't matter if you'll eat something...'

'I told you, I want toast and a cup of tea. Make the toast now, because there's a basketful of ironing to do later, and you can do your share.'

I turned away to slice the bread, feeling the sense of injustice building inside me.

Thoughts of Duncan Coulson flashed into my mind. Now there was a lad going places! If my father had a bit more gumption, he might do something of the sort, but all he did every day was to go down the docks and wait for someone to give him a job that paid a few pennies.

Damn Pa and his drinking! It wasn't fair on the rest of us. My elder sister Sadie had left home the second she could and sometimes I wished I could, too, but Robin and Ma wouldn't manage without me.

Hot water stung my hands as I washed plates and mugs. The flat iron was heating on the range. I took Robin's shirt out of the basket; by the time I'd pressed his trousers, two blouses for Ma, a dress and my skirt I'd had enough.

'You haven't finished,' Ma said as I turned to leave the kitchen.

'I'm not doing Pa's things! Besides, I've had enough. I'm tired and I want to go to bed.'

'All right, have it your own way. I was too tired to do it all, but I'll press a shirt for him. You know what he is like if he wants a clean shirt. You can finish the rest tomorrow. And don't say you won't, because you will. You're my daughter and you'll do as I tell you for as long as you live here.'

* * *

I woke when Ma screamed, jumped out of bed and went to the top of the stairs, listening to the row between them. Pa was drunk again and he had just hit my mother. His drunken rages were happening more often of late. Ma should stand up for herself more, but she just seemed to take it.

Hearing another terrible scream from my mother, I ran down the stairs and through the parlour into the kitchen.

'Stop it, Pa! You'll kill her before you're done.'

Pa's head came round to face me. His eyes looked strange, wild.

'Who asked your opinion?' His words were slurred into one another. 'Interfering little bitch. I'll teach you to keep your nose out of my business!'

'No, Michael. Leave her alone. She doesn't know what she's saying.'

'It's about time I taught her some manners...' He lurched towards me, intent on striking out with his fists. 'Come here, you bitch!'

I backed away. He was going to beat me the way he beat Ma! I wasn't going to stand there and take it the way Ma did. I needed a weapon, something to defend myself with from his hammer fists. I was near the black cooking range, where a pan of water was simmering; Ma had it ready for my father to wash when he came in from the docks.

Without thinking of the consequences, I picked up the pan of simmering water and threw the contents over Pa as he advanced on me. He screamed in shock as the hot water went over him, onto his face, through his clothes, scalding his skin.

'What have you done? You wicked, wicked girl!'

Stunned and scared, I watched Pa stumbling about the room, hands to his face, moaning and cursing.

'I didn't mean to do it. I didn't think...'

'Away and get your sister Sadie. I'll need her to help me.'

I retreated towards the door, as Pa crashed about the kitchen, still screaming and cursing. Turning from the scene of pain and chaos, I ran down the lane to Sadie's house, which was at the far end of the grimy street. The smell of thick smoke issuing from the chimneys of the other houses stung my throat; I could hear a foghorn out on the Thames, but all I could see in my head was the shock on Pa's face. I hammered at Sadie's door and her husband Ben opened it.

'What's up, lass? Come away in, you're shaking like a leaf.'

'It's Pa. He's hurt bad. Ma needs Sadie to help her.'

'What happened to him?' Sadie came to the door. Four months pregnant with her first child, she placed a hand affectionately on the bump. 'He was drinking again tonight, wasn't he?'

'He...he scalded himself with the pan of hot water,' my gaze dropped as I lied.

Sadie made a shushing noise between her teeth. 'I knew he would do something daft one of these days.' She looked at her husband. 'I suppose I'd better go if Ma needs me.'

'Do you want me to fetch the doctor, Sadie lass?' Ben Masters was a North Country man who had traded the mines of Newcastle for the docks of London after serving his time in the army during the war.

'There's no money for doctors. Pa hasn't been right since he came home from the trenches. He thought he was entitled to a hero's welcome after what he'd been through out there and all he got was to stand in line with a hundred others begging for work on the docks. It hurt his pride and that's why he went on the drink.'

'He's a fool. We all have to stand in line for work down the docks these days, and his attitude doesn't help.' Sadie looked tired and distressed as she listened to her husband. 'Want me to come with you, love?'

'We'll be all right, Maggie and me.'

Sadie fetched her shawl. I had come out without one and shivered as we walked back together, feeling frightened and guilty. If anything happened to Pa, they would likely throw me in prison for a long time. I was silent all the way home, holding back as my sister went inside the house. From upstairs I could hear the sound of Robin crying.

'I'll go up to him. You help Mum.'

I ran up the stairs, feeling glad that I could be of some use without facing my father again. He had never seemed to like me much and now he would hate me. I wished I could go back to before I'd flung that water over him. I should have found something else to defend myself with—something that wasn't so terrible as a pan of hot water.

'What's the matter with Pa?' Robin asked as I went into the bedroom. 'He's been swearing something awful.'

'He got some hot water over him,' I said. I put my arms about him. 'He's in pain right now, but he will be better soon. Try to go back to sleep Robin. You can't do anything to help him.'

'I'm hungry. I've only had a bit of bread and scrape for me tea tonight.'

'That's because Ma had no money. She was relying on Pa to bring his wages home. If there's any money left, I'll go down the market and buy some food tomorrow, love.'

Robin whimpered a bit and then settled down, his eyes closing as he drifted into sleep. The noise from the kitchen had lessened considerably, though now and then I heard Pa yell out.

I sat on the side of the bed waiting and listening as Robin slept. Someone else had come into the house now. That was my brother-in-law's voice, and another man. Ben must have fetched the doctor even though Sadie had told him there was no money to pay for his visit.

I was afraid to go down and find out what was happening. It was not until an hour later that I heard the voices get louder and then the door shutting with a bang. Sadie, Ben, and the doctor had all gone. Then the sound of slow footsteps coming up the stairs made my heart thunder in my chest. Ma entered, a lighted candle in her hand.

'I'm sorry. I just wanted to stop him hitting you, Ma. When he turned on me, I lost my head...'

'Your trouble is that you don't think, Maggie. What you did was cruel. Scalding is one of the worst things that can happen to anyone.'

'I'm sorry. How is he? He isn't dead, is he?'

'The doctor gave him something to knock him out until the pain eases,' Ma said on a sigh. 'He's given me a balm to treat the worst of the burns. Fortunately, the water wasn't as hot as it might have been but it was bad enough. We've left him on the sofa for tonight. If he's better in the morning, Ben is going to help me get him up to bed. He was in a lot of pain, Maggie.'

'Yes, I know. I wish I hadn't done it.'

'God knows how we'll manage now. It was bad enough when your father gave me a few coins occasionally, but now he can't work. You will have to find work, Maggie.'

'But I already work in the bakery, Ma.'

'You'll have to do an evening job as well. Don't look at me like that, girl. You brought this on yourself. I need more money coming in and you're the only one fit to work in this family now.'

'Yes, I know. I'll do what I can. But there's only one sort of evening job I'm likely to get, and that's behind a bar. You've always been against me taking that kind of work.'

'That was then, this is now, and things have to change.'

'I'll look round on Saturday afternoon and see what I can find.'

Ma sighed. 'Don't blame yourself too much, Maggie. I've often wanted to hit back myself, but your Pa was never like this until the war. They call it the Great War, but I think it was a wicked war. It's more than six years now since he came home at the end of it, and he can't let go. He drinks to forget the things he saw and we have to remember that, girl.'

'Yes, Ma. I really am sorry...'

'Sorry isn't much good to him, is it?'

2

I spent the whole of my free afternoon traipsing round the various alleys and lanes in the area, close to what had once been called St. Katherine's docks, but was now just a part of the London docks. Once upon a time there had been a hospital here and more than a thousand homes, which were torn down to build the docks. Houses, pubs and various shops had sprung up in the area from here to the Tower, and it was close by that I finally found what I was searching for. I'd tried several pubs, asking for work behind the bar in the evening, but now I was standing in front of a small café on the waterfront. When I went inside to the steamy warmth, the tables were almost all occupied: sailors and dockers, working men with grimy faces and hands.

A couple of young sailors whistled at me as I went up to the serving counter. My cheeks were warm but I was used to being called after in the streets where I lived, perhaps because I had thick fair hair that waved onto my shoulders and greenish blue eyes.

'Evening love,' the man behind the counter grinned. He was a large man with a huge belly and receding hair. 'Come for a cuppa, 'ave yer?'

'I certainly wouldn't mind one. It's cold enough outside, but I really came in to see if you had an evening job going spare.'

'Grab her, Billy Biggins,' one of the men sitting close by yelled out. 'Yer trade will shoot up if she starts working 'ere. I'll be in every night fer a start.'

'In that case I ought to say no,' Billy said and winked at me. 'What makes you ask for an evening job, lass?'

'My pa had an accident. He can't work for a while. I do a day job at a bakery but Ma can't manage on what I give her.'

'That's a bit rough on you, lass.' He poured a cup of tea, pushing the sugar bowl towards me and shaking his head as I reached for my purse. 'Keep your money. What's your name, lass, and how old are you?'

'I'll be seventeen in a few weeks' time, and my name is Maggie Bailey.'

'You'd be Michael Bailey's lass then? What happened to your pa, Maggie?'

'He was going for me ma, and I flung a pan of hot water over him. It wasn't boiling, but it was hot enough to hurt. He's got red patches all over the top half of his body, on his face an' all —.'

'Good God!' Billy's face registered shock at my open admission. 'It's a rare temper you've got on you for a bit of a lass—though you've got guts, I'll give you that much.'

'I was that mad at him for hurting me ma, I didn't think but it was wrong and I'm lucky he's no worse. Ma says he might have died if the water had been boiling, and it might have been.'

'Well as it happens you've come at a good time, Maggie. My wife Ann is having a baby in a month or so, and she won't be able to do much in the café. I need help with making the sandwiches, cooking bacon and serving the customers but mainly the washing up. Do you think you can do that?'

'I'll be pleased to, sir. I promise I won't let you down, and I wouldn't throw hot water over you!'

'You would regret it if you did. But I need a girl with spirit to stand up to my customers. You will have to behave yourself mind.'

'I shall. When can I start, please?'

'You can start tomorrow. Ann will show you what you'll be doing—if you've no objection to working on a Sunday?' I shook my head vigorously. 'Right then, lass. We'll see you tomorrow morning bright and early.'

'Thank you so much! You won't regret it!'

I felt as if I were dancing on air as I ran all the way home. Bursting into the kitchen, some of the pleasure drained out of me as I saw Pa half lying, half sitting on the old sofa that had been brought in from the parlour for his use.

'What are you looking so happy about? I'll flay the skin off your back when I'm on my feet. You wait and see if I don't.'

His threats sent shivers down my spine. He was a bully and handy with his fists and his belt, and he wouldn't hesitate to use them on me when he was better.

'I didn't mean to hurt you the way I did, Pa. I just wanted you to stop hitting Ma.'

'Interfering little bitch! Keep your nose out in future and remember I haven't finished with you yet.'

'You shouldn't hit her like that! She isn't well and one of these days you could kill her.' I faced him stubbornly, unwilling to let his threats frighten me.

'I'll do for you first!' The words contained such hatred, but he had never liked me.

Ma was upstairs, tucking Robin into bed. He was coughing and looked unwell, his cheeks unnaturally high in colour.

'What's wrong, Robin love?' I sat on the edge of his bed and took his hand in mine. 'Don't you feel well?'

'I've got a pain in me chest, Maggie,' he said, his little face working with distress. 'Ma says I've got to stay in bed for a day or so, and it's the Sunday school treat tomorrow.'

'We'll see how you are in the morning.' Ma ruffled his hair. She turned to me, a mixture of hope and resignation in her eyes. 'So how did you get on then, lass?'

'I've got a job in a café that stays open late at night. I've got to go in in the morning and Mrs Biggins will show me what to do.'

'A café? Well, that's better than a pub. What are they going to pay you?'

My mouth fell open. 'I never asked, Ma.'

'Well, there's an idiot! Still, they're bound to give you something, and anything will be a help.' She pushed me before her as we left the room, lowering her voice. 'I think Robin needs the doctor but I've got no money. You gave me all your wages last night, didn't you?'

'You know I did.'

'I had to pay two weeks on the rent and we needed some coke for the fire. It's been hard going these past years, and now with your Pa laid up the way he is...'.

'I wish I hadn't done it. I'll work hard and make it up to you, I promise. And you can have the money I've saved for my coat for Robin.'

'It's a shame, because you needed that coat. But Robin needs the doctor more. I'm not blaming you for it all, Maggie. What happened was your father's fault. If he hadn't been drunk, he wouldn't have hit me and you wouldn't have thrown that water over him. I don't know what they did to him out there in the trenches but it must have been pretty bad. He was a good man to me before he went out there.'

* * *

Ann Biggins was a pretty woman with dark hair and eyes and a friendly smile. She looked me over and nodded her head in approval when we met that morning.

'It isn't going to be easy for you working here, Maggie, but I'm glad to have you. I'll show you what to do and then we'll see how you go on for a couple of weeks.'

'Does that mean I'll be let go after that?'

'Not if we all get on together. It might be you who wants to leave us at the end of that time.'

'Oh no,' I said. I had taken to both Bill and his wife immediately. 'I don't think I shall want to leave you, Mrs Biggins.'

'Well, let's see how we go on. I've a feeling we shall do very nicely together.'

It was easy to make the sandwiches, because I'd done them often enough for Robin at home, though it wasn't often I was able to fill his with nourishing cheese and pickles, or the streaky bacon oozing with fat that the working men enjoyed.

'We have ham sometimes, and beef now and then', Ann told me. 'But the most popular are the cheese and pickle and the bacon. The other thing we get a lot of call for is egg and chips, and sausage, egg and chips.'

My stomach rumbled at the thought of all that delicious food and I wished I could afford to take a bit of it back for Robin. Maybe with some decent food inside him he wouldn't be so vulnerable to chills and childhood diseases that he brought home from school.

'Are you hungry, Maggie?' Bill asked, making me blush because he must have heard my stomach rumbling.

'There wasn't much for breakfast this morning...'

'There wouldn't be with your pa off work. Come on then, lass, show us how good you are at cooking bacon, eggs and sausages, and then you can eat them.'

'Really?'

I found it simple enough to cook on the large iron range, because it was just like the one at home only bigger. Within a short time, there was a plateful of sizzling hot food, which I devoured in minutes, leaving only the sausage, which I surreptitiously removed from the plate and wrapped, in a clean handkerchief.

'Well, if that tasted as good as it looked, I can see the customers coming back for more.' Bill's chins wagged as he laughed. 'I suppose we ought to talk about wages, lass. What about five shillings a week to begin with, and another two if we keep you on after the trial period? Oh, and you can cook yourself a meal before you start.'

He was being extraordinarily generous. I suspected that he had offered more than the going rate because he felt sorry for me.

I should be working long hours, but with the promise of five shillings a week and a meal, I couldn't have been happier as I left the café and began to walk home. A heavy wagon was rumbling down the cobbled street, pulled by two large black horses. They belonged to the local brewery and had shining brasses on their harness and headbands. As I passed the market, I saw old women selling flowers from wicker baskets, and a Pearly King and Queen were singing for pennies for the poor of the East End. Maybe it wasn't so bad round here after all. At least folk helped each other.

Approaching the corner shop, I noticed a board outside with a deep black band all the way round it. The news bulletin said that Queen Alexandra, widow of King Edward VII had died on 25th November. She'd lived for several years after her husband but now she was gone.

A woman stood next to me, reading the headlines. She looked at the board and shook her head over the news.

'That's sad that is, lass. Still, it comes to us all, kings or coalmen!'

'Yes, I suppose it does.' I'd read in the paper once that Queen

Alexandra was a lovely person, always giving things away, and I thought it was a pity that she'd died.

'What yer, Maggie!'

For a moment or two I stared at the young man who had spoken, hardly recognising him at first, because he'd shot up and his shoulders had broadened since I'd last seen him. He was dressed in working clothes, but they were clean and there was something about him that made me look twice.

'You're Jack Holmes, and you sat two rows behind me in the third year in church school.' The teacher had kept him down, because he hadn't been paying attention to the lessons. He was the kind of lad that was always up for a lark and the others had looked up to him.

'Yeah,' he said, his merry blue eyes going over me. 'How yer doin', Maggie?' He had dark wavy hair and a nice mouth.

'Not so bad. I've just found myself a job at Bill Biggin's café.'

'I thought you worked down the bakery?'

'I do but I need a second job in the evenings. Pa had an accident and can't work for a while.'

'I've seen yer pa hanging round the docks but not these past few days. Is there anything I can do to help? I could manage a couple of bob if you're short?'

'No, thanks. I'm getting paid five shillings a week and that's more than Pa was bringing in when he was working.'

'I reckon he got most of the rough jobs—stuff no one else wanted to do. Yer pa ain't easy, Maggie. A lot of the men don't like him. Sorry, but it's the truth.'

'It's all right, I don't like him much either.'

Jack was amused. 'I like you,' he said. 'You're bright and pretty. If you need anything any time, you ask me.'

'Maybe I will,' I said, because Jack's grin was infectious. 'And maybe I won't...'

'You're a tease Maggie Bailey!'

'Am I? Even if I am I haven't got time to talk to you.'

'Right, well, I'd best get on,' he said but he didn't look offended. 'It's the kids Sunday school treat this afternoon and I said I'd help out. Will you be bringing Robin, Maggie?'

'If he's well enough. He wasn't too good yesterday, but he says he feels better this morning. I know he won't want to miss the treat.'

'You bring him,' Jack took a paper twist filled with sweets from his pocket and offered them to me. 'They're Fox's glacier mints, try one. Don't forget what I said about the treat. We're having lots of games, and there's a donkey cart for the kids to ride in. Robin would never forgive himself if he missed that, would he?'

* * *

I gave Robin the sausage from the café when I found him outside in the backyard. He'd come from the lavatory, which was just a couple of boards over a hole in the ground and emptied by the night soil man. Robin was washing his hands under the tap at the back of the house. To find my brother washing his hands voluntarily was a rare occurrence.

'Where did you get that?' he asked in-between bites of the sausage. 'Does Pa know?'

'It's nothing to do with him. I cooked it at Mr Biggin's café and he let me bring it home for you.'

'I thought you worked in the Bakery?'

'I'm going to work at the café at nights but I'll be taking you to the Sunday school treat this afternoon. There's a donkey cart and they're having lots of games and things.'

'And the tea. I don't want to miss the Sunday school tea. They'll have cakes and ham sandwiches and jelly. I am better, aren't I, Maggie?'

'Yes, you seem better to me. Come on then, let's help Ma with the chores and then we can get off when we're done.'

After dinner, I fetched my coat and Robin's, wrapping him up warm in his knitted scarf and shabby cap. His eyes were glowing with anticipation and there were two pink spots in his cheeks. I squashed my doubts about the wisdom of taking him out in the cold wind, knowing that he would be miserable if denied his treat.

'Come on, Maggie,' he pulled at my arm. 'We'll be missing it if we're not quick.'

'Come on then. I'll be back at half-past four, Ma, because I've got to be at the café by five.'

Ma nodded to me. She was carrying the dishes through to the scullery to wash them and hardly noticed us leave.

It was bitterly cold out, but the sun had poked its way through the grey and that made it feel better. Robin was excited, running ahead of me down the cobbled street to the church hall, which wasn't much better than a tin shack and had once belonged to a brewery.

Robin had a wonderful time at the treat. He was one of the first in line for a ride in the donkey cart, and it was Jack Holmes who was in charge of the donkey. He gave Robin an extra turn.

'It's perks of the job, to do a favour for yer mates,' he said and winked. 'Can't say anythin' wrong with that, can yer?'

'I can't but I think some of the others might. Come on, Robin, there's plenty more to see and do.'

After the donkey cart there were games of running, climbing frames and swings, also several stalls where the children could exchange tickets for sticky sweets or small toys. And there was a lucky dip, from which Robin triumphantly pulled a small wooden fire engine. And then of course there was the tea, with piles of ham or cheese sandwiches, pork pies, sausage rolls, jam tarts, fruit cake and red jelly.

It was just gone half-past four when I told Robin we had to leave. The party was still going strong and he was reluctant.

'I've got to get to work. I'm sorry, Robin. I promised Ma I would see you safe home and I'll be late for my first evening at the café if I don't go now.'

'Why don't I take Robin home for you?' offered Jack who was standing nearby.

I hesitated because Robin was enjoying himself so much. I didn't know Jack that well, but everyone seemed to like him and I thought he could be trusted to take care of Robin.

'Will you make sure he wraps up well before you leave? He catches cold so easily. Don't let him go out without his scarf and cap.'

'I've brothers of my own and they've got little ones.' Jack ruffled Robin's hair. 'We'll be all right, won't we young-un?'

'Yeah, we're all right. Please let me stay, Maggie.'

'All right. Behave yourself then and don't give Jack any trouble. I'll see you in the morning.' I nodded to Jack. 'Thanks for looking after him.'

'No trouble. You get off and don't give us another thought. I'll see him home safe, I promise.'

* * *

The café smelled warm as I opened the door. Bill was serving at the counter. He smiled, encouraging me as I went round the back to take off my coat and put on the large apron that swamped me.

'Get yer tea then, lass,' Bill said. 'There's a beef pie tonight if you've a taste for it. Or you can do yerself a fry up if you'd rather.'

'I'd like a slice of the pie and some mash,' I said and helped myself. I took it into the back kitchen to eat it. Ann was standing at the table ironing a shirt.

'I wondered if you would come again. Bill could do with some help and I can't stand on me feet like I used ter. You'll be a big help to us, Maggie.'

'Thank you,' I said and cleared my plate. 'I'll take this to the scullery and make a start on the dishes, shall I?'

'You do that, Maggie. When you've finished you can give Bill a hand out there. I'm tired and I'm off to bed now you're here.'

I went into the scullery, where the dishes had been piled high. There were some old newspapers to put the scraps in, and I paused to read the top one. There was an article about someone called Josephine Baker. The headline said that she had wowed the crowds in Paris with her witty dancing, and the photograph of her looked indecent, because she was wearing hardly anything. I looked at the date; it was October 1925, which was quite recent. Some of the others went back to 1922! Bill must keep his papers a long time. I hoped I would get a chance to read some of them now that I was working here, but I had no time for reading at that moment. I had to work to earn the meal I had just eaten. For the first time in years, I didn't have a stomach-ache because I was hungry.

3

It was nearly midnight when I crawled into bed on a bitterly cold night towards the end of November. I was sleeping in what had been Sadie's room now. I seemed to get home later and later every evening, because there was always another job to do at the café and I didn't want to disturb Robin.

Falling instantly asleep, I dreamed of Christmas, which was less than a month away. It was the first year that I would be able to buy Robin something good for his Christmas gift. I'd managed a trip to Bermondsey market and was looking forward to seeing Robin's face when he opened his presents.

Because I was so tired it was a while before I stirred, even though I was being shaken hard. I opened my eyes sleepily, looking at Ma in bewilderment.

'Is it time to get up?'

'It's five o'clock. I would have let you sleep for another hour, but Robin is ill. He's been coughing half the night, keeping your father awake. He kept me fetching and carrying for him for ages but he has gone off at last and I don't want Robin to wake him. You'll have to see to your brother. Make him a warm drink and see if he'll settle. If not, we may have to fetch the doctor, and it's foggy out.'

I jumped out of bed and pulled on the dress I'd worn for work the previous evening. I could hear Robin whimpering in the next room and hurried to his side.

'What's wrong, love?' I asked as I placed a hand on his forehead. He was burning up!

'I feel bad,' Robin said tearfully. 'Me head aches and me throat is sore. I don't like it when you're not here, Maggie.' He always wanted me there even though at almost eight years of age he was old enough to sleep alone.

'I didn't want to wake you when I came in, love.' He felt hot and damp to the touch. 'I'll make you a warm drink. That will ease your throat, darlin'.'

This wasn't the first time he'd suffered with a nasty chill this winter, but he seemed poorly. I didn't want anything to happen to Robin; he was far too precious! However, when I gave him the warm, milky drink he swallowed it all and appeared easier, drifting off to sleep.

There was no point in going back to bed even though it was early. I might as well dress properly and then make breakfast for Ma and me before I got off to work.

* * *

If anything, the fog was worse when I left the bakery and walked to the café, the pavements really icy now and treacherous underfoot. The barrow boys were already packing up their goods, laughing and calling to one another cheerfully despite the chill. The windows of the café were steamed up and running with water as I went in, but it was comforting inside, because Bill had the big round-bellied stove burning.

'Oh, it's lovely in here!'

'Got to keep the customers happy! I think some of them only come in nights to get warm.'

Some of our customers were vagrants who had no homes to go to and lived on the few pence they could earn doing odd jobs on the waterfront. They stayed to the very last minute, because it was warm and comfortable in the café, and most of them would sleep under the bridges at night. Bill knew them all by name, and what had brought them down to this level.

There was Old Tom, as he was known, his greasy grey locks hanging about a face lined with sorrow. He'd lost his home and all his family in the war and had lived on the streets ever since, his mind wandering at times. I liked him and was glad when Bill told me to give him an extra cup of tea with his meal, because he seemed so sad and lonely. Some of the others were surly devils and I didn't enjoy serving them, but none of them ever bothered me, perhaps because they knew that Bill would bar them from the café if they did.

'I wasn't sure you would come tonight, lass. It's a terrible night, not fit to send a dog out. It's a wonder your Ma didn't make you stay at home.'

'I thought you might need me,' I couldn't tell him that Ma couldn't afford for me to have even one night off.

'Ma kept Robin home this morning because of his chest.'

'Got a cough, has he? I've got something that might help. Let's hope you don't take ill, coming out on a night like this.'

The terrible weather made little difference to our trade. If anything, the customers stayed longer, preferring to sit in the corner near Bill's stove and drink tea rather than venture outside into the freezing night. I had hoped it might clear when I was ready to leave, but if anything, the fog was worse.

'I can't see across the street,' Bill said when he looked out. 'I don't think you should walk home in this, lass. You can sleep on the sofa in the parlour if you like.'

Ma might worry if I didn't get home but if she were asleep, she might not even know I hadn't returned, and it *was* a terrible night. 'Are you sure?' I asked, tempted to stay in the warm.

'Wouldn't say if I wasn't. Ann will give you a blanket and a pillow. It's best if you stay, Maggie, in weather like this.'

'I'll stay then. I'll help out until the last minute, and then go through but if it lifts, I'll be off early in the morning so as not to worry Ma.'

I finished the washing up before going through to the parlour. Bill had spoken to his wife and she had brought out a pillow and two blankets. She made a wry face as she put her hand to her back.

'I've been feeling a bit off all day. I've got another month to go but if I get much bigger, I'll never make it. I keep thinking I've got my dates wrong and the baby will take us by surprise.'

'I should think that would be a relief. You've been suffering a lot recently.'

Bill came through to join us. 'I hadn't the heart to throw Old Tom out,' he said. 'I've let him to sleep in there by the stove, Ann. I'll see he goes first thing in the morning, whatever the weather.'

'You're too soft for your own good, Bill Biggins. You keep the door to the café shut, Maggie. I don't think Tom's the sort to sleep walk but you never know.'

'He wouldn't hurt a fly and he likes Maggie.' He gave Ann a look that took in her weariness. 'It's up to bed for you, love. You look worn out. Goodnight, Maggie.'

I wished them goodnight and then sat down on the sofa after they had gone. After looking about me so that I would know where I was if disturbed in the night, I lay down and was soon asleep. I slept soundly for some hours, waking suddenly when I heard a noise close by and then the light came on. I blinked as I saw Bill in his night-clothes, a thick dressing gown over his night-shirt.

'Sorry to wake you, Maggie, but I think Ann has started the baby. I need to go for the doctor. Will you go up and sit with her until I get back?'

'Yes, of course. Has the fog cleared?'

Bill looked out of the window. He was pulling on a heavy over-coat. 'It looks a bit better though it's still a rough night. I'll be back as soon as I can.'

I heard him speaking to Old Tom as he went through the café but then a scream from upstairs made me bolt up them. There were two bedrooms, but it was easy enough to find Ann's because the light was on and she was making a terrible howling noise.

She was sitting up, bolstered by a pile of feather pillows against the brass and iron bedstead. I went straight to her, taking her hand and holding it as she panted, her teeth bared.

'Is there anything I can do to help? I'm sorry but I've never been round a woman giving birth before. I've no idea what you need.'

'We shall need a lot of hot water, lass,' the voice made me swivel round in surprise. Bill couldn't be back that soon! I gasped as I saw it was the man I thought of as Old Tom, but looking very different to the way he usually did. He had put off his filthy and torn coat and rolled his sleeves up to his elbows. I had time to register that his shirt looked surprisingly clean before he spoke again. 'Don't look so surprised, lass. Didn't Bill tell you I used to be a doctor? If he'd told what was wrong, he needn't have gone out on such a filthy night. I've brought more babes into this world than a few. Get off and put some pans of water on to heat.'

'No...' Ann was looking at him in fright. 'Don't leave me, Maggie... I don't want him near me.'

'It's all right, Mrs Biggins,' Tom said in a soft persuasive voice. 'I really do know what I'm doing. I've scrubbed my hands in the sink downstairs, and by the looks of things you can't wait for the doctor your man's gone to fetch.'

Bill might have known that Tom had once been a doctor but he hadn't trusted him to look after his wife, and nor did she. I suppose they'd both thought he was past it.

I looked at Ann and saw what he'd already seen; the child's head was visible between its mother's thighs and had a mass of black hair. Throwing Ann an apologetic look, I headed for the stairs.

Ann was screaming like a banshee again when I carried the steaming kettle and a bowl upstairs a little later. I was just in time to see Tom bringing the baby out. He turned with a grin on his face as I entered, showing me the little wriggling body covered in its mother's blood, and then laid it in Ann's arms. A short time later Tom dealt efficiently with the afterbirth, turning to me at last with a nod of satisfaction.

'You'll need to bathe the child in a minute, when they've got to know each other a bit,' he said. 'I'll leave you to finish up here. I think you can make them both comfortable now. I've done all that needs doing for Mrs Biggins, except clean her up, and I think she would rather you did that, Maggie.' He clearly knew that she'd accepted his help only because she had no choice.

'Thank you...' Ann called to his departing back. 'I'm sorry for what I said at the start.'

Tom shook his head but didn't look round as he went out. I saw what needed doing for Ann and set to work cleaning her up and removing the bloodied sheets, which had been folded under her and were simple to get out.

'You needn't do anything with them; they're old ones I saved for this. Just throw them out in the yard and Bill will burn them later,' Ann said. 'You'd better take the babe now and make her clean for when he gets back.'

'She's a little darling,' I said as I picked up the baby, 'but she did come quickly. I thought you would be ages in labour, like Ma was with Robin.'

'I've been in pain most of the night and the afternoon too if I'm honest,' Ann admitted with a wry look. 'I ought to have said something before but I was sure it couldn't happen for another two or three weeks.' She looked at her baby anxiously as I started to bathe her. 'There's nothing wrong with her, is there? She doesn't look weak or...' She broke off as her husband came into the room, smiling at him in her delight. 'Come and meet little Katie, Bill. She decided not to wait for you to get back.'

'How did you manage that?' He looked at me but I shook my head. 'Not you, then.'

'It was Tom,' his wife told him. 'You knew he used to be a doctor, didn't you?'

'Yes, but I thought him too old.' Bill looked bewildered. 'Well, I never. I saw him shuffling off down the road as I got back. Silly old fool, why didn't he stay around to be thanked? I should have given him a good breakfast at the very least.'

'Maybe he didn't want to be thanked,' Ann said. 'You'll have to do something for him when he comes in, Bill.'

'I certainly will! The doctor's wife told me he couldn't come. Apparently, he'd been up all night with a patient. She advised me to get a midwife.'

'Well, I don't need one or him either. All I want now is a nice cup of tea and some sleep. Would you put the kettle on, Maggie?'

'I'll do it now, and then I'll be on my way.'

'It's much better out now,' Bill said. 'I'm glad you were here, Maggie.'

'It's Tom you need to thank,' I reminded him. 'But I was glad to do what little I could.'

'I'll thank Tom when I see him. Don't forget that cough remedy for your brother, lass. It's on the side in the parlour.'

'No, I shan't forget, thank you.'

I ran down the stairs, leaving them together. It took only a few minutes to fill the kettle and place it on the range. Leaving the house, I found that it was much milder out, and it had been raining a little, which had cleared away the fog. It was nearly six o'clock and I would have to hurry or I wouldn't get to our house before it was time to leave for the bakery.

Ma was just coming downstairs when I rushed in at the front door. She gave me a hard look.

'Where have you been all night, my girl?'

'I stayed with Ann and Bill for the night, slept on their sofa, and it's a good job I did. Ann had her baby this morning.'

'So you helped her out, did you?' Ma's expression lightened. 'Well, I suppose I can't nag you too much; it was a foul night but I was worried when you didn't come in.'

'I'm sorry if you were worried, Ma. But you would have had more to worry about if I'd had an accident, wouldn't you?'

'Yes, I suppose so,' she said with a sigh. 'Your brother has been coughing again for the past hour. Will you make him a hot drink, Maggie?'

'Bill gave me a bottle of cough medicine last evening. It's only half a bottle but it may help Robin to settle. I'll give him a spoonful and then come down and make him a drink. I haven't got time to go back to bed now even if I wanted to.'

'You'll make yourself ill if you're not careful,' Ma said, 'but I've been up half the night with your father again.'

'Is he still in pain from what I did?'

'It still hurts a bit I think, but he hasn't been able to sleep without getting the drink inside him for years. He keeps asking me for whisky but I don't have any to give him. All I have is some ale. I warm that up for him and it settles him for a bit.'

'Why do you put up with it, Ma?'

'Because he was a good man to me once. I wasn't from round here, Maggie. I was a country girl. Michael was a travelling man then. I met him at the midsummer fair and I fell for him the minute I saw him. He loved me then...' Her eyes were misty with tears. 'When the war came, I begged him not to go. There were other men, younger than he was, who got out of it one way or another but he was on fire to sign up. He was a fine brave man when they sent him out there but don't you remember him the way he was?'

'I sort of remember,' I said. She seldom talked to me like this and I wished she would tell me more so that I could understand why she stayed with him. 'But he's so violent now, Ma. Robin is frightened of him.'

'Yes, I know. That's the thing I can't forgive him for—making the child afraid of him.' Ma rubbed at the bridge of her nose tiredly. 'Go up to your brother then, Maggie. I'll get the range going for breakfast.'

Robin's face was pale with bright pink spots on his cheeks; it was obvious that he was feeling unwell again. I tipped a little of the medicine into a spoon and held it to his lips. He swallowed obediently.

'Where did you get that, Maggie?'

'Bill had some medicine left over from when he'd had a chill, and he gave it to me. If the weather hadn't been so bad, I'd have been home earlier.'

'I'm glad you waited until the fog went,' Robin said. 'I don't want anything to happen to you, Maggie.'

'Why should you think it would?'

'My mate at school...' Robin hesitated. 'Something bad happened to his sister when she was going home from her job in the pub one night a few weeks back. He didn't tell me what it was, because his pa would thrash him if he mentioned Sally's shame, that's what Terry said, but it must have been something bad.'

'Do you mean Sally Green?' I knew she hadn't been into the bakery recently, but I didn't know something had happened to her. Sally was a pretty, pleasant girl with fair hair and I liked her. 'I am sorry she's in trouble but why should that affect me?'

'Terry said he was forbidden to talk about it, but he told me because we're best friends. If it happened to her, Maggie, it could happen to you.'

'Well, don't worry about it, love. Nothing will happen to me I promise you. I always run all the way home.' I bent and kissed him. 'Would you like some cocoa or a cup of tea?'

'Can I have cocoa? Will you make it with milk?'

'Half milk, half water,' I told him. 'I don't think there's enough for all milk, but it will be nice, because I've got a lump of sugar for you. I've got a sausage to cook for your breakfast, too.'

Robin's face lit up at the prospect of the treats I had saved for him, and he had stopped coughing for the time being.

I returned to the kitchen. The range threw out some heat because Ma had stoked it up ready. There were some cold potatoes left over from the previous night's supper and I put them into the pan with Robin's sausage, cooking them until they were crisp and brown, mouth-wateringly good. I made the cocoa then hurried upstairs to my brother's room with the tray as I heard Pa stirring.

'That looks smashing,' Robin said, face lighting up as he saw the fried potato and sausage. 'I don't know which to have first—the drink or the food.'

'You eat your breakfast first. The drink is hot. It will be cooling while you eat. I'm going to get ready for work now.'

I washed in cold water in my room because I'd heard Pa go down, heard him cursing and shouting and I didn't want to fetch hot water for myself when he was in the kitchen. The sound of his raised voice going on at Ma about something echoed through the house, and after saying goodbye to Robin, I slipped out of the door without going back to the kitchen.

* * *

'Maggie...wait up a bit!'

I glanced over my shoulder and saw Jack Holmes trying to catch me up.

'Haven't seen you around for a while. You used to come to the singing at the church hall sometimes?'

'I don't have time now. I work every evening—including Saturday and Sunday.'

'That's not very fair on you.'

'I've got to do it. At least until Pa goes back to work—and I don't know when that will be.'

'Is he still laid up then?'

'He isn't in bed all the time, but he isn't in a very good mood. I'm not sure if he's in pain or just bad tempered.'

'I know he's got a temper on him.' Jack shook his head when I lifted my brows at him. 'It doesn't matter, Maggie. I don't tell tales out of school. It's a pity you don't get any free time these days. I was going to ask you to come to the pictures with me one evening. Or a dance at the Pally if you'd rather.' He grinned suddenly. 'They're all doin' the Charleston up the Pally.'

'Do you mean it?'

'Yeah, of course.' Jack grinned. 'I'd like to take you out, Maggie —when you can spare the time.'

'I don't have to work from one o'clock on Saturday until five. Is that long enough to see a film? I've never been to the pictures. I've seen pictures of the actors in the papers and Sadie sometimes has those magazines about film stars—Greta Garbo is lovely but I've never seen her on the screen.'

'We could probably watch the matinee main feature. We wouldn't see the whole bill but we could go anyway. '

'I'll have to ask Ma,' I said but there was an excited feeling way down in the pit of my stomach. 'I sometimes do the ironing on a Saturday, but she might let me go for once.'

A bakery van wagon rumbled past. It was painted a rich green with gold lettering on the side and pulled by two magnificent horses, their tails and manes braided and shining. One of them lifted its tail and steaming excrement plopped out on the road. Seconds after the wagon had moved on, a lad darted out and scooped up the dung with a shovel and pail. Horse manure was much prized for back gardens or the church allotments. In the distance I could hear the rattle of the trams and a car was back firing; the streets were getting so congested with traffic that they were painting white lines all over the roads these days. 'You ask her then, Maggie,' Jack said, 'and then we can go out somewhere.'

The bakery shop was just across the road. Jack stopped walking. 'I'll wait for you to come out tomorrow morning if you like. You can tell me what she says then.'

'Yes, all right. I'll tell you tomorrow.'

* * *

I couldn't wait to finish my day at the bakery so that I could hurry to the café and see Ann and Bill's baby. The bakery was just a job to me, though I enjoyed serving the customers, but Bill and Ann were becoming like family. Bill greeted me with his usual cheery smile.

'Ann wants to see you before you start. Up the stairs with you, lass. I'll give you a shout when your supper is ready—pie and mash all right for you?'

'Lovely. Thanks, Bill. I'm longing to see the baby. Oh, I meant to say that cough medicine worked a treat for our Robin.'

'That's good, lass. Off you go now. Ann's waiting for you.'

I ran upstairs, pausing outside Ann's bedroom to watch her nursing the baby. There was a clean white candlewick counterpane on the bed and flowers on the dressing table. The room smelled of cologne and babies.

'Come in, Maggie. She's nearly finished her feed but I don't mind you watching. She's a greedy little devil, can't seem to get enough.'

'Has the doctor been to see you?' I reached out tentatively to touch Katie's little fist with my fingertips.

'He came eventually this afternoon. Had a look at Katie and me and said everything was fine. No thanks to him.'

'It's a good thing Tom was here.'

'I'm not sure what we would have done without him. Katie was so determined to be born, but Tom did everything so easily. I've told Bill that he ought to have free tea as often as he likes it, and a hot meal once a day when it's cold like this.'

'He'll probably come in this evening. I've always liked him, but I didn't realise how clever he was until last night. And under that old torn coat his clothes were clean, and he looked younger than I'd imagined him to be.'

Ann nodded, putting the baby over her shoulder and patting her back gently to bring up the wind. 'I wanted to see you, Maggie. I know I told you we would have a trial period, but it goes without saying that we want to keep you on. I wondered if you might like to come and work for us here all the time—day and evenings until nine. Bill can manage after that, and I should be able to help him once Katie is asleep.'

'I should like it but I get five shillings a week from the bakery.'

'Bill said we could pay you ten shillings and sixpence for the week.'

'I'd like to work here all the time, but I'll have to ask Ma first.'

'You do that, Maggie.' Ann held out the baby. 'Do you want to hold her for a moment?'

'Yes please.' Katie smelled of milk and talcum and she smiled up at me, then burped. 'I'm not sure if that was a smile or the wind.' I heard Bill calling to me from downstairs. 'I'd better go now.'

Katie back in her mother's arms, I ran down the stairs again. Bill had my meal waiting on a plate in the kitchen.

'It's odd Tom hasn't been in today, isn't it?' Bill said looking thoughtful. 'I wanted to thank him for what he did for Ann last night.'

'He's probably a bit embarrassed about it.'

'Well, I dare say he'll come in when he's hungry. I've given him a cup of tea and a cheese roll many nights when he hasn't had a penny to bless himself with, but this deserves more. I dare say I'd have coped when I got back, but Ann says he was marvellous. A proper doctor and decent with it. Seems a shame that he gave it all up, doesn't it?'

'Yes, but I suppose he couldn't face people after his family died.'

'It was a gas explosion in the building where they lived. Probably caused by a leaky gas pipe and a flying bomb going off nearby. His wife, three children and mother were all asleep in their beds; they didn't stand a chance. He was working at the infirmary, got home the next morning and found a big hole where his house used to be.'

'That's so very sad. I suppose tragedy changes people. Ma says me pa was different before the war. I suppose we ought to make allowances for him.'

'Yes, well, we all have to do that,' Bill said. He turned his head as he heard a shout from the café. 'Sounds as if the natives are getting restless...'

He went through to the café and his cheery voice came back to me as he talked and joked with the customers. As soon as I had put the dirty plate into hot water to soak, I followed him.

Six men had come in together and the orders were flying. Two of them wanted pie and mash, which was easy to serve but the other four asked for either bacon rolls or sausage, egg and bacon with a plate of bread and butter.

I disappeared into the kitchen once more, getting on with the frying while Bill served them mugs of hot tea. I could hear a lot of laughter and chatter, but as I picked up the tray to carry in the hot food, everything suddenly went quiet. Putting the tray on the bar, I looked at Bill and was surprised to see that he was looking a bit green in the face.

'Has something happened?'

'There was an accident on the docks this afternoon,' one of the customers answered, because Bill clearly couldn't. 'Several men were hurt, lass—and one of them was killed.'

'It was Tom,' Bill said in a choked voice. 'He wasn't even work-ing, but he saw what was happening when the hoist chain gave way and he rushed forward to push a group of men out of the way. The load of steel girders fell on him. A few of the others were hurt but they say a lot more would have died if he hadn't done what he did.'

'Tom was killed...' Tom's sudden death would have been hard enough to accept if the previous night hadn't happened, but remembering how gentle he'd been with Ann and the baby brought tears to my eyes. 'That's terrible...'

'Aye, lass, it is,' one of the other men said on a sombre note. 'Everyone liked Old Tom. He went on the drink sometimes, but we've all done that from time to time.'

'It's a great shame.' Several voices echoed Bill's sentiments.

Bill and I glanced at each other. Everyone had looked on Tom as being a down and out but he had been a hero twice in the space of a few hours and now he was dead. All I could do was stare as the tears trickled down my cheeks and into my mouth.

'I never got to thank him.' Bill said, 'and now I never shall.'

'No...' I had admired the way Tom had delivered Ann's baby and had wanted to tell him so; now he was dead. The tears stung my eyes as I picked up a tray of dirty plates and escaped to the kitchen.

4

It was obvious something was wrong! Ma's eyes held a guilty, frightened expression as she sat at the kitchen table the next morning. She turned her head aside as I entered, getting up to make the tea.

'What's wrong, Ma?' I started to cut the bread.

'You sit down, Maggie. You work hard enough as it is....'

Taking the big brown pot from her hands, I set it down on the kitchen table. 'Sit down, Ma. I can make a bit of toast, just like always. Now tell me what's wrong?'

'It's your wages,' she said, shame in her eyes. 'There were four shillings in the pot where I always put the money you give me and now it has gone.'

'All of it? Pa took it, didn't he? Where is he?'

'I don't know. I must have fallen asleep and when I woke his side of the bed was cold. I looked for the money when I came down, because I was going to the market this morning.' Her shoulders dropped and she looked so defeated. 'I've thought before that a few pence had gone missing but this time he took it all.'

'Ma! Why didn't you hide it in a different place?'

'I didn't mind the odd sixpence now and then.'

Anger worked inside me. All the hours I put in to get extra money for us and she let him take sixpence when he pleased—from my wages!

'In future I'll keep what I earn and give you what you need before I go to work in the morning. If you can't be trusted to look after it, I'll do the shopping. I can get most of what we need from Bill's suppliers. It will be cheaper than you can buy down the market. I'm not going to work so that he can drink himself silly and then knock you about when he gets back.'

'Don't talk to me like that!' Her head came up. 'You will give me the money same as always.'

'No, Ma, I won't. I don't have to live here so don't threaten me. Ann Bailey has asked me to work for them full time at the café, and I've decided that is what I want to do. I dare say they would let me sleep in the kitchen on the sofa if I asked.'

'Maggie!' She stared at me in horror. 'I can't manage without your money. You know I can't.'

'I know that, Ma. I shall give you the rent money each week when it's due, but I'm not giving it all to you—because he just takes what he wants and we have to go without.'

'You shouldn't be so hard on him, Maggie. He has suffered more than you will ever know.'

'I don't care! A lot of men suffered in the war, but they don't take the food out of the mouths of their children.'

'Maybe you're right,' she said with that defeated air. 'I'm useless these days...'

'You shouldn't let him put you down. You're not useless but you let him take advantage. It is time you stood up to him.'

'He'll just hit me harder.'

I made toast for us both, spreading it with the last of the jam.

'Jack Holmes asked me to a matinee at the pictures, and I'm going this Saturday.'

She was surprised by the change of subject, her gaze narrowed, still defensive. 'You're a bit young to start courting—not seventeen yet.'

'I'm not courting, just going to the pictures. It's time I had a bit of fun.'

'There's no talking to you now, is there?'

'I'm old enough to walk out with a lad if I want.'

She sensed my defiance, accepting that something had changed between us. 'Jack's not a bad lad, sensible from what I've seen. I suppose... as long as you don't misbehave. Don't let me down, Maggie.'

'Leave off, Ma. I know what I am doing.'

'Get off to work then. They may ask you to work out your notice at the bakery—a week or maybe two.'

'Bill knows that. He wants me to start as soon as possible, but he accepts I have to work my notice.'

We heard Robin calling from upstairs. Ma got to her feet. 'I'll go up to him.'

I snatched my coat from the hall peg and went out. Jack was standing on the pavement at the opposite side of the road. He arched his brows as I crossed the road. I nodded and he gave me the thumbs up.

'She said yes then?'

'As long as I behave myself, as if I wouldn't!'

'Course you wouldn't do anythin' daft. I wouldn't neither, lass. You're seventeen next birthday and I'm not nineteen yet. We don't want to end up getting wed in a hurry, do we? I want me own business and you've got your family to think of. Don't stop us being good friends though, does it?'

'No, 'course it doesn't. I really want to go to the pictures with you. What's on then?'

'I'll have a look today and tell you tomorrow.'

'Good.' It looked as if Jack was intending to walk me to work every morning and that gave me a warm glow. 'I'm leaving the bakery soon. Going to work in the café from seven in the morning until nine at night.'

'That's even better then. We'll have longer together in the mornings, because I go that way as well, and I might be able to walk you home some nights.'

'Are you laying claim to me then?'

'Reckon I might as well. You'll be my girl, won't you, Maggie?'

I was bursting with pride and happiness, but tried not to smile too much as I said: 'Reckon I might as well, Jack. We'll see how we go anyway. Here we are then. I'll look for you in the morning.'

* * *

My boss wasn't pleased when I told him I was leaving the bakery. He frowned as he said: 'Is it any use me offering you more money? I was going to anyway when you were seventeen. I would rather not lose you, Maggie.'

'No, please don't do that.' My feeling of elation disappeared as I realised, he was upset. 'I'm sorry, but it's done now.'

A look of annoyance came into his eyes. 'I had high hopes for you, Maggie, but I suppose if you've made up your mind that's it.'

'I'm sorry, Mr Shirley.'

'Oh well, I'll have to look out for another girl. I'll expect you to work out the week, Maggie.'

'Yes, of course, sir.'

I was relieved that he'd accepted it without forcing me to work more than the week, because now that I knew my leaving annoyed him, I thought it best to be away.

* * *

I yawned, feeling heavy-eyed when I came down that Saturday morning. This was my last day at the bakery. I would be glad when the morning was over, because then I would be free to spend the afternoon with Jack. He'd told me that the program showing that afternoon was a Western starring someone called Bronco Billy, followed by a new Charlie Chaplin film.

Jack didn't walk me to work that morning, because he had a second job that he did on Saturday mornings. He hadn't told me much, but it was something different to the work he did on the docks, and it paid well, because Jack always had money in his pocket.

The bakery smelled delicious, warm bread and cakes making my stomach rumble, but I wasn't allowed to eat during working hours. I was busier that morning than usual, because a lot of the customers popped in to say goodbye.

'We shall miss your smile,' several of them told me, and that made me feel a bit weepy.

At half past twelve, which was half an hour before I usually finished, Mr Shirley came up to me with my pay envelope.

'You can get off now, Maggie. I've put a little bit extra in your wages, and I wanted you to know that if things don't work out in your new job you can always come back. It will be seven shillings and sixpence a week when you're seventeen.'

'Thank you, Mr Shirley.' I was surprised that he should give me extra. 'I don't think I shall change my mind, but if I do, I'll come and ask.'

I was feeling pleased as I left, carrying a large loaf for Ma and a couple of stale sponge cakes for Robin that I planned to make into a trifle. I had an extra half an hour to make the treat for Robin's tea, and then I could smarten myself up for the outing with Jack.

'Ma, I'm home,' I cried rushing into the house. Pa came out of the kitchen. His expression told me that he was in one of his foul moods. 'Where's Ma?'

'She went over the road to see some friend of hers that's ill,' he said, glaring at me as if it was my fault. 'Why she has to fuss with other folk when she's a family to look after I don't know.'

'Ma always helps anyone she can,' I said defensively. Going past him into the kitchen, I started to set out the ingredients to make the trifle. He stood and watched, his eyes dark and brooding. 'I'll make a cup of tea in a minute, Pa.' I was trying to appease him, just the way Ma did when he was in a mood and I felt angry with myself. Why did we all do everything he wanted all the time? What kind of a man was he to make his family fear him?

'What's that rubbish you're making now?'

'A trifle for Robin. I thought it would do him good and it's a treat. He doesn't get many treats these days.'

'Blaming me for that are you?'

'I didn't say it was your fault.'

'But you thought it. I've seen the scorn in your eyes when you look at me, girl. I know what you're thinking.'

'I'm not thinking anything,' I said, nerves jumping as he moved towards me. 'I'm sorry for what I did.'

'You will be! I've bided my time and now my chance has come.' He made a grab at me but I stepped back, tried to dodge past him. He caught my arm, twisting it behind me until I cried out, and then he thrust me away so that I fell against the range. It burned my arm and made me wince. He had done it deliberately. 'Know what it feels like now, do you?' His gaze narrowed, fixing on the flat iron that had been left to heat on the top of the range. 'How would you like to feel that iron on your face, girl?'

'You wouldn't...' Surely he couldn't mean it? He reached out for the iron. My stomach twisted with nerves, but even as his fingers touched the iron, a small tornado came at him from behind, shoving him hard so that he lost his balance and put his hand out to the stove to steady himself. He cursed as the heat seared him, turning to his son with a yell of rage. 'You little runt! Want some of what I'm going to give yer sister do yer?'

'Leave him alone, Pa,' I moved defensively in front of Robin. 'If you touch him or me, I'll have the constable to you. They'll lock you up for brutality. You'll go to prison I shouldn't wonder.'

'Bitch.' His eyes narrowed as he looked at me, measuring my determination. Then he saw the wages packet that I had automatically laid on the shelf without thinking when I came home. 'That's your money, is it? Well, you can just give it to me to make up for your lip, my girl.'

'That's Ma's money! You can't take that!'

I tried to stop Pa as he made a lunge for the money, but he hit me hard across the face, knocking me against the kitchen table. Then he snatched the packet from the shelf, pushing past Ma as she came into the room.

'What's wrong?' she asked as he rushed out and the front door banged behind him. 'Have you been upsetting your pa again, Maggie?'

'It wasn't Maggie's fault,' Robin defended me. 'He was hitting her. He was going to burn her face with the iron; he said so.'

'What did you do to provoke him, Maggie?'

My arm was hurting where I'd burned it on the range and my face stung. I turned away to wet a cloth in the sink, wringing it out before holding it to my face.

'I asked you a question.'

'I said I was making a treat for Robin, and that he didn't get many these days.'

'Have you burned your arm—or did he do it?'

'Pa did it,' Robin said. 'I pushed him when he was going to put the iron on her face and he burned his hand, then he took Maggie's wages.'

'He'll be off to the pub then.' Her shoulders sagged, a look of defeat in her eyes. 'I thought you were going to keep your wages, Maggie? Now he's taken your money once he'll do it again. I've got a bit of lard in the pantry. I'll spread it on your arm to take the sting out and we'll put a bandage on it.'

I took the cold cloth from my cheek. 'How can I go out with Jack now?'

'He won't take any notice. Tell him your father did it. He'll understand.'

'No, I'm not going with him looking like this. You'll have to tell him I can't, Ma. I don't want to see him...'

'Don't be a little fool,' Ma said sharply. 'You've been looking forward to this all week. We can rub a bit of rice paper over the mark. That will cover it up.'

'It won't. You know it won't.' The tears were spilling over. 'Why does he always have to spoil things? There was an extra two shillings Mr Shirley gave me in that packet. Why should he spend it all down the pub?'

'Don't ask me,' Ma sank wearily down on the chair. 'Go with your young man or don't but don't make things worse. I've enough to put up with as it is.'

'I'm sorry.' She looked so tired! 'Don't worry. I'll still have my wages tonight.'

'Well, make sure you don't leave them lying around. Now go upstairs and get changed. If you give up your treat, you're only letting your pa win.'

I nodded and took the cloth from my cheek. 'Does it look awful?'

'It feels worse than it looks. Let me see to your arm and then go and get ready, girl. Jack isn't going to bother about a little thing like that if I know him.'

* * *

I was waiting for Jack outside the house at half past one. He came over to me grinning but his expression changed as he saw my face.

'What's wrong, Maggie? Did you hurt yourself?'

'I had an accident...' I couldn't look at him as he tipped my chin up towards him. His eyes were narrowed, angry.

'Did your father do that?'

'He was in one of his moods.'

He deserves a good hiding!'

'I said something he didn't like.'

'I bet you didn't say anything much. Brutes like him hit first and think afterwards. One day he'll get what's coming to him!' Jack had such a look on his face that I felt scared.

'You won't do anything—anything silly?'

Jack gazed down at me, then bent his head to kiss the mark on my cheek very softly. 'If I had my way I'd take a whip to him,' he said gruffly, 'but that wouldn't do any good and I'd end up going down the line for it but someone will do for him, you'll see.'

'Don't, Jack,' I said, feeling cold of a sudden. 'Sometimes I hate him, but I wouldn't want him... well, you know.'

'That's why he gets away with it. If your Ma had stood up to him years ago, he might never have got this bad. She lets him hit her and now he has started on you.'

'Let's forget about him. Do I look awful? Would you rather not take me out today?'

'You'll always look nice to me, Maggie. Come on, or we'll miss the first picture and I like a good Western...' He grinned at me. 'I like the Keystone Cops, but they aren't the same without Fatty Arbuckle but you know what happened to him, don't you?' I shook my head and Jack pulled a face. 'He killed a woman by raping her and they put him on trial—three trials he had, but in the end he got off. They stopped all his films though. So they should after what he done!'

'Maybe he didn't do it if he got off in the end?'

'I reckon there was some funny business. There's no smoke without fire. I don't like blokes what treat a woman bad. If I had my way, I would string them up!'

I tucked my arm into his, smiling up at him and yet a sense of menace... of foreboding ... loomed at the back of my mind.

* * *

It was a good outing after all. Jack had bought a packet of toffee, which we shared as we sat in the darkened cinema, watching the pictures flicker on the big screen, and listening as the piano player made the music sound darker and darker once the cowboys and Indians started shooting at each other.

The chase was very exciting, and it was nice seeing the hero get the girl at the end. After the Western there was a short cartoon followed by an interval when the lights went up. Unfortunately, we had only seen half of the main feature when Jack told me it was time to go.

'It's not fair on you having to leave now. Why don't you stay and I'll go on my own?'

Jack wasn't having any of that, insisting not only on leaving with me but walking me to the café as well. 'I can't fetch you home tonight,' he said. 'But if you leave at nine tomorrow night, I'll be waiting for you.'

'Yes, all right. Bill says that tomorrow is the start of my new hours. I'm going to have Saturday afternoons off so we'll be able to go out now and then, if you want?'

'Of course I want.' He grinned and turned away with a wave of his hand. 'See yer tomorrow, Maggie.'

* * *

Bill looked at my face and then at the bandage on my arm as I took off my coat. However, he made no comment, merely pointing to the menu, which was advertising beef stew and dumplings as the main dish, besides all the usual favourites.

'What do you fancy, lass?'

'Can I have some of the stew?'

'Help yourself. Had a good afternoon, did you?'

'It was lovely. Jack liked the Western but I thought Charlie Chaplin was very funny.'

'Yes, so I've heard. It's an age since I took Ann anywhere. We're always too busy.'

'I could look after the café one night if you like.'

'I don't think so, lass, you couldn't manage on your own. Mind you, if we could get a bloke in to keep an eye on the rougher sort it might be all right. I'll think about it. Ann could do with a change.'

We were very busy that night, and it was half past ten before Bill told me to go home.

'If this happens often, I shall have to pay you extra,' he said and chuckled, 'but usually the business tails off around nine.'

That was true, though when it was cold some of the customers kept drinking more and more tea as an excuse to stay by Bill's fire. I didn't like leaving the warmth to walk home myself. It was very dark out, because there was no moon that night, the sky having clouded over earlier in the day. We still hadn't got proper street lighting like they had up West, and there was only the occasional lamp that worked to guide the late-night traveller. Some of the shops and houses were showing lights, but there were patches of dense shadow that were pitch black. Once or twice, I had an odd feeling that I was being followed and I walked more quickly, breaking into a run as I neared our house.

There was a light still on in the kitchen. I hesitated but as I was debating whether I should go straight up the stairs, the door opened and Ma came out.

'Oh, it's you, Maggie. I thought it might be your father.'

'Hasn't he come in yet?'

'No, not yet. It's the first time he's been out late since...the accident. I suppose he's drunk all the money away. If he had spirits, he might be lying on a bench somewhere, sleeping it off.'

'I couldn't stop him taking the money, Ma.'

'Just be careful not to put it where he can see it in future. Go on up then, girl. You won't change anything standing there and you have to be up early in the morning remember. You're no better off than you were at the bakery working part time at the café.'

'Yes, I know. But Bill and Ann are really nice to me, Ma.'

'Well, you've made your bed so you can lie on it,' Ma's harshness told me that she hadn't forgotten our quarrel and the way I'd stood up to her.

* * *

When I went down to the kitchen in the morning Ma was already there. There was no sign of Pa and judging by Ma's anxious expression he hadn't come home all night.

'I've never known him to stay out all night before,' she said. 'I'm worried about him, Maggie. He's come home late and drunk often enough, but it isn't like him to sleep rough.'

'Maybe he just fell asleep somewhere. I'm sure he's all right.'

'Much you would care if he wasn't!'

'That's not fair. I don't like his violence but I wouldn't wish harm on him.'

'Wouldn't you?' Ma looked at me hard, and then relented. 'Sorry, Maggie. I'm being harsh on you and it isn't your fault. You couldn't have stopped him taking the money.'

'Try not to worry too much, Ma. I'm sure he'll be back in time for his dinner.'

'I wish I was as confident. I feel something has happened to him —something bad.'

'Why don't you go down the police station? If he got into a fight he might have been kept in the cells until he sobered up.'

'Yes, I've thought about that,' she said. 'I'll go when Robin has had his breakfast.' A smile relaxed her face. 'What time will you be home tonight then?'

'About half past nine I should think.' I stood up, hesitating before picking up my coat. 'I'm sorry I threw the water over Pa, and I'm sorry I argued with him yesterday. I hope he will turn up soon.'

'Get off to work then. We don't want you getting your wages docked because you were late.'

'I shan't be late.'

'I nearly forgot,' she said. 'A lad called to see you yesterday— Duncan Coulson. I told him you'd gone to the pictures with a friend and he seemed disappointed.'

'Did he say what he wanted?'

She shook her head. 'Get off then or you'll be late and get the sack!'

I reached into my coat pocket. 'This is for you, Ma. Five shillings from Bill last night. Next week it will be ten and sixpence.'

'Sixpence more than you were getting, and you working an extra day for it,' she grumbled. 'Still, if he feeds you, I suppose that's worth something.' She hesitated, then, 'I'll take a shilling. You keep the rest. If your pa wants it, he'll take it from me. You can be responsible for the money now, girl. You wanted it that way. Now you can try managing and see how you like it!'

* * *

I found my first whole day at the café hard going. The morning was the busiest part of the day with lots of men I'd never seen in the café before coming in for their breakfast. The night time customers were less demanding than these new ones, who wanted serving quickly and spoke harshly if I kept them waiting.

'They're always like that,' Bill told me when things eased off a bit. 'Some of them have been working night shifts in the factories and they want something quick before they go down the docks to get in line. If they're late they're unlikely to get any of the better jobs.'

'Don't they sleep at all?'

'Maybe for an hour or two before they clock on again, that's probably why they're so bad tempered, lass. Tired men don't watch their tongues.'

'Don't they earn enough in the factories?'

'What is enough? None of them earn more than a few shillings a week, maybe a pound at best. They all know they could get stood off at any time so they earn what they can while they can.'

'I've heard my father say it's difficult getting work down the docks. I always wondered if he said that because he didn't want to work.'

'Don't misjudge him, lass. It's being treated like dirt that turns men bitter. Some of the men wait all day and never earn a shilling

—soul destroying that is. But I think things are pretty bad for working men in most places so there's no point in grumbling about what we can't change.'

'Yes, it must be hard,' I said. I considered telling Bill that Pa hadn't come home all night but decided against it. He must have enough problems of his own, because I could hear the baby crying and knew that Ann had been up with her most of the night.

'By the way, there was a girl attacked down by the waterfront last night. You be careful when you go home, Maggie.'

I remembered the feeling of being followed the previous night. 'I might have someone to walk home with me this evening.'

'Got a boyfriend, have you? Jack is it, the one you went to the pictures with?'

'He's just a friend,' I said and blushed.

The café was starting to fill up again with men who had come off the early shift and wanted something to eat before they went home for a few hours. I was kept busy making bacon rolls while Bill dispensed tea and gossip to the regulars. They grumbled about the state of the country, the wages they were paid and the weather; it didn't change much from customer to customer.

* * *

When I went out into the street that evening, my heart lifted to see that Jack was waiting. He came towards me with a smile on his face.

'Right on time then, Maggie.'

'Yes. Bill knew you might be here and he said he wanted me to have someone walk me home because of what happened last night.'

'Yes, I heard that there was a girl attacked. It happened a couple of times some weeks back but it has been quiet for a while and we all thought it was over. Some of the men were talking about getting a vigilante group together.'

'Don't you get involved, Jack. I don't want you in trouble with the police.'

'Don't you worry your head about me, love. We know how to look after our own round here. The dockers might be a rough lot and a bit foul mouthed some of them but they're decent when it comes to what's right, and they don't hold with men that prey on innocent girls. There are plenty of girls what do it for a few coppers; there's no call to go raping decent ones.'

'Is that what happened? I knew a girl had been attacked but Bill didn't tell me it was rape.'

'Best you do know,' Jack said looking grim. 'At least that way you'll watch out for odd blokes if I can't walk you home some nights.'

'I wouldn't speak to strange men anyway.' I hesitated, then, 'You haven't heard anything about me pa, have you?'

'Why do you ask?'

'He didn't come home last night. Ma was worried about him.'

'He probably got drunk and slept it off somewhere.'

'Yes, that's what I told Ma. I expect he'll be there when I get home.'

'Let's hope he's in a better mood then.'

'Yes,' I agreed and hugged his arm. 'It's real good of you to walk me home, Jack.'

'I wanted to. It means we can have a bit more time together. I heard about a tea dance on Saturday afternoons. Do you fancy going? It won't be like the Pally but it might be all right—probably a bit posh for us but we could try it if you like?'

'I can't dance. I wouldn't mind making an idiot of myself up the Pally, but not at a posh place. Why don't we just go for a walk this week? We could go somewhere and have a cup of tea or something. You don't have to spend money on me all the time. We might take a bus and look at some of the sights—Big Ben and the palace or Hyde Park.'

'Would that be all right with you?'

'Yes, why not? It would give us lots of time to talk.'

'You're easy to please. Most girls want to go to the pictures or a dance.'

'Been out with a lot of girls, have you?'

'One or two but you were always the one I wanted for my girl. Ever since school. There won't be no more now that you've said you'll be my girl, Maggie.'

'There hadn't better be,' I teased. We had reached the end of my street. 'I'd better go straight in. Ma will be in a bother if Pa hasn't turned up by now.'

'I expect he came back when he was hungry.' Jack hesitated, then bent his head and gave me a quick peck on the cheek. 'See you tomorrow.'

'Thanks for walking me home, Jack.'

He waited on the other side of the road until I let myself in.

There were voices in the kitchen. Pa must be back, because one of the voices was a man's. I was on my way upstairs when the door opened and Ma came out with her visitor. Not Pa, but Eric Pearson from three doors down the street. He was a large, thickset man who worked down the timber yard and was better off than most of his neighbours.

'I thought I heard you come in, Maggie. Mr Pearson has been helping in the search for your father but so far there's no sign of him.'

'I saw him leave the King's Head last night,' Mr Pearson said. 'Michael was pretty drunk, but he could still walk. What happened to him after that I don't know. Your mother has tried the infirmary and the police station, but so far she hasn't had any luck.'

For the first time I began to feel worried. Pa had been drunk often enough, but he had always come home.

'I wish I could do more to help, but I have to be at work again in the morning.'

'You have enough to do,' Eric said. 'Don't worry about it, Maggie. We'll find him.'

'I hope so. I'm going up now, Ma. We've been busy all day. I'm tired to death.'

'It's harder work than the bakery then? I thought so. You'll wish you were back there before long.'

* * *

I hoped Pa might have turned up by the time I came down the next morning, but Ma's face looked grey and the shadows under her eyes were darker than before.

'I'm sorry, Ma,' I said and fetched my coat from the peg in the hall. I wanted to tell her how much I loved her, how I wished I could make things better for her, but couldn't find the right words.

Jack walked to the café with me. He tried to tell me that Pa would turn up soon enough, because he wanted to comfort me, but I was beginning to think the same as Ma.

It was another busy morning at the café, which pleased me, because it saved me thinking and worrying. In fact, I didn't think about Pa much at all until Eric Pearson walked in at three o'clock that afternoon. As soon as I saw his face, I knew something was wrong.

'Is it my father? Has he been hurt bad?'

'No, lass. I'm sorry, it's your ma.'

'Ma?' I stared at him in bewilderment. 'What's wrong with her?'

'My wife went over an hour ago to see if there was anything she could do and found her lying on the floor. She called the doctor out straightaway, but... I'm sorry, Maggie, she died before they could take her to the Infirmary.'

The floor moved under my feet. I grabbed at the counter as my head swam, staring at him in disbelief. It was such a shock that I could hardly take in what he was saying.

'But she wasn't ill... I know she was tired, but she's often tired. I don't understand. What happened to her?'

Eric looked awkward. 'I don't know how to tell you, lass. Someone thought they saw your father go into the house half an hour earlier, but if he did he must have left before Mary went over. Someone had been there, and whoever it was had hit your mother over the head with the poker. Mary says she thinks your mother's silver candlesticks have gone from the parlour, the ones her posh cousin gave her.'

I felt sick. None of this made sense. I was suddenly conscious of Bill behind me, pushing me down into a chair. My head was going round and round. This couldn't be happening. Not to Ma... not to Ma!

'Take a deep breath, lass,' Bill's voice said. 'I'll fetch you a drop of brandy.'

He was back with it in seconds. He put the glass in my hand and told me to drink it all. I obeyed him, choking on the fiery spirit as it stung my throat, but in a moment or two the faintness had cleared.

I looked into the faces of the men watching me anxiously. 'You're saying that Ma was murdered, aren't you? And... my father... it was him that...'

'Eric doesn't know that for sure,' Bill said. 'If it was him, he'll be found and...' He broke off, but we all knew it would mean a hanging. 'No one knows for sure what happened, lass.'

'I hope they hang him,' I said and the bitterness in my voice shocked them all. 'He was always hitting her. That's why I threw that hot water over him. I wished I hadn't done it, but now I wish it had killed him! I'd rather he was dead than her. I would rather be in prison than have him kill her!' I felt a scream building inside me. Ma couldn't be dead. She couldn't!

'Ah, don't take on like that, lass,' Bill said. 'You don't mean it; you know you don't.'

I couldn't answer him, because I'd just started to realise what all this meant. Ma was gone. She wouldn't be waiting for me when I got home. I wouldn't see her, talk to her... touch her ever again. 'Where is she?' I asked at last. 'I want to see her.'

'The police came and took her away,' Eric said. 'There will be an inquest and then they'll let you have the funeral when it's officially known what happened to her.'

'Robin will be home from school soon...' I looked at Bill, confused, uncertain. 'I don't know what to do.'

'Sadie knows what has happened,' Eric said. 'She said she would meet him when he comes back from school and give him his tea. She'll keep him with her. She said to tell you not to go home alone.'

'You can stay here for the night if you like,' Bill said. 'Unless you want to go to your sister now?'

'Could I? I don't want to lose my job. I'll come back after I've seen Sadie.'

'No, you take the rest of the day off,' Bill said. 'I'll need you in tomorrow as usual if you feel up to it.'

'I shall be here. I'm sorry about this but I have to think about Robin. He's closer to me than he is to Sadie.'

5

Sadie's eyes were red with crying. She hugged me tight when I walked in, and then sat down at the kitchen table, her face working with distress.

'They're saying it was Pa. Did you know that?'

'Mary Pearson thought she saw him go into the house earlier, but she isn't sure it was him,' I said. 'But I wouldn't put it past him. He was hitting her the night I threw that hot water over him.'

'You threw that water over him? Ma never told me that bit. She said it was an accident. You said he'd done it himself that night. Why did you lie to me?'

'I was too ashamed of what I'd done. Now I wish it had been boiling. If I'd killed him, she might still be alive.'

'She would have hated you for it. She loved him. It didn't matter what he did to her, she went on loving him. She used to talk to me about when they were young sometimes. I was on the way by the time they got married. I think she was a push over for him right from the word go. Her family cut her off. They were posh, you know, at least her cousin is posh. I've never seen her, but Ma said she's got money. Grandmother died when Ma was young, and

Grandfather died soon after she ran off with Pa. He wrote her a letter, telling her she was a wicked girl and had broken his heart.'

'She never told me any of this, only a little bit about her falling for Pa, and that was after I threw the pan of water at him. Why didn't she tell me anything?'

'I was the eldest. Things were so much better before the war. There was more money in the house and she used to sing while she worked. She often told me things. You were too young then, and when Pa came home afterwards...it all started to go wrong, didn't it?'

'I wish I could have done something to make it better for her. She was so tired, so unhappy...'

'You did your best, love. You couldn't have worked any harder, and I always thought Ma was a bit rough on you. Pa too... but he was like that with all of us when he came home after the war.'

'What do you think will happen now? I mean if Pa...' I broke off because it was too hard to say the words.

'If he killed her?' Sadie took the kettle from the range and poured the boiling water into a large brown pot. Her hands were shaking as she brought it to the table. 'The police will find him and he'll be put on trial. If he's guilty...' Her face crinkled with anguish. 'He might hang, Maggie.'

'What about Robin? What shall we tell him?'

'We can't keep it from him, he's bound to hear the truth from someone.'

'It will break his heart. He's only a child.'

'Maybe you should take Robin away for a while. It's not going to be easy for any of us to live here after what has happened—especially if Pa murdered her.'

'Don't! I can't bear to think about what he did—hitting her so hard. How she must have suffered.' Tears were trickling down my cheeks. Sadie had poured us both a mug of tea but neither of us had touched it. 'I've got a decent job at the café but I couldn't afford to take Robin on a holiday.'

'I know. It's up to you what you decide but where are you going to live? You can't go back there alone. It would be dangerous until they find Pa, because if he did kill Ma he might come after you. Besides, I don't think the landlord would let you stay on. I can have you both here for a while, but when the baby is born...' Sadie let the words hang in the air. 'It isn't that I wouldn't have you around, love, but well, you know. We want some privacy. Ben likes to have the run of the house.' She blushed. 'We haven't been married that long and...'

'You don't have to explain. I can stay at the café for a while—until I know what's going on anyway. If you could keep Robin with you for the time being?'

'Yes, of course I will, for a while.'

'I might be able to find somewhere for Robin to stay with me. So that we could keep the family together.'

'I'm not sure we shall be here that long. Ben wants to emigrate to America. They've been asking for people for Australia in the paper, but he wants to go to America. He's been on about it for ages, thinks it would be a better life for us out there. I've only stayed because of Ma but now...' She looked a bit uncomfortable as though she realised that she was abandoning all responsibility towards Robin and me. 'Well, Robin is closer to you than to me. I think I'd rather make a new life for us somewhere else. If I were you, I should do the same.'

Sadie sounded selfish and she was a bit, always had been, but she was my sister and even though I didn't often see her, I loved her and I'd miss her.

'Yes, I know what you mean, but I'm not sure I want to go away.' I glanced at the mantle clock. 'Robin will be out of school now. I think I'll walk and meet him. I want to tell him myself.'

* * *

Jack was waiting outside Sadie's house when I left for work the next day. It was a bitterly cold morning, dank and miserable, smoke from the factory chimneys hanging in the air instead of drifting away. The smell from the river was bad, and the pavements were greasy underfoot, litter lying in the gutters. I grimaced as I saw a dog tossing a dead rat in the air, playing with it like a child with a toy.

'You haven't slept all night,' Jack said. 'Are you sure you want to go to work today?'

'There's no point in staying home. I should be under Sadie's feet, and I don't feel like going back to our house. Not until...'

'They catch him?' Jack's expression was grim. 'It won't be long, Maggie. He won't be able to hide in this part of London, not after what he's done. Some of the men are talking about giving him a good hiding.'

'I wish they would,' I said fiercely. 'I'd like him to suffer the way she did, Jack. She made excuses for him all the time, but I think he was a bully. Sadie says he'll hang, but I think that's too good for him.'

Jack nodded. 'How are your family taking it?'

'Sadie is very upset. She keeps crying and setting me off. Robin has been very quiet. He hasn't cried that I know of, but he looks bewildered, frightened. One of the other boys had told him before I got to him. He asked me if Pa was going to come and kill us too. I told him he was safe, because Pa hadn't meant to do it. That he'd probably been drunk and just hit Ma too hard.'

'Is that what you really think?'

'Pa could get very violent when he was drunk but he couldn't have stayed drunk for two days on my wages.'

'Maybe he wanted more money and your Ma wouldn't give it to him?'

'Yes, that might be the answer. Mary Pearson told her husband that my mother's silver candlesticks had gone. Her cousin sent her them after she married; they were special to her I think.'

'Your ma wasn't from these parts, was she?'

'I think her family came from somewhere away—the West Country, Sadie said. Ma never talked to me about her past, though it seems she used to tell Sadie things.'

'It's going to be hard,' Jack said. 'Things will get more unpleasant until this is settled. You may have a visit from the police.'

'They came last night, asked us if Pa was violent at home. When I told them what happened last time he attacked her, they seemed to think it was an open and shut case.'

'That's what everyone thinks,' Jack said, giving me an odd, considered look. 'Your pa had made a bit of a name for himself, Maggie. He was often violent down the docks, and that's why he didn't get as much work as he might have. Folk round here reckon he deserves what's coming to him.'

We had reached the café, I hesitated, then reached up to kiss him on the cheek. 'I might stay at the café tonight, if Bill says it's all right, but if you come in for a cup of tea at nine we can talk.'

'I'm not sure if I can make it tonight, but if not, I'll come and see you tomorrow. Don't worry, Maggie, things will sort themselves, you'll see.'

I nodded but didn't reply, merely running across the road to the café, where the windows were streaming with heat from inside. I didn't see how any of it would get sorted. Ma was dead and the world had turned upside down.

* * *

'Ben took me into the house to fetch some of Ma's personal things,' Sadie said. She had popped into the café to see me the next day. 'You've got Saturday afternoon off, haven't you? I think you should come round, Maggie. Robin is going to a friend's house for the day and we need to talk.'

'Yes. I was going out with Jack, but I could see him after.'

'Right,' Sadie looked at me thoughtfully. 'He could come for tea if you like, but I want an hour or so on our own. I think there are things that you ought to know.'

'Like what?'

'I can't tell you now. You come on Saturday and we'll talk then.'

'Yes, all right. I was going to come anyway. You haven't heard anything I suppose?'

'Ben says the police have been all over the docks asking questions about Pa, but so far they don't seem to have come up with any clues.'

'Yes, that's what I've heard. Jack says the police are idiots. No one talks to them, but he thinks Pa will be found soon. Most of the men round here are keeping an eye out for him.'

'I hope they're not going to take the law into their own hands,' Sadie said looking worried. 'I mean we don't know it was Pa that killed her, Maggie. We've only got Mrs Pearson's word for it that she saw him go into the house.'

'Who else would do a thing like that?'

'I know it seems as if it was Pa, but Ben says it's wrong to condemn him without a hearing.'

'Yes, I suppose so but if he did it, I want him punished.' I gave her a defiant look. 'I'll see you on Saturday then.'

'Right. Don't forget that you can ask Jack for tea if you like.'

'I shan't forget. I haven't seen that much of him this week. I think he's been working. I know he does odd jobs for someone. He wants to have his own business one day.'

'He sounds a bright lad. You want to hang on to him, love.'

'You said I ought to take Robin away somewhere.'

'Well, it's up to you, Maggie. I just thought it might be better for both of you.'

After Sadie had gone, the café was a bit quiet so I went through to the kitchen. Ann was nursing the baby and looking washed out, and the kitchen smelled of urine. She obviously couldn't cope with all the work Katie had made for her.

'Shall I rinse those bits through for you?' I asked, looking at a tub filled with the baby's napkins and clothes.

'Would you mind? I could do with some help, if Bill isn't busy.'

'He can cope for the moment and you look shattered.'

'She was awake crying all night, but you must have heard her crying?'

'Yes, I did. I didn't sleep much either but I'm used to it. I'm one of those folk that don't seem to need it. I often used to get up early at home and do a few chores before...' I choked on the words. Picking up the bucket of dirty nappies, I said, 'I'll take these through to the washhouse then.'

When I came back from the yard, having hung the clothes out to drip some of the wet out of them, Ann had gone upstairs and Bill was in the kitchen. He looked at me oddly.

'There's someone to see you in the café, lass.'

'Is it Sadie again?'

'It's the police.'

'They've got him, haven't they?'

'I'm not sure. The constable wants to talk to you.'

I went through to the café. The young constable looked so serious that I suddenly felt sick, knowing what he was going to say before he spoke.

'You're Miss Maggie Bailey?'

'Yes.'

'I've been to see your sister. She wasn't at home so I thought I'd better come here. We need someone to identify a man's body. We think it is Michael Bailey. Would you be willing to do it, miss?'

'I... I'm not sure,' I said, my mouth dry. 'What happened to him?'

'He met with some kind of an accident,' the constable replied heavily. 'We found him on a bit of waste ground near the docks. We think he'd been there a few days, but we can't be sure how long, because it's been so cold of late. We're pretty sure it's him, but we need someone to identify him.'

'You can't ask Maggie to do that,' Bill said from behind me. 'I knew him well enough. I'll do it if you like, or there's her brother-in-law if you need one of the family.'

'I could ask Mr Masters,' the constable said, 'If Miss Bailey doesn't feel up to it?'

'No, don't ask Ben. I can do it. Shall I come with you now?' I looked at Bill apologetically. 'I shan't be long and we're quiet today anyway.'

'You'll want to see your sister afterwards. Come back for the evening rush, lass.'

'Yes, of course,' I promised. I took a deep breath as I turned to the police officer, my head up. 'I'm ready.'

* * *

'So it's over then?' Sadie looked so pale and sick that I told her to sit down. She put her hand on her swollen belly as if to protect her unborn child from all the evil things that were happening to our family. 'I kept hoping they would find him alive and he'd say it was all a mistake, that he didn't hurt Ma.' She caught back a sob. 'Why did it have to happen, Maggie?'

'The police say he didn't have a penny on him. If he took those candlesticks he must have been robbed of them. He couldn't have spent all the money in the time. The police think he has been dead a couple of days.'

'So it would have been the day after she was killed...'

'Or that night,' I agreed. My hands shook as I filled the kettle and set it on the range. 'His face was bruised, Sadie. He'd been beaten to death with an iron bar or something of the sort. I knew it was Pa but his face looked a terrible mess.' It had shaken me to see Pa like that and I'd cried, something I hadn't expected. 'If he killed Ma he deserved it but we shall never be sure now, shall we?'

'I've thought it over and over and the more I think about it the less I believe he did it. Ma would have given him whatever she had. He could have taken the candlesticks months ago if he'd wanted, but they were her pride and joy, and he left them be out of respect for her feelings. Why would he suddenly change his mind?'

'I still think it was Pa. I don't know what happened afterwards, or where the candlesticks went, but I think he killed her in a temper. Perhaps he didn't mean to do it, but you don't know what he was like of late. He was really going for her the night I stopped him, and he threatened to put the hot iron on my face the morning he went off in a temper. I think he would have done it if Robin hadn't pushed him against the stove.'

'Well, we shall never know for certain, but in a way I'm glad it happened like this, Maggie. I would have hated all the business of a trial, and if they'd hung him...' She closed her eyes for a moment. 'At least this way we can put it behind us. I suppose we can have both the funerals together.'

'You're not going to have them buried in the same grave? Sadie, you can't!'

'Why not? It's what she would have wanted, and it will cost less, Maggie. I fetched her box from the house and there's nothing of any value, no trinkets of any kind. I know she had a couple of rings and brooches once, but they've all gone, been taken to the pawn shop I expect.'

I hated the idea of my parents being buried in a single grave, but my sister was showing practical good sense and I knew Sadie was right; it would cost less.

'I have a few shillings.' I offered.

'Ma had a policy to cover a funeral. There's just enough if we wait and bury them together.'

'Is that what you wanted to tell me?'

Sadie shook her head. 'There are some letters in the box, letters from Ma's cousin. Her name is Beth and she has been asking Ma to visit her for ages it seems. She wrote only a few weeks ago and asked if you and Robin could visit her—'

'Ma's cousin asked for us? That means Ma must have kept in touch with her over the years.'

'Yes. I think she did,' Sadie agreed. 'I believe she is older than Ma and she has property of her own, though I'm not sure what— but she sounds as if she has money. She says she's thinking of retiring soon, because she hasn't been feeling too well, but she doesn't give details so Ma must have known all about her. I think she must have sent Ma money now and then, just a few pounds, because she says she isn't going to send any more until one of us goes to see her. You might get on all right there, Maggie. She might ask you to stay with her if she's lonely.'

'Ma never told me any of this.'

'Ma needed what you earned,' Sadie said. 'She couldn't have managed on Pa's money even when he was working. She couldn't afford to let you go, Maggie.'

I felt hurt and angry. Ma had taken me for granted but never told me anything and it wasn't fair.

The kettle was hissing as it boiled and the smell of cooking pervaded the air. Everything was normal and yet so different.

'I know. I'll look at the letters when this is all over, Sadie. I don't feel like it just now.'

'I know you are upset, Maggie, but you'll have to do something,' Sadie said. 'Unless you want to go on sleeping on Bill Biggin's sofa?'

'No, I don't. I think I might go back to the house for a while. Until the landlord throws me out anyway.'

'Stay there on your own? It gave me the creeps just going in with Ben to get her box. You can't sleep there, Maggie.'

'Why not? Pa isn't going to come after me now, is he?'

'I wouldn't get a wink of sleep thinking of you there. If you want to fetch anything, I'll come with you on Saturday. I suppose we'll have to clear it out anyway. We might get a few pounds for the furniture.'

'Yes, I suppose so. All right, I'll wait until Saturday and then see how I feel but I don't see why I can't stay there until I get notice.'

* * *

Sadie was on edge the whole time we were at the house, but apart from a few shivers when we went into the kitchen, I didn't feel any different. Ma had never hurt us while she was alive and I didn't see why I should be afraid of her now she was dead.

'I think we should go through the chest in Ma's bedroom,' Sadie said. 'If there's anything of value there, we ought to take it now, because once people know the house is empty there may be a break in.'

'It won't be empty. I'm going to sleep here tonight.'

'Oh, Maggie. I don't think you should. If you don't want to stay at the café you could sleep on our sofa for a while.'

'No, I'm going to stay here until the landlord puts me out. It will give me a chance to decide what I want to do, Sadie.'

'I don't like the idea, but if it's what you want... but I'm not coming back here again once we've got Ma's best things out. It gives me the shivers.'

I was silent for a moment. Maybe Sadie was right and we ought to sort things out.

'Let's go through Ma's things together,' I said. 'You might want some of them and I'll keep some. If I have to give up the house, we can sell the rest of it then.'

'That's fair enough. I'd like her silk blouse if you don't mind, and that silver hand mirror. I know the glass is a bit spotty but Ben says I can get that done.'

Ma's chest yielded very few treasures. Sadie took the blouse she wanted and the mirror. There was also a nice leather handbag that Ma must have had for years and never used, and some smart gloves.

'Do you want these?' Sadie asked trying on the gloves.

'No, you can take them if you want them. I would like to keep Ma's sewing box if you don't mind, but I don't think there's anything else other than the furniture. We can sort that out if I have to give up the house.'

'All right,' Sadie agreed. I could tell she had hoped to sell everything but she didn't argue. 'I suppose we could get rid of the rest of her clothes. There's nothing else worth keeping, but we might get a few pence for them on the market.'

'Do you want to do that, or shall we burn them? I wouldn't want to see anyone else wearing Ma's dress.'

'No, you're right,' Sadie agreed. 'Do you think we should go through Pa's things?'

'Ma pawned his suit the other week. We can take the rest of his stuff down the market if you like.'

'Let's do it now,' Sadie said. 'I don't want to come back again unless I'm forced.'

Pa hadn't owned very much. There was a pair of working boots that had some life left in them, a couple of threadbare jackets, a pair of old trousers and some shirts.

'I don't think these are worth selling,' Sadie said. 'Ma didn't have much but Pa seems to have had even less.'

'There's something in the pocket of this jacket,' I said and fished inside it. I brought out a bunch of old keys, some pebbles and a small leather box. Opening it, I saw it contained a tiepin, which looked as if it was made of gold and had a pretty red stone set in the bar.

'That might be worth something,' Sadie said. 'We could pawn that, Maggie.'

'I think we should give it to Robin. We've both got something of Ma's. I think Robin should have this.'

'Yes, all right,' Sadie agreed. 'But I would like the best teapot from the dresser in the parlour. Ma never used it but I always liked it. And there are some cups and saucers that match it.'

'Take them when we go downstairs,' I said. 'Look, let's leave these clothes for now. We've sorted out anything any good, and I can put the rest out in the yard another time. I'll probably put them under the copper to burn when I do the washing.'

'So you're really set on staying here?'

'Yes, I am. I shall ask Robin if he wants to come with me, but if he doesn't, I shall stay here alone for the time being.'

Sadie stared at me as if I were mad, but I was determined. It didn't make any difference to the way I thought about Ma's murder whether I was in the house or not. It was a good house, one of the best in the street, and I wasn't going to give it up without a fight.

* * *

Robin shook his head when I asked him if he wanted to come back to the house with me. He shuffled his feet and looked down at the floor, but wouldn't speak. He was becoming increasingly quiet, and though he hadn't shown any emotion when we told him that Pa was also dead, I had seen his eyes darken with fear.

When I showed him the gold tiepin and told him it was his, he spoke for the first time in days. 'I don't want it,' he said in a small voice. 'It was Pa's. I hate him. He killed Ma and I'm glad he's dead.'

'We don't know for sure that he killed Ma,' Sadie said. 'You're upset, Robin. This has all been too much for you. I think we've all been to hell and back this week.'

'I'll sell the pin and keep the money for you, Robin,' I said. If Robin felt that way, he would never want the pin, but the money would be his—or I would spend it on things he needed and he would never know the difference.

'Don't want it. Don't want anything of his.' Robin burst out wildly. He turned and ran outside to the yard.

'I'd better go after him.'

'Leave him for a while. He'll get over it.'

'I wish I hadn't offered him the pin now.'

'You keep the money,' Sadie said. 'You'll need it until you sort yourself out, Maggie.'

I didn't answer. I would sell the pin and use the money for my brother. He needed clothes for school and shoes.

I told Jack what was on my mind when he came to Sadie's house. He had come too late for tea but he walked me back to the café, and offered to sell the pin for me.

'If there's anything else I can do for you,' he said. 'I can sell bits and pieces from the house, or old clothes.'

'We're going to burn most of the clothes. They're not much good anyway,' I said. 'I'm keeping the furniture for the moment, because I'm going to stay at the house until the landlord throws me out.'

'You can't stay there alone, lass!' Jack was shocked at the idea. He looked at me the way Sadie had when I told her.

'I don't see why I shouldn't. I shall lock the door all the time. Ma never did that. If she had she might still be alive.'

'No one locks their door in the lanes,' Jack said. 'It's not often that strangers come round thievin' and hurtin' folks. It wouldn't have kept your pa out, would it? He would have broke the door down if she'd tried to shut him out.'

'If it was him that killed her. We'll never be sure now. Pa didn't have the candlesticks,' I said and frowned. 'He didn't have any money either. That's a bit odd, Jack. He couldn't have spent the money for those sticks so soon, could he?'

'He might have been robbed,' Jack said. He sounded a bit odd and didn't look at me. 'Did the police ask if you had any idea of a motive for the beating?'

'No; they seemed to think it was a robbery. The candlesticks were worth a few pounds. If Pa was mixing with vagrants, it's likely that they set on him to take the money.'

'Yeah, that sounds about right. Well, it's a good thing it's all over, isn't it, Maggie? You wouldn't have felt safe until he was out of the way.'

'No...' I was a little unsure, because Sadie had put doubt in my mind. 'I wish the police had arrested him though. We'll never know the truth now—never know whether he killed her or not.'

'He did it all right!'

'How can you be certain of that?' His eyes avoided mine. 'How would anyone know that?'

'The word is that he did it. I don't think you need to doubt it, Maggie. Don't start feeling sorry for him now he's dead. You wouldn't have been safe while he was around.'

I had an uneasy feeling that Jack knew more than he was saying. I remembered him telling me that the men on the docks were all for teaching Michael Bailey a lesson. Had that got out of hand? Was it a revenge beating rather than a robbery? My blood chilled and for a moment I felt swamped with guilt and regret. I'd been angry with Pa, had said he deserved to be punished, but I hadn't wanted him dead—not like that! Not in my heart. I had said it to Jack though, said it in anger and hatred. It was as if the Almighty had listened and struck Pa down, but I knew it wasn't God's hand that had beaten Pa senseless.

* * *

Was Jack involved with the men who had beaten my father to death? And was there another reason they had decided to take the law into their own hands? A reason other than the suspicion that he had murdered his wife?

I remembered all too clearly Jack saying that Michael Bailey deserved a good thrashing, and I'd agreed, because I'd felt bitter and had wanted him punished but I hadn't wanted him murdered.

It had upset me more than I'd expected, seeing Pa lying there in the mortuary with his head bashed in, but then I'd hardened my heart against him, because I believed he'd killed Ma. But supposing he hadn't? Supposing Mary Pearson had been mistaken and it was someone else she'd seen going into the house that morning? Yet Jack had seemed to think that the lanes round the docks were a safer place now that Michael Bailey was dead. Did he suspect that my father was the man who had attacked those girls, or did he know it was him? Was he one of the men who had taken the law into their own hands?

The thoughts went round and round in my head endlessly. If it was true that Pa had raped that girl, I should be glad he was dead and out of the way. On the other hand I didn't want to believe he had done such a thing.!

I went down to the kitchen. I'd scrubbed the floor before going to bed the previous night and there was no sign of the blood, nothing left of the pain that Ma must have endured before she died. A picture of her last moments rushed into my head and I felt faint. In that moment I knew how Sadie felt about coming here, and I was shaking from head to foot. I took a deep breath. I had to get a grip on myself because I was determined not to let silly fears drive me away from my home.

Just as the kettle was boiling, I heard a sound that seemed to come from outside the front door. I went through the parlour, listening for a moment before I called out, 'Is anyone there?'

There was no answer and after a moment of hesitation, I opened the door. A parcel wrapped in newspaper was lying on the doorstep. Feeling the weight and the knobbly shape as I retrieved it, I knew it was Ma's candlesticks.

I wished I'd been a bit quicker getting the door open. It was strange, the sticks being returned. Unless, it wasn't a thief who had taken and then returned them, but someone looking out for Michael Bailey's family.

If a group of local men had gone after Pa, giving him the thrashing they felt he deserved, they wouldn't have left something valuable lying around for a vagrant to find and steal. If that was what had happened, it meant that Pa had taken the sticks and... someone had brought them back to me. Someone who knew me well perhaps?

I took the parcel back to the kitchen, deciding to leave a little earlier than I need so that I could call round and see Sadie. We would have to tell the police that the sticks had been returned, and I didn't have the time to visit the police station.

There was another reason why I didn't want to leave at my usual time. I didn't think I could face Jack until I had sorted this out in my mind.

6

'Where did you get these?' Sadie stared at the beautiful silver candlesticks, seeming bewildered. I had unwrapped them and placed them on her kitchen table without saying anything. 'They weren't in the house the other day when we were there. I'm sure they weren't, because I looked. I told the police they had been stolen!'

'They were stolen but someone brought them back. I found them on the doorstep early this morning. I had got up to make a cup of tea because I couldn't sleep—'

'I told you that you wouldn't be able to, and this just proves it isn't safe. You never know who is about.'

'No one that means me any harm. And it wasn't the house or Ma that kept me awake. I was thinking about other things—about the future.'

Sadie wouldn't understand about Jack and the other men getting together to teach Pa his lesson. If she even suspected he was involved she would go to the police and I didn't want Jack to be arrested.

'Anyway, I have to get to work. You can take these into the police station and tell them what happened, can't you?'

'Yes, I suppose so,' Sadie said reluctantly. 'But why are you going into work so early?'

'Because I need to make up some time. I've had a lot of time off since I've been working at the café and I don't want to lose my job.'

'You haven't thought any more about leaving London then?'

'I'm not sure. We'll see when the funerals are over.'

'Well, it's up to you, but Ben says we're definitely emigrating once the baby is born, so you'll have a few months to get Robin settled. I suppose he could go on the Parish if you can't find him a place to live.'

'He won't do that! What an awful thing to say!' I glanced at my brother, who was thankfully still sound asleep on Sadie's sofa. How could she say such a thing? 'If it means going to the country for his sake, then I'll go.'

I caught a satisfied look in my sister's eyes and knew that Sadie was trying to push me into the decision. She didn't want Robin to go to a home any more than I did, but she wanted me out of London, because she thought it safer in the country.

'But I'm going to think about it first, all right?'

'It's your decision, but you don't belong here, Maggie. None of us belong here. The docks are not such a wonderful place to live, are they? If I didn't have Ben, I would take the opportunity. Ma's cousin wants you to stay with her. I should have thought you would jump at the chance.'

I shook my head and left Sadie's house without waking Robin.

* * *

Jack was waiting when I left the café that evening. He looked at me oddly as I joined him.

'Is something wrong, Maggie? You weren't there when I called for you this morning.'

'I came to work early. I want to make up for the time I've lost. We're having the funerals on Friday. I'll need the morning off for that.'

'Yes, I know. I shan't be there, Maggie. I can't manage it but if you need money I can help.'

'Money isn't everything, Jack.'

He had an odd expression in his eyes. I wondered if it was guilt. 'There is something wrong, isn't there?'

'Someone brought Ma's candlesticks back early this morning— left them on my doorstep. Who would do that, Jack, and why?' He couldn't look me in the eye! He did know something about what had been going on! What part had Jack played in Pa's murder?

'Maybe they couldn't sell them. The police would have told the pawnbrokers to be on the lookout for a pair of silver sticks. It would be too dangerous to sell them or to keep them, so it was probably the safest thing, giving them back.'

'Yes, that's a possibility, but if Pa took them, if it was him that killed Ma, they must have been taken from him when he was attacked.'

'That's another way of looking at it,' Jack agreed. 'So what are you getting at then?'

'I wondered who brought them back to me, Jack, and if that person was involved in Pa's murder?'

'Does it matter who brought them back? You wanted your pa punished—said hanging was too good for him. Happen some people thought the same way as you, perhaps for other reasons.'

I stopped walking and took hold of his arm, making him look at me. 'I know I said those things when I was angry, but I would rather the law had punished him, if he was guilty. If you know anything else I ought to, Jack, I should be glad if you would tell me.'

He was silent for a moment, then, 'Do you really want me to tell you?'

'Yes. It would settle things in my mind.'

'It was your pa attacking those girls. He'd been under suspicion for a while, before he killed your ma. He did it again the following night and they caught him. He'd been seen drinking at a pub, not local but at the other end of the docks. Some of the men went down there to find him and teach him a lesson, and they saw him stalking a girl. It was meant to be a lesson, Maggie, but one of the men lost his head and went in too hard.'

I felt as if someone had thrown a bucket of cold water over me. I had known it in my heart all the time, but it was still shocking and horrible. It was shameful! My pa doing things like that. I felt angry and disgusted and glad he'd been punished.

'Were you with them when they killed him, Jack?'

'Not that night. I joined in the first time they got together and went looking for him, but that night I had to work. I swear I wasn't there, Maggie. I wouldn't have let them go that far if I'd known, and it *was* me that let it be known you could do with those candlesticks. I don't know who had them, but whoever it was, he wouldn't have dared to sell them. If the police traced them to him, he would be hung for murder.'

'I'm glad it wasn't you,' I said and gave him a wan smile. 'I wish it hadn't happened the way it did, but then again, I'm glad it didn't come out about him being the rapist. Sadie is upset enough as it is and Robin hates his father.' I hated him too at that moment. Remembering the times he'd tried to get into my bedroom, I shuddered at the thought.

'You're not going to tell Sadie what I've told you?'

'No. I had most of it worked out in my head this morning, but I didn't tell her when I gave her the sticks.'

'You gave them to Sadie?'

'Do you think I could keep them, knowing or suspecting what I did?'

'I suppose not, but you'll find it hard to keep that house going on your wages, Maggie—that's if your landlord will let you have the tenancy. The money those sticks might have fetched would have paid your rent for six months.'

'I know.' I frowned, because I wasn't sure what to do for the best. 'I haven't made up my mind what to do yet, Jack. Once the funerals are over, I'll be able to reason things out more clearly. At the moment all I can think about is Ma and what that devil did to her.'

'Maybe your ma knew what he'd been doing,' Jack said. 'Had you thought about that, Maggie? She might have accused him of it—'

'—and that might be why he killed her and took the sticks,' I finished for him, because it made sense. 'I wondered why he'd done it, because he'd used his fists on her before but never the poker. He must have lost his head...' Perhaps when she'd looked at him, he'd felt shame and it had driven him wild.

'Well, we can't know all of it, but I do know he had the sticks on him, and that should settle your mind on what happened at your house. It was Michael Bailey that murdered your ma and ran off with her candlesticks. I reckon he got what was coming to him!'

'Yes, it does settle my mind, thanks,' I said. 'And I'm glad you weren't involved in the beating.'

We had reached the house now. Jack stood there looking down at me awkwardly. I hesitated, then. 'Shall you be here in the morning?'

'If you want me to be?'

'Yes, I do. I was just too mixed up this morning, but I'm settled in my mind now.'

'Goodnight then, lass.'

The chill struck as I entered the house. I must have forgotten to bank the fire up before I left that morning. I locked the door. I had to light the stove again, and it took a while before it got going enough so that I could make a hot drink, but while the kettle was boiling, I ran upstairs to my parents' room and collected everything I could find of Pa's. I took it all out into the shed in the back yard, pushing everything under the copper with a bit of wood and paper to make it catch.

I felt better now there was nothing left in the house to remind me of Pa. I hated him, hated what he'd been, what he'd done to my mother—and to those girls. I would never tell anyone else what I knew, but I wasn't going to feel guilty about his death ever again. He'd deserved what he got!

It was only as I tumbled into bed that I remembered the next day was my seventeenth birthday. Not that it mattered. Ma had never made a big thing of my birthday anyway.

7

Robin had made a birthday card for me at school. Sadie brought it round to the café in the middle of the morning.

'I thought you might call this morning,' she said. 'I hadn't forgotten it was your birthday, love. I've got a little present for you.' She offered a parcel. Inside was a pretty pink scarf. 'It's not much, but I wanted you to have something.'

'Thank you. Jack bought me a pair of gloves. They're made of leather and very smart. I shall look posh when I wear them and this scarf.'

'Well, you won't wear them on Friday,' Sadie said. 'Your coat is grey and I've sorted a hat and gloves for you. They belong to Ben's Aunt Jean. She works up West in an office and has some good clothes. She was happy to lend them to me. I've borrowed some things for myself as well.'

'What about Robin? He's only got his school things.'

'Robin isn't coming to the funeral, Maggie. He shouted at me when I told him he ought to and ran out of the house. He came home later but he was so upset that I told him he needn't. He's going to stay with some friends on Thursday night and come back to me on Saturday.'

'Yes, perhaps that's best. It might be too much for him.'

'It's more than I want,' Sadie admitted. 'It would have been bad enough with Ma dying like that—but Pa as well and not knowing what really happened.'

'I think you know. You just don't want to admit it.'

'You sound hard,' Sadie said, staring at me as if she was disappointed in me. 'You be careful, Maggie. Don't get bitter over this. After all, you can't be sure it was Pa killed her, and I for one don't believe it.'

I wanted to tell her the truth but I didn't. Let her keep her illusions if she wanted to, but I knew and I hated what my father had become.

* * *

Friday was a cold, dank, miserable day. It didn't rain but the moisture gathered on the church windows, and the trees were dripping as we went outside after the service to see the coffins lowered into the ground. I kept rubbing my hands together despite the gloves Sadie had borrowed for me.

Sadie stepped up to the grave, scattering some earth on the coffin. I followed her, fallen leaves slippery underfoot. The gravestones nearby looked old, covered with moss, the inscriptions almost worn away by rain and time. Ma and Pa had been tucked away in an odd corner, out of the way of decent folk I thought, but we were lucky that they had let us bury Pa here at all, because most folk thought he was a murderer.

'Bye, Ma,' I whispered, my throat tight, eyes stinging. 'I'm sorry I didn't tell you I loved you.' I stepped back, blinking so that I wouldn't cry. I had cried all my tears in the night.

Sadie had decided to put on a bit of a do at her house, just for the friends and neighbours who had called to ask what they could do to help at this sad time. I stayed for half an hour, and then told my sister I had to get back to the café. It wasn't true, because Bill had insisted I didn't return until the evening rush, but I felt too miserable to stay there and listen to everyone praising Ma and trying to avoid mentioning Michael Bailey.

Most of the people in the lanes had a good idea what had happened to him and why. So why didn't they just say it instead of behaving as if everything was normal? It was false and horrible to pretend everything was as it should be, and it brought a bitter taste to my mouth.

I was glad to get back to work. Bill looked at my face as I walked in and set a plate of pie and mash with onion gravy in front of me.

'Get that inside you, lass,' he said gruffly. 'You'll feel better soon.'

'I'm just glad it's over.' Violent shudders took my body and my hand shook as I reached for the mug of hot tea, he had put in front of me. 'It was horrible, Bill.'

'Yes, lass, I know, but you have to put it behind you now. Think of the future. You can't help the dead. Look after the living.'

'Robin has been quiet since the murders happened...brooding, not like himself at all. I have to make him smile again, but I don't know how.'

'It will soon be Christmas. We shall close the café for a day, and Ann wants you to bring Robin here for dinner. We'll make it a family do. What do you say?'

I took my time to answer. I'd planned to make a nice Christmas for Robin at our house, but wasn't sure that he would come. I had tried to get him to come home with me a couple of times but he'd refused to budge from Sadie's house.

'Yes, I think we should like that,' I said at last. 'I'll ask Robin tomorrow when I see him. Jack is taking us both out for tea at a posh place he knows of up West. He says it will do us both good to get away from the docks for a while, see something different.'

* * *

The afternoon up West was a success. Robin was excited by all the bright lights and the wonderful shops, including Selfridges and Harpers, which we ventured inside but didn't buy anything, because it was all too expensive. We took a tram past the theatres, seeing the brightly-coloured posters for shows with Noel Coward and other stars. There was a new Charlie Chaplin film on at a big Odeon cinema, and a Rudolph Valentino film was on at another. The shop windows were decorated with lights and Christmas trees. A brass band was playing carols somewhere, the atmosphere of excitement evident in people's smiling faces. Robin held on to Jack's coat as we mingled with the crowds, wanting to see everything, as we munched roasted chestnuts out of a paper bag.

Oxford Street had once been the slum area called the St Giles rookery, where the poor had lived in terrible squalor. It had been haunted by the worst kinds of criminals, a place of despair where few outsiders dared to venture, but you would never know it now. Shops and posh restaurants had sprung up and the whole area thrived.

Jack bought Robin some sweets and a small toy from one of the costers who had barrows outside the railway stations. I bought a ladies' magazine to read when I was in bed at night. It had stories about families, and showed pictures of girls in the new shorter dresses with dropped waistlines, that the magazine described as frivolous but all the fashion. Some of them had been designed by someone called Coco Channel. I didn't know who she was, but the article said she was a French designer. I liked her things because, although they were expensive anyone could wear them, unlike the very smart clothes rich women wore.

I noticed one woman getting out of a large, sleek car. She was wearing a fox fur and had several large diamond rings on her fingers. She went into one of the exclusive jewellery shops in Bond Street and her chauffeur drove away. I wondered what it must be like to have that much money, but I couldn't imagine it. One of her rings would keep a family for a year at least; perhaps more because I didn't know what something like that was really worth. When I looked in a jeweller's window, I gasped at the price ticket on rings with much smaller stones.

We went on a long bus ride, looking out of the dirty windows at ancient buildings, St Paul's cathedral and Westminster; places that Robin had never seen and I'd seen only rarely. After that, Jack took us to a nice teashop, where they served tea in posh cups and cream cakes . The waitresses looked very smart in their uniforms and bustled about, serving the hordes of customers more quickly than you would think possible.

'One day we'll go to a posh hotel and have dinner,' Jack told me as we caught the tram to go home afterwards. 'When we get engaged. I'll be giving you a ring too.'

'Oh yeah?'

'Yeah.' His look was confident, almost cocky. 'You'll see, lass. I'm going places. All we can do today is look in the windows of these shops, but one day we'll be able to buy nice things. One day I'll buy you a fancy diamond ring.'

'All I want is enough money to pay the rent, feed us and a little bit extra when we need it.'

'You'll have more than that one day, Maggie.'

I smiled but I didn't really believe him. People like us didn't often get the chance to earn enough for diamond rings, and to be honest I wasn't bothered. All I wanted when I married was a man who treated me right and came home with his wages in his pocket.

Bill had given me an extra couple of hours off so that we need not rush back, and I was feeling better than I had since Ma was murdered.

'And when is that going to be? I don't recall you asking me?' I said in a cheeky voice that made him look at me.

'I didn't. Can't afford it yet, Maggie love. I need to work hard and set myself up in a trade. When we do get married, I want a nice house so that you have somewhere decent to live—and you won't need to worry for money either.' He sounded so confident at that moment that I almost believed him, but not quite.

'That will be nice. As long as I'm not an old woman by the time it happens.' I enjoyed his teasing, although at the back of my mind there was a little niggling doubt. Since he'd told me about what had happened to my father, I'd thought he might be hiding something from me. Had he told me the whole truth about that night?

'It will be sooner than you think. I've been working two jobs for a while now—the docks and another little thing I've got going. I'll be my own boss in no time.'

I wondered what his second job was, but I was feeling too content to ask at that moment. It had been such a wonderful afternoon, and it was good to see Robin smiling again. For a while at least we had managed to shake off the shadow of the past few weeks.

I had told Robin about going to Bill's for Christmas and he looked pleased, but when I asked him when he was going to come home with me, he shook his head.

'Don't want to go there,' he said, his eyes dark with fear. 'Never. Don't want to go in that house again, Maggie.'

'Then you don't have to. I'll look for somewhere else we can be together.' I'd have liked Sadie's house when she left but knew there was no chance of getting it. It was one of the better ones and the landlord could let it a hundred times over.

'I'd come with you then,' Robin slipped his hand in mine. His expression was trusting, a little pleading and it caught at my heartstrings. 'I'd rather be with you than Sadie but not at that house.'

'Then I shall give it up as soon as I can find somewhere else,' I promised.

That night I asked Bill if he thought I would be able to find somewhere for Robin and me to live in the area.

'Not sure about that, lass. Landlord told you to move, has he?'

'Not yet. I think he may have been waiting for the funerals to be over. I was going to leave the rent with a neighbour and ask if I could stay on, but Robin won't come back there, so I shall just have to find somewhere else.'

'Before the war there used to be rooms in the tenements,' Bill said, 'but some were destroyed by the Zeppelin airships when the Germans bombed us. Terrible that was, especially that explosion at the Silvertown munitions factory—seventy-three killed and 400 hundred injured. It won't be so easy to find a place now. You couldn't afford any of the new housing they've built on the other side of the river. Besides, most would think you're too young to be a tenant on your own. It's families that get first chance. I think your only choice is to go into lodgings, if you can find someone willing to take you.'

'Lodgings?' My heart sank. I didn't fancy the sound of that; there would be too many rules and regulations. 'Well, I shall have to think about it, ask around.'

'I'll ask as well,' Bill said and frowned. 'You're a good worker, Maggie. We don't want to lose you.'

Bill was being kind as usual. There were plenty of people who would like to work here.

Sadie had mentioned putting Robin on the Parish, and I

suspected that a lot of people would think he'd be better off in a children's home. It wouldn't be easy keeping us both in lodgings, because it would take all our money for meals; it was much cheaper for me to cook our food and keep house. I wasn't sure how I would manage, but I would keep us together somehow.

* * *

I found a letter through the letterbox when I got home from work at the end of that week. It said that we were up to date with the rent and could stay at the house until the twentieth of January.

'I doubt if it will be that easy to rent the house,' Sadie said when I told her that we been given until the end of January to move. 'Who wants to live in a house where a murder's been done?'

'It doesn't make any difference to the house,' I said. 'I'm sleeping there and it isn't haunted. I found it a bit difficult at first, because it seemed cold and empty, but I don't take any notice now.'

'Have you got rid of Pa's things?'

'I burned them all.'

'And Ma's?'

'I burned the rags. I might be able to use some of the other things—cut the dresses up and make them over for myself.'

'What about the furniture when you leave?'

'If I get a house, I'll need some of it, if not we can sell it. If anyone wants to buy it.'

'The stuff in the parlour is quite good,' Sadie said looking thoughtful. 'The mattresses will go to the rag and bone man I should think. You might get a couple of pennies for them.'

'If we have to go into lodgings, I'll take my share of the money and Robin's. I've asked around but so far nothing has turned up that sounds right for both of us. I could get a room easily but they don't want Robin. They all say children are too much bother.'

'He can stay here until the baby is born. After that...' She shrugged her shoulders. 'Ben wants to go as soon as I'm up and about so you should fix up something before then.'

'I'll find something. It's early days yet. I want to stay near the docks if I can but otherwise, I'll have to look further afield.'

'You could always go to Ma's cousin.'

'You wrote and told her what had happened, didn't you?'

'Yes, a week ago. I haven't had a reply.'

'Maybe she wouldn't want us now. A visit is one thing, having us living there is another. It's a lot for anyone to take on and I'm not going without Robin.'

'Well, you might be right about her not wanting you,' Sadie said. 'It does cast a bit of a shadow—Ma being found like that and folk suspecting Pa. I've had a few funny looks when I've been down the market recently. If I wasn't having the baby I'd be off now, but Ben says it is best to wait until I'm over it.'

'The customers are all right with me down the café. Not so judgmental but then all our customers are men.'

'You're right, it's the women that are the worst. A couple of them were whispering the other day. I nearly hit one of them. She hinted that there was more to Pa getting killed than I knew, as if he were some kind of criminal.'

'Well, maybe there was more than we know,' I said. I debated whether to tell her the truth but decided against it, because she would get upset. 'Just ignore them, Sadie. Put it out of your mind.'

'The way you have?' Sadie gave me an odd look. 'I wish I could be more like you, Maggie. I just keep thinking of him the way he used to be, and of Ma. I cry a lot.'

'I think of Ma too. But tears won't bring her back. I've got to think about Robin and me. You and Ben will be out of it, starting a new life in America but we've got to find a future for ourselves.'

8

I was determined not to let the misery of the past few weeks overshadow the Christmas I had planned for Robin. Jack had sold Pa's tiepin to a pawnbroker for me. He gave me two pounds for it, because the stone was a ruby. I bought a silver pin from a stall on the market for five shillings, which I was going to give to Jack. The rest of the money and my tips from the customers at the café went to buy several gifts for my brother.

First of all I purchased the practical things like a new pair of boots and a thick jacket to replace his old one. Then I bought sweets, nuts, oranges, and some small toys: a monkey on a stick, a second-hand set of tracks and a clockwork engine to run on them, also some books with pictures of animals, a box of paints and a drawing book.

I took the parcels to Sadie's early on Christmas morning, and we all watched as Robin tore off the wrappings with cries of glee. Sadie had bought him a jumper from the second-hand stall on the market and also some sweets.

'You spoil him,' she said as she saw all my parcels.

'He could do with some spoiling,' I replied. I gave Sadie a box of handkerchiefs, and also a packet of cigarettes for Ben. In return I received a pair of wool and Lyle stockings, which was just what I needed.

'We'd better go now,' I told Robin when he had finished unwrapping his gifts. 'Are you going to take your things with you or leave them here?'

'I'll take the engine, but we'll leave the rest here for when I get back.'

'Yes, all right. You won't need your sweets, because Ann will have plenty of nice food.' Robin smiled at me, clearly still excited by the best Christmas morning he'd ever had. For today at least the shadows had been banished.

The parlour behind the café was looking festive. Bill had brought in a tree from the yard. He dug it up from his patch of garden and replanted it after Christmas each year, and Ann had decorated it with candles, strings of tinsel and small parcels wrapped in bright paper. Under the tree were parcels for each of us from Bill

He had bought a lovely soft red jumper for me and a mystery story by Agatha Christie, because he said I was always reading old newspapers and it would give me something better to do in my spare time. He gave Robin a beautiful tinplate toy car and he presented his wife with a pretty blouse. She also had a lovely silver locket and chain he'd given her earlier, but she'd saved one parcel to open with us.

I had given them chocolates and a tiny bottle of brandy, which Bill made a big fuss of and declared he was going to drink it all by himself after dinner.

The dinner was roast goose with baked potatoes, stuffing and three vegetables, followed by trifle, mince pies and sweets that Bill called petite fours. We three had a glass of wine, and Robin had a sweet fizzy drink of pop that went up his nose and made him sneeze.

After dinner we sat by the fire and played silly games, and each time a winner was declared Ann took a parcel from the tree and gave it to the person who had won. It didn't take me long to work out that Robin was winning most of the games and I came in a close second, but as the gifts were little packets of sweets, I gave mine to Robin on the way back to Sadie's before going home on my own.

* * *

The house seemed a dark and lonely place, but I refused to let myself think of Ma. I went into the kitchen, setting the fire ready for the morning. Just as I was about to go up to bed, having decided that there was no point in staying up by myself, I heard a knock at the door and went to stand just inside it, as I asked, 'Who is it?'

'It's Jack,' his voice called to me. 'I saw your light on and thought you were back. Can I talk to you for a minute?'

Jack grinned at me as I unlocked the door, and the smell of strong drink was on his breath. I frowned, feeling a bit reluctant to let him in when he'd been drinking, but then so had I and it was Christmas.

'I brought your presents,' Jack said. 'Can I come in for a while?'

'Yes, of course you can,' I said and stood back for him to enter. 'I've got something for you too. I was just off to bed, but I can make some tea if you like. I don't have any wine or anything.'

'That's all right, I brought a bottle of sherry,' Jack said, producing it from under his coat as I led the way. 'And these are for you, Maggie.' He handed me two parcels.

I thanked him and gave him his gift, then fetched two small glasses from the dresser in the parlour. Jack opened his parcel and declared the tiepin was just what he wanted, then drew the cork from the sherry, pouring us both a glass.

'Here's to us, lass,' he said. 'Drink up, there's plenty more.'

The sherry was sweet, much nicer I thought than the wine Bill had served at dinner. I finished my glass before opening my parcels. Jack had bought me a silver locket on a chain, very similar to the one that Bill had given his wife, and a small bottle of lavender water.

'Oh, Jack! I've never had anything so lovely.'

'I wanted my girl to have something nice,' he said and poured me another glass of sherry. 'I couldn't afford Channel Number Five or diamonds this year, but I will one day. Drink up, lass. I've been waiting to celebrate with you all day. I couldn't ask you to my house because Ma had all the family round. Besides, you were invited out for the day but I've been thinking about you all the time, wishing we could get wed soon. I'd like us to be together—Robin and all.'

'Oh yes!' I smiled when Jack poured another drink, because the picture he had conjured up was so enticing. Jack, Robin and me all together; it would be perfect. 'I wish it could be like that, Jack. It would be so nice.' Perhaps it was all the wine and sherry I'd drunk, but the future looked warm and cosy, all my problems gone. 'I know we have to wait for a bit, but perhaps not too long.'

Jack sat down on the old sofa. It was stuffed with horsehair and had gone lumpy and hard. He patted the seat beside him. I finished my third glass of sherry and went to sit next to him. I knew he was going to kiss me. I lifted my face for his kiss, closing my eyes as his lips touched mine.

He tasted of sherry and a stronger spirit beneath it, but the feeling it gave me to be kissed like that was spreading through me, warming me right down to my toes.

'I do love you, Maggie,' Jack said and his voice was a bit slurred as he nibbled at my neck. 'You're so lovely. I want you to be my wife. I want you so much...'

Jack's hands were moving at my breasts, caressing me through my dress, arousing such lovely feelings deep down inside me. I snuggled up to him, vaguely aware that I shouldn't let him do it, but it was Jack and I liked him. It was just nice to lie there, warm and cosy, and let him kiss me and touch me. I tensed a little when he slid his hand up under my skirt, touching my thighs, and then he caressed me between them, his fingers seeking out the warmth of my secret places. No one had ever touched me that way before and it made me tingle all over.

'Let me love you, Maggie,' he murmured huskily against my hair. 'I'll be careful, nothing will happen.'

My mind was telling me to say no, but my body was saying, *yes please*! I was too content to deny him; just lying there as he moved my knickers out of the way and then lay on top of me. I could feel something hot and warm poking at me, and then he was pushing inside me and I tried to cry out to him to stop as I suddenly realised that he was going much too far. He smothered my cry beneath a kiss and I couldn't struggle, because I was trapped beneath his body on the sofa.

All my pleasure in what I'd thought of as a nice cuddle had gone when I felt the sharp pain of his entry tearing at my hymen. I was frightened now, but my sobs were muffled by his bulk as he thrust into me a few times, and then it was over as suddenly as it had begun.

I lay still and tense, as I understood what had happened. Ma had warned me often enough, but she'd never told me what men might do to me, just that I shouldn't let them kiss me.

I felt numb, disappointed that Jack had taken advantage of me that way. The kissing and touching had been nice, but the rest had been uncomfortable and had left me feeling empty.

Jack moved away. I lay with my eyes closed, refusing to look at him for the moment. I was angry with him, because he'd always said he wanted to wait and I'd trusted him. I'd been foolish to let him in at this time of night, especially when I knew he'd been drinking.

'Look at me, Maggie,' he said, and then, as I reluctantly did so. 'I'm sorry. I didn't mean to go that far but it was so lovely... you're so lovely.'

I sat up, common sense asserting itself. There was no point in making a fuss about it now.

'Let's hope nothing happens.' I wanted to rage at him, to hit him and make him suffer for his selfishness, but it was too late. 'I'm not ready for a baby yet. I'm too young and I've got Robin to think of.'

'It won't happen,' Jack said but didn't sound as convincing as usual. 'But if it does, you know I'll marry you, Maggie. I love you.'

'I care about you too.' Jack had an infectious charm that made him hard to resist, even when he'd done something you didn't like. 'It's happened now and we can't do anything about it.'

'I shouldn't have come. I've been drinking a lot.'

'Well, you did and I let you in, so that's my fault. You'd better go now, Jack. I've got to get to work in the morning.'

'All right. You're not mad at me, are you?' He looked anxious, contrite.

'No, not really.' I was angry with him but even more so with myself. 'I'll see you tomorrow, Jack.'

I got up and went through to the hall, leaving him to follow. He looked a bit sheepish as I pushed him through the door.

'I'm really sorry.'

'Goodnight, Jack. Happy Christmas.'

I locked the door after he'd gone and stood against it, eyes closed for a moment. I wasn't going to cry over it. I'd cried too many tears of late. I would pray that nothing happened, but if it did then I would have to do something about it. I had no idea what women did to get rid of babies they didn't want or couldn't afford to have, but I knew that it happened.

* * *

I woke with a headache the next morning. As I doused myself with cold water at the sink, I tasted the awful bitterness on my tongue and knew it was my own fault for drinking too much of that sweet sherry Jack had brought. Because it was sweet and warmed my throat, I hadn't realised that it would make me tipsy. In the cold light of day, I knew that I had made a big mistake. If I were pregnant, it would be terrible. I would lose my job and be stared at in the street.

'*Open the door, you slut!*'

I could hear Pa's harsh voice as he tugged at the bedroom door handle. He had called me a slut often enough, and now I had proved him right.

'It wasn't my fault...' I spoke the words aloud to the empty house, but the truth was in my mind. I had let Jack in.

I left early for work. The house was cold and seemed to echo with voices accusing me. I didn't want to see Jack this morning and I couldn't face Sadie yet. She had eyes like a hawk and she would know something was wrong. My shame hung over me like a black cloud, because I knew I'd been stupid. Jack would think I was easy now and he wouldn't respect me.

The weather had turned colder again and the roofs of the houses were white with frost, icicles hanging from guttering where the water dripped. The pavements were treacherous and you had to be careful where you stepped, because some of the kids had been making a slide. I shivered and tucked my hands into the sleeves of my threadbare coat.

I tried not to think about what would happen if I was already carrying Jack's baby. It couldn't happen just like that surely? Just once? It took ages for some women to have their first child.

I could hear Katie crying as soon as I entered. Billy was standing at the counter. He looked tired and yawned as he saw me.

'I'm glad you're in early, Maggie,' he told me. 'Could you help Ann with the child? She has been crying for most of the night— soon after you left. Neither of us got any sleep.'

'Yes, of course I will.' I went through to the kitchen.

Ann was nursing the baby, but she looked so tired and Katie sent up a fresh wail as her mother tried to hush her.

'Give her to me for a minute. You look exhausted. Sit down and rest for a while.'

Ann put Katie into my arms and the miracle happened. Her wailing stopped immediately. She smelled of sick and urine and I took her to the table to lay her down on a towel while I changed her nappy. The soiling smelled strange and unpleasant and it was a yellowish colour, which didn't look natural.

'I think she may be sickening for something,' I said. Katie was looking miserable but she didn't cry. I changed her nappy for a dry one. I thought her bottom looked sore.

'Do you think we should have the doctor?' Ann looked anxious. 'She cries so much that I didn't think there was anything different this time.'

'She is very hot and her nappy doesn't look right. I think she might have a tummy upset. Robin often had them when he was little. We used to get a mixture from the corner shop in the lane, and that mostly settled him but perhaps you should have the doctor?'

'Will the shop be open?'

'Yes, I should think so. Do you want me to get her something for a colic?'

'Did it help Robin?'

'Ma said it mostly cured him in a few days. He would start to improve almost at once.'

'Would you mind fetching a bottle? How much is it?' I told her sixpence for a small bottle and a shilling for the large. Ann extracted a shilling from her purse and handed it to me. 'Tell Bill where you're going. You can have your breakfast when you get back.'

'All right. I'll be as quick as I can.'

I pulled on my coat and went back into the café. Bill nodded when I explained what I was doing. It struck cold outside after the warmth of the café and I decided to run to keep myself warm. A man was pasting bright advertising posters on a wall. He had just put up one for Gold Flake cigarettes, and there was another for Airship chocolates. I'd never seen any of those and I wondered what they were like. Was it a special kind of chocolate or just a picture on the box?

I saw Jack as I went into the shop. He was just coming round the corner and I thought he might be waiting when I left the shop, but there was no sign of him.

9

Jack was waiting outside the café when I left that evening. He looked a bit sheepish as he stood at the other side of the road.

'I wasn't sure if you would be talking to me today?'

'It was my fault too,' I said. 'We had both been drinking. If I hadn't had the sherry on top of the wine Bill gave me, I would have stopped you.'

'You know I love you, Maggie.'

Jack looked so handsome and so contrite that I couldn't be angry. He smelled lovely and I thought he had slicked his hair back with some kind of oil. He had obviously changed out of his work things before coming to meet me and I thought it was his way of saying sorry. My anger had gone anyway. The feeling I'd had in his arms when he'd kissed me was so lovely I didn't even wish it hadn't happened that much. I just hoped there wouldn't be a baby.

'Did you see me this morning when I went to the shop? I had to get some medicine for Katie. She kept them awake all night, but she seems to have settled for a bit. I think she had a bad tummy.'

'Babies are like that,' Jack said and looked gloomy. 'Ma had ten of us, and the house smelled of nappies and washing for years. I was the second youngest and I remember the baby crying all hours until it died. Five of Ma's babies died.'

'I am so sorry. I didn't know that you'd had all those brothers and sisters.'

'The ones that died were all girls. Ma said it didn't matter because girls were more trouble and her lads would look after her in her old age. She were that bitter when my brothers got married and went off to different parts of London. I'm the last one at home now.'

I had seen Mrs Holmes in the market a few times, but she had never spoken to me. She was a small woman, plump with wiry grey hair and a thin mouth. I thought that perhaps Jack didn't have much of a home life.

'What will she do when you leave?'

'I don't know.' Jack frowned. 'I suppose I shall have to help her out, though my brothers never send her a penny. Ma has a bitter tongue. She drove Pa to his death and she sent my brothers running for their lives. I'm the only one she can't get over, because I tell her straight.'

I wondered if Jack was telling me all this, because he wanted me to understand why he couldn't get married just yet. Of course he had to help his mother! We both had our responsibilities and neither of us was ready to marry right now.

'Sadie and Ben are going to America when she is over the baby. Someone has to look after Robin. I want to do it but I can't have a baby. Unless I'm married.'

'I've told you I'll wed you if it happens,' Jack said, but I sensed his unease and I knew he didn't want it to happen until he was ready.

* * *

'You haven't been round since Christmas!' Sadie said when I visited the next Saturday afternoon. 'I was thinking I would have to come to the café to find you.'

'Is something wrong?'

Sadie put a hand to the small of her back and sighed, obviously wanting to impress on me that she was nearly seven months gone and feeling the strain. She had put on an awful lot of weight in the last few weeks and her skin was a funny putty colour, her hair hanging in lank rats' tails.

'I have been feeling unwell,' she told me and sighed. 'I do care about Robin, Maggie. You know I love him but I could do without having to look after him. I know you work hard, but you could take his washing home with you. I've got enough to do.'

There was a whine of self-pity in her voice that reminded me of Ma sometimes. It was a disloyal thought, but I couldn't help feeling it was just like her to push it all on me. When I thought about it, Sadie had always been selfish but she and Robin were all I had left of my family.

'I've been giving you money for his keep.'

'It's his washing that bothers me. I can't keep him much longer, Maggie. I know I said he could stay until the baby was born and we were off to America, but I felt well then. Robin was coughing all night. He kept Ben awake and he was pissed off when he went to work. He thinks it is time you took Robin with you.'

'I am trying to find somewhere for us both. Robin can't help coughing. I'll get him some mixture from the shop and bring it back. If you give him a spoonful every now and then it will help but don't give him too much. It says on the bottle that you mustn't give more than one dose every six hours, because it is strong.'

'It would be good to get some sleep. Ben won't put up with many sleepless nights, Maggie. If the mixture doesn't work you will have to find somewhere quick.'

'I'll go and get the mixture now.'

I left Sadie's house feeling anxious. Ben was usually good-natured and understanding. If he had told Sadie that Robin had to go, he meant it. As I approached the shop, I saw Robin hanging round with some older lads. They were playing hopscotch on the road. He wasn't wearing his scarf or cap.

'Robin, come on love, I'll buy you a treat,' I called to him. He hesitated and then came to me. I took off my scarf and wrapped it round his neck. 'What do you want, love? An apple or some sweets?'

Robin opted for the sweets but in the end, I bought both.

When we went back out into the street the Sally Army brass band was playing hymns, and people were singing along. Robin wanted to stop and listen to them. His hand crept into mine as we stood together in the cold wind, listening to the music and the singing.

'Do you think Pa is in Hell?' Robin asked me. His eyes were dark with fear as he looked up at me, his face pale. 'People say he killed Ma. Do you think he did, Maggie?'

'I don't know, love,' I said and squeezed his hand. 'Pa got violent when he had too much to drink, but I don't think he meant to kill her. Perhaps he just hit her too hard.'

'I hate him,' he said. 'I want Ma...' A tear rolled down his cheek. 'Sadie isn't like you, Maggie. I don't think she likes me much.'

'She gets tired with the baby coming,' I said. I bent down so that I could look into his face. 'Whatever happens, Robin, remember that you are my brother. I love you and I always shall. I am going to find somewhere for us to live and then you will be with me.'

'I love you, Maggie.'

'I love you too. You are my special person. Never forget that, Robin.' I hugged him and gave him a penny to put in the Sally Army tin. The man shaking the tin smiled at him and he ran back to me, his tears apparently forgotten.

I took Robin back to my sister's house and gave him some of the cough mixture. He went to sit by the parlour fire and I followed Sadie into the kitchen.

'I'm not surprised Robin coughs all the time if you let him go out without his scarf and cap. You know his chest is weak.'

'I can't be watching him all the time,' Sadie said and her eyes snapped with temper. Her pregnancy was making her worse and she'd always had a temper—a bit like Pa. 'I'm telling you, Maggie, if you don't get him away from here, I shall have to think of something myself!'

'Don't you dare put him on the parish!'

'Find somewhere then,' Sadie yelled. 'I'm warning you; I can't keep him much longer. I'm so tired I don't know what to do with myself half the time.'

I walked out of the house, feeling so angry that I left the scarf she'd given me lying on her sofa. Did she imagine that I hadn't tried to find accommodation for us both?

I could have wept when I got home that night. I had walked and walked for two hours, the biting wind nipping at my ears and turning my nose red. The house was freezing cold when I got in and it took me nearly an hour to get the fire going enough to boil a kettle. In another half an hour I would have to be back at work and I still hadn't been able to find lodgings that I could bear to take. I had been offered one room for us to share, but the house reeked of stale cabbage and the landlady's breath had smelled of strong drink.

I wasn't going to take my brother to a house like that, because I knew he would hate it. Sadie would just have to keep him for a bit longer.

I wished that Robin wasn't frightened to come back here, because I might have been able to stay on a while. I didn't know what I was going to do if I couldn't find a decent place for us to live soon.

* * *

'I would offer you a room here, Maggie,' Bill said when I told him how I had spent my afternoon off. 'But Katie will be needing her own room soon. It doesn't seem worth it just for a few weeks, because I would have to ask you to move out again.'

'I didn't expect you to offer me a room. I just thought you might know of someone who wanted a lodger.'

'Most would take you, Maggie. You know the problem.'

'Yes, I do...' I turned away feeling the tightness in my chest. It seemed as if no one wanted a lad in the house, because they were too much trouble. Several people had suggested I take Robin to the church hostel, because they would find him a good home. The only woman who had offered us a room was a dirty slattern I wouldn't trust. I would have to be desperate to take the room I had been offered, but in another week, I would be homeless myself. Sadie wouldn't want me as a second lodger; I was going to have to find something even if it did smell awful.

As I went to bed that night, I suddenly realised that my period had been due a day or so earlier. I hadn't given it a thought, but lying awake in the darkness I realised that my problems could be about to get so much worse.

* * *

I didn't say anything to Jack when he walked me to work the next morning.

He'd been a bit subdued lately. I wondered if it was because he was worried in case, I was pregnant. I wasn't sure yet. I could just be a bit late. I thought about what I ought to do for the best. If I was carrying Jack's baby he might marry me, though I had sensed he wasn't keen on the idea. What alternatives did I have?

One girl in the lanes had stuck a bit of wire up inside herself to try and kill her child, instead she'd ended up giving herself a kind of blood poisoning that had killed her and she'd suffered a lot of pain. I didn't fancy trying that method. There were other things I might try though, like drinking hot gin and sitting in a hot bath. I wasn't sure it would work, but I knew of other girls who had done it.

It was probably better to do it sooner than later, and it had to be done before I was forced to move into lodgings. I dared not start having a miscarriage in someone else's house; they would throw me out for certain.

When Jack told me he couldn't meet me on the Saturday the second week after Christmas I knew it was my chance. I could fetch the tin bath in from the yard, heat the water, and I would have the gin as well. It might not work, and if it didn't, I would have to consider asking Jack for some money so that I could go somewhere and ask for help from one of the women who did that sort of thing. I knew they existed, that they got rid of babies for girls in their dark little back rooms, but I would have to ask someone. People didn't talk about it openly, because both the abortionist and the mother could go to prison if the police found out.

I called at a pub on my way home from the morning session at the café and bought a small bottle of gin. The woman behind the bar gave me a hard look but didn't refuse to serve me. I slipped the bottle into a bag I'd brought specially for the purpose and hurried home, praying that no one had seen me buy the gin. I had hoped my courses would start and I wouldn't have to do it, but they hadn't and it seemed the best way out to me. I might not be pregnant. I couldn't be sure but I had to be certain that if I was, I lost it quickly, before anyone guessed, including my sister. Besides, the baby was hardly there yet, not a proper person, if it was there at all.

It took quite a while to fill the bath with really hot water. I dipped a toe in it and gasped, realising that I would scald myself if I got in that and added a saucepan full of cold water. Then I heated some of the gin in another pan and climbed into the bath.

The heat with the combination of the hot gin was overpowering. My head swam after I drank it, but I sat it out until the water started to get cooler, and then climbed out of the bath. I was feeling so dizzy that I wrapped the towel round me and just sat in the chair by the range for a moment, trying to get some energy back.

If that didn't work nothing would! My head was muzzy and when I heard someone at the door, I ignored it. Let whoever it was go away!

Whoever was there was knocking again, harder now, seeming determined to gain entry. I pulled on Ma's ancient dressing robe. It was years old and far too big for me, but it would do for the moment, and I could throw it out if I got blood all over it.

I went through the parlour to the front door. My head was swimming as I called out to ask who was there.

'It's Sadie. Let me in, Maggie. I have to talk to you.'

'I'll come and see you later.'

'No! I want to come in now. What's the matter with you?'

I opened the door reluctantly. Sadie pushed past me and went through the kitchen. She looked at the bath and the steam dripping everywhere, and then at the half-empty bottle of gin on the table.

'What have you done?' she cried, whirling on me in shock. 'Maggie! You stupid fool! Who was it—Jack Holmes?'

'I don't know what you mean.' I was so ill that I could hardly look at her let alone answer her. The room had started to whirl and I clutched at the table as I fell, knocking the gin bottle flying. I heard the smash of glass and then everything went black.

When I came to myself, I was lying on the sofa. Sadie was holding a glass of water and Ben was standing beside her, looking at me oddly.

'What?' I asked defensively as I sat up. 'So I fainted...' I took the glass of water and drank it all, giving it back to her empty. 'Could I have some more please?'

'You stupid, stupid girl,' Sadie shouted. 'What would have happened if I hadn't come?'

'I expect I would have managed. You didn't have to drag Ben here.'

'He should marry you,' Ben said. 'Sadie told me what you'd done, lass. I'm not condemning you—you're not the only one to try to get rid of a baby. It's the father's fault. Do you want me to talk to him?'

'I haven't told you who the father is,' I said, but there was no sense in denying it. It was best to get the arguments over now and be done with it.

'There is only one lad you've been hanging round with,' Ben said. 'If I have a word with him, he'll do the right thing by you, Maggie.'

'I'm not sure I want to marry him.'

'You slut!' Sadie slapped me hard across the face. 'You will marry him if I have to take a stick to you. What would Ma have said? Have you thought about that?'

'Several times,' I said, putting a hand to my cheek. 'I think she would have slapped me—just the way you did.'

'You deserve it,' Sadie said. She put a hand to her back, a look of pain on her face. 'You are a selfish, wicked girl! How are you going to look after Robin? You can't even look after yourself. I don't need this, Maggie. I've got enough to put up with as it is.'

'If I could get rid of it, I could take Robin away somewhere. I can't find lodgings here.'

'And you won't anywhere else.' Sadie's eyes were bright with anger. 'You're too young. No one will let you rent a house and land-ladies don't want a child in the house when you're out at work, and once they discover you're having another they will throw you out in the street.'

'Maggie feels bad enough,' Ben told her. 'Make a cup of tea and talk this out sensibly between yourselves. I'm off to find Jack Holmes. He got her into this mess and he can get her out.'

'No. Please don't,' I cried but Ben ignored me. He closed the front door with a bang as he went out. 'I was going to tell Jack if this didn't work. He isn't ready to get married yet. He has to help his mother and he needs to save some money before we get married.'

'You should have thought of that before you let him have his way with you,' Sadie said. She gave a moan of pain and sat down on the sofa. 'I feel awful and it's all your fault. I thought you were sensible and that I could trust you to look after Robin. You've let me down, Maggie, and you've let yourself down too. I'm ashamed of you! You'll be ruined. No other man is going to look at you now—unless you want to earn your living on the streets! Is that what you want?'

'You know it isn't. Stop going on about it, Sadie. It only happened once. I had a little too much to drink and... it was nice and I didn't think he would go all the way.'

'You little fool. Ma warned you often enough. I heard her.'

'I know.' I looked at her resentfully. 'It is all right for you.'

Sadie gave a yelp of pain. Her eyes widened in fright. 'I've got a terrible pain in my back. I think it is the baby...'

'It can't be,' I said feeling scared as I saw her flinch and pull a face. 'You're not due for several weeks yet.'

'Do you think I don't know that? Get some clothes on, Maggie. I need to get home and I'm not sure I can manage it alone.' She wailed, the tears starting to pool in her eyes. 'It hurts. It hurts bad. I want Ben.'

'I'll get dressed and see you home,' I said forgetting that I had been faint a few minutes earlier. 'Then I'll fetch Old Sally to you. She will know what to do.'

'Ben was going to pay for a doctor,' Sadie said. She watched as I pulled on my dress. 'He didn't want Sally near me because she is so dirty. Hurry up, can't you? I want to be at home. It's all your fault, upsetting me like this, and leaving me to look after Robin. I told you I was ill and you haven't done a thing to help. You didn't even call for his washing today.'

'I've been looking for somewhere we can stay,' I protested, but my sister wasn't listening. Her face had gone white. She was in terrible pain!

* * *

It was difficult getting Sadie down the street to her house. She leaned on me hard and she was heavy, but I did my best to support her, though she almost stumbled twice. As we got near to her house a neighbour saw us and came out to help. I found it easier with two of us and I helped half-carry my sister up to her bedroom.

'Pull those best covers off,' Mrs Wayman directed me. 'Where did you put the old sheets, Sadie love?'

'In the bottom drawer of the chest,' Sadie said through gritted teeth. 'Hurry up, Maggie! I want to lie down.'

'I'm working as fast as I can,' I said and dragged the eiderdown back, throwing some blankets after it to the foot of the bed. The old sheets were on the top of some other stuff in the chest. Sadie had put them there in readiness. I spread them over the mattress, covering her best sheets so that the blood wouldn't stain them, though if Katie's birthing was anything to go by it would go clear through to the mattress.

As soon as I had finished, Sadie sort of staggered to the bed and flopped down. For a moment or two that seemed to ease her, but then she pulled her knees to her chest and started screaming.

'You had better go and fetch Old Sally,' Mrs Wayman told me. 'And if you can find Ben, tell him to come home as soon as he can.'

'I'll go for Sally first,' I said. 'Then I'll look for Ben but I can't search for long, because I have to be back at work.'

I hurried down the stairs and left the house. I could hear Sadie screaming as I shut the door behind me.

10

It was easy to find Old Sally, because she was sitting at home, nodding by her fire. She woke up as I banged at her door and came to answer it, rubbing at her eyes. I saw that her apron was grimy, and her hands didn't look very clean either, but I did as I had been told and asked her if she would go to my sister's house.

'Ah, I bin expecting 'er to drop her pup sooner than she thought,' the old woman said, grinning at me with toothless gums. 'Right, you get back and tell 'er I be on my way, lass.'

'Mrs Wayman is with her,' I said. 'I have to find Sadie's husband.'

I sped away before she had time to say anything, making a mental vow that I wouldn't ask Sally to assist when I gave birth. I thought of Old Tom, as we'd called him, with regret. If he hadn't been killed on the docks, I would have known where to find him, because on such a cold day he would have been sitting in Bill's café drinking tea.

Now, where would I find Ben? He had gone to look for Jack, but since Jack wasn't at home he might have had to search further afield. The only thing I could do was to try Jack's home and see if Ben was still there.

Jack's cottage was better than some of the others in the lanes, and had once belonged to a ship's captain so the saying went. It had stood at the corner of St. Peter's Lane for more than two hundred years and had a low, sloping roof and small paned windows. I hesitated outside for a moment and then hammered on the door with the black iron knocker. After a moment it was opened, and a woman looked out.

'What do you want?' she demanded. 'I told the other one he wasn't here. He thought I was lying, but it's the truth. You're Michael Bailey's girl—the one my Jack has been hanging round with, aren't you? I warned him you would be trouble. Has he knocked you up already?'

'I'm not looking for Jack. I need to find Ben. My sister has gone into labour.'

'I told him he might find Jack at the timber yard. He has been working all hours of late—at least that's what he tells me. What would I know? He might be anywhere. He never tells me anything. I'm only his mother.' Her eyes narrowed as she looked at me with dislike. 'If you're thinkin' my Jack will marry you, he won't. I'll have some say in that, and I'm not havin' a murderer's daughter in my house.'

'You might have no choice,' I retorted before I could stop myself. 'Unless you want Jack to move out when he marries me?'

* * *

'I should never have said it.' With a little shock I was back in the present, dragged back by the grief that had gripped me once more. I looked at the sofa and saw that Thomas was lying with his eyes closed. The fire had burned low so I got up to put another log on and gave it a little stir.

'Could you do with a cup of tea, lass?'

'I thought you were asleep?' I turned to look at him.

'I've been listening all the time.' He sat up and then stood. 'I've got a gas ring. I'll put the kettle on. It will be a long night else. I think you have a way to go yet?'

'Yes, I do,' I said and sighed. 'Are you sure you want to listen to my troubles?' He'd been doing so for what seemed like hours and there was so much more to tell—things I didn't want to say or remember.

'The Lord put me on this earth to help others and I do it to the best of my ability but I want to hear your story, Maggie.'

'You are very kind,' I said. 'Will you tell me your full name please?'

'It is Thomas Carter. Some people call me Tom, but I prefer Thomas, as I was christened.'

'Thomas...' I smiled. 'It suits you. If you really want to hear I shall continue. Sadie suffered terribly, because the baby was so early and they had to turn it in the womb. I caught the sob in my throat. 'I suppose with it coming so early it was inevitable.'

Thomas turned to look at me, sympathy in his eyes. 'Did she lose the child?'

I nodded, feeling the knot of misery inside. 'Of course she blamed me...'

* * *

I didn't manage to find Ben, even though I searched until the last moment. In the end I told some of Sadie's neighbours to pass on the word that the child had come early if they saw him, and I went to work.

When I left work that evening, I called at the house. Ben came to the door. The look on his face was so anguished, so angry! He looked as if he had been crying.

'Sadie...' I asked scared that my sister had died giving birth. 'I tried to find you but I couldn't.'

'I was off on a wild goose chase,' Ben said bitterly. I had never seen him like that and it made my stomach spasm with fright. He was usually so easy going. It had to be something bad! I waited with bated breath as he spoke again, 'The baby came too soon. It never drew breath. I had a son but he didn't live. The doctor says that Sadie was so badly damaged inside she may not have another child.'

'Ben...' His pain was so raw that I wanted to weep for him. 'I am so sorry... so very sorry. I don't know why it happened.'

'Sadie blames you,' Ben said, eyes hard and unforgiving as he looked at me. 'You upset her and she has not been well for a while. It is too much for her looking after Robin. Mrs Barlow has taken him with her for a couple of nights. You should find somewhere you can take him. Sadie won't have him here—or you. As soon as she is better, we are leaving this wretched place!'

The door slammed in my face. I stared at it for a moment, feeling as if I had been punched in the stomach.

Oh Sadie, no...please don't blame me...please don't blame me. My throat closed as I felt the hot sting of tears. Ma had turned against me and now my sister. I didn't want to lose her too, but she would hate me from now on. She had wanted her baby so much. Why did she have to lose the baby? It was so unfair.

I turned away and walked back to the house, feeling the knot of misery growing tighter inside me. *I didn't mean to hurt you, Sadie.* I felt alone, shut out from the only family I had ever known. Sadie was my sister. I loved her. I would have tried to comfort her if I could, but she didn't want me near her, and that hurt so much. Ma had told her things she hadn't told me, and even Pa had treated Sadie with respect. Why was I the one everyone hated? What had I done that was so terrible?

It was as I reached my front door that I heard my name called and saw Jack coming towards me. I waited for him, too numb to give him a smile.

'Ma said you came to the house, Maggie,' he said, looking anxious. 'Did you need to see me urgently?'

'I was looking for Ben. You had better come in, Jack. I do have something to tell you.'

Jack followed me in. The ache in my chest kept nagging at me and the tears were very close. It wasn't fair of Ben and Sadie to blame me for the loss of their baby. Sadie had worked herself into a temper over something that had nothing to do with her. I could understand their grief over losing the child, but it wasn't fair that I should be blamed.

'Do you want a cup of tea?' I asked and moved the kettle on to the stove. It was still warm because I had kept it built up in case, I needed more hot water. I opened the range door and put some coke on the fire. 'It won't take long to heat, unless you have something stronger?'

'Sorry, I don't.' Jack looked down and saw the broken glass where the gin bottle had smashed. 'Have you been drinking this rubbish? This cheap stuff is rotgut, Maggie.'

'I hoped it would work,' I said. The bath was still full of water that was now cold and would need to be emptied. 'I had a bath as hot as I could and drank gin but nothing happened to me. Sadie came and found me when I was feeling faint and then her baby came on suddenly. It was stillborn. I think Ben hates me now, and I am sure Sadie does.'

'Why? It wasn't your fault.' Jack's face was ashen as he took in what I was saying. 'You tried to get rid of the baby—our baby? But nothing happened. Is that what you're saying?'

'I am two weeks late and I always come regular.' I shrugged my shoulders. I hadn't known for certain I was pregnant but I'd done it anyway, because I thought it would work sooner rather than later, but what did I know of things like that? I was still an ignorant girl! 'You told me you don't want to get married yet, and your mother made it plain I wouldn't be welcome.'

'What did she say to you?' I told him and he swore. 'The old bitch! I should leave her to rot in her own mess.'

'But you won't, because she is your mother.'

'Something like that, but she will have to learn to watch her tongue in future. If she talks like that to you again, I will leave her.'

'I shan't give her the chance.'

'I can't afford two houses,' Jack said. 'But I can marry you, Maggie. I've enough saved to take care of you and the baby—maybe your brother too, though it will be a tight squeeze.'

'I won't have him put in a home, Jack.'

'No, I don't suppose you will. All right, I'll find a corner for him somewhere. I might be able to board the attic and make room for a bed up there.'

'Robin might like that if we made it nice. Are you sure you want to take us on, Jack? It will spoil your plans for the future. You wanted to save for your own business.'

'What else can we do?' he asked and frowned. 'I love you, Maggie, and I got you into this trouble. It is up to me to look after you.'

'That is why Ben came looking for you, to force you to marry me. I am glad he didn't find you. I wanted to tell you myself...' I hesitated then continued: 'Drinking gin didn't help but there are women who do it for money.'

'Back street butchers,' Jack said and scowled. 'That happened to a friend of mine's girl. He didn't want to get married so he paid for her to have the baby aborted. She turned septic inside and died. I'm not having that happen to you, Maggie.'

'Jack...' I felt my throat tighten and the tears trickled down my cheeks. The way he was looking at me broke through the fog of misery. Jack did care about me; he hadn't just used me. 'Thank you. I didn't want to push it on you, but there isn't much else I can do. Sadie won't be here much longer and she hates me anyway. I'll keep working at the café for as long as I can so we can put a bit of money by.'

'Your hours are long at the moment. You won't be able to do so many as the time goes on, but while you can I shan't say no to the money.'

'When can we be married?'

'As soon as I can get a licence. It won't be a fancy church do, Maggie. We shall need the money when the baby is born and you can't work. I'll take you out to a fancy restaurant afterwards, and you can have a pretty dress, but that's as much as I can afford.'

'I might have a dress that will do. It was Ma's from when she was young. It is a bit yellow but if I dip it in the blue it will come up lovely. I would rather have new shoes and a hat. I would like a felt cloche with a bow at the side, and a pair of shiny black ankle-strap shoes.' I'd seen some shoes in a magazine one of the customers had left behind at the café and had been secretly hankering after them ever since.

'I expect we can manage them,' Jack grinned. 'Don't look so down, Maggie, love. It will be all right once we're wed. You can have Robin with you and Ma will look after him when you're not around. She can do something to earn her keep for once.'

'Don't put it to her like that please. I've already got off on the wrong foot with her.'

'She told me. I got it in the ear, but I shan't put up with it in future. You will be my wife and she will have to accept it, whether she likes it or not.'

'I have another week at the house...'

'Why pay the rent when you don't need to? Pack what you want tonight and come home with me. You can sell what you don't want.

I'll come tomorrow and clear it out with a mate. We can get a few bob for some of that stuff in the parlour.'

'I suppose Sadie is entitled to something...'

'Didn't you tell me she had the candlesticks?'

'Yes, but...'

'But nothing,' Jack said, his mouth set in a stubborn line. 'She has had her share. You and Robin are entitled to the rest. You leave her to me, Maggie. You said she hates you, so let her stew in her own juice. She doesn't care about you so why should you bother about her?'

11

Mrs Holmes stared at me with dislike when Jack took me into the kitchen. My gaze travelled round the large room. At least it smelled clean, faintly redolent of herbs and baking, not that awful stale cabbage odour that I had found so repulsive elsewhere. The furniture was pine and the dresser was set with good quality blue and white pottery. There was an air of well-being about the cottage. No one went short of anything in this house. I noticed small luxuries that Ma had never had, like an American clock on the wall, shining horse brasses nailed round the fireplace, and a beautiful yew wood grandfather chair by the fire. There were other small treasures elsewhere that I would become familiar with in time, but that night it was just a general feeling of comfort that struck me.

'What have you brought her here for?'

'Maggie is my girl.' Jack gave her a hard look. 'You might as well accept it, Ma, because she is staying. We shall be wed as soon as I can get the licence.'

'Knocked 'er up, 'ave yer?' she grunted. 'You're a fool, Jack Holmes, just like yer father afore yer. He never could keep it in his breeches either. How we're goin' ter manage with another two mouths to feed I don't know.'

'You've not gone short of much yet, Ma,' Jack told her. 'It will be another three soon. I'm going to make a place in the attic for Maggie's young brother.'

'I'm not 'aving a lad in the house! They make too much noise and mess.'

'He won't cause you any extra work,' I said before Jack could speak. 'I shall look after him I promise.'

'What about when you're laid up with the child and can't work?' She glared at us. 'It's me that will 'ave the bother of the lot of yer then. I tell yer, Jack. I won't stand for it.'

'Then Maggie and me will find somewhere else. I can't afford to keep two houses so you'll have to shift for yourself. I suppose you can get a job scrubbing floors somewhere.' He picked up my bags and looked at me. 'If we're not welcome here, we'll go elsewhere...'

'You can't leave me on my own!' his mother screeched.

'I can—and I'll be taking the things I've bought with me,' Jack said. 'That clock for a start and a few more bits and pieces; the treen tea caddy and the silver kettle on a stand you're mighty fond of cleaning.'

She stared at him for a long moment in silence, then, 'You wouldn't really walk out on me, after all I done fer yer?'

'I think the shoe has been on the other foot for a while now. It's your choice, Ma. Either you make my girl welcome or I walk—and I shan't come back once I go.'

'So you'll run out on me like your brothers did...'

'You drove them away with your tongue. Make up your mind, Ma. Either you are civil to Maggie and her brother when we fetch him, or we'll go somewhere else.'

Her mouth went hard with temper. She didn't want to give in and a part of me hoped she wouldn't. I didn't want to live here with this bitter woman, but unless she refused to have us, I had no choice. I wasn't surprised when she turned away with a muffled curse.

'You'll 'ave it yer own way same as always. I still say you're a damned fool and that's the truth of it...'

'I'll take you upstairs,' Jack said and winked at me. 'You will have my room and I'll sleep on the settee down here until we're wed.'

The rooms upstairs had low ceilings that dipped away at the corners and the walls were rough plaster that had been painted smooth over the years, but it was warm and clean, and the large bed looked inviting. There was a lowboy under the window; made of mahogany with brass handles, it had a touch of class about it and was obviously old. Another tall chest stood to one side of the bed.

'I'll put some of my things into the hutch. You can have the chest for your bits and pieces, Maggie.' He pulled open the top two drawers and took out the contents, dumping them into an oak hutch; that too looked old and had the same air of quality as the lowboy.

'Where did you get these things? They are better than anything Ma had, or Sadie for that matter. I've never seen anything quite like them.'

Jack hesitated then. 'I've told you that I work extra some nights and weekends? Well, I clear houses for a furniture dealer. He buys the stuff and sends us to clear it for him. Sometimes I see something I fancy and he lets me have it a bit over cost. I bought these things and the clock downstairs from Eddie, and a few more things. We could have furnished a house for ourselves cheap if we had to, but it is best this way. I know Ma isn't easy, but she is a good cook and you'll be all right once she gets used to you.'

I doubted that I would ever get used to Mrs Holmes and her bitter tongue, but there was no point in complaining. Jack had promised to marry me. I had a roof over my head and somewhere for Robin to sleep. It was enough.

* * *

Bill looked dubious when I told him I had moved in with Jack and his mother. His brow furrowed as I explained that we were getting married quite soon.

'I suppose you know your own mind best, lass but you're a mite young for marriage.'

'I didn't have a lot of choice. I couldn't find a decent place to take Robin and my sister won't keep him much longer. Besides, I like Jack. He's generous and he's cheerful.'

'Like I said, you know your own mind best. I would have given you a room here if I could but there isn't enough space. Now that Katie has started to sleep better at nights, we shall be putting her cot into the spare.' His expression softened. 'Ann reckons that medicine you fetched has made all the difference. She wants you to pick up another bottle tomorrow.'

'Does she need another bottle already? It's strong stuff, Bill. Tell Ann to be careful with that medicine. You shouldn't give more than the recommended dose every so often. Katie is only a little one.'

'I expect Ann has read the instructions. She is good with her learning; better than me, I reckon. I left school when I was nine to look after my ailing mother. Ann went to school until she was fifteen. They wanted her to stay on and do school teaching with the young ones, but Ann wanted to make something of herself. She went into a posh office and I dare say she would have been there now using one of them fancy typing machines if I hadn't happened along.'

'I think she was lucky you did. I bet she likes being married to you more than working in a stuffy office.'

'Get along with you,' Bill grunted. 'It's going to be a stinger tonight. I dare say we shall be filled up afore it's dark.'

Bill was right. The customers started piling in to get a place in the warm. Some of them ordered food, but a lot of the time we were busy serving hot tea.

Jack was waiting for me at nine. 'I thought I'd better come and meet you to make sure you didn't get lost on the way home, Maggie.'

'I'm glad you did,' I said. 'You look pleased with yourself?'

'I got five pounds and ten shillings for that stuff I sold for you. Do you want it, or shall I keep it for you?'

'You keep it until we need it. If I had it, I would probably give some of it to Sadie. I bet she will ask when she knows the house is empty.'

'Well, don't you give it to her. I'll put it in the lowboy upstairs, because that locks, and I don't want Ma getting' her hands on our money.'

'When can we fetch Robin? He could sleep on the chair in the kitchen until you've got the attic boarded for him.'

'It's best if you wait until we're wed,' Jack said and his grin broadened. 'I've booked us up for this Saturday. I didn't see the point in waiting more than a week. We'll have the ceremony at the Register Office. I've asked a couple of me mates to be witnesses. I thought Ben and Sadie should know so I called to tell them and give them the time. Ma won't come but that doesn't matter. I sent word to my brothers. They can come if they want and stay away if they don't. There will be a bit of sherry at home for them afterwards, and I'll take you out at night. We'll go to a nice restaurant and have that posh meal I promised you.'

'I shall look forward to it,' I said and then thought of something. 'I seem to remember that Ma had to sign a paper when Sadie got married. I'm not sure who should sign for me. I don't know if Sadie would do it.'

'Sadie or Ben will do. We'll need your birth certificate too. You leave it all to me. There's nothing for you to bother your head over, Maggie. You just tell Bill you want the whole Saturday off for once.' He smiled down at me. 'Your sister is getting better so there's nothing for you to bother your head over. I've told them we'll be taking Robin as soon as I've fixed the attic.'

'You are so good to me!'

Jack was so confident, so sure of everything he did. I hadn't been convinced at the start that I really wanted to be with him, but I had begun to realise how lucky I was that he had picked me. He was good looking with his dark hair and eyes, and he could charm anyone when he set his mind to it. I was looking forward to being Jack's wife.

* * *

Ma's white dress had been washed and dipped in water with the blue bag. The yellowing had all gone and it fitted me perfectly after the waist was taken in an inch or two. On the morning of my wedding I put it on with the hat and shoes Jack had bought for me. I was feeling very smart when I went down to the kitchen.

Jack's face lit up when he saw me. 'You look beautiful, Maggie. You know I love you?'

'I love you too, Jack,' I said and gave him a quick hug. 'Shall we go?'

Jack took my hand. I glanced at his mother, but she turned her back on us, pretending to be interested in scrubbing the pine table.

'Will you change your mind and come?'

She glanced at me and I saw temptation in her eyes. 'Waste of time,' she muttered. 'I'll be cookin' a bit for Jack's brothers if they come back later.'

'Thank you,' I said. 'It's good of you to bother.'

She didn't answer and Jack hurried me out of the house. We ran hand-in-hand to catch the tram at the end of the road.

'Eddie and Spiker will meet us there,' Jack said. 'I asked Ben if he would come. He says your sister is still getting over the baby so I dare say it will be just us and me mates.'

'It doesn't matter,' I said, but there was a small voice inside my head that was telling me I wanted my family to see me married. 'What about Robin?'

'I'll fetch him round when we get back. No sense dragging him all the way to the Register Office is there? He will be happy to get a taste of Ma's sausage rolls and cakes. I gave her a few bob to put on a bit of a spread in case any of my brothers turn up.'

I nodded. It would be stupid to make a fuss now. I had thought Ben or Sadie would come to the Register Office and bring Robin with them, but why should they? Sadie blamed me because she had lost the baby. She and Ben hated me because of it. I should have known they wouldn't want to see me married, even though Ben had insisted Jack must marry me.

Jack's friends were waiting for us. Eddie was dressed in a smart striped suit with lounge lizard, two-tone shoes. I thought he looked like a Spiv, his hair plastered to his head with oil that smelled like violets. Spiker was wearing a suit of sorts, but it had seen a lot of wear and needed a press. He hadn't shaved and his breath stank of strong drink. I didn't much like the way he looked me up and down but he was Jack's friend and we needed two witnesses so I had to smile and act as if everything was perfect.

The ceremony was brief. I hardly knew we were married when I walked out with Jack a few minutes later. Eddie threw a handful of rice over us and gave me a small parcel.

'For the blushing bride,' he said and kissed my cheek. He smelled so strongly of violets that it made me choke.

'You are very kind, Mr...' I floundered because I didn't know his name. He shook his head, giving me a look I thought was rather odd.

'Just call me Eddie, everyone does. Take care of her, Jack. You've got a good one there.'

Jack looked at me on the tram back to the lanes. 'All right, Maggie? You're a bit quiet?'

'It was so quick! I don't feel married.'

'Well, you are. It's all legal and done proper,' he said and took my left hand. He kissed the finger with his ring. 'I'm going to look after you, love. I'm sorry it wasn't a church do with all the trimmings, but with the baby coming it seemed best to get it over.'

'I just wish Sadie and Robin had been there...'

'Your sister is still in bed so Ben said,' Jack told me. 'I'll take you home and then I'll fetch Robin round. You'll feel married when we have our night out, and then we'll be sharing your bed from now on.'

'Yes, I know.'

Jack was looking at me so hotly that I felt warmed right through. What did it matter if my sister hadn't wanted to see me wed? Robin would be living with us from now on and I would forget about Sadie. After all, she would be leaving the lanes for good soon.

I opened the parcel Eddie had given me on the way home. It contained a beautiful little silver jug. It was such a pretty shape and had a pattern engraved on it. Jack looked at it thoughtfully.

'I reckon that's old, Georgian probably, and real silver.'

'It's lovely. It must have cost a lot of money.'

'Eddie probably got it cheap. A lot of the time when we clear houses there's no one interested in the stuff and he gets it for next to nothing. I reckon that's where I'm headed. As soon as I know a bit more about the stuff and what it's worth, I shall start up me own business. I just need to buy a van.'

'That will cost a lot of money, Jack.' I'd seen adverts for Ford's popular car and that cost nearly nine hundred pounds; a van would probably be more. A gallon of petrol cost nearly two shillings after the recent price rise. 'You've spent too much on me—the new shoes and my wedding ring...'

'Don't you bother your head over that, love. I had a bit of luck this week.'

'What do you mean?'

Jack grinned and touched the side of his nose. 'You want to know a lot, Maggie. Eddie took me to the new Greyhound racing track. I put five bob on a dog and won a pound, and I won ten bob on another.'

'Gambling? Is that a good idea, Jack?'

'It was only a bit of fun and I was lucky. The winnings paid for your shoes so don't look at me like that, love. I've got more sense than to gamble regular—though if you're in the know it isn't much of a gamble.'

I asked him what he meant but he shook his head and changed the subject, telling me about a new Clara Bow picture that was coming soon. I'd loved my first visit to the cinema and knew I would enjoy it whatever he took me to see. Besides, I didn't want to spoil things on our wedding day so I let it go, but I didn't like the idea of his gambling.

* * *

When we got back to the cottage, we found a house filled with people, all of them strangers to me. Jack's brothers hadn't bothered to come to the ceremony at the Register Office, but they were all seated round the large, scrubbed pine table tucking into the food and sherry Jack had provided. Their wives were there too and about six children, all under the age of nine from what I could see. The men greeted him with shouts and laughter, pushing a drink into his hand and mine.

'I never thought I'd see the day,' one of them said and laughed loudly. 'My little brother a married man.'

'This is Sam,' Jack said obviously pleased. 'This is his wife Jane and his eldest Sarah—and this is Bob, Tony, George and Eric....'

The introductions went on and on until my head started spinning. There were so many of them and they were so noisy that I could hardly hear what anyone was saying. I wanted to remind Jack of his promise to fetch Robin but he was laughing and joking with his brothers and the wives were talking at me and over me.

I tried to reach Jack, but they weren't having any of it. I was made to sit and tell them who I was, where I met Jack, where I worked and a lot more. Then I was given the presents. They had all brought us something: a set of spoons, a carving knife and fork, some pillowcases and towels.

It was past four o'clock and most of the food had gone by the time they left. Jack was sitting in a chair, an empty glass in his hand, his eyes closed when I started to clear the mounds of dirty dishes and glasses. Mrs Holmes had already made a start with the washing up. She made no comment, as I picked up a cloth and dried the ones she had washed.

'Is there anything left for Robin? Jack was going to fetch him round but he forgot about it.'

'There's a cake or two in the larder. I know what my lot are. Show them a table filled with food and they will clear it. I put a bit by for later; the lad can have that if he likes.'

'Thank you. You cook so well. I've never tasted better pastry, and that Victoria sponge was delicious, so light and soft.'

'You're a bit of a cook yourself?'

'I cook bacon sandwiches and fried egg and sausage at the café , but I've never cooked cakes the way you can.'

'I'll teach you if you want,' she said. 'It's best you learn the way Jack likes his food. I shan't always be around to do it.'

'You'll live for years yet.'

'Mebbe and mebbe not. I don't come from a line of long livers. Me ma died when she was forty-three, me Pa fifty-six.'

'That doesn't mean you won't live longer.'

'Best to be prepared, if you want to learn?'

'Yes, I do please. Where did you learn?'

'I was in service afore I married. Worked my way up to Cook I did—and I'd 'ave done better to keep as I was, but Jack's father was a charmer. I couldn't resist him. I had to marry him because they would 'ave turned me off once I was in trouble.'

'Oh...' It was the longest conversation I'd had with her and I was wondering what to reply when Jack put his head round the door. 'I'm off to fetch Robin now, Maggie. Get yourself ready and we'll be off out when he's sat down to his tea.'

'All right, I'll just finish this first. We can't leave all the work for your ma.'

'You're the only one that thought of it,' Mrs Holmes said as Jack went off. 'They are a right selfish lot my boys married. I tried to warn them, but they would 'ave their way. You've done your share, Maggie. Go and make yourself look pretty for Jack when he gets back.'

'All right, thanks,' I said. Most of the work was done. She had only the wiping down of the sink to finish.

I ran upstairs and changed out of Ma's dress, putting on my Sunday-going-to-church outfit. I brushed my hair, pinched my cheeks and licked my lips, dabbing a little of the scent Jack had given me for Christmas behind my ears. I was back downstairs

when Jack returned some minutes later. He was alone and he didn't
look pleased.

'Where is Robin?'

'He has gone to stay with a friend. Apparently, it is his friend's
birthday and he was invited to tea and to stay the night.'

'Oh...' I felt disappointed because I had been looking forward to
showing Robin where his own little room would be in the attic. 'I
won't be able to fetch him tomorrow but you can collect him for
me, can't you?'

'Yes, I'll do that, Maggie. You look a treat. Come on, we'll catch a
tram and go up West for our night out.'

* * *

Jack really spoiled me that evening. He took me to an Italian
restaurant. There were starting to be a lot of them in London now,
run by Italians who thought England was a better place to live. This
one was small and intimate, the table lights giving it a cosy feel and
the red cloths so smart and pretty. Vine leaves twined across the
ceiling and there were baskets with wine bottles and bunches of
imitation grapes hanging over the counter. I liked the smell of rich
food issuing from the kitchens. I had never tasted anything like the
dishes they served us, and I was curious about what was in some of
them. For me the problem had always been how to put enough
food on the plate for my brother and Ma. Savouring the taste of
delicious sausage, spaghetti and meatballs in a tomato sauce made
me curious. There was such a lot about food I didn't know and I was
discovering an interest that I had never suspected.

'How did you know about this place?' I asked Jack.

'Eddie brought me here when I started to work for him. It opens
your eyes to the way the other half lives, Maggie. This is good but

there are better places—places where it costs more than you would need to feed a family for a month for just one meal.'

'But that's a wicked waste. The ingredients are just the same, it's just the way it has been cooked.'

'It's the learning behind it,' Jack said. 'Everything in life is a matter of what you know, and sometimes who you know. If you look down at the ground and work your guts out, you'll die afore your time and you'll never know about the good things—like my pa. Meeting Eddie was the best thing that ever happened to me, Maggie, apart from you, of course. I want the things he knows how to get. I've been working for him part time, but he says he'll take me on full time now I'm married. He has got some special jobs coming up soon and he says I am the man for him.'

'Are you sure you trust him? I thought...well, he looked like a Spiv...'

Jack was amused. 'Eddie likes his suits and them fancy hand-made shoes of his are a bit flash, but I don't care what he wears. I can earn twice as much working for him as I could at the docks. Eddie has always been fair with me, Maggie—and yes, I trust him.'

'You know him best.' The wine had gone to my head and I felt a bit giggly. 'I've had enough to eat. Shall we go home now?'

'If you're ready,' Jack said and his hot eyes made me tingle all over. He reached across the table and took hold of my hand, stroking the back with his finger. 'I love you, Maggie. What happened at Christmas was daft. I'd had too much to drink. It won't be like that this time, I promise.'

'I like it when you kiss me...' I felt a bit shy as I looked into his eyes. My stomach was starting to spasm and my breath came in funny little gasps. I wanted to lie in bed with him and feel his flesh touching mine...to kiss him and touch him.

Jack called the waiter and paid him. He held his hand out to me, his fingers closing over mine as I reached for him.

'I reckon it's time I showed you how it feels to be married proper-er,' he said and I smiled. I was at that moment as happy as I had ever been.

* * *

Jack made love to me slowly unlike the first time. He had undressed me, removing my clothes piece by piece, his eyes feasting on my body as if he were starving. He kissed my shoulder as he removed the dress I had been wearing, making me tremble with anticipation. My bodice and petticoat came off next and then my drawers. My stockings were the ones Sadie had given me at Christmas. I should have liked to wear silk, but they were too expensive.

'Jack...' I whispered, because I felt strange with him looking at me. 'Am I all right?'

'You're more than all right,' he said huskily. 'You're beautiful, Maggie. I've dreamed of you like this but it wasn't as good. I love you so much. I would kill anyone who tried to take you from me!'

He was so fierce that for a moment I was shaken, but then I laughed. 'Silly! No one is going to try. I love you, Jack. I don't want anyone else. I promise there won't ever be anyone else.'

'I'll be good to you,' he vowed and reached out for me.

He picked me up as if I weighed no more than a feather and carried me to the bed, placing me amongst the sheets as if I were something precious... special. My heart turned over. Jack had won me. His tenderness, his concern, his decency in marrying me when he could have just walked away and left me to sort myself out, had proved his love.

Jack was a charmer. His loving that night was tender and sweet, drawing every response from me that a woman in love can give. I was his completely, my body thrilling to his touch—an instrument that he played at will. I arched beneath him, meeting his urgent thrusting with an equal passion, wanting his loving, wanting him deeper and deeper inside me. I cried his name aloud, my nails scoring his shoulder as I reached for something and found it.

As the waves of pleasure broke over me, I clung to him, licking the sweat from his shoulder, tasting him as he had tasted me, knowing that nothing could ever be as wonderful again. Yet it was, again and again that night as he took his fill, teaching me so much that I had never known... initiating me into pleasures that I had not known existed.

Afterwards, my face buried in his chest, I asked him why he was such a good lover. 'You must have been with other girls,' I said inhaling the scent of him. He tasted salty, a little like shrimps. 'I'm not your first. I couldn't be...you know just what to do.'

'Look at me, Maggie,' he commanded and I lifted my head. He tangled his fingers in my hair, his face so close to mine that I felt his warm breath. 'You're not the first, but you're the last. I swear it on my life. Do you believe me? You're not just a girl to me, Maggie Holmes—you're my life.'

'I believe you. I shall always be yours.'

'You had better remember it,' Jack said and then kissed me. 'Get some sleep, lass. It will soon be morning and you have to work.'

I settled into his arms, feeling thoroughly loved. I wished there was no work. I wanted to lie in this bed and make love with my husband forever, but I knew Jack was right. Life didn't stop just because I had fallen in love with the man I'd married. I had to work and look after my brother.

* * *

'You get off, Maggie,' Bill said to me at eight that evening. 'You should have taken the day off. It isn't often a girl gets married.'

'It's the one and only time for me,' I said and laughed. I had felt like laughing all day. The customers had been teasing me, and most of them had left me a tip. They couldn't afford to buy presents but a few pence by their plate was meant as a gift and at the end of the day I had three shillings. It would come in useful and I was pleased. I could afford to buy Robin a present, something special to celebrate him coming to live with us. I wasn't sure what it would be, because I was going to ask if he wanted a football or a cricket bat. It would be his choice. Maybe he would choose a visit to the cinema; he had only been once and he had never forgotten it.

Jack wasn't waiting for me when I left the café, but he wouldn't expect Bill to let me off early. I was lucky to have such an understanding employer. I had taken a day off for my wedding at short notice, but Bill hadn't grumbled. He and Ann had given me thirty shillings as my wedding gift.

'You can buy something you need,' Bill said. 'If we'd given you a present it might not have been what you need.'

The money was so unexpected and wonderful. As much as I would earn for three whole weeks, and mine to spend as I liked. It felt like Christmas and my birthday all rolled into one, only better, much better. Nothing had ever been this good before. I couldn't wait to get back to the cottage. I was bursting with excitement when I rushed in, full of my good fortune and eager to share my news.

Jack was sitting at the table drinking a glass of beer. His head came up as I entered and I saw an odd look in his eyes, guilty or afraid. It couldn't be because he was having a drink. He seldom drank too much and he didn't become violent when he'd had a few, just a bit soppy.

'What's wrong?'

'Sit down, Maggie. I've got something to tell you. I'm sorry, love, this isn't going to be easy.'

'You've lost your job?'

'No, nothing like that...' Jack stared down at his glass. 'It's your sister and Ben, they've upped and gone.'

'What do you mean? Sadie was still ill. You told me!'

'It was what Ben said but he must have been lying. They left this morning first thing.'

'Robin...where is Robin? She wouldn't have taken him. She didn't want him.'

'No, she didn't take him...' Jack could hardly look me in the face. 'Last night when I went to the door Ben answered. He didn't ask me in. I asked for Robin and he told me—'

'He was staying with friends for the night. You told me. Is he with his friends now? Have we got to fetch him?'

'He wasn't with friends, Maggie. Ben told me that Sadie took him to the church home. I didn't want to spoil your wedding day so I made something up. She gave him away, signed a paper giving up all rights to him.'

'She can't do that!' The scream built inside my head. I felt shivery as if I'd been dipped in a bath of cold water. 'It isn't legal. It can't be! She wouldn't do that! She knew he was coming here. She knew...' I ran at Jack, pulling at his shirt as he got to his feet. 'We have to go and get him back. He will hate it there! They don't know him. They can't look after him the way I do. He will cry and wet the bed and they will be cross with him, but he can't help it and he only does it when he's scared. '

'Sadie left you a letter. Jack placed it on the table. 'It explains—'

'What do you mean? How can she explain what she's done? He can't stay in that place, Jack. We have to get him back.'

'We can't, Maggie. Sadie signed for him and she's his sister. We can't get him back. I went round there first thing this morning and asked. They told me it is all perfectly legal. His sister signed him away and they won't give him back to us.'

'But he's my brother too and I want him back. I didn't sign. She can't just sign him away. I have rights too. I am married now and I have a home. I can look after him. They must give him back to me. They must!'

'You don't have the right,' Jack said. 'I am sorry, Maggie.' He took my hands as I grabbed at him wildly, trying to pull him with me, to make him help me fetch Robin back. 'Sadie is his sister... you aren't...'

'What do you mean? Of course I am Robin's sister. I've always been his sister. I love him and he loves me. He will be miserable in that place.' I was so upset that I couldn't take in what he was saying. I could only think of Robin's pain. He would be feeling so lost and alone... he would think we didn't love him.

'Yes, I think he will at first,' Jack said. 'Read your letter, Maggie. It will explain better than I can.'

'No!' I took the letter and tore it across and then threw it on the fire. I didn't want to read Sadie's excuses. 'I don't care what Sadie says. She hates me. She sent Robin there to punish me because she lost the baby.'

'It's on your birth certificate, Maggie. Your mother wasn't Jane Bailey and your father is...unknown.' Jack looked grey in the face. 'I saw it when Ben gave it to me. I didn't think it mattered, love. I thought Sadie would just let you have Robin, because she wasn't bothered what happened to him, but, according to Ben, she says you can't be trusted. She says it is for the best this way, because you aren't Robin's sister and you aren't her sister either.'

'Don't lie to me!' I screamed at him. 'It isn't true...' Yet even as I denied him something deep inside told me that he was speaking the truth. It was the reason Ma had told Sadie things she hadn't told me... the reason Michael Bailey had looked at me that way. He hadn't seen me as his daughter. 'It isn't true...' I said but I was crying now rather than screaming, all the fight knocked out of me. 'It isn't true...' I sat down at the kitchen table, feeling the hopelessness sweep over me, my hands to my face. 'Robin loves me. He wants to be with me...'

'You should have read what she says in her letter. Sadie didn't know who your real parents were. She says your Ma's cousin may know, and she wrote an address down for you. She says she doesn't hate you—'

'She is lying! She did it to hurt me, Jack. You know she did.'

'Maybe she did,' Jack said because he could see that I wasn't going to change my mind. 'It doesn't make much difference. I tried to get Robin back for you, Maggie. I'm sorry. If I hadn't insisted that we leave him there until we were married it might not have happened. I should have fetched him the next day and brought him here. Sadie wouldn't have done it then.'

A moment or two earlier I might have agreed that it was his fault. I had wanted to scream and hit out then, but now I just felt sick and tight with misery. All the time I had been planning treats for Robin once he was living with us and he didn't know what I had planned. He must be frightened and in terrible distress. One sister had gone off to live with someone he hardly knew and the other one had given him away.

'He must think that no one loves him. Can you imagine how he feels...how lonely and frightened he must be?'

'Yes, I can, but what can we do? I told them he had a home with us but they wouldn't listen. They said they had plans for children like Robin. They said he would be given a new life, a good life somewhere away from London—maybe in Canada or Australia.'

'I saw something about that in the papers,' I said feeling hollow. 'It's a scheme to send orphans to other countries where they need to increase the population... but Robin belongs here with us. I have to get him back, Jack. I have to!'

I turned towards the door. Jack was with me as I went out.

'I'll come with you,' he said, 'but I know the answer you'll get. If

I could have moved them he would have been waiting for you at home. I tried love, honest I did.'

'I have to try myself, Jack,' I said and my voice broke on a sob. 'I have to try...'

'I know you do,' he said and looked wretched. 'I shan't forgive myself in a hurry. If I'd done what you asked—'

'No! It wasn't you. Sadie hated me. She wanted to hurt me. She was jealous because I was getting married and she knew this was the one thing that would ruin everything. She might have done it anyway. She has spoiled it all...'

'Not everything,' Jack said and there was a plea in his voice. 'You've still got me, Maggie.'

'Yes, I didn't mean that,' I said, but my heart was breaking. I loved Jack and it could all have been perfect, but Robin was gone and that hurt me so much. He would be crying, thinking that no one loved him.

'I care,' I whispered. 'I love you, Robin. I don't know how but I'll find you...one day I'll find you, my darling....'

12

'And did you manage to see him when you went to the home? Did they allow you to say goodbye?' Thomas asked as I came to a halt, the tears streaming down my face. I shook my head. 'That's a proper shame. You weren't the only one to suffer like that, Maggie. Quite a few children got caught up in that scheme. Some were orphans, some of them from families who couldn't afford to look after their children. I've heard of parents who thought they were just sending their lads for a holiday and discovered the truth too late. Some of them didn't know what they were signing.'

'Sadie knew,' I said, bitterness in my voice. 'She did it to punish me. She knew I was getting married and that Robin would have a home with us. It was because of the baby.'

'That is sad,' Thomas looked grave. 'What have you done to try and find him?'

'I went to the home every Saturday for weeks, asking them where he'd gone, begging them to give him back, but they wouldn't. I was told to write to the Bishop and to government ministers. I wrote letters to everyone I could think of but I never got any answers. I kept writing week after week but it was as if I didn't exist. Whatever I did it wasn't enough.

I wasn't his sister and I had no rights. It didn't matter that I loved him....' My voice broke as the tears came. *'Love doesn't count...'*

'Did you come to us? We've managed to trace a few of the children who were taken but didn't get sent abroad. We do try to find people in all sorts of circumstances.'

'Molly told me to come to you—'

'Molly?'

'Jack's mother. She told me to call her that...later, after she got used to having me about. I did ask once but the woman I spoke to told me I had left it too late.'

'She shouldn't have done that,' Thomas said. *'It is never too late, Maggie but tell me what happened later, after that day...'*

* * *

'You've got a light touch with the pastry,' Mrs Holmes remarked, as I finished making the apple pie we were to have for supper that Saturday night. 'And your Victoria sponge is as good as mine. I reckon I've taught you all I can, Maggie. If you want to learn more you should get a book, or take one o' them courses.'

'What courses?' I asked, going to the oven to put the pie onto the middle shelf. I washed my hands at the sink, drying them on a towel as she fetched out a newspaper. I put a hand to my back. It was the end of April now and I was nearly five months gone. I'd been right to think I'd fallen for a child that first night, but I no longer regretted it. The baby was mine and the thought of it growing inside me had helped me to get through the dark days after Sadie betrayed me and sent my Robin away.

Robin was the only one I missed. It seemed to me now that my family had never really cared for me. None of them had wanted me except Robin. I didn't even know where Sadie was; she'd said they were going to Australia but hadn't told me where or said goodbye to my face. I suppose I might have tried to find out who my real mother was but I'd burned Sadie's letter and I didn't know the address of Ma's cousin—only she wasn't my mother and the cousin wasn't a relation so why should she care about me? Maybe if I hadn't burned Sadie's letter...but I had and Jack didn't remember the address so it was hopeless.

All I had now was Jack, the baby and Jack's mother. She was all right with me these days, telling me to call her Molly and giving me cooking lessons. I think it was the cooking that had made her less hostile towards me; she liked it because I was interested in learning, but I still got the sharp edge of her tongue more often than not.

Sometimes I got a backache when I had been standing for a while and I was feeling tired. 'Where does it say about the cooking courses? 'I asked her.

My eyes had been drawn to an article about the unrest with the miners. They were demanding more money and the bosses and government were talking about it being an outrage and standing firm.

'They say the miners will strike. I think they are entitled to a bit more by the look of it. It's hard enough to feed a family when you get decent wages. They've been asked to take a pay cut, and that isn't fair on a working man.'

'They are fools if they strike,' she said harshly. 'The government will break them. The bosses and them lot always win in the end, you mark my words.'

I nodded, reading down the page until I found the advert for the cooking courses. 'This sounds interesting but I couldn't afford it. You have to pay fifteen shillings and you go to a cooking school every day for two weeks.'

'You've got a bit put by. You won't be able to work at the café forever, Maggie. Besides, you're too bright to be wasting your time there. You could find a good job in a proper restaurant. I shouldn't wonder if you got twice what that Billy Biggins pays you.' She looked at me hard. 'You want to think of the future, girl. Don't put all your trust in men. They let you down.' She sounded bitter and I knew she hadn't forgiven Jack for bringing me into her home but we were stuck with each other and we made the best of it.

'I should like to work in a teashop. There's a lovely one across the road from the cinema Jack takes me to sometimes. We've never been in but it's all done out in that new style—Art Deco they call it —and it's real expensive. We could make a fortune, you and me together.'

She shook her head firmly. 'You don't want to be thinking about me. You think about the future, Maggie. After the baby comes...'

'But I shall have to look after it, and there's my job. I can't let Bill down.'

'He works you to death and pays half what you're worth,' she said. 'If you've any sense you will give notice before the baby is born. I dare say I could look after the child sometimes if you wanted to better yourself, and once you're earnin' good money you could pay someone if you had ter.'

'But you said it was too much to expect you to look after the baby.'

She made a tutting sound. 'I say a lot of things. I'd want a bob or two for it, mind. Jack can pay me. He seems to have plenty of money in his pocket these days.'

'Yes, he does.' I sometimes wondered where Jack got his money from. I knew he had several five-pound notes in the drawer upstairs, and he was always generous to us. 'You don't think...Jack wouldn't do anything daft, would he?'

'Like what?'

'I don't know...' Jack had been a bit odd recently but I didn't want to tell his mother. I would be sure to get a tongue lashing for it. 'You'll watch the pie, Molly? I ought to leave now or I shall be late.'

'You tell that Billy Biggins you want a rise.' She glanced at the clock and scowled. 'You've got another twenty minutes yet, girl. Sit down and have a cuppa with me.'

'Ann asked me to get a bottle of that medicine for Katie. If the shop is busy, it might make me late.'

'She uses a lot of that stuff. You bought a bottle for her a week ago.'

'Yes, I did. I shouldn't have thought she would use it all that quick. We used to have it for Robin but Ma was careful with it...' Pain lanced through me. I only had to think of Robin to start up the ache inside me. Time didn't ease the way I felt, though everyone said it would.

'Don't take on so, lass. He'll be all right.' Molly saw my expression. 'You've had no reply to your letters?' I shook my head. 'Why don't you try at the Sally Army? I've heard they find folk what are lost.'

'I could try them...' I remembered the day Robin and I had stood in the cold and listened to them singing hymns and the hurt twisted inside me like a knife. 'I'll try anything.'

'He is probably settled and happy by now,' she said. 'Children soon get over things. You shouldn't torture yourself.'

'I can't forget him just like that. You don't understand.'

'I understand right enough. I lost five children, all of them girls. You wait until you hold your baby in your arms, Maggie. You'll know how I felt then when I lost mine. Robin isn't your real brother. You've seen the birth certificate. Jane Bailey wasn't your mother.'

'I should have guessed. I was never loved in that house—except by Robin. He loved me. I thought Sadie did, but after she lost the baby, she hated me.'

'Well, write another letter or go to the Sally Army, but stop fretting over it, Maggie. If you're not careful you'll bring a miscarriage on yourself and you will lose the baby. You don't want that, do you?'

'No, I don't,' I said and sniffed. I wiped my face. 'I'd better go if I am going to get that medicine.' I fetched my coat. It wasn't cold out but it might be when I came home later. 'Tell Jack I'll be home a bit earlier this evening. Bill says I can finish at eight most nights. Katie sleeps through now and Ann can help him a bit in the evenings.'

Molly said something I didn't hear as I went out. I walked to the corner shop and looked for the medicine Ann wanted. The label was a different colour and I asked the man behind the counter why it had changed.

'It's a bit stronger. You need to give smaller doses. Read the label, Maggie.'

'It's not for me. Mrs Biggins uses it for her Katie.'

'It's a bit strong for babies that young. You tell her to be careful with it, lass.'

'Yes, I will. Thank you for telling me, Mr Hopkins.'

'That's all right. I wouldn't want her to overdo it.'

I paid for the medicine and left the shop, thinking about what Molly had said about the Sally Army. Had I got time to pop in before I went to work? I decided that it would be cutting things too fine and hurried on towards the café. I didn't want to be late.

It was warm inside the café, though Bill hadn't got the big stove burning, just the range in the kitchen. He was busy so I went straight through and put the bottle on the sideboard. Ann came in just as I was tying on my apron. She saw the medicine and looked pleased.

'Thank you, Maggie. Is it still a shilling?'

'Yes. Mr Hopkins said to be careful with it. He said they've made it stronger and you should give a smaller dose or not use it so often.'

'Oh, I had better read the instructions,' Ann said and gave me the money. 'Katie sleeps so much better now I have this...' She started back up the stairs, taking the bottle with her.

* * *

Jack was home when I got back that evening. He smiled at me and put a little package on the table in front of me.

'What is this? It isn't my birthday.'

'I can buy a present for my wife when I want, can't I?' He caught me round the waist, putting his hand to my swollen belly. 'Maybe it is something for the little one.'

I opened the small box and found a silver rattle with a coral teething ring. 'Oh Jack, you shouldn't have spent so much money on something like this,' I said. 'The baby isn't even born yet.'

'I wanted you to have it. It didn't cost much. Besides, I earned a bonus this week. Eddie looks after me.'

I sensed something wasn't right. I didn't know what was different, but Jack had changed recently. He had plenty of money in his pocket, but he wasn't as settled as he had been. He couldn't sit down in the evenings and went off after he'd had his supper. Jack always said it was business, but sometimes I knew he'd had a few drinks when he came to bed. He wasn't violent and we still made love often. He was as gentle and loving as he had always been, but I knew he was hiding something.

'What is it, Jack? What is worrying you?'

'Nothing is wrong. I'm not worried about anything. Why should I be?'

'I don't know. Is it something to do with your work. You haven't been gambling at the greyhound track?'

'No, I've only been the once. Nothing is wrong, love. Ma said you were upsetting yourself earlier. She thinks you should give up working at the café so much—and I can afford it. Tell Bill you can only do part time from now on.'

'I don't know...' I hesitated, because Molly had set me thinking earlier when she showed me the cooking courses. 'Are you certain it wouldn't put too much on you? I could keep on as I am for a bit longer.'

'Why should you? Tell Bill you'll do mornings through to three o'clock and then come home. If he doesn't like it you can leave. We can manage on what I bring in now.'

'I'll talk to him. Have you had your supper?'

'Yeah, and that apple pie was smashing. Ma says you're a good cook.' He grinned in his old way. 'I told you she would come round. She says you're a hard worker and I did well for myself. She likes you better than any of the other wives.'

'I did well for myself too,' I said and bent down to kiss him. 'If you're quite sure, Jack. I'll speak to Bill tomorrow.'

* * *

I left a bit earlier than usual the next morning so that I would have time to call in at the headquarters of the Salvation Army. It was a big, square, ugly building with the name painted on a board out front. I tried the door tentatively. It was unlocked so I went inside. I could hear someone laughing somewhere and then a girl came out from behind a screen and went to the counter.

'I don't know if I've come to the right place...' She turned to look at me and I saw her face was burned on one side. I couldn't help staring because she would have been so pretty if she hadn't had that awful scar on her face. 'I'm sorry...I was looking for someone who might be able to help me find my brother.'

'We might be able to help. Mrs Douglas isn't here at the

moment. She deals with missing people inquiries. Give me your name, and his name, and I'll tell her when she gets back.'

'His name is Robin Bailey and my sister signed for the church home to take him early in January.'

'So it's nearly five months then.' She frowned. 'It's a long time. Why didn't you come sooner? If he went in a home they ought to know where he is.'

'They won't tell me. They say he's being well looked after but they won't say where he is.'

'Then I shouldn't think we can find out. Besides, he's probably better off.'

'I didn't think you could help. I'm sorry I wasted your time.'

'You didn't give me your name...'

I walked out without looking back. It was like banging my head up against a brick wall. No one really cared! I felt the lump in my chest as I walked away from that ugly building. I should have known better than to ask. The Sally Army and the church were all on the same side.

I was feeling upset and angry as I went into the café. No one knew what it meant to me to lose Robin. Even Jack thought it was for the best, though he'd never actually said it to me, but I knew he was secretly glad that we didn't have Robin to look after. The sickness was churning inside me, because I couldn't bear the thought of my brother alone, perhaps coughing... he would cry for me and I wouldn't be there to comfort him.

Bill wasn't in the café when I went in. A couple of customers were sitting there but they didn't speak, which was strange because they usually had something to say even if it was only to ask for another cup of tea.

'Where is Bill?'

'He went through to the back,' one of the men said. 'I think summat's up with the little one. I reckon they've got the doctor with them.'

'Do you want anything before I go and see?'

Both men shook their heads so I went through the back into the kitchen and took off my coat. I got the frying pan out, preparing to make myself a bit of breakfast as I always did and then Ben came down the stairs. The doctor, a small, wiry man in a dark coat, followed him into the kitchen.

'Maggie bought it yesterday,' Bill said in answer to something the doctor had said. He gave me such a look that my heart slammed against my chest. 'Where did you get that medicine, Maggie?'

'From the shop on the corner,' I said. 'I always get it there. I know it has been changed, because I asked about it and they told me it was stronger. You have to give smaller doses. I told Ann...' My breath caught as I saw Bill's face. 'Why, is something wrong?'

'Katie is very ill,' the doctor spoke because Bill was obviously upset. 'She has been poisoned by whatever is in that foul stuff you bought. It should never have been given to a baby of six months. It is for adults not babies and I wouldn't recommend it to anyone, because it has laudanum in it and that is dangerous stuff unless you know how to use it.'

'But...we used to give it to Robin and he was all right.'

'It isn't the same as the other stuff,' Bill said. 'The ingredients have been changed and it's too strong for babies.'

'I told Ann it was stronger,' I said but the way he looked at me I was sure he didn't believe me. I shivered, because this wasn't the genial Bill I knew. He looked hard and angry. 'I wouldn't lie to you, Bill. You know I wouldn't—'

'Ann said you told her it was just the same.'

'No, I told her Mr Hopkins said to be careful with it.'

'He shouldn't have sold it to you for a child,' the doctor said. 'I'll be having a word with him on my way home.' He glanced at Bill.

'There isn't much I can do. I'm sorry. You will just have to wait and see if she pulls through. The mixture I gave Katie will ease the pain in her stomach, but she is very ill. You can call me again if you need me. I'll pop back later and see how she is...'

'Thank you,' Bill said. 'You can see yourself out.' He waited until the doctor had gone and then looked at me. 'Why didn't you tell me it was a different medicine, Maggie?'

'I told Ann. We were busy in the café and I didn't think to tell you. Ann said she would read the label.'

'She must have forgotten. I know she is sometimes tired, though not as much as before because Katie sleeps so well.'

'Is Katie really poorly?'

'She has been sick several times in the night. The doctor says that is good because she has to get that stuff out of her system. He gave her something he said would line her stomach, but she brought it up again and she is crying. He says she has pain in her stomach.'

'I'm so sorry. Shall I go up and see if I can help Ann with her?'

'No, I think you had better stay away from her, Maggie. Ann is very upset. Get your breakfast and then come through to the café.'

Bill left me and I heard voices murmuring in the café. I felt shocked, stunned to think that the medicine I'd brought for Katie had made her so ill. The doctor had said she was poisoned, but I couldn't believe he meant it. It couldn't be poison. The medicine was there for everyone to buy and in the past, it had seemed to help Katie. What had they put in it to make her so ill? I had never dreamed it could harm her.

I didn't fancy a big breakfast after what I'd learned so I just made a bit of toast with butter and jam. Bill looked at me hard as I went into the café a short time later. I sensed that he was trying to decide whether or not I had lied to him. Surely, he couldn't think I had neglected to tell Ann about the new brand of medicine?

* * *

I didn't see Ann that morning. I knew she came down to the kitchen because I heard her talking to Bill. I was serving in the café and I couldn't hear what they were saying, but he seemed odd when he came back at about two in the afternoon. I finished serving the last customer and took his money. For once the café was completely empty.

'Maggie...' Bill said. 'I am sorry. I don't know quite how to say this... but Ann doesn't want you here any more. She told me to get rid of you.'

I stared at him, shocked and disbelieving. 'You are giving me the sack? What have I done? I swear to you on my baby's life that I told Ann to be careful.'

'She says you didn't and she doesn't want you in her kitchen.' Bill went to the till and took out some money. 'I'm going to give you thirty shillings. It's your wages for this week and a bit more.'

I stood there in silence, unwilling to take his money. He needn't have paid me any extra but he had because he knew that Ann was lying. He believed me, because he knew I was telling the truth but she was his wife and he had to do what she wanted. I took the money reluctantly.

'I didn't make your baby ill. I'm sorry the medicine harmed her but I didn't know. It should have something on the label to warn people.'

'It isn't proper stuff like they have at the chemist,' Bill said. 'The doctor told me they have a lot of trouble with these herbal remedies. He called it rubbish. It's cheaper than the medicine he gives out and people buy it, but it can do more harm than good sometimes. It kept Katie quiet, but it was harming her.'

'It was good for Robin but that was before they changed it. Ann asked me to get it for Katie. Why didn't she call the doctor before?'

'That might be my fault. I'm not blaming you, Maggie. I just can't keep you here. Ann is in such a state. I think she might go for you if she saw you.'

'I'd better go then. You've been good to me, Bill, and so has Ann. Please tell her how sorry I am about Katie.'

'When she is over this,' he said. 'I'll give you a reference if you need one. You've been a good worker.'

'I'll ask if I need it. I'd better go.'

I walked out, my head down. Ann had made up her mind I was to blame. When I reached the other side of the road I glanced back. I saw a face at the upstairs window and knew it was Ann. She wanted to make sure I had gone. I lifted my head proudly. I had told her what Mr Hopkins said about the new stuff being stronger. If she hadn't taken the time to read the instructions carefully it was her fault Katie was ill.

I took my time walking home. What was I going to tell Jack and Molly? I decided I wouldn't go straight back to Molly's house. I could go to the market and visit a couple of shops I had in mind.

* * *

Molly looked at the material I'd bought from the market, and the Butterick dress pattern for a maternity gown.

'I wondered when yer would get round to it,' she said. 'You're bursting out of everything you've got, girl.'

'Well, I hadn't got the time to make a new dress before. Sam's wife has a Jones sewing machine. Do you think she will lend it to me?' Sam was her eldest and friendly enough but his wife didn't often visit us.

'I should think so. You'll have time on your hands now—unless you can find a new job.' Molly thought I had been treated unfairly, and she said I was right to take the extra money. 'Make him pay for the way he treated you, lass. I should like to give that wife of his a piece of my tongue.'

'Please don't,' I begged. 'She is upset as it is.' It was nice that she was standing up for me but I didn't want her to go for Bill over it, and she would if I let her.

'You're upset too,' Molly grumbled. 'He had no right to throw you out like that and I've a good mind to tell him so.' She turned away to put the kettle on the hob. 'But I dare say you'll find another job if you need it.'

'I called in at the bakery on my way home. Mr Shirley said he would take me back like a shot if it weren't for the baby. He said once I've had the child, he will be glad to take me on and he'll pay me eight shillings a week. It isn't much but it's better than nothing.'

'Thinks he wouldn't get a fair day's work out of yer at the moment I suppose. Well, there's plenty more fish in the sea, Maggie.' She hesitated, then, 'Why don't yer sign onto that cookery course I told you about? Once you've done somethin' like that you'll always 'ave it behind yer.'

'Do you think I should?'

'Why not? I'll lend yer the money if you're short.'

'I've got the money. What would Jack say?'

'He doesn't 'ave ter know.'

'I couldn't not tell him. It wouldn't be right.'

Molly snorted in disgust. 'Do yer think he tells you everythin' he gets up ter? It's best not ter tell a man too much, sets 'im thinkin'.'

'I don't know. Perhaps he doesn't tell me everything, but I wouldn't want to lie to him…So you think I should do the course?'

'Which one will yer take? There were more than one as I recall.'

'The baking course. I can cook a dinner but I want to make fancy cakes. The sort I could sell in a teashop.'

'I was thinking yer might like ter go as cook for a mistress, but if it is a tea shop yer after.'

'I don't suppose I'll ever have my own shop,' I said. 'But I would like to work in a place like the one I told you about up West.'

'Well, you never know, you might 'ave yer own one day. Stranger things 'ave happened, mark my words.' She shook her head as I put the pinking scissors to the material. 'Not like that, you daft lump! You have to cut it on the bias or you'll never get it right. Come here and let me show yer...'

I let her take over. I would need the dress if I was going to take the cookery course. At the café the big apron had covered my swelling belly but without it my condition was obvious.

'I'll go and sign up in the morning then,' I said. 'Jack may not approve but it's something I've been wanting to do for a while.'

* * *

Jack was angry when I told him about Katie and losing my job and then he frowned.

'After the way you've slaved for him! He's got a damned cheek if you ask me. Do you want me to go round there and give him one?'

'No, of course I don't, Jack! Please promise me you won't go near him. Ann was upset over Katie. I can't blame her. Perhaps I shouldn't have taken the medicine for her after Mr Hopkins told me it had changed. In a way it is my fault that Katie is ill.'

'Don't be daft! If anyone is responsible it is the person who made that stuff up, or Ann for giving it to her baby. From what you told me she gave Katie far too much all the way through just to keep her quiet.'

'I did think she gave Katie too much. I told both her and Bill at the start that they needed to be careful—and I did warn her that the new stuff was stronger.'

'If she had anything about her, she would admit it,' Jack said. 'It's just as well you've left there, Maggie love. I didn't like you walking home alone at night and I couldn't always be there to fetch you.'

'I'm sorry about the money, Jack. I know we needed it. I'll go back to work as soon as I can. Molly says she'll look after the baby for a few hours a day so I can do part time anyway.'

'We don't need money that bad, and if things go right for me you won't have to work at all.' Jack kissed me. 'Once I've got a bit more behind me, I'll be able to keep you in style.'

Jack was always talking about how things would be wonderful one day, but I wasn't sure if I believed him. It was hard for people like us to better ourselves. 'You don't mind me taking the cooking course, do you?'

'Not if it is what you want. I like good food so it won't be wasted.'

'I should like to work in a teashop but with my own cakes, not the sort of stuff the bakery sells. Do you remember that posh shop up West, near where we went to the pictures?'

'Yeah, real fancy stuff. No call for that round here. People couldn't afford it.'

'Not at the prices they charge up West,' I agreed. 'But you can make things nice without charging the earth, Jack.'

His gaze intensified. 'So you want to own a teashop, do you? Well, we shall have to see,' he teased. 'Maybe when I've got me own van you can have your shop.'

'Oh Jack! You'll never have one of them furniture vans. They must cost so much money.'

'I reckon I shall need at least a hundred, maybe two to set up on me own. I'll want a van and a store to put the stuff in, and then I need money to buy things. You can't always sell everything straight away.'

'Two hundred pounds?' I stared at him in disbelief. 'That is so much money. You will never save that much. It is impossible!' I couldn't even visualise that amount of money. 'Only rich people can afford things like that, Jack.'

'It will take me a while. I know it seems impossible but Eddie has asked me to do some special jobs. If I do them, I shall start to earn big money. I really want to set up for myself, Maggie.'

'You can have the money I was going to use for the course if you like?'

Jack laughed and shook his head. 'You keep your money, Maggie. Do the course if you like. It may help you get a job after the baby is born. I don't think you'll get your teashop just yet but you never know.'

* * *

I enrolled for the course the next morning. The woman taking the bookings looked a bit surprised, because she could see I was having a baby, but I told her I was quite sure I wanted to do it.

'Married women don't often take our courses,' she said. 'Most ladies do not wish to work once they are married—and these are professional courses you know. It isn't like jam making at the Women's Institute.'

'I would expect them to be professional when I am paying for them. Is there something wrong with my money?'

'No, of course not, Mrs Holmes. I'll put you down to start next week.'

I thanked her and left. She had been smartly dressed and I'd got the impression that my fellow students would be of a better class— young ladies from middle class families was the way she had put it. Well, they would just have to put up with a cuckoo in the nest, because I wasn't going to let that snooty receptionist put me off. I was really looking forward to learning all the new techniques I'd read about in the leaflet she had given me once I'd paid my money.

I'd never even seen fondant cream icing or made a meringue, and I certainly had no idea what a Baked Alaska was, but I was going to enjoy finding out.

When I got back from the college Molly grinned at me. She pointed to something on the table. I picked it up and discovered it was a large apron, but much nicer than the one I had used at the café.

'I washed it and ironed it for yer,' she said. 'I wore that when I was cook at Lady Marsh's house. Very particular she was about how her servants were dressed. I had three of them given me. I was supposed to give them all back when I left but I kept this one. I thought it might come in handy. It will be just right for yer cookery course.'

'I shall wear it with pride,' I said. 'I've got a head start on the others because you've already taught me such a lot.'

'I don't know about all that fancy stuff you're going to learn,' she said after looking at my leaflet. 'You'll never use that knowledge round here but if it's what yer want to do...'

13

Mr Hopkins looked at me anxiously when I entered his shop that morning. He waited until the other customers had gone out and then he asked me if I knew anything about Katie Biggins.

'I haven't been round for a few days,' I told him. 'Bill was angry when the doctor said that medicine had poisoned her and he gave me the sack.'

'You did tell Mrs Biggins it was stronger, didn't you?'

'Yes, I told her but she says I didn't.'

'I'm sorry, Maggie. I shouldn't have let you buy it, because I thought it wasn't suitable for a child that young. I hope the baby gets better. When I heard she was ill I took all those bottles off the shelf. If it made her ill, it might do the same for others.'

'It might have been all right if she'd listened to what I said, but it's probably best to be on the safe side. I would never have hurt Katie on purpose. Ann should have known I wouldn't.'

I left the shop feeling thoughtful. It was odd having so much time on my hands; when I'd done most of the chores in the morning, I hardly knew what to do with myself. It would be all right once I started the baking course, but for the moment I felt strange.

* * *

I decided I would buy a few flowers from the market and visit the graves. It still hurt me that I wasn't Jane Bailey's child. Ma had been the only mother I'd known, and when I was small and things were better, she had been kind enough.

I bent to lay my flowers on Ma's grave, feeling the familiar ache inside. The wind whipped into my face, blowing hair into my eyes. Here amongst the mouldering gravestones, there was no sense of peace for me, only bitter regret.

'Who am I, Ma?' I asked. 'Why didn't you tell me instead of Sadie?'

I regretted now that I had tossed Sadie's letter into the fire. I should have kept it and written to Ma's cousin. Not that it really mattered who my mother had been. She hadn't wanted me or she wouldn't have given me to Jane Bailey to bring up. The person named as my mother on my birth certificate was Elspeth Grange, but I had no way of knowing whether it was my mother's true name or just something made up. Where the name of my father should have been written it just said *unknown*. How could she not know the name of my father, unless she was the kind of woman who went with men for money?

My throat felt tight as I bent by the tiny grave that held Sadie's baby. A part of my sister's heart would always be buried here with her first child.

'I'm sorry, Sadie,' I whispered. 'I didn't mean you to lose your baby. You didn't have to take Robin away from me just because your child died.'

I got to my feet and gave a little cry of surprise as I felt my baby kick. It was the first time I'd felt it like that and I put my hand to my swollen belly. The reminder of new life growing within me made me smile. I had to count my blessings and think of the future. I had

Jack and I had my baby. I wouldn't give up trying to find Robin, but I knew with each week that passed it was becoming less and less likely that I would ever find him.

'Well, Mrs Holmes,' the cooking instructor asked, her eyes on my bulge. 'What are you hoping to gain from this course? Most of my young ladies are intending to make a career out of cooking, and some of them will be giving lavish dinner parties. I am not quite sure what your expectations are?'

I felt the eyes of the other young women on me and for a moment I wished I'd never enrolled. They were all from better class homes and some of them spoke as if they had a silver spoon in their mouths. They must wonder what a girl like me was doing here.

'I want to learn to cook beautiful cakes and puddings, because one day I am going to have my own teashop.' I heard a titter from the back of the room and guessed it was Myrtle Fairborn. She had come into class wearing a dress that must have been bought from an exclusive designer and a diamond engagement ring that looked as if it was worth a small fortune. 'Nothing wrong with that, is there?'

'Nothing at all,' Miss Ransom replied. 'I think it is laudable, though you may find it difficult to achieve once you have your child to look after.'

'My mother-in-law will help look after the baby,' I said. It was highly unlikely I would ever have my own shop but I wasn't going to admit it in front of this snooty lot!

'I shall collect the money for ingredients at the end of class,' Miss Ransom said. 'As you know, we charge two shillings a day—which means I want a pound from each of you.'

I stared at her in dismay, because I'd only brought the two shillings for today's ingredients. 'I can pay for today,' I said, my cheeks hot as I heard the titter again. 'I'll bring the rest tomorrow. I didn't realise that we had to pay it all at once.'

'Nor did I,' another voice said from behind me and I turned round to see a girl with soft fair hair and blue eyes. 'I brought the money for today and my tram fare. I shall have to bring the rest tomorrow.'

'You should have been told when you signed,' Miss Ransom said, annoyed. 'Very well, but these things are expensive. I cannot afford to pay for your ingredients so if you don't bring your money, you will not be able to cook tomorrow.'

My cheeks were burning as I took my place at the large, scrubbed pine table and waited for the lesson to begin.

'Don't mind her,' a voice said beside me and I saw the girl with fair hair. She smiled at me. 'My name is Belinda. I think it is wonderful that you want your own teashop. My Aunt runs a small hotel at the seaside. She used to do all the cooking herself, but it is getting a bit much for her now so she sent me here to learn. I am taking this course and then two others, and then I'll go back home and work for her.'

'That sounds lovely,' I said. 'You don't live in London then?'

'No, I live in Yarmouth—that's a place on the East Coast. It's always been a fishing port, and it's at the mouth of the River Yare. You can get to the Norfolk Broads from the Yare and in the summer, we get people coming down for holidays, as well as the day-trippers.

August is packed out with the Bank Holiday and all the schools closed. Aunt Beth doesn't cater for the holidaymakers much, though we take a few in the summer. Her customers are mostly travelling salesmen and permanent residents, but she has a bit of a name for good food, which is why she wanted me to take these courses.' Belinda's grin lit up her face. 'She is paying for it and I get a chance to visit London and go to the shows. I reckon you're lucky to live here all the time. There's so much going on.'

'I suppose it is all right if you can afford to go to the pictures and the theatres as much as you want,' I said. 'Most people I know only get to go to the musical hall or the dance hall once in a while.'

'Be quiet if you please. I cannot begin if you insist on talking to each other.'

Belinda winked at me as the instructor began telling us that we would begin that morning by making a sherry gateau.

'Many of you will be familiar with cake making but we shall begin with beating the butter and eggs together and then add the sugar with the other dry ingredients. The more air you get into your mixture during this first step, the lighter your cake will be.' Her sharp eyes passed over us. 'You all have your recipes. Does anyone want to ask questions? I shall be walking round, watching you and I will show you anything you are not sure of. No questions? Very well, you may begin.'

Everyone looked at the instructions they had been given and the ingredients. It was evident that some of the girls were experienced in making this first part of the gateaux, but Belinda stood staring at hers as if she were lost.

'Making a plain sponge is easy,' I told her. 'Watch me.'

I creamed the butter and eggs with a fork, using the wrist action that Molly had taught me and whipping it until it was soft and fluffy before adding the sugar and flour and a small amount of sherry. Belinda watched and then started on her own. I waited until she had finished, giving her a nod at each stage, and then we took our sponges to the ovens together. Myrtle put hers in just before us. She gave me a look of dislike but I ignored her.

Miss Ransom was instructing us about how much sherry to put into the whipped cream that would bind the sponge layers.

We were all busy whipping our cream with the whisks provided. I had never used a whisk before. It had a springy circle of twisted wire at the end of a wood handle and I wasn't quite sure how to use it until I saw one of the other girls.

'I haven't whipped cream before,' I told Belinda. 'We never have anything like this, just butter cream with icing sugar, only Molly makes it with half margarine most of the time.' I had thought that delicious, because at home we'd never had anything half as good.

'Aunt Beth does a lot of fancy stuff for her guests,' Belinda said. 'It don't half make your arm ache!'

'The cream needs to be soft and light,' Miss Ransom said, stopping next to me. 'If you over whip you may end up with a buttery substance. Yes, that is just about right, Mrs Holmes. You had better take your sponges out now, ladies.'

I hurried over to the oven and took out both Belinda's and my cake, closing the door quickly. Myrtle went to the oven a second or so after me and I heard her make a sound of disgust.

'You should have waited for me! Look what you've done to my cake.'

'I was very quick. You heard Miss Ransom remind us.'

'You did it on purpose,' Myrtle said and glared at me.

Her cake had sunk in the middle. Miss Ransom went to look at it.

'It may be the result of putting in too much sherry,' she observed. 'You can still use the cake, Miss Fairborn. If you cut a thin layer from the top and add an extra layer of cream, it will not show once the whole thing is covered in cream and nuts.

'She did it on purpose...it was the loss of heat in the oven.' Myrtle glared at me again.

'She is a misery,' Belinda whispered. 'I bet her cake would have sunk in the middle anyway. I don't know why she is here. She will employ a cook when she gets married anyway.'

'She doesn't like me. I'm not her sort,' I said and Belinda winked.

'Shall we walk to the tram stop together?' Belinda asked as we took off our aprons. 'What did you think of it today then?'

'I thought what Miss Ransom said at the end was interesting. I've always believed it was what you did with the ingredients that counted. Most of what you put into the cakes or puddings is the same. It's just how you flavour things.'

'Yes, but it's knowing how to make light pastry and sponges too,' Belinda said. 'I wasn't sure at first, but I reckon she knows what she's talking about. We shall get on all right with Miss Ransom.'

'Yes,' I agreed. 'I think I am going to enjoy the next two weeks.'

We started to talk about other things. I discovered that Belinda was a great reader. She liked Agatha Christie's books, but she hadn't read the one Bill had given me at Christmas. I said I would bring it for her and she promised to bring me a book by P.G. Wodehouse that she said was about someone called Bertie Wooster and his butler Jeeves. It didn't sound that interesting to me, but Belinda said it was funny so I agreed to read it, though the only time I had was on the tram coming to the course and going home.

At the first tram stop we parted, because we were going different ways. I stayed on the tram as Belinda got off. I was thoughtful as I stared out of the window at the shops and the people scurrying home. I had learned something in class today, but more importantly I had made a new friend. I didn't know then just how important meeting Belinda would turn out to be.

* * *

'Is that all yer brought home for two bob?' Molly snorted with disgust as I put what was left of my cake on the table in the kitchen. 'Daylight robbery if yer ask me.'

'What do you think of it?'

Molly sliced a bit and ate it, licking her fingers afterwards. 'Nought wrong with that, lass,' she said. 'Not that it ain't a waste of money learning to cook somethin' like that. Who has the money to buy fancy stuff round 'ere?'

'I doubt if many people could afford it, though I would be selling it by the slice, not the whole thing. I suppose I would have to go further afield to find customers, in a classier part of town. Not that it is going to happen for a while. Maybe one day.'

'Pigs might fly,' she muttered and pulled a face. She seemed in a bad mood and I wondered what had upset her.

'Is something wrong, Molly?'

'Nothing for you to bother yer head about. 'What are yer giving Jack for his tea?'

'I thought sausage egg and chips,' I said and saw her disapproval. 'It's easy and I've been on my feet most of the day at the cookery class. I'll make a meat pie at the weekend.'

'It's not much of a tea for a man after he's worked all day. I'll get a bit of fish from the market in the morning. I can make a fish pie for tomorrow evening. I didn't go shopping today, because I've no money in my purse.'

'Didn't Jack leave anything for you this week?'

'He must 'ave forgot. Can yer lend me ten bob until he pays me?'

'Yes, of course. I'll fetch you some from the drawer.'

I went upstairs and shook the key from the vase on the windowsill. I unlocked the drawer and took ten shillings from the money we had put by, then frowned as I looked at it. I was sure there had been at least six or seven of those big white five-pound notes, but now there were only three. I hadn't touched them, because I had my own small store of money, but I was sure there were fewer than there had been only a few days earlier. At one time Jack must have had nearly fifty pounds, but there was less than half that now. I asked Molly about it when I went downstairs.

'Of course I haven't touched your money,' she said looking indignant. 'What would I want to do that fer? I've always managed on what Jack gives me. I'm no thief! '

'It isn't my money it is Jack's and I didn't think you had stolen it,' I said. 'I just wondered if you knew what he had done with it, because I am certain there was more there, because he is saving for his own business.'

'Pig's will more likely fly,' Molly snorted. 'Ask him about it yourself when he comes in.'

* * *

'I needed some money for something,' Jack said when I mentioned it that evening. 'I don't have to ask you if I want money. I earned it and I'll spend it as I please. So stop nagging, Maggie.'

'I didn't mean to nag.' It wasn't like him to snap back that way. He must be tired or worried about something. 'I'm sorry, Jack. It just bothered me when I realised the money had gone. I even asked Molly if she had touched it.'

'She'll be sorry if she does,' he muttered and pushed his chair back with a scraping noise. 'I'm off out. It may be late when I come in so don't wait up for me.'

'Where are you going? You haven't eaten much supper, and you haven't tried the cake I made.'

'I don't fancy that creamy stuff. Give me an apple pie or the treacle tart Ma makes any day.' He reached for his jacket and went out. I was still staring at the door he had just slammed when Molly came in from the scullery.

'Where has he gone at this hour? He hardly lives 'ere these days. What's the matter with him? Yer 'aven't quarrelled with him, ave yer?'

'He was cross because I asked about the money. I wasn't nagging, just worried, but he got into a bit of a temper and went off.'

'Men, they're all the same—all trousers and no brain,' Molly said and sniffed in disgust. 'I thought Jack was better than most but he'll be gettin' into bad ways. If it's not the drink or women it will be gambling. You mark my words, lass. It will be one of them three...'

* * *

'It's your last day,' Belinda said when we met on the last morning of the baking class. 'I'll be off home next week, because my other courses are only for one day each. I shall miss you, Maggie.'

'I'll miss you too. I've really enjoyed these past two weeks. I've learned a lot of things I never thought I would know. I am not sure if I'll ever use some of them, but even Jack liked the Queen's pudding we made yesterday, and I took some meringues and almond macaroons to the church home for the kids the day before.'

'They would love them if they got them, but I doubt if the kids saw one of them. I should think the people who run it scoffed the lot.'

'I should hate to think that,' I said. 'I was going to take whatever we make today there this afternoon, but if you think the kids won't get them, I might as well give them to a neighbour.'

'Don't you take them home? My landlady has been giving mine to her family and customers all this week. She says she will employ me if my aunt doesn't, but I know Aunt Beth will be pleased to have me back. I went to the Post Office and phoned her yesterday evening. She is really busy and can't wait for me to come home. She thinks she will have to take on more help if things stay the way they are.' Belinda looked at me thoughtfully. 'I know you're married and all that, but if ever you need a job or a friend, remember me.'

'I'll give you my address. We can write sometimes if you like.'

We had to stop talking then, because Miss Ransom had started to tell us about the special fruitcake we were going to make. 'It's what a lot of people call a Simnel cake and it is special for Easter.'

We worked for most of the morning. When the cakes were made and decorated, Miss Ransom inspected them all. She chose Myrtle's as being the most attractive and we all had a small piece to try.

'Yours was as good as hers and I'll bet it tastes better,' Belinda said as we walked to the tram stop later. 'She just picked Myrtle because her mother is rich and she gave Miss Ransom a donation to help set up the college. They are friends from way back.'

'It doesn't matter. I got to keep my cake intact to take home.' We looked at each other as we reached Belinda's stop. 'I suppose this is goodbye but I'll write to you when I can.'

'It was lovely meeting you. I meant it when I said I'd miss you. If ever you need a friend, just remember me.'

'I shan't forget.' I said and gave her a quick hug on impulse. She hugged me back. 'Take care, Belinda. I hope everything goes well for you.'

Once off the tram, I started to walk home, but at the last minute I took a detour. I had made a new friend in Belinda, but old friends had been on my mind. Even though I'd had an exciting time earning my certificate as a cake maker, I hadn't been able to forget Bill and Ann, and their daughter Katie. I had decorated my cake with little yellow chicks and chocolate eggs and I thought I would take it to the café as a gift for Katie.

The café was almost empty when I went in. Now that the

weather was milder, the windows were dry and it seemed cooler inside. One old man sat in a corner drinking tea and Bill was standing behind the counter looking moody.

'I came to ask about Katie. Is she any better?'

'She isn't much better. The doctor says he thinks she will live but if you ask me, she's not right by a long chalk. She cries all the time, doesn't give us a moment's peace,' he said and glanced over his shoulder. 'You shouldn't be here, Maggie. Ann hasn't forgiven you. Katie isn't getting on as she should and the doctor said it is because that medicine was drugging her, making her sleepy, and now she is having to get used to going without.'

'I am sorry.' I put my basket on the counter. 'I brought a cake for Ann and Katie, if you think Ann would accept it?'

'She wouldn't. I know you mean well, Maggie, but I must ask you not to come here again—unless you need a reference? Ann is so tired and nervy. If she saw you...' He shook his head. 'None of this is your fault but Ann blames you and I can't change her.'

'Get her out of here! I told you I don't want that wretched girl coming here again.'

Ann's voice was sharp with hatred as she came into the café. Her eyes had dark shadows underneath and she looked ill. Obviously, she hadn't been sleeping. I thought that if she went on this way, she would be the one who needed the doctor next.

'What are you waiting for?' she screamed at me. Suddenly, she flew at me, going for my eyes with her fingers. She was like a mad woman, her eyes wild and dark with hatred. She spat in my face. Bill pounced on her dragging her off me.

'Get out of here,' he shouted at me as he struggled to contain his raging wife. 'Stay away like I told you. I don't want you upsetting my wife. You've done enough damage.'

'My baby is dying! I'll kill you...if I see you again, I'll kill you.'

'I'm sorry,' I said. 'I never wanted to hurt Katie or you.'

I felt terrible as I retreated, still hearing Ann's hysterical screaming even after I left the café. Bill must be having a terrible time with her. She seemed as if her grief over her sick child had almost driven her out of her mind.

I wished I hadn't gone near the café, but I had wanted to make them a gift to apologise again for my part in Katie's illness. It had been a stupid gesture and for two pins I would have thrown the cake away. However, I couldn't bring myself to waste something that had cost two shillings to make.

My cake had rich marzipan in the middle and I knew it was no use taking it back for Jack. He'd hardly touched the cakes I'd taken home. He had been in a strange mood for a week or two.

There didn't seem much point in taking the cake to the church home if it wouldn't be given to the children. Instead I decided to take it to Sadie's neighbour, Mrs Wayman. She had three children and she wouldn't turn her nose up at a cake like this, because she must find it a struggle to put enough food on their plates.

I hadn't bothered to go back to the lanes since my wedding. Several people were standing in the street gossiping as I walked towards Maisie Wayman's house. One or two held up their hands in welcome, others just stared, their gaze following me down the street.

Mrs Wayman looked at me suspiciously until I showed her the cake and explained, then she smiled. 'I've always said you were a good girl, Maggie. Some folk round 'ere are too quick to take sides. Sadie had been poorly for a while. It was no surprise to me that her babe came too soon. She was alus frettin' and carryin' on.'

'Sadie was upset over Ma and Pa...'

'Of course she was, you too. I didn't approve of her putting Robin in a home. She never ought to have done that, lass.'

'No, she didn't. He was supposed to come and live with me.' I fought the tears. 'How are your children?'

'My Trevor has won a scholarship to a specialist school. I'm not sure if he can go, because the uniform costs too much money, but it was good him winning it. Jeanie leaves school in the summer. She will be going to work in a shop where they pay good wages, and that will be a help, especially if this strike comes off.'

'What's that then? I read something in the papers about the miners going on strike, but how will it affect you?'

'Haven't you seen the latest headlines in the paper? They are talking about making it a general strike—that's all the key workers, Maggie. The tram drivers, train drivers, dockers, postie, milkman, baker...the lot of the daft hapeths. You name it, they're all in it together. Call themselves men! They're like a load of kids playing truant, if you ask me. Have they given a thought to their wives and kids if they strike? Where is the money coming from to buy food and pay rent? I told my Charlie he was to go to work regardless but he said the others would lynch him if he broke the strike so I suppose we'll 'ave to manage as best we can. I shall be grateful for your cake, Maggie. It is probably the last treat we'll get until this nonsense is over.'

'But that will mean chaos. We shan't be able to buy bread or milk, or anything.'

'That's the least of it. Goodness knows what will happen if they can't unload the ships or get cargoes loaded. We'll have food rotting on the docks and people will fight if they see their kids going without.'

'I'd better do a bit of shopping for flour and stuff. We can make our own bread, but we'll need flour and the shop will soon run out if there's no lorries to deliver it to them.'

'I wish I could do the same. I 'ave just enough to manage on each week. What I'll do when Charlie's wage stops, I don't know.'

'Will the unions pay anything? They call the men out and I thought there was some sort of provision for strikes?'

'It will be a couple of bob a week, like as not, and how are we supposed to manage like that?'

'I don't know. Let's hope the strike doesn't last long.'

I was thoughtful as I called at the shop on my way home and bought extra flour, eggs, sugar and margarine. I was lucky to have a few shillings extra in my pocket so that I could stock up the larder, but most of the women in the docklands were like Mrs Wayman. They spent every penny they got each week, only managing to buy clothes and extras by paying the tallyman a few pence a week or hocking their husband's best suit to the pawnbroker. The pawnbrokers would be busy these next few weeks. It was the only way most folk would manage.

* * *

'Well, I reckon it's daft,' Molly said as we sat at the kitchen table that evening and ate the supper she had cooked. 'It's hard enough for most folk to manage with a wage comin' in every week. What are they goin' ter do if there's nothin' at the end of the week?'

'That's their hard luck,' Jack said. 'It will be better for Eddie and me. I'll be earning extra for strike breaking.'

'What?' Molly stared at him from the other end of the table. 'You'll never do that, Jack. Go against your mates and all them poor devils what are goin' without to make their feelings known! There will be some as end up starvin' if I'm any judge.'

'More fool them then. I reckon what the miners do is their problem. We've got to keep things going or London will be at a shut down. Food will be rotting at the docks and on the farms. I'll be driving lorries bringing food into the city.' He glared at his mother. 'I'll be earning double time every run I make through the docks. I'm not turning that down so you needn't look at me that way.'

'There will be fighting and bitterness. You want to think on what it will be like when the strike is over. You'll be a black-leg and they will hate you, especially if they know you made money out of it.'

'I don't care what the fools think. I've paid Eddie a deposit on one of his vans. 'If I earn extra this way, I can pay for it faster and then I'll be me own boss.'

'Is that where the money went?' I asked. 'I know you want your own business, Jack, but are you sure you want to do this?'

'Someone has to do it. They will be bringing in all sorts from the country: doctors, lawyers, gentlemen's sons from the university. Why shouldn't we make something from all this?' His expression was belligerent. Strike breaking went against the grain, but the extra money he would earn tempted him.

'I'll be glad when you get away from that Eddie. Once you've got your own van you can work for yourself,' I said to him.

'I'll still be working for him some of the time, but using me own van and charging by the hour.' Jack got to his feet. 'I've done all right with Eddie, and if you don't like what I'm doing, you can lump it. I'm off for a drink.'

'Do you have to go? I hardly see you these days, Jack.'

He looked at me and for a moment he hesitated, then, 'I'm doing this for you, Maggie. I don't want my wife going to work once the baby is here. The more money I can earn now the better it will be for all of us. Besides, Eddie says that it is a chance to earn some really big money.'

Molly gave a snort of disgust and took some dirty dishes through to the scullery. She was banging the pots loudly when I went to help her after Jack left.

'His father would turn in his grave! I never thought our Jack would go against what he is—against working folk.'

'He doesn't see it that way. If it is true that all those professional people will be helping to break the strike it makes sense for Jack to earn what he can.'

'Don't let the folk round 'ere 'ear yer say that, Maggie. When they haven't a crust to put in the mouths of their babes, they'll remember what Jack did in the strike.'

'I don't suppose it will last long. A day or so and it will be over.'

* * *

The General Strike was called at midnight on the 3rd of May 1926 and a state of emergency was declared. For nine days Jack didn't come home. I was nearly out of my mind with worry by the third day, but from reading the British Gazette, of which Mr Churchill was the editor, I saw that a lot of the men manning the trains, buses and lorries bringing food into London were working day and night.

Jack was out for what he could get, but some of the men doing the kind of manual work they had never done in their lives looked to be enjoying themselves. The undergraduates seemed to think it was a lark and there were reports of scuffles between them and working men. Lorries, buses and cars braved the wrath of the strikers, often accompanied by an armoured car. On May the 8th a detachment of Grenadier Guards with twenty armoured cars escorted 100 food lorries from the docks to Hyde Park.

A crowd had gathered to jeer them and some people threw missiles, but the only real trouble was in Glasgow, according to the Gazette. Up there it seemed the bitterness had been intense and several people were hurt. In London there were fights amongst the strikers and the strike-breakers but we didn't hear of anyone actually getting killed, though there was a bit about a policeman having his helmet knocked off and some other minor incidents.

I did my shopping in the market the same as usual. Some of the fresh food was scarce in the first few days, but gradually the food got through and things were almost back to normal.

Several emergency kitchens had been set up. Some of them were especially to feed the workers the government had brought in, and these were run by people from the upper and middle classes, and the food was well cooked and served. The Sally Army was giving out soup and bread to the families of the strikers. I saw queues of women and children when I walked back from the market, but not many men. Most of them were too proud to take what they thought of as charity.

After nine days the General Strike was over. It was clear that food and services were getting through and the TUC realised that they had taken on more than they were prepared for in calling for support for the miners. However, the miners themselves were too stubborn and their action continued.

'I dread to think what their families are going through,' Molly said as we read the headlines in the paper. 'Poor devils. It's the wives and children I pity. They are the ones that suffer. They will lose in the end and this will all be fer nothin.'

'I was talking to Mrs Wayman this morning on my way back from the market,' I said the day after the strike was declared over. 'She says folk are getting up a collection to send to the Welsh miners to help the families out. The government may have broken the strike in the towns and cities, but that doesn't stop common folk feeling for their own.'

'We'll give them a few bob. Take a bit from Jack's money. He won't know any different with all the money he's been making these past few days.'

'I gave her half a crown. I wouldn't touch Jack's money, besides, he hid the key somewhere different so I couldn't take it if I wanted.' It was uncomfortable with Jack away. I couldn't help wondering what had happened to him. I knew that he might have been working too hard to bother to come home, but I still couldn't help feeling anxious. 'I wish Jack would come back. I don't understand why he couldn't pop in for a cup of tea. He has to eat somewhere.'

'Ashamed of himself I shouldn't wonder. Once folk round 'ere realise what he has been doin' he will find himself shut out. If he goes down the pub to drink, they will send him to Coventry. I warned him but he wouldn't listen...' She broke off as we heard the doorknocker. 'Now who's that? No one knocks round 'ere.'

I got up and went to the door. My heart jerked with fright as I saw the police constable standing there.

'Is it Jack? What has happened to him? Has he been hurt? He was driving food lorries to help break the strike and...'

'You would be Mrs Holmes?' the young officer looked slightly uncomfortable. 'May I come in, ma'am? I have something to tell you and you won't want all your neighbours listening in.'

I stood back. My mouth was dry and my stomach was tying itself in knots. I put a protective hand to my swollen belly. Something bad was coming!

'What is it, Maggie?' my mother-in-law asked and glared as she saw the policeman. 'What does he want?'

'I don't know. I think it's something to do with Jack. Has he been injured?'

The policeman removed his helmet. 'You said your husband had been helping to drive food lorries to break the strike?'

'Yes, that is what he told us, but we haven't seen him for some days.'

'I'm not surprised. He and his friends know we're on to them.'

'What do yer mean? Our Jack wouldn't do anythin' the wrong side of the law.' His mother looked angry but I felt shivery all over.

'I am afraid that is just what he has done. A lorry carrying beer and cigarettes went missing. Jack Holmes was the driver. We have reason to believe that he and that boss of his Eddie Carver have been profiteering from the strike by selling stolen goods at inflated prices.'

'No!' I sat down as my knees turned to jelly 'Jack wouldn't do that, he wouldn't. He works hard and he's saving for his own business. He wouldn't deal in stolen goods. I don't believe it.'

'It wouldn't be the first time. We've had our eye on Mr Carver for a while, Mrs Holmes. He sells second-hand and antique goods, but some of the goods were never paid for by Mr Carver. He has a team of men breaking into empty properties when the owners are away and clearing out the contents. He specialises in silver, things like that clock on the wall and brass...' His eyes went to the horse brasses nailed to the chimney surround. 'Would you like to tell me where these things came from?'

'The clock belonged to my grandfather,' Molly said. 'The horse brasses have been here since afore my husband died.'

'I'll take your word for it, ma'am,' the young constable said. 'I shall want to question Mr Holmes when he gets back. At the moment I'm just making enquiries about a missing lorry and the contents. If your husband can provide an answer, I'll be glad to let it go at that but Mr Carver may be in trouble, because we were about to make an arrest when the strike started. It took over everything for a bit, but now it is finished we shall be asking Eddie Carver to accompany us to the station to answer a few questions.'

'Jack wouldn't steal! I know he wouldn't do anything like that. He just works at the clearing business for Eddie.'

'Well, he'll be needed to answer questions. If you will tell him we were here looking for him, Mrs Holmes.' He put his helmet on, the strap under his chin. 'I am sorry to be the bearer of bad news at such a time, ma'am.'

I went to the door with him, standing against it after it was closed, gathering my breath. Molly was still sitting at the table, seemingly stunned.

'Do you think it is true? Surely Jack wouldn't. He wouldn't do anything that stupid?'

'I knew he was up to somethin',' Molly said angrily. 'You wait until he gets back. He will feel my hand round his ear! We're decent folk! It was bad enough he were willing to break the strike fer money but stealin' is somethin' I don't hold with, Maggie. If them things he brought 'ere are pinched he can just get rid of them.'

'The silver jug Eddie gave me as wedding present. Do you think that came out of one of the houses he stole from? I thought there was something odd about Eddie and Spiker on my wedding day, but Jack had said they were his friends. Did he know what he was doing all this time?'

'It stands ter reason he must 'ave done. I thought he was too flush with money. No one round these parts has a bundle of five-pound notes in the drawer. We'd better hide some of the things Jack brought home, and that money. If the police search the house, they will want ter know where it came from.'

'I don't know where the key is to the lowboy upstairs.'

'I'll soon fix that...' Molly went to the drawer and took out a heavy knife. I followed her upstairs. She approached the piece of furniture I had so admired when I first saw it, inserting the tip of the knife and twisting it. The drawer released and she pulled it open. All the money had gone. 'That rotten little bugger has taken it —every penny! Have yer noticed anything else missing?'

'I don't know.' I glanced round. 'Yes, a silver pot and the jug Eddie gave me. They were on the windowsill.'

'Jack must 'ave taken them. Now why would he do that?'

'I don't know. Do you think he has run off? No, he wouldn't just go and leave us. Molly, he wouldn't leave me to have the baby alone, he wouldn't take everything of value.'

'If he knew they were on to him he might. He would need money on the run. He's been gone nine days, Maggie. I thought it was strange him staying away all that time but now I can see why. He's took what he can sell easy, and the money. I don't know about the lorry what went missing, but I'd bet my last penny that he's done a runner.'

I sat down on the edge of the bed and stared at her. Jack had been behaving so strangely of late. Now I knew why!

'He must have discovered what was going on in the last few weeks. I am sure he didn't know when he went to work for Eddie full-time.'

'He's made a right mess of things. I've got half a crown in my purse. How much have you got, Maggie?'

'A pound and a few coppers,' I said feeling hollow inside. 'I'll find work. Don't worry, Molly. I'll go and find work first thing in the morning.'

'In your condition?' She looked sour. 'Who do you think wants a woman nearly six months gone with child? When the baby is here, you'll find it hard enough to get work, but for the moment it is out of the question. I'll have to take in washing. It's what I used to do afore Jack started giving me good money. I'll go to the laundry and ask in the morning. You can keep the house, cook and shop until it's too hard fer yer.'

'It isn't right that you should have to work to keep me, Molly.'

'Life ain't about what's right or wrong. It's about payin' the rent and puttin' food in our bellies. When you've had the child, you can find work and I'll take care of the bairn, but until then it's washing and ironing other folk's' clothes for us.'

* * *

I sat on the bed after Molly went downstairs, trying to take in what had happened. Jack had been so good to me, wedding me when he didn't have to, buying me presents and giving me a home but it had all been based on lies. 'Oh, Jack,' I whispered as the rain battered against the windowpanes. The wind was howling in the eaves, an eerie, haunting sound that seemed to add to the feeling of foreboding that hung over me. 'Why did you do it? We could have been so good together.'

I had thought things would be so nice for us. Jack was going to work for himself and I had been planning to go back to the bakery after my child was born. I had wanted to work and save for a while, my dream of owning and running a teashop a bright star on the horizon.

It would never happen now.

I felt so helpless. Always before I had been able to work, but Molly was right. I had tried some of the shops in the lanes and they had all turned me down.

What we would do if Molly couldn't get washing, I didn't know. Our money wouldn't last long and then we should have to start selling the few items of value Jack had left behind.

15

'It was a thoughtless thing he did,' Thomas said. He was opening the curtains, letting the light of morning flood into the drab room. 'It must have been hard for you with the baby coming. You needed your husband there and the last thing you wanted was to have the worry of having no money hanging over your head.'

'It was worse for Molly.' I got to my feet. 'It is time I did something to help. Shall I make breakfast?'

'You can put the kettle on. I'll go and fetch us something from the shop in a minute. 'What do you mean, it was worse for Molly?'

I filled the kettle and put it on the hob. 'There's some bread I could toast. If you have butter or jam it will do.'

'We'll have some marmalade and there's butter,' he said. 'I like my butter, Maggie, fresh from the farm if I can get it. You still haven't told me why it was worse for Molly. You were the one who had lost your husband, and you were carrying a child.'

'Molly was worn out,' I said and my throat caught as I remembered. I sat down and he set about making the toast. 'She never told me...almost until the last. I helped as much as I could by doing the ironing, but I *couldn't handle those heavy sheets. She wouldn't let me try, but it was too much for her. She didn't tell me she was ill, but I should have seen it. I should have noticed the signs.'*

* * *

For the next few weeks, I expected Jack to come walking in and tell us that he had got caught up in some business or other, but the days passed and there was no sign of him.

A couple of times as I walked home from the market, I felt I was being followed. I looked over my shoulder, feeling nervous but I couldn't see anyone.

Molly didn't believe me. 'Imagination, girl,' she said. 'No man is going to follow a lass what's near her time. Unless it were Jack?'

'No, I don't think so.'

Once I had caught a glimpse of a man's face in a shop window. I thought it might have been one of Jack's friends, not Eddie but the other one—Spiker.

'You don't think it was someone with a message from Jack?' I asked after a moment.

'Wishful thinkin',' she said. 'Jack will come back when he's ready.'

'I hope so,' I said, but I had a horrible feeling that he had gone for good. Sometimes I thought he had simply walked out on me and at others I thought he was dead. I cried myself to sleep night after night, but I tried not to let Molly see how upset I was. She was worried too but she made out it was nothing and Jack would come back with a grin on his face.

The feeling of being followed ended after the first month. If someone had been watching me, they had stopped. I wished Jack would send us word if he was hiding somewhere. Even a card with his name on it would do, just something to tell us that he was still alive.

* * *

I came home from the market that morning feeling so weary that I could hardly stagger into the house. I had been walking round and round the stalls looking for the cheapest food I could buy and my back ached so much that all I wanted was to sit down. Molly scolded me as she saw the tiredness in my face.

'You will kill yourself, lass, and the babe too,' she said. 'I know you're angry with Jack. I could kill the daft lump, but the child is innocent.'

'Don't scold me, Molly. I'm not trying to take it out on the baby. You can't do the shopping and all that washing.'

The house smelled of wet washing and the steam was rising from some sheets she'd washed that morning as they dried round the fire. Once upon a time I had quite liked washing day, but that was when it had happened once a week; now we had washing drying every day and I hated it.

'Make that the last time you go to the market. We'll 'ave to buy from the corner shop until after the baby is born.'

'You know they charge more than the market. I picked up some bargains this morning. I've got some rag end of lamb and enough vegetables to keep a stew going most of the week.'

'You're a good manager,' Molly said. 'Jack didn't know how lucky he was. I could take my dolly stick to him for what's he's done to you, lass!'

'He didn't know it would come to this. I'll be all right, Molly. I'm just sorry I can't help you more with the work.'

'You put your feet up and rest. I've done the washing. I'll see to a bite of supper in a minute; just a bit of bread and an egg will do fer now.'

'I'll start the stew later,' I said and got up. The pain shafted through me and I yelled out, clutching at myself. 'It's too soon. It can't be the baby, Molly. It is too soon...'

'I've been telling you not to overdo it. You wouldn't listen and this is the result. Up the stairs with yer and I'll fetch Old Sally to yer.'

'Not her,' I begged. 'Please not Sally. She's so dirty and I'm sure she killed Sadie's baby.'

'Don't talk such nonsense. I can't do it all by myself, Maggie. I need help and Sally is the best round 'ere. Just hang on fer a bit and I'll bring 'er round.'

'Please don't leave me. I can manage if you'll sit with me.'

Molly ignored me and went out. I felt panic sweep over me. Supposing she didn't come back? Supposing I had the baby while she was gone?

I pulled myself up the steep stairs to the bedroom I had shared with Jack, feeling terrified. Sadie had had her baby with only Sally for company and her child had died. Now it was going to happen to me.

'Where are you, Jack?' I muttered. 'Damn you for leaving me alone when I needed you! Damn you for promising it would all be wonderful and then running out on us.' I screamed his name, panting like a wild thing as I finally made it to the bedroom and flopped down on the bed. 'I hate you...I hate you.'

I tried to lie down on the bed but I couldn't keep still. The pains were coming so fast that I didn't know what to do with myself.

'Damn you! Damn you!' I yelled. 'I hate you.'

I got up and walked about the room, each step seeming laboured and slow. I was in so much pain and so frightened. When I felt the water running down my leg, I thought I had peed myself, and then I realised that my waters had broken. The baby was almost ready to be born. I crawled back on the bed, lying on my back and drawing up my knees, opening them, feet flat to the bed. I caught hold of the metal bed rail behind my head and held on, pushing down as the pain ripped through me again.

'I hate you, Jack!'

I was screaming as someone came into the house downstairs. I pushed harder, hoping that my baby would arrive before that filthy old crone got her hands on me.

'I'm coming, lass.'

A woman ran up the stairs and entered the bedroom. It wasn't Sally but Mrs Wayman, the woman I had given a cake to when I finished my cooking course.

'Molly looked done in,' she said. 'I told her to sit down and rest for a bit. She said she would go to fetch Sally when she had got her breath back. I'll look after you, Maggie. I've seen a few babies into the world in my time.' She approached the bed and looked down at me. 'It looks as if you've done most of the work yerself, lass. I can see the head already. You left it a bit late to send fer anyone.'

'I didn't realise. My back ached when I was down the market but I just thought it was to be expected. It wasn't until I got home that it became so bad, I couldn't stand it.'

'You shouldn't be down the market in your condition, but I suppose Maggie can't do everything. Your husband should be here.' She rolled up her sleeves. 'You haven't heard from him I suppose?'

'I hate him. I hope I never see him again!'

'We all feel like that at times like this,' she laughed. 'I swore I would never let Charlie near me again, but I've 'ad six though only three have lived past their first birthday. Push a little bit harder, love. Yer almost there...'

'Is it coming?' I craned to see and then felt a whooshing sensation as in a mess of blood and water my baby came shooting into the world. Mrs Wayman scooped it up and, in another second, she had cut the cord and was wrapping the baby in a towel that had been lying on a chair. 'What is it?'

'You've got a lovely little girl,' she said and smiled. 'It's just as well it was a girl, Maggie. Boys are often more trouble, both when you're giving birth and when they grow up. She is beautiful, but she was certainly in a hurry to be born.'

'She is like me. I'm always impatient.' She put the baby into my arms. 'Thank you so much for coming. I didn't expect it.'

'You helped me,' she said. 'I know some folk think you got what was comin' to yer, marryin' that Jack Holmes, but we can none of us help where we love, girl.'

'I did love him. I'm not sure how I feel now. I'm not certain I would forgive him if he came back.'

'Happen he can't,' Mrs Wayman said as she took my baby to wash her. 'He was mixing with wrong uns by the sound of it from what I 'ear. That Eddie Carver hit a policeman when they tried to take him in, split the poor young devil's 'ead open. He'll go down for attempted murder as well as thievin' I reckon. Happen your Jack didn't know what they were up to until they snatched that lorry of beer and fags. If he threatened to go to the coppers they might 'ave done fer him. He were alus a charmer. I can't see Jack runnin' off and leavin' yer alone. Unless he had no choice.'

'The clothes are in that top drawer,' I directed her to the chest. 'I bought a shawl and a few nice things when I had a bit of money.'

'This is pretty,' she said as she took the shawl and a long gown from the drawer. 'You might want to save it for the christening? There's another one here not so posh.'

'Yes, that one will do, and her nappies are in the next drawer down. It is a good thing I bought her things when I had the money. I wouldn't be able to get much now.'

'I saw the washing downstairs. It's no wonder Molly is worn out with that lot.'

'She will be able to stop as soon as I can find a job.'

'By the looks of her she ought not to have started it. Isn't there something you could sell?'

'I suppose we could sell the wall clock. I hadn't thought about it, because it was Jack's pride and joy.'

'I should think that might fetch five pounds, maybe a bit more. I've always wanted somethin' like that, but I've never been able to afford it.'

'You can have it for three pounds,' I said. 'I know it is worth more, but you've been good to me.'

'I don't want anything for a bit of a good deed. I'll ask Charlie if he's got anything put by, but I doubt it. Maybe in a few months, if you've still got it then.'

'Yes, all right. The clock would be one of the last things I would sell, because I know Jack likes it but we may have to sell something, until I get on my feet and start work again. I agree that all that washing is too much for Molly.'

'She was havin' a job ter breathe when I saw 'er,' Mrs Wayman said. We heard a door bang downstairs. She looked over her shoulder. 'That sounds as if it's Molly and Old Sally now. I'll go down and tell them the good news and then I had best get off. Charlie will be home soon wantin' his tea.'

I thanked her again and she shook her head. I heard her go downstairs and voices talking. Sally sounded put out because she had been called out for nothing, but the sound of her voice got fainter and I thought Mrs Wayman had taken her with her.

Molly's footsteps were slow and heavy as she came upstairs. She seemed to pause outside the door before she came in. I looked at her face, feeling uneasy as I saw how red she was, an unhealthy colour I didn't like in her cheeks.

'Sit down, Molly. You look worn out.'

'I went too fast. To tell you the truth, Maggie, I've found the washing a bit too much for me. I think I shall make this the last lot. You'll be up and about soon, and then I can take care of the baby while you're at work.' She came to look at the child in my arms. 'She's a beauty. Mrs Wayman said she was and she's right. I can see Jack in her.'

'She has his eyes.'

'Yes, she does.' Molly sat down. I saw her chest heaving and felt worried, but she shook her head before I could ask. 'I'll be all right in a bit. This breathlessness comes and goes.'

'Why didn't you tell me before?'

'You've enough to worry about as it is. Anyway, now you know. If anything happens, you must move from 'ere and see if you can find that cousin of yer ma's—'

'Jane wasn't my mother.' It still rankled that no one had told me and I spoke with a touch of bitterness.

'She was yer ma as much as she could be,' Molly said. 'I never told yer, but I tried to rescue Sadie's letter from the fire. I saved a scrap of it. I think it said something about Eastbourne but I can't be certain, because most of it disintegrated in me 'and. You could always start there.'

'She probably wouldn't want me now I have a child. Sadie wrote to her after Ma died, if she had wanted to see me, she would have come looking. It wouldn't be hard to find me. Anybody in the lanes would tell her where I was living.'

'She might not have been able to. Well, you must do as you please, but I wouldn't sit round here waiting fer Jack ter come back if I were you.'

'This is his home. What would he think if he came back and found it empty?'

'Serve him right,' she said. 'Besides, the rent is too much fer yer ter manage alone. Yer will have ter pay someone ter look after the baby. Sell what's left and go to the country. Things might be cheaper there. Yer might find a job as a housekeeper. If you asked round, yer could find someone to mind the babe and live in, at least until you could get enough money fer that teashop. Yer want ter look fer a place with a couple of rooms over the top, Maggie.'

'I'm not sure.' This cottage had been lived in by generations of Jack's family. Did I have the right to sell what belonged to him and leave an empty shell? He would come back to find new tenants living in his home and he would hate me. I looked at her hopefully. 'Maybe you will feel better once you don't have so much work to do.'

'Happen I shall. I can breathe proper now. I'll go down and make the tea.' At the door she stopped and looked back. 'What shall you call her?'

'I was thinking Beth,' I said. 'I don't know why but I like the name.'

'Beth is a good name,' Molly agreed. 'It sounds classy. You think about what I said when the time comes, Maggie. Beth deserves a better life than either of us ever had, girl. If she is as clever as her ma, she could go places.'

The door closed as Molly went out. She seemed so certain that she wouldn't live much longer and it frightened me. Molly hadn't wanted Jack to marry me and she wasn't the easiest person in the world to live with, often grumbling and telling me off for the smallest thing but she was all I had except for my child. If anything happened to Molly, I would be alone.

I prayed that she wasn't really ill. She had been doing too much! All that washing and turning the big, heavy mangle had been hard work and it had tired her out. She would soon start to feel better once she stopped doing so much work. I could work my hours at the bakery and still do most of the housework and cook the evening meal. I just needed Molly to keep an eye on Beth and feed her while I was at my job.

'Don't die on me, Molly... please don't leave me.' I whispered a prayer.

'Where are you, Jack? Damn you! Why aren't you here when I need you? You promised to take care of me. You broke your promise...'

Supposing he couldn't come back to us? Eddie Carver was a rogue and a violent one according to gossip. Had he killed Jack when he threatened to tell the police?

Mrs Wayman had suggested it and it could be true, and yet why had Jack taken all his money from the drawer? If he had planned on coming back, he wouldn't need to do that, and that made me think he had been planning to leave me.

* * *

I was up and about within two days. I felt a bit wobbly when I came downstairs the first time, but I couldn't let Molly struggle up the stairs with drinks and food for me, and Beth needed attention. Her nappies had to be washed and so did her clothes.

Molly shook her head over me. 'You'll do too much too soon and make yourself ill, and then what shall we do? You've got to be the breadwinner in this family, Maggie. My working days are done.'

'You've brought up a big family and had all those children. It is about time someone took care of you.'

'Jack was supposed to do that,' she said bitterly. 'He promised so much and then he let me down—you and the baby too. I should've known he was too much of a charmer.'

'Maybe he couldn't help it. Have you thought that he might be dead, Molly?'

Her face turned white for a minute, then she shook her head.

'No, not him. He's too sharp for that, Maggie. He knew it was all coming down like a pack of cards and he legged it, leaving us to struggle on alone.'

In my heart it was what I thought. Jack had run out on us, on his mother, his baby and me.

* * *

16

'I've looked out a few things I had for my little uns,' Mrs Wayman said when she popped into the bakery that morning in late September. 'I know yer working now, Maggie, but it can't be easy fer yer. With Molly and the baby to feed and no man to bring in a wage.' She looked at me curiously. 'I suppose you've never heard anything of your man? It's some weeks since he disappeared now.'

'Nearly four months.' The time had gone so fast, because I never got a moment to myself. It had been spring when Jack left and now it was autumn again and every day was a long hard struggle for both Molly and me. 'At first, I kept thinking he would walk in and ask what all the fuss was about, but I am beginning to think he can't. He must have been in an accident or something.'

'He was caught up in that nasty business with the strike,' she said. 'Charlie says he was a black-leg, but I told him he must be wrong. Jack Holmes wouldn't turn his back on his mates, would he?'

'I don't know. Jack didn't always tell us what he was doing.'

'Charlie said that bloke he worked for, Eddie Carver, has been arrested and tried for thieving. They reckon he'll go to prison for a long time.' Mrs Wayman frowned. 'He might have murdered your Jack. You should go to the police and tell them Jack is missing, Maggie. Hanging isn't good enough for the likes of that Eddie Carver!'

I was thoughtful as Mrs Wayman left the baker's shop. She genuinely thought Eddie might have murdered Jack. I was too frightened to ask the police, because I couldn't be sure Jack wasn't involved in all the thieving his boss had been doing. I didn't want the police searching the cottage and upsetting Molly, or taking away any of the more valuable items.

We were just about managing to keep up with the bills, but it wasn't easy. I had to buy special feed for Beth so that Molly could give her a bottle when I was at work.

Beth was nearly always asleep when I got home from work. I fed her during the night and on Saturday and Sundays I was able to take her out with me, strapped in a shawl in front of my chest. She was easy to carry while she was small, but one day soon I would have to start thinking about a pram for her, and I had no idea where the money was coming from for that!

'Maggie, you can start washing the shelves down now,' Mr Shirley told me, bringing me out of my reverie. 'When you've done them, you can go home.'

'Thank you,' I said. He had been good taking me back, but he expected a full day's work for his money and I seldom got home before six in the evening.

A late customer came in just as I was finishing and it was actually past six before I was able to leave that evening. I hurried home, knowing that Molly would have put the fish pie in the oven and if I was late it would spoil. She got a bit cross if I was over my time, and was becoming increasingly irritable.

Molly was sitting in her chair by the fire when I got in, Beth in a cot beside her. I smiled fondly at my baby. She looked pink and soft and beautiful and I wanted to pick her up and cuddle her, but she was fast asleep and I knew I shouldn't disturb her.

'Has she been good today?' I asked. Molly didn't answer. I looked at her. Her eyes were closed, but I felt a horrible sickness in my stomach because I knew she wasn't asleep. I touched her cold hand. She looked peaceful, as if she had just sat down to rest for a bit and gone to sleep.

'Oh, Molly,' I said as the tears caught in my throat. 'What am I going to do without you?' In death she looked younger; the lines of care had vanished from her face. 'Molly, I wish you could have stayed longer...waited until Jack came back.'

I'm not sure how long I knelt beside her, feeling the pain of grief and loss. Molly hadn't wanted Jack to marry me, but in the end, she had been my friend.

* * *

I was grateful for the help Molly's sons gave me arranging her funeral, but I didn't like the way they kept picking up things and looking at them, as if mentally adding up the value of Molly's personal goods. Nothing was said about it, however, until we got back to the cottage after the funeral.

'What are you going to do now, Maggie?' Sam asked. 'You won't stay here? I don't see how you can afford a house like this on what you earn. With Jack gone you need to find a couple of rooms somewhere.'

'I haven't decided yet. Jack might come back and expect to find me here.'

'If he's alive he'll be the other side of the world by now,' Sam said and frowned. 'He was in deeper than you might think with that Eddie Carver. No, I think you should consider giving up the house, Maggie. I've thought of taking it over myself.'

'So it would remain in your family?'

'It usually gets passed down to the eldest son and that's me. I wouldn't have said if Jack were still here, but you can't afford to stay here on your own, can you?'

'No, I suppose not. When do you want to move in?'

'In another month. That should give you time to look round for something else.'

'Yes, I suppose so...' I was numb, unable to think clearly. 'What about the furniture? Jack bought some things...'

'You'll sell them I expect? I'll give you a fair price. Ask someone what they are worth and I'll pay the same or a bit more. I don't want to be hard on you, Maggie but if I don't take the house someone else will when you can't pay the rent.'

'I know what they are worth. Jack told me. I'll want twelve pounds for everything—the furniture and the smalls, but not the clock.'

'Twelve pounds is a lot without the clock. Throw that in and I'll pay you tomorrow.'

'Ten pounds but not the clock. I am sorry, but I have promised that to someone.'

'Go on, Sam,' his wife said. 'There are some nice pieces here. Give Maggie the twelve pounds she asked for. She's entitled to her share of Molly's stuff too, same as your brothers. If anyone wants something from Molly's bedroom they should say now.'

The other wives, and the brothers, Bob and George, followed her upstairs. Sam was looking a little smug, pleased with himself.

'Twelve pounds it is then, Maggie. I'll bring it tomorrow. Ma said you were good to her. You deserve something to keep. He took a wedding ring from his pocket. 'I took it off afore she were buried. It's no good to her in the ground. You keep it in memory of her. The others will go through her bits upstairs. You should go with them if you want anything.'

'This is enough,' I said and slipped Molly's ring on to the middle finger of my right hand. 'Thank you, Sam. I'm sure I could get twelve pounds for that stuff so you don't have to buy it unless you want to.'

'The money should be enough to keep you going for a while. Shall you stay round here?'

'I am not sure. There doesn't seem much point now.'

If Sam hadn't wanted the cottage, I would have stayed in the hope that Jack might come home. Molly had told me to make a new life for myself, and I was beginning to think it might be for the best. She had thought my mother's cousin might live in Eastbourne, but I didn't even know her name.

I regretted my action in throwing Sadie's letter into the fire, but it was too late to worry about that; besides, if Ma's cousin had wanted to find me, she would have done it by now.

I had a month to decide what to do for the best. After Molly's family had gone, leaving me with piles of dirty dishes to wash I stood with my hands in water and thought about what I really wanted to do.

I would have a few pounds in my purse. Enough to take me away from London and keep Beth and me for a few weeks, but after that...I would have to find work and a place to live.

17

I received a letter from Belinda two days later. She was full of news about her aunt's hotel and the guests. She liked doing the cooking but they were so busy that her aunt was thinking of taking on another cook part time. She talked of walking by the sea, of going to shows on the pier and a new boyfriend who had taken her dancing.

It was like a breath of fresh air blowing through the clouds, another world far away from all the pain and problems of the past months. I smiled as I folded it and put it carefully into my purse. Then I went upstairs to start packing Beth's things. I had found two large leather bags in the cupboard. They would hold most of my clothes and Beth's.

My packing done, I took Beth and went round to Mrs Wayman's house. She invited me in for a cup of tea.

'I came to tell you I am going away,' I said. 'I want Charlie to come and fetch the clock you liked. I am giving it to you as a present.'

'You can't do that, Maggie. You need all the money you can get, lass.'

'I want you to have it. You helped me when Beth was born, and I have some money.'

Mrs Wayman looked at me in silence for a moment, then got up and went through to the scullery. She came back with a small pram; it was the kind that you could lift off the wheels and use as a cot and had obviously seen a lot of wear, but it had been cleaned, the metal parts oiled.

'I was going to bring this round. Charlie cleaned it up for yer. I used it for all my babies. I thought it would be useful for your Beth. Will you take it in exchange for the clock?'

'Yes, of course I will. It is just what I need. I can put Beth in that and balance the bags on the handle when I take her to the train. Thank you so much.'

She smiled, obviously relieved, because an exchange was not charity. 'I'll send Charlie to fetch the clock tonight. When are yer leavin'?'

'Tomorrow. I have a chance of a job if I leave now. I was going to stay another month, but I've decided there's no point in waiting. I am going to tell Mr Shirley when I leave you. He won't be pleased, but I can't help it. If I wait it may be too late.'

* * *

'Where are you, Jack?' I asked. 'Why did you leave me?' I paced the floor of the bedroom I had shared with Jack for such a short time. Outside the wind was howling; it rattled the windowpanes and whistled in the eaves, sounding eerie at times. 'I can't stay here alone, I have to go.'

It was foolish to have doubts. I had given up my job. Tomorrow I would say goodbye to all that I had known and begin a new life in Yarmouth. I must not be afraid. I must not look back! Inside a child was weeping, begging to be loved, for someone to come and kiss me and tell me everything was all right.

No one would come. I was alone apart from my child. I had made the right decision. There was nothing for me here. I should move on. So why was I tortured by doubts and why did I feel so afraid?

'You're not a child, Maggie Bailey. You're a woman, and you have a child to care for. It's time you moved on. Jack has gone. He left you. If he had cared he wouldn't have gone without a word.'

Restless and angry with myself, I took my bags downstairs ready for the journey. I would slip the key through Sam's door on my way to the station. These regrets were stupid! I had burned my boats and there was no going back.

* * *

The first thing I noticed as I got off the bus was the tang of the sea. It was salty and the wind was quite strong as it blew in off the sea, but there was also the underlying smell of fish and what smelled like open drains.

'Here, let me give you a hand with those bags,' a man said as I struggled with my pram, Beth and the bags. 'Have you come for a holiday, missus?'

'No, I'm hoping to find work,' I said and thanked him as he set my pram straight and handed me the heavy bags. 'Tell me, what is that smell...strong fish.'

'It's the herrings. You can smell it worse at this end of the prom-enade because of the smoke houses. They land the catch here and the herring is gutted and smoked in them lanes.' He pointed to a mass of what looked like back-to-back houses so close together that it would have been impossible to take a horse and cart through. 'Girls come from all over to work there, a lot of them from Scotland, but it's hard work, love, and not as much of it going as there used to be years ago.'

'I'm a cook. I've got a certificate. I'm hoping to find a job in a hotel.'

'You should have come earlier in the year,' he said. 'Hotel keepers hire new staff in the spring usually. You want to walk in that direction. Most of the hotels are further into the town.'

'This is on the sea-front I think.' I looked at the address I had written down. 'The Sunny Cliff Hotel...'

He looked thoughtful. 'Yes, I do know that one, it's a nice clean place, busy all the year round. You've got a fair walk, missus. You should have stayed on the bus for at least another two stops.'

'Oh, I wasn't sure. I didn't know where to get off. I just asked for the sea front.'

'Just keep walking along the promenade and you'll come to it in time,' he said. 'It's past the Britannia Pier, I know that much. Ask someone else when you get a bit further along.'

'Thanks, I will.'

I walked away from the area that smelled so strongly of fish. The houses got better and more prosperous looking as I left Old Town behind. The town had spread out in the past century as Yarmouth developed as a seaside resort and the coming of the railway had made it easier for people to visit. It had suffered damage from the Zeppelins during the war, particularly the harbour, but there was no sign of that here. The beach was quite stony in parts, though as I'd come on the bus, I had seen sand dunes. The sea appeared grey and a bit choppy, the sky darkened by clouds. On the horizon I could see vessels that looked as if they might be herring drifters, their nets spread wide; gulls circled overhead calling loudly.

Now I could smell something nice. I wasn't sure if it was fish and chips or something different, but it was definitely food and it made me feel hungry. I had brought a buttered roll and some cheese with me, but it seemed ages since I had eaten.

I kept walking, taking in all the sights. I saw a man selling candy floss and toffee apples, and another man was giving a handful of children donkey rides on the beach. Because it was the end of the season and a lot cooler than of late, there were only a few brave souls sitting in the striped canvas deck chairs. I did see one man emerge from the bathing huts and make a dash for the sea in his bathing suit.

Everything was so different, more open and newer than London. The sea was restless, angry, the people, strangers to me, hurrying by. I began to feel apprehensive. Supposing Belinda's Aunt didn't like me? She might not want to take on a woman with a small child. I might have to find work gutting herrings. I hadn't liked the smell of the strong fish and I might go back to London rather than face that! Looking about I saw lots of cafés, bars and shops. Surely I must be able to find work somewhere here? I passed a cinema and saw they were advertising the latest Charlie Chaplin film and a Western. Jack had loved a good Western. I shut the thought out before the tears started. Jack had deserted me!

When I found Sunny Cliff Hotel, I stood staring at it for ten minutes before I dared to cross the road. I was so nervous that I almost turned tail and ran, because it looked so posh. How had I imagined I would get a job here? If I had known where to go, I might have tried to find lodgings for the night and returned to try my luck in the morning, but it was all so new and bewildering.

I crossed the road and went up the steps to the front door. It wasn't easy getting the pram up them, but then a man came out and gave me a hand, carrying the pram into the rather daunting reception area.

'Ring the bell and someone will come,' he said. 'Excuse me, I have an appointment. I expect we may meet again.'

'Thank you.'

I approached the reception desk feeling apprehensive. He had said ring the bell but I wasn't a guest. I was looking for work and I wasn't quite sure what to do. As I hesitated, a woman came through from the back. She had dark grey hair tightly rolled into a bun at the nape, thick glasses and a long nose.

'May I help you? Do you have a booking?'

'No. I came...' I faltered because I suddenly realised, I didn't know Belinda's aunt's full name. 'I was looking for a job as a cook. I know Belinda. She told me her aunt needed extra help in the kitchen.'

'Indeed.' The woman looked down her nose, unsmiling. 'And who might you be?'

'I am Mrs Maggie Holmes. I come from London. Belinda and I took a cookery course together. We got on so well she told me to come if I needed a job, and her letter said her aunt was so busy she needed more help.'

'You have a small child,' the woman said, eyes narrowed in suspicion. 'How do you expect to work and look after a baby?'

'Beth takes the bottle. I shall find someone to take care of her while I work. I really need this job. My husband...is dead and I had to leave the cottage. Belinda's letter....' My voice trailed off as I realised that I had come on a wild goose chase. I shook my head as I apologised: 'It was silly of me to think I could find work here. I'm sorry for wasting your time. Could you direct me to a lodging house that would take me and the baby please? I'll get a room for the night.'

'And what will you do then?'

'I don't know. I might look for a job somewhere here, or go back to London, I suppose.'

'Wait there one moment,' the woman said. 'I'll be back soon.'

I stood waiting as she disappeared through the back. I supposed she had gone to find Belinda's Aunt. Obviously, I didn't stand a chance because of my baby. They wouldn't be so fussy in the herring sheds but I would still need a room and someone to look after Beth while I was at work. It had been mad to come here!

After a few minutes I heard voices and then Belinda came running from the back room. 'It is you, Maggie!' she cried and threw her arms round me. 'I didn't believe Aunt Beth, but it is true. When did you get here?'

'I got off the bus about an hour ago. I chose the wrong stop and had to walk a long way. I should have written to you first, but when I got your letter, it seemed like a chance of a new life.'

'Oh, Maggie,' Belinda said. 'Aunt says your husband is dead. I am so very sorry.' She saw the pram and stopped to peep in at the baby. 'She is lovely. I've thought of you so often. We had such fun together.'

'I should have asked before I came. If you can tell me a cheap place to stay, I'll find somewhere for tonight at least.'

'You can stay with me at my home. My sister and her husband have a room going spare. She is expecting her first but not for a few months yet. I think Hetty would look after your little girl for you while you're at work if you wanted. It will be good practice for her.'

'Your sister? I don't remember you talking about her in London?'

'Didn't I? I thought I had mentioned her once or twice, but maybe it was to one of the others?'

'Yes, I think it must have been. We talked about cooking most of the time.'

'We got told off for talking too much! Are you hungry? Come into the kitchen with me and I'll make you a sandwich and a cup of tea.'

'Will your aunt mind?' I looked at the woman standing near the counter. 'I didn't know what to call her.'

'I always call her Aunt Beth, don't I?' Belinda laughed again. 'She is Miss Beth Brown. Aunt Beth was my mother's sister. When our parents died, she helped Hetty and me through school. Hetty worked here until she got married, but her husband owns two herring drifters and she doesn't need to work now. She was thinking of taking a female lodger, just to make herself some money for extras. She will be pleased if I take you home. I'm always going on about you.'

'Will Miss Brown mind if you give me something to eat?'

'No, of course not. You don't mind Maggie having something to eat, do you, Aunt?'

'Can you bake as well as Belinda claims?' Miss Brown's question startled me.

'I can cook most things,' I replied. 'I like making fancy cakes, but I can do a meat pudding or a roast. Whatever you want.'

'I might ask you to do a bit of cleaning,' she said. 'My regulars like good food and I can't stand on my feet too much these days. I'll give you a try, a few hours cooking but you'll help with the bedchambers too. Making beds and sweeping the carpets, a bit of polishing, and toilet cleaning as well.'

'I don't mind what I do, Miss Brown. I need a job and somewhere to stay. If Belinda's sister will take me in and look after Beth, I shall be pleased to work for you.'

'Why did you call her Beth?' There was a strange, slightly challenging look in her eyes for a moment.

'I thought it was a nice name. It just came to me when she was born. I suppose it might have been because Belinda was always talking about you when we were cooking together.'

'Take your friend and give her something decent to eat, Belinda. You will need tomorrow to settle in and find your bearings, Mrs Holmes,' Miss Brown said. 'I shall expect you at seven sharp the following day. Your hours will be seven until two and three until half past eight in the evenings. I shall pay you ten shillings a week and your food. Is that acceptable to you?'

'I am grateful, Miss Brown.'

Her mouth drew into a prim line, as if she did not like to be thanked. 'It is for a trial period of a month. If you meet my standards, I'll talk to you then about staying on.'

'Thank you, you are very kind.'

'Nonsense! I expect my staff to work hard, Mrs Holmes. I do not give favours, even to Belinda. You should not expect time off in the busy periods unless it is absolutely necessary, and you will let me know immediately if you do need time off for anything.'

'Yes, of course. I shall try not to let you down.'

'See that you don't! 'Go along then, Belinda. You still have dinner to cook remember.'

Belinda winked at me as she picked up my bags. 'Aunt's bark is worse than her bite,' she whispered as she took me through a room at the back of the desk and then into the large kitchen. It was spick and span, the scrubbed pine table so large that I wondered how anyone ever managed to carry it here. The dresser and shelves were filled with good quality blue and white earthenware and there was a big cooking range and also a smart new gas cooker and refrigerator. Copper bottomed pans hung from hooks above the range, and the floor was covered in dark red tiles, which looked as if they were scrubbed and polished every day. There was a warm feel to the room and the smell of herbs and baking was delicious.

'What a lovely place to work! So big and light with all those windows over the sink.'

'There's a garden we can walk in when it gets too hot in the summer,' Belinda said. 'The guests don't use the kitchen garden, though some of them wander in from time to time. They soon realise and go off again. It gets very hot in here so we need somewhere we can go when it is unbearable.'

I went to look out at the small, enclosed garden. I could see an apple tree and some fruit bushes as well as a plot for herbs.

'Well, it seems wonderful to me. I shall enjoy working here with you.'

Belinda looked thoughtful. 'I'm so sorry about your husband. What happened?'

'There was an accident,' I said vaguely. 'And then, after Beth was born, Jack's mother was ill. I came home and found her dead in the kitchen. I couldn't have afforded to pay the rent there and pay to have Beth looked after so I thought I would try further afield, and then your letter came. It all sounded so good, I just packed up and came. I know I should have asked but I wanted to come at once in case the job was taken.'

'I am glad you did. Aunt would have kept managing herself, but it is too much for her these days. Seeing you standing there and knowing that you can cook lovely cakes made up her mind. She knows I can do a bit, but even though I took that course I am not as good at the fancy stuff as you, Maggie.'

I turned to her eagerly. 'I didn't get much chance to use my skill once I finished the course, but I love doing it. I'll do whatever you or Miss Brown want me to do. I am just pleased to have a job here. Do you think your sister will mind looking after Beth?'

'I am sure she will enjoy it. Hetty gets a bit lonely sometimes with her husband away at sea. Besides, we've needed an extra pair of hands for a while.'

'It looks as if I've come to the right place then.'

'Yes, you have,' Belinda said and glanced at my Beth as she started to grizzle. 'Does she need feeding?'

'I gave her a bottle on the train. She will be due for another soon, but I have to make it up, and I need to warm the water.'

'I'll warm the water for you,' Belinda offered. 'I should like to see you feed her. She is lovely but I'll bet you're hungry too. Will a chicken sandwich do? I've got to make a start with the dinner soon.'

'I'll make my own sandwich and then I'll feed Beth. After that, I'll give you a hand with the vegetables. What are you having?'

'Glazed carrots and white cabbage in black pepper butter, also, boiled, small potatoes with mint, and there's a choice of a beef and ale pie, which is already in the oven, or pork chops.'

'What is for afters?'

'Apple snow and an almond tart with home-made strawberry jam filling.'

'Sounds delicious. Why don't I give you a hand with them once Beth has settled? The sooner you are finished for the evening the sooner we can go to your home.'

* * *

Belinda's home was in the second line of houses, separated from the sea by the first line hotels and guest houses. It was a red brick modern house with three large bedrooms and a smaller one that Hetty was turning into a nursery; it also had electricity and a real bathroom! She looked a little uncertain when Belinda first took me in, but when she saw Beth fast asleep, she melted.

'Isn't she a little darling?' she said, 'and she seems good too. Did she cry much on the journey?'

'Most of the time she is as good as gold. That doesn't mean she can't kick up a row when she wants to.'

Hetty put her hand to her stomach. You could just see a gentle mound under her loose dress. 'I know they can be little monsters. A friend of mine had her baby three months ago and she has had a bit of a time with him. He screams for hours sometimes.'

'That is so tiring. I've been lucky so far. Beth never seems to mind anything much, as long as she is fed on time.'

'Well, I suppose you can have the spare room. I'll keep an eye on Beth while you are at work. How much is Aunt paying you?'

'Ten shillings a week.'

'That is a bit mean,' Hetty said. 'She gave me twelve and sixpence. When she decides to take you on full-time you want to ask for a rise. Anyway, I'll charge you six shillings a week for your bed and looking after Beth. If you want meals, it would be extra.'

'Miss Brown is giving me my meals,' I said. 'I shan't want to eat here, but if I do, I'll buy my food.'

She nodded and looked pleased.

I wasn't sure how long Hetty would be content to look after Beth, but I would make the most of it while I had the chance.

* * *

The next day was spent walking round the busy seaside town. It was warmer again and more people were on the beach, in the cafés and on the piers. There were shows going on most nights of the week. One of them was called Old Fashioned Music Hall and the poster said that one of the singers would perform favourites made popular by Marie Lloyd, who had died in 1922 aged fifty-two. Valentino had died this year too; his death had been mourned by thousands of women.

There was a nice atmosphere everywhere you went. People seemed happier, more relaxed than in London. I could see why they liked to come and visit; it was obviously a good place to set up a business. Some of the shops catered for the holidaymakers, and they were more expensive than the ones the locals used. I had to search to find the shops I could afford to patronise, because they were often tucked away in side streets. I didn't want to buy souvenirs and new clothes, but I did need somewhere that I could buy Beth's powdered milk, concentrated orange juice and the creams and talcum I needed to keep her sweet.

In one of the back streets there was a little shop with a *To Let* sign in the window. I pressed my nose against the glass, shading my eyes with my hand and thinking that it was just the right size for a teashop. However, there was no point in hankering after something I couldn't afford to have. When Jack was earning a lot of money, I'd thought it might happen one day, but it had been a dream based on stolen goods.

I walked away from the shop, then turned and looked back. There were rooms over the top and they were empty. It was just what I needed for Robin, Beth and me but I couldn't afford to take it.

To set up a teashop properly, I would need far more money than I was likely to have in my pocket. To achieve a dream like mine I would have to scrimp and save for years, and then I still might never get there.

18

My first task the next morning was to help prepare the tables in the dining room. After that I went to the kitchen. It had been thoroughly cleaned and looked spotless. Belinda and I were kept busy cooking and serving large fried breakfasts from a quarter to eight until just after nine o'clock. The guests had grapefruit first and toast after with marmalade and everyone had a choice of coffee or tea. We had rows of little individual metal pots with a metal jug for the milk and a pot for the sugar. I thought they were the kind of thing I would like to serve with my cakes and wondered how much they cost, and if you could buy them cheaply from a wholesaler. I was learning about these things now and I listened eagerly to everything Miss Brown told us.

After breakfast, I went upstairs with another girl and she showed me how to make the beds the way Miss Brown liked them. We then swept carpets and polished brown wood furniture. It was all basic, plain stuff, nothing like the fine mahogany lowboy and chest Jack had bought for our bedroom at the cottage. There were a few ornaments but not many signs of flowers or anything that might have made the place look more homely.

Miss Brown, as I came to know over the next weeks and months, believed in keeping things clean and neat. She served good food and, I was told, her cakes and puddings were considered some of the finest available on this part of the coast. Non-residents sometimes came in for tea, which was served in the big drawing room at little tables dotted between the comfortable chairs and sofas. However, there were no frills. She did not have a bar in the evenings and no alcoholic beverages were served in the lounge although guests were allowed wine with their meals, which they bought by the glass.

Her guests were not permitted to take an unregistered person to their rooms, and the door was locked at ten thirty at night. Guests had to leave their rooms by ten o'clock in the mornings but they could return at any time after eleven thirty when they could sit in the public rooms while their own were being cleaned. Most of the guests were single gentlemen who came and went on business, because she catered more for the professional guests than the holiday folk, but she did occasionally have a family to stay or a married couple. Single ladies were not encouraged. Her rules were strict and her lodgers respected them. Perhaps, I suspected, because her charges were reasonable and the food was good.

Yarmouth or Great Yarmouth to give it its full title was on the east coast of England and popular with holiday makers in the summer. Then, as I learned from Belinda, the promenade was filled with families enjoying the sea air and all the entertainments to be had, theatres, piers and lots of delicious foods on offer. However, Miss Brown preferred her regular guests because they filled her rooms all year round.

Keeping a lodging house was hard work unless you had enough staff. Miss Brown had done much of the work in the kitchen for years, but now she was no longer a young woman and she preferred to linger in reception and talk to her guests when they came in or went out.

'You are lucky to have Miss Brown for your aunt,' I told Belinda one evening as we walked home. 'Do you know why she never married?'

'She could have married when she was in her late twenties, but her fiancé was killed in some kind of accident,' Belinda told me. 'His family owned this hotel and he left everything to Aunt Beth. She buried herself in work and found a life for herself here.'

It was easy to see what had made Miss Brown the way she was. Her manner was often sharp, and she expected us to work hard for our wages. After I had been working for her a month, she raised my wages to twelve and sixpence.

'If you wish to work on a Sunday, you can earn double money,' she told me. 'Belinda likes to go to church and she will not do Sunday lunches or teas. As you know we have a cold supper on Sunday, so your hours would be from seven until two and from three until five.'

'When Pa was ill, I had to take on two jobs. We lived near the docks and I worked in the bakery in the daytime and then at a café at night. After Ma died, I got married and things were a bit better.'

'What was your mother's name, Maggie?'

'Jane Bailey.'

I had the oddest feeling as I told her that she already knew, but she merely nodded.

'You may have read in the paper that she was murdered.'

'I seldom read that kind of thing, Maggie. I am very sorry. It must have been a terrible time for you.'

'It wasn't as bad as it might have been, because I had Jack.'

She didn't say anything more, just looked at me and then Beth. I told her that I would be happy to do the hours, though I might need to bring Beth to work sometimes, because Hetty liked to go to church on Sundays too and it would be awkward for her to take the child with her.

'Does she cry much?'

'Hardly ever,' I said. 'I could put her pram in the annexe off the kitchen and if I feed her in my lunch break, she wouldn't be any trouble at all.'

'Bring her in on Sunday and we'll see how we go on,' she said.

I took Beth in the next Sunday. She was as good as gold and I sailed through the day easily, pocketing my extra money.

However, the following Sunday Beth was a bit restless, crying instead of sleeping. I thought she might have a bit of a cold, but I wasn't sure what to give her for it. After what had happened to Katie, I didn't trust the herbal medicines that Ma had always given us at home, and I didn't think Beth was ill enough to call out the doctor.

She cried all the time. I was preparing and cooking lunch. I picked her up twice and got her off to sleep, but once she was back in her pram she started to grizzle again. Miss Brown came in as I was clearing up the surfaces after getting the roast into the oven.

'Is something the matter with Beth? I've heard her crying several times.'

'I think she may have a bit of a cold. She is flushed and miserable, but I don't think it is anything serious.'

'You've got the puddings to make,' she said in a sharp tone. 'You can't work with a baby crying all the time. I shall take her into my sitting room. If she continues to cry, I shall ask the doctor to call. You can't be too careful with babies, Maggie.'

'Are you sure you don't mind? I did say she wouldn't be any trouble...'

'Well, she is today. Leave her to me and get on with the work..'

She wheeled the pram away. I wondered if this meant the end of my job and listened for the sounds of crying but heard nothing for the rest of the morning. When it was time for my lunch Miss Brown brought Beth back to me.

'She settled well once I rocked the pram. All she wanted was a little attention.' To my surprise there was a smile in her eyes, as though she'd enjoyed having Beth.

'My sister would say that I should give her away, because it is too hard to look after her, but I shall never give her up!'

'Nor would I if she were mine,' Miss Brown said and her expression became sad. 'I never married but I should have liked children. Belinda and Hetty have been like my own, but I never had the pleasure of them when they were babies. I should count it a pleasure to look after Beth on a Sunday.'

'Are you sure you don't mind? The extra money is so welcome.'

'You should start an account at the Post Office. If you save a few shillings a week it will soon count up and then you always have something for a rainy day.'

'Could I do that? I thought you needed a lot of money to have a savings account.'

'The banks require a larger deposit and all sorts of things, but the Post Office is for people like us, Maggie.'

'What do I do? I've never had any money to save before.'

'I will pick up a form when I am out shopping tomorrow,' Miss Brown said. 'I can show you how to fill it in and then you can take it to the post office in your lunch hour one day and sign it while you're there.'

I thanked her, surprised at the change in her. She'd seemed aloof, as if she wanted to keep her distance, but now the barriers had come down.

* * *

After I finished cleaning bedrooms one morning, I came downstairs to discover that two people were waiting in reception. They had rung the bell but no one had come. I apologised and asked them to wait, going through to Miss Brown's sitting room. She was sitting in an armchair, her eyes closed. She held earphones against her ears and I could tell that she was listening to the wireless. I touched her arm and she jumped, opening her eyes to look at me.

'What is wrong, Maggie? I was listening to the music. The BBC has started to put out concerts regularly now as well as the newscasts.'

'I saw it in the paper, but I've never heard the wireless. No one had them where I lived.'

'Here, listen to this,' she said and handed me one of the earphones . 'Isn't that lovely.'

I was entranced. 'That is beautiful... I didn't know people could play that kind of music. It's better than you get at the cinema.'

'They will have music like this in films soon,' she said. 'But you must have wanted me for something?'

'There are some people waiting in reception.'

'My goodness! I didn't hear them. I must go. You can listen to the wireless for a moment if you like.'

I sat down in the chair she had left and put the earphones on. The music sounded even better when I had two instead of holding one to my ear. I got carried away and was still sitting there when Miss Brown came back. I jumped up thinking she would be cross but she just smiled.

'You're like me,' she said. 'I could listen to music for hours. Unfortunately, you will have to go and help Belinda with the lunches; she can't manage alone but you can come and listen now and then when you have time. You can borrow my books too, if you like reading?'

'I love to read when I have time. It isn't often I get a chance, but I've read some Agatha Christie and P. G. Wodehouse.'

'There are lots of them in my bookcase, and poetry too. You might like poetry if you try it, Maggie. Those Reader's Digest books also have a lot of interesting things in them.'

'Thanks, but I'd better get on.'

'I suppose you must.'

I had the oddest feeling that she was reluctant to let me go.

* * *

I had come to Yarmouth just as the season was drawing to an end. During the winter some of the cafés and small guesthouses closed, but we kept going and were as busy as ever.

In December the papers were filled with stories about the famous author Agatha Christie. She had gone missing and for several days the police feared the worst, but then she turned up safe and sound in a hotel. She didn't explain why she had disappeared, and everyone said it was a mystery just like her books.

At Christmas time Miss Brown brought out a large box of decorations, glass balls, silver tinsel and candle holders. A huge tree was delivered and Miss Brown, Belinda and I decorated it together in the evening. The guests thought it was lovely and small gifts began to appear underneath it.

I was very surprised on Christmas day to discover that several little parcels came my way. I had suspected that Miss Brown, Belinda and Hetty might give me something and I had bought gifts for them. However, there were chocolates, a tiny bottle of perfume, scented soap and a pink artificial silk scarf from the residents. Also, a knitted coat and bonnet for Beth and a small teddy bear.

'But how did they know my name?' I asked Miss Brown when she brought them through to the kitchen and placed them on the table as I ate my share of the Christmas dinner I had cooked. Belinda was having hers at home with her sister and brother-in-law but Miss Brown had paid me extra to come in and cook for the residents.

'They often ask who has cooked something when it is particularly good,' she told me with a smile. 'I always tell them truthfully and it is usually you, Maggie. You are an excellent cook, my dear. In fact, I have decided to put your wages up to a pound a week.' I started to thank her but she shook her head. 'You could easily earn that or a bit more at some of the larger hotels in town. We are lucky to have you. The residents wanted to show their appreciation. Some of them bought gifts, the others clubbed together to give you this...' She placed a five-pound note on the table in front of me.

'That is too much...' I gasped, feeling overwhelmed. 'No one has ever given me so much money.'

'It was the residents that thought of it. I bought you a present. It is a fully-fashioned twinset, Maggie. I think the size is correct, but you may change it if the colour is wrong for you.'

I opened her bulky parcel and found the most beautiful jumper and cardigan I had ever seen. The wool was soft to the touch and the colour was a pretty blue. I stroked it reverently with my fingertips. I had bought her some scented soap and felt amazed that she should give me something like this expensive twinset.

'It is beautiful! I've never had anything like this to wear not even when I got married. I can't thank you, or the residents, enough.'

'You have worked hard since you came here. I trust you, Maggie, and I like you. I want you to stay with me. Have you thought what you'll do when Hetty doesn't feel like minding Beth any more?'

'I shall have to find someone to mind the child. I can afford to pay five shillings a week to the right person now. I suppose I could put a card in a shop window and see what happens.'

'You don't have to do that just yet. I wouldn't mind looking after

Beth for a few hours each day. It won't make any difference to your wages. To be honest I enjoy having her, Maggie. I've taken her out to show the customers a few times. They all think she is lovely. They know you are a widow and they want to help as much as they can.'

Tears pricked behind my eyes. 'I was so lucky when I came here,' I said. 'If I'd thought about it a bit more I might have stayed where I was and taken in lodgers, but I had to decide quickly. I am glad I did. Living with Hetty and coming here to work, it's like coming home.'

When I thought about it I remembered that Jack's brother hadn't given me much time to decide. He'd seemed determined to take over the cottage when their mother died. I wasn't sure he would have let me stay even if I'd wanted to. Without Jack I had less right to it.

Where the hell had he gone? Sometimes I thought he would turn up or get in touch, but at others I believed he must be dead or in so much trouble that he dared not come back. It made me sad and angry by turn, because I missed him but I was angry that he'd risked everything. Surely, Eddie couldn't have forced him to do things he knew were wrong.

I had no idea where to look for him and wouldn't dream of asking his former boss. It was his fault that Jack had disappeared and I didn't want anything to do with him or his bad ways.

I knew I was lucky to have this place. There was no one else who cared for us now. Even if I'd managed to find my real mother, it was unlikely she would want to see me. She must have given me away, or perhaps she'd died. There was no way of finding out. I didn't know where to start. Sadie hadn't left a forwarding address, or if she had it was in the letter that I'd had thrown on the fire. I did regret that, because it might have told me things I needed to know, but it was too late. I just had to make the best of what I had. I'd decided to make my home here and thought myself lucky.

'I am glad you feel that way,' Beth told me. 'I love Belinda and Hetty dearly, but if I'd had a daughter I should have wanted her to be like you. You are brave and honest, and I honour you for the way you just get on with your work and never make a fuss about anything I ask you to do. Hetty and Belinda would never clean toilets, but you do them, and people tell me how clean they are when you've finished.'

'I'm used to hard work. I was brought up to it.'

'I'm sorry for the life you've had, Maggie. I hope you will continue to find happiness here with us.'

She was looking at me so oddly. I thought she was going to tell me something, but then she turned and walked away.

What was she holding inside? What was the secret she wanted to share but couldn't?

19

I had taken an hour off to get my hair cut into the new shorter bob that everyone was wearing these days. Some women were having theirs shingled, but I decided that that was a bit too far for me. My hair was thick and heavy and it clung damply to the back of my neck when it was hot in the kitchen. I closed my eyes as the first lengths came off, because Jack had always loved my hair.

Jack had been missing for well over a year now and he wouldn't know I'd had my hair cut. So many months had passed that I had begun to shut his memory out of my mind, not wanting to remember. If he cared about me, he would have come looking for me long ago! Jack would have found me if he'd wanted to, so he either didn't or he was dead. Either way he was lost to me and I'd settled into my working routine.

My life in Yarmouth had become comfortable and familiar. I worked hard but the job was satisfying and I had friends. My search for Robin continued, but I wouldn't let myself look back.

The old Maggie had gone. When I looked at my reflection in the hairdresser's mirror that morning, I hardly knew myself. I looked like one of those flapper girls in the magazines and newspapers the guests left lying around in their rooms.

'It suits you, madam,' the hairdresser told me as he showed me the back with his hand mirror. 'Not everyone can wear this style but you can—beautifully if I may say so.'

I thanked him and paid his fee. It was autumn 1927 now and we'd had a busy summer, the town thronged with happy faces as people enjoyed the seaside air, but the weather was milder than usual for this time of year, and there were still some holidaymakers about. Only a few brave souls were on the beach, but there were plenty of attractions. People liked to visit the museums down at the South Quay, the monument to Lord Nelson and other places of interest.

As I walked back to the hotel, I kept glancing in shop windows and laughing at my reflection. Was it really me?

'Maggie! Maggie Bailey, is it you?'

I turned as I heard myself addressed by my maiden name, staring in surprise as the man walked up to me. I hadn't seen him for almost two years and I hadn't thought about him either.

'It is you!' He stared at me as if he couldn't believe his eyes.

'Duncan Coulson,' I said and smiled. 'What are you doing here?'

'I might ask the same of you. Don't you remember I told you I was going to be apprenticed as a boat builder? I work and live just outside Yarmouth, but I had to come in today to do an errand.'

I started to shake my head, then nodded as the memory slotted into place. 'Yes, I do remember you telling me but I had forgotten. A lot happened after you left, Duncan.'

'I read about your mother and father in the local paper my sister sent me.' He glanced down at my left hand. 'She said you had married but I wasn't sure. Congratulations.'

'I'm a widow now,' I told him and wondered why I had said it. I couldn't be sure Jack was dead. 'I have a child, she is just over a year old, and I work at Sunny Cliff Hotel as a cook and cleaner.'

'You're a widow?' Duncan didn't seem to have registered the rest. 'I should say I am sorry. It must have been difficult for you, Maggie.'

'It was for a long time, but it is much better now. I'm getting on well and I like my job. I've just had my hair cut at the hairdresser. I've never been to a hairdresser before in my life, but my employer said I should because it would feel cooler in the hot kitchen and when the weather is warm.'

'It suits you; you look different, a woman. You were just a girl when I left, Maggie. I wanted...' his words died away, as if he were not sure of them. 'Do you work every day?'

'Yes. I finish at five on a Sunday, but not until nearly nine every other day. Why?'

'Would you come out with me? There isn't much happening on Sunday nights, no dancing anyway, but we could go for a walk and a drink.'

I hesitated, because I wasn't sure that I wanted to change my life. Then a flicker of rebellion stirred. Jack had promised so much and then let me down. Why shouldn't I enjoy myself once in a while?

'Yes, all right. I should like that, Duncan. There is a brass band concert on the promenade. I sometimes go and listen to that; it's the Sally Army. They sing hymns but I don't mind that, do you?'

'I wouldn't mind anything with you, Maggie. Shall I wait outside the hotel for you when you're done?'

'Yes, please.'

He seemed reluctant to walk on. 'You must know I've always cared about you, Maggie. I would have asked you out before I left the docks, but I knew it would be a year or two before I could ask anyone to marry me.'

'We don't know each other well enough to talk about things like that yet, Duncan,' I said. 'You can take me out on Sunday, but I am making no promises.'

How could I when I didn't know if Jack was alive or dead?

'I know that, Maggie but I've never stopped thinking about you. I didn't think you were old enough to get married when I left, and I blamed myself when they told me you had married, but I kept hoping they were wrong and you would be waiting for me when I got back.'

'I might have waited if you'd asked. But this is just a walk and a drink. No promises, Duncan.'

'Not yet. I'll make you care about me, Maggie. You wait and see. No one has ever treated you as good as I shall now that I've got another chance with you...' His gaze was so intense that I felt a prickling sensation at my nape.

'I have to go,' I said. 'I shall see you on Sunday.'

I left him standing there. I knew he was watching me walk away but didn't look back. The look in Duncan's eyes had told me that he wanted me, making me aware that the feelings I'd experienced with Jack were not dead.

Was it wicked of me to feel excited? My husband had been missing for well over a year. Was I wrong to want to live again in another man's arms?

I warned myself to be sensible. I would meet him that Sunday, but it was just a walk and a drink. I didn't have to go out with him again if I didn't want to. I could step back at any time, but my instincts were to make the most of the chance that had come my way.

* * *

I took my best dress to work on Sunday. I had cut it out at home and made it myself, working on it for an hour or so when I had time.

The skirt was shorter than I'd worn before, though it still wasn't anywhere near as skimpy as the Flapper girls were wearing this year, but it was in the style Coco Chanel had made popular, and the skirt came to just below the knee. My legs were brown where I'd sat in the garden in the sun during my lunch break and I didn't need stockings. With my hair shorter and wearing the low-waisted dress, I felt very smart as I came out of the cloakroom.

'That is a pretty dress,' Aunt Beth said as she saw me. 'Are you going somewhere special this evening, Maggie?'

'I'm going for a walk with someone; a friend I used to know at school in London. Duncan is apprenticed at a boat builder just down the coast and we met the other day. We shall probably watch the concert and then have a drink later.'

'What about little Beth? You can't take her to a pub, Maggie.'

'We could sit outside somewhere,' I said. 'There's a place near the pier where we could buy a drink and take it outside to look at the sea.'

'Why don't you leave her with me for a few hours? It will be much nicer for you and your young man if you haven't got to bother with a child.'

'He isn't my young man. Just a friend from school.'

'I am sure he is very nice,' she said. 'You must bring him to see me another day. Run along with you now. I can look after Beth for the evening. You enjoy yourself, Maggie. You deserve a night off.' Aunt Beth smiled at me.

I hesitated, but she seemed determined to have her way. It would be nice just to relax and have fun for once without having to think about the baby.

'If you're sure,' I said, 'but you've had her most of the day.'

'I love looking after her,' she said. 'Go and have a good time—and bring your young man to see me another day.'

I thanked her and went out of the front door. Duncan was

standing just across the road. I waited for a bus and someone on a motorcycle to go by and then ran over to him. His gaze went over me with appreciation. He had his hand behind his back and when he brought it forward, I saw that he had a posy of roses.

'I hope you like roses?'

I held them to my nose, inhaling the perfume. My heart raced as I saw the heat in his eyes. In that moment he seemed so intense that he almost frightened me.

'They are lovely,' I told him. 'No one has ever given me flowers before.'

'Not even your husband?'

'For my wedding, of course.'

'You should have flowers every week,' Duncan said. 'I've got a cottage, Maggie. My garden is full of flowers just like this. It isn't much yet but one day I'll have a big house.'

'Are you enjoying being a boat builder?' I asked, because it made me uncomfortable when he talked this way. It was much too soon!

'Yes, I love it. I always wanted to work with my hands, making things. Working with wood is such a good feeling. We build wherries and other small sailing boats. It is a satisfying job. I know it will be a while before I am earning much, but the money is regular.'

I felt that he was building up to something and I tried to turn him. 'Miss Brown, I call her Aunt Beth because she prefers it, owns the hotel where I work. She offered to look after Beth for me this evening.'

'Oh...your child. You said she was just over a year old, didn't you?'

'Yes. She is beautiful, Duncan and she knows it. Everyone spoils her rotten, but she makes you want to laugh. You should see the old-fashioned looks she gives people when she doesn't approve.'

'I suppose she keeps you busy, what with working all hours and a child to look after too.'

'I don't have a lot of free time. I don't mind, because I love her and I love the work I do.'

'You married Jack Holmes, didn't you?' A nerve flicked at the corner of his eye. 'What happened, or can't you talk about it?'

It was my chance to tell him the truth, but the truth wouldn't come. 'Jack was helping break the strike, driving food lorries...I'm not sure...' We could hear the sound of the brass band playing. I took his hand, tugging at him. 'Come on, let's hurry or we shall miss it. Jack doesn't matter.'

Duncan let me hurry him along the promenade. We reached the small crowd gathered on the prom to listen, and when I dared to look at Duncan again, he was smiling.

We joined in the singing. Duncan had a strong, musical voice and I felt proud of him as I saw people turn their heads to look as he sang the hymns with gusto. Afterwards, some people clapped and I thought they were applauding Duncan as much as the brass band.

When the concert was over, we strolled along the front. We went on the pier and Duncan asked me what I wanted to drink. I asked for a sweet sherry, because it was the only thing I could think of. He bought a half of beer for himself and we sat at a table near the railings and looked at a sailing ship on the horizon.

'My boss says that it will all be steam and diesel engines in a few years,' Duncan said. 'Our skills will be lost then but I think people will want small sailing boats forever. Trevor says that his sons don't want to follow him into the business. I might take it over from him when he retires.'

'Would you like that?'

'Yes, I think so. I did think I might move on somewhere, but I like it here. It is a good place to live. Yarmouth is busy, especially in the high season when the holidaymakers come, but where I live it is quieter, nicer, I think. I don't have a sea view but it isn't far to walk to the beach and the bus runs right past my house. It is only twenty minutes or so to get into town.'

I fingered the stem of my glass, which was empty. Duncan looked at it.

'Would you like another sherry, Maggie?'

'No, thank you. One is plenty. I think I should get back to the hotel. It is well past Beth's bedtime and it disturbs her when I take her home. I have to be at work again at seven in the morning.'

'You don't have to,' Duncan said suddenly. His gaze was hot as he looked at me, intensely passionate. 'If you married me, you could stop work—at least, you need only do a few hours if you wanted to for a bit of extra money for yourself. In another year or so I'll be earning enough so you wouldn't have to work at all.'

I wasn't expecting him to ask me just like that and it shocked me. Yes, I'd known him for years at school and I'd sensed he was sweet on me then but we hadn't met in a long time and I'd changed. It was too sudden, even for an old friend.

'Duncan...' I wasn't sure how to answer him. If I told him the truth about Jack, he wouldn't ask me out another day. 'We don't know each other well enough to think about getting married yet.'

'I know what I want,' Duncan said and his eyes blazed at me. I felt a spasm of desire mixed with fear. I was flattered by his attention, but this was wrong. Jack might still be alive! 'Maggie! I would marry you tomorrow—as soon as we can fix it up anyway. I suppose you had a church wedding last time?' I shook my head and that seemed to please him. 'We could have a proper white wedding if you like, Maggie. I've got a few bob put by for the house I'm going to buy us, but I could buy you all the pretty things you need to get married.'

I had a lump in my throat as I remembered my wedding day. I'd worn one of Ma's old dresses cut down to fit me with a new hat and shoes. For a moment I was tempted, after all who would know? I could have a life of being looked after but something held me back. Maybe Duncan had been carrying a torch for me for years, but it was too quick for me.

'I'm sorry, Duncan. It is a bit too soon for me to think about getting married just yet.'

'You're still upset over Jack.' A sulky look crept into his eyes.

'No...not really. I did love him, but I want to move on. I want a future, Duncan, but I don't know you yet.'

'I shouldn't have spoken so soon, but I wanted you to know how I feel,' Duncan said. 'I thought it was too late but now there's a chance and I have to tell you, because I lost you last time through waiting and not telling you how I've always felt about you. I want you to be my wife, Maggie. I love you and I'll be good to you. I swear you wouldn't regret it.'

'What about Beth? Would you want to raise another man's child?'

'She's your daughter so I'll love her,' he said and his eyes seemed to beg me to say yes. 'At least say you will think about it, Maggie ...please?'

'All right, I will think about it.' I knew it was wrong to make a promise I couldn't keep, but I liked being with him. 'I have to get back now, Duncan.'

'I'll walk you back,' he said and smiled. 'You're my girl now, Maggie. As soon as you're ready I'm going to have the banns read. We'll be married in church and I'll be real good to you.'

I tucked my arm through his as we walked back to the hotel. I felt guilty but I wouldn't let my guilt intrude. Duncan was the kind of man I should have married: steady, dependable and loving. Jack was just a memory now. He'd left me to fend for myself. I didn't owe him anything and yet I felt a queer little pain inside whenever I let myself think of him.

Outside the hotel Duncan hesitated and then kissed me on the cheek. I knew he wanted to take me in his arms and kiss me properly, but he couldn't do that in the street with people walking by.

'I've promised to work extra hours this week,' he said. 'Shall I come next Sunday, Maggie?'

I should have said no, but it was too hard. I was young and I wanted some fun and excitement in my life. If I let this chance of some happiness go, I might never get another.

'Yes please,' I said and gave him a quick kiss on his cheek. 'I shall look forward to it, Duncan.'

'Don't forget I think the world of you, Maggie.'

Aunt Beth greeted me with an expectant smile. 'Well,' she said. 'Did you have a lovely time, Maggie? Beth was as good as gold. I gave her some milk and read her a story and she went off like a lamb.'

'It was so kind of you to let me go. I had a good time. Duncan told me all about his work, the boats he is building and his hopes for the future. He has his own cottage and he brought me these roses from the garden.'

'Roses. That sounds promising,' she said. 'He'll be asking you to marry him before long, you see if I'm not right.'

'I don't think I should get married again.'

'Nonsense! It would be such a waste for a pretty girl like you, Maggie. I wasted my chances, clung to my memories and refused every offer I got—and there were several. The hotel must have been an incentive for some of them, but others were genuine. I could have married but I didn't...' The expression in her eyes at that moment was sad, haunted, and I thought a little guilty, as if she had a secret she was afraid to share. 'Don't you waste your chances, Maggie. If he asks you, say yes.'

'I could work part time,' I said and blushed as she gave me a sharp look. 'Duncan did hint that he would like to get married, but I don't know him well enough.' Except that I'd seen him at school every day for years of my life. Of course I knew him. He was safe, dependable Duncan.

'No one is saying you should rush into anything. You bring him to meet me next time, Maggie. You can make a special tea and we'll have it in my private sitting room.'

Aunt Beth seemed as if she truly cared about me, about my future. For a moment I felt close to her, as if we had known each other all our lives.

20

I thought about Duncan a lot that week. He was an energetic, ambitious man and he loved to talk about his work. When he spoke of things he loved, his face came alight and I found him interesting. I knew that I would enjoy being his lover and his wife but it was stupid to hanker after something that could never be. I couldn't marry unless I knew for certain if Jack was dead and I might never know the truth of his disappearance.

That Sunday we went for a walk on the beach and Duncan kissed me under the pier. He held me close, his lips demanding, insisting on a response, which I gave willingly. He had brought me some chocolates this time, and said that if I could get off an hour earlier in the week, he would take me to the cinema to see a new Greta Garbo film.

I told him I wasn't sure I could ask for time off, but when I took him back to meet Aunt Beth, she gave us sherry and almond comfits and told Duncan that I could go early on the Tuesday night if he wanted to take me somewhere nice.

After that I just couldn't tell him that I didn't want to see him again, and why should I? Jack had deserted me.

I had such a lovely time at the pictures that it became a regular thing. On Sundays we went for walks and a drink, and sometimes we would have a nightcap with Aunt Beth when we returned. On Tuesdays we went to the pictures or one of the musical shows. I had discovered a love of music and I decided that one day I would buy myself a gramophone so that I could collect the kind of records I liked. I told Duncan that I should like one and he looked pleased.

'I knew how much you liked the music, Maggie,' he said. 'I bought a gramophone from the second-hand shop last week. I was going to give it to you for your birthday, but you can have it now if you want?'

'You keep it until my birthday. You are very thoughtful, Duncan. It is exactly the present I would choose for myself.'

Duncan looked down at me, his eyes intent on my face. The hot look he gave me made me tremble and desire pooled low in my abdomen.

'You know I love you, Maggie. You don't remember when we were at school and we sat in the playground and talked about what we would do when we left school. I think I fell in love with you then. I came to your house before I left the lanes. I was going to ask you if you would wait for me...to tell you I would come back in a year and marry you, but you had gone out to the pictures.'

'Ma said you called but you didn't leave a message.'

'It wasn't the kind of thing I could say to anyone else.' His eyes were so dark and intense that I shivered. 'Will you marry me? Please say yes, Maggie. Even if you don't love me now, you will soon. I'll be so good to you.'

It was wrong of me to let him go on hoping. I wanted to tell him, but when I started to speak, he grabbed me and kissed me, almost as if he knew what I was going to say.

'Don't answer now,' he said urgently. 'Think about it and tell me next time.'

'Yes, I will,' I said. That Sunday I made up my mind that I would find the courage to tell him the truth.

* * *

There were now two babies at Hetty's house, her son Tim was now a few months old. Beth was teething and kept me awake several nights on the run making me tired. My restlessness would pass in time, but I couldn't help thinking it would be nice to be in my own home, especially when Beth's crying woke Hetty's baby on Friday night.

She came downstairs to the kitchen looking pale and tired. A few minutes later Belinda followed her down.

'Poor little Beth,' she said. 'Is she ill, Maggie?' She went to put the kettle on. Hetty was trying to quieten her son, who was screaming at the top of his voice. 'I'll make us all some tea. It is enough to put anyone off having children at all with these two. I'm dead tired and you both look like death warmed up.'

'Tim has been fretful all night,' Hetty said and looked at me as if it were my fault. 'If you can't keep Beth quiet at nights you should look for somewhere else to live, Maggie. I am sorry, but I need to sleep and she has kept us all awake the whole week.'

'Not every night,' I said but she left the kitchen without answering.

'Hetty doesn't mean it,' Belinda assured me. 'She is over-tired and worried about Tim. He hasn't been well. I think it is just a bit of a chill, but Hetty worries with her husband away most of the time.'

'Yes, of course she does.' I didn't argue with Belinda, but it wasn't the first time recently that Hetty had hinted I should leave. 'She only took me in out of kindness. I suppose it is time I looked for a place of my own.'

'I should miss you,' Belinda said. 'I can't say I would move in with you, because Hetty likes me to help her with Tim sometimes and I pay her a few shillings for my room and keep. Besides, you might get married soon. You've been going with Duncan for a couple of months now and he is serious.'

'I don't want to get married, not yet anyway,' I said. 'You're engaged. When will you get married, Belinda?'

'Not until next year. William is saving for a house. Anyway, I don't want to give up working for a while. Aunt Beth paid for my training and once you are married you never know how soon you'll start a family. Another year is plenty soon enough for me. It's different for you, Maggie.'

Beth had quietened. I put her back in her cot. 'What makes you think it is different for me?'

'You've already got Beth. It makes sense to get married if you can, Maggie. You need a man to look after you so that you don't have to work all the time. It is hard looking after a child and working full-time when you're on your own. If Aunt Beth didn't love your little one you wouldn't be able to do it at all. Hetty can't look after a baby and a small child. I know you might find someone else, but it wouldn't be easy. I shouldn't say but my aunt isn't as strong as she used to be. I know she is only in her mid-forties but she gets tired easily these days. It was all right her looking after Beth when it was just once a week, but it is every day now.'

'Are you saying it is too much for her? She hasn't complained.'

'No, she wouldn't, because she loves having Beth with her, and she knows how difficult things are for you.'

'I see...' I turned away so that Belinda couldn't see my face. She was my friend and she wasn't being unkind, but clearly, she was concerned for her aunt's welfare. 'I shall have to see if I can find someone to take care of Beth sometimes and I'll look for somewhere to live.'

'I'm sure Hetty didn't mean it. Don't tell Aunt I said anything, because she would be cross.'

'No, I won't,' I said. 'And don't look so worried, Belinda. It isn't your problem. It's mine and I'll have to work it out for myself.'

* * *

'Would you mind if I popped out for a while when I've finished for the morning?' I asked when I saw Aunt Beth that morning. 'I have to look for somewhere to live. Beth kept us awake again last night. She woke Tim and Hetty was so tired she asked if I could find somewhere else.'

'Well, I suppose it is a bit much with two children crying,' Aunt said. 'No, of course I don't mind, Maggie. You can leave little Beth with me. It will be easier for you if you go alone.'

'Are you sure it isn't too much for you? You must tell me if it is, because I don't want to take advantage. You've had her a lot recently and looking after a small child is tiring.'

'I never heard anything so ridiculous in my life! What put that into your head? Did someone say something?'

'No, of course not,' I said but I couldn't look at her. 'I've got to help Belinda with the breakfasts now. Thank you for all you do for me.'

I went through to the kitchen. Belinda looked at me oddly, but didn't say anything as I got on with my work. After breakfast I went upstairs and started on the bedrooms and toilets. It was past eleven when I finished. Beth was engrossed with a pile of brightly-coloured bricks in the annexe. She clamoured when she saw me and I picked her up, giving her a cuddle before I went into the kitchen.

Belinda wasn't there so I made a start on the vegetables and then looked at the meat pie in the oven, which was cooking nicely.

Today, the residents could choose between steak and kidney pie, a quiche or ham and a jacket potato. Belinda had made a start on the deserts but I made a treacle tart and an upside-down apple cake. I had just popped the apple cake into the oven when Belinda walked in. I could see from her face that something was wrong.

'What is it?'

'I've just had an argument with my aunt. You told her what I said to you, Maggie. You promised you wouldn't but you must have said something. She told me to mind my own business. I wasn't interfering. She does look very tired sometimes.'

'She offered to look after Beth while I popped out to see if I could find somewhere to rent. I asked if she was sure it wasn't too much trouble. I promise that's all I said to her.'

'Well, she accused me of all kinds of things, including being jealous of you,' Belinda said and looked disgusted. 'I'm not jealous, Maggie, even if she does make more fuss over your little girl than she ever did of Hetty and me. I just thought she had been looking weary recently and I wondered if it might be running about after Beth. She doesn't put her in her cot and leave her to get on with it the way you do. She runs after her all the time and I think it is too much for her.'

'It probably is too much for her to look after Beth as often as she does, but she fetches her into her sitting room without asking me, Belinda, and she insists on showing her off to the customers and giving her cake and drinks of orange juice and milk. It has been lovely for me bringing her here, but if it is upsetting you, I can find somewhere else to leave her. I suppose she won't want to be cooped up in a cot soon. I don't know if there is a nursery locally where I can leave her. I should prefer somewhere there are other children. She won't go to school until she is five.'

'Some schools take them at four,' Belinda said. 'But don't take her away just yet, because Aunt Beth will blame me.'

'I'll make sure she doesn't. I'll look for somewhere to live today, but when I get settled, I'll find someone to take care of Beth while I am at work.'

'You don't have to move out.'

'I think it is for the best. Hetty is fed up with us being there. I shall try to find a cottage if I can. I know there is one down the smelly end, because I saw a card in a window. I don't really want to go there, but if I can't find anywhere else it will have to do.'

'No, don't go down there with that lot,' Belinda said. 'They can be a rough crowd, Maggie. The men work hard and some of them come home drunk at nights, and some of those herring girls use awful language.'

I smiled because what she was describing was very similar to the life I had known before I came to the hotel to work. Here I had learned that there was a gentler way of living, a world that held so much promise if only I could hold on to it but it wouldn't worry me if my neighbours got drunk sometimes, and bad language was something I'd grown up with even if I didn't use it myself.

'I've finished all I need to do here,' I said. 'You can manage to serve up if I'm not back in time, can't you?'

'Yes, of course. Don't hurry,' she said. 'I'm sorry if you thought I was getting onto you earlier, Maggie.'

Belinda was hard working, good-natured and generally easy going. We had gone out a few times together before I started courting and we got on well. She wasn't as good at making fancy cakes as I was, but she cooked a good plain meal and one day she would make someone an excellent wife. Belinda had no ambitions; she was content with her life, spending her money on nice clothes and the things she enjoyed. I didn't want to fall out with her.

'Of course not,' I said. 'I'm only going to look in that shop where they have cards in the window. If there is anything going at a price I could afford it is sure to be there.'

'You never know, you might just be wasting your time moving.'

'What do you mean?'

'You could always get married.'

'I've only just met Duncan again. It's far too soon,' I said, but I couldn't help thinking about it as I left the hotel and walked the two streets to the shop advertising properties to let. I had been out with Duncan many times and if you thought about it, I had known him longer than I'd known Jack before I married him. I hadn't had much choice with Beth on the way, but afterwards, as I lay in his arms, I'd known it was the right decision.'

It was stupid to look back, to hanker for something I couldn't have. Jack had gone. I had to accept that he wasn't coming back, either because he couldn't or because he didn't want to. If I'd known for certain that my husband was dead, I could have grieved and moved on, but this way I was stuck in limbo.

I studied the cards in the shop window. The cottage down what the locals called the smelly end was still available but there was nothing else that I could afford. One or two better cottages were available for short-term lets to holidaymakers, but they were far too expensive and the owners wouldn't let me have them on a permanent basis.

I retraced my steps, feeling undecided. The shop in the back street, which had rooms over the top, had been let to a new tenant months ago. I thought of it wistfully and wished that I had been able to seize the opportunity when it was available, because it was now a cake shop and always seemed busy.

* * *

Aunt Beth was sitting at the table, a cup of tea and a piece of sponge cake in front of her. My Beth was sitting on her knee being fed with pieces of the sponge; she was gurgling with pleasure and they both looked happy. It was a pleasant scene and something seemed so right about them. I couldn't put my finger on it, but seeing Aunt Beth and my daughter together gave me a feeling of coming home at last.

Belinda glanced at me as I entered and poured me a cup of tea. 'Any luck?' she asked.

'The cottage I told you about is still available.'

'It must be awful or it would have gone by now,' Belinda said. 'Besides, it smells horrible down there, especially when the wind is from the sea. You don't want to live near the smoke houses! You would hate it there, Maggie.'

'Yes, I should, but there isn't anywhere else and I have to find somewhere. I can't stay at Hetty's much longer if she doesn't want me.'

'You could always come here to me,' Aunt Beth surprised us both. 'Well, why not? You could have the annexe bedroom. You know I don't like letting that to guests, because it is too close to the kitchens and the smell of cooking seems to get in there sometimes.'

'I couldn't afford to pay what you get for it when you do let it,' I said and glanced at Belinda. She tried to hide it but I could see she was annoyed that her aunt had offered me the room. 'Besides, Beth might cry and upset your customers.'

'The annexe is out of the way of the rest of the hotel. It makes perfect sense, Maggie. It would save you the journey back and forth every day, and it would be company for me. I miss you and Beth when you leave at night—Belinda too, of course.' She smiled at her niece. 'You can pay me whatever you give Hetty if it makes you feel better.'

'Maggie's baby will be here all the time then,' Belinda objected. 'You look so tired, Aunt Beth. You really shouldn't offer to do so much for Maggie. You will wear yourself out.'

Aunt Beth glared at her. 'I thought we had all this out earlier. I think you are being very foolish, Belinda.'

'You are the one who is foolish—'

'How dare you speak to me like that?' Aunt Beth demanded. 'I am perfectly well and I shall do what I please.'

'Please don't quarrel over me. There is no need to get upset, Belinda. I shan't take your aunt's room, because I am going to get married...' I was horrified the moment the words left my lips. 'At least, I shall if Duncan asks me again.'

'Maggie, that is wonderful,' Belinda cried. 'I am so pleased. I am sure it is the best thing for you. You'll have a home of your own and if you work part time it won't be so much for Aunt to do.'

'Are you sure it is what you want?' Aunt Beth asked, concerned. 'Take no notice of this silly girl! You weren't sure you wanted to marry him, Maggie. After all, you don't know him well, do you?'

'I've known Duncan most of my life,' I said and suddenly it was all so simple. At least it was if I smothered my conscience. Jack must be dead. He would have contacted me by now if he was still alive, so there was no reason I shouldn't marry again. 'We were friends at school. He didn't ask me before he left London to work here, because he couldn't afford to be married. If he had I should probably have said yes, because I liked him and I know he is in love with me.'

Aunt Beth still looked anxious. She seemed as if she wanted to say more, but then shook her head, as if deciding it wasn't the right time. I could see that my decision had pleased Belinda. Clearly, she thought I'd taken advantage of my position here. A thought struck me as I saw an odd look in her eyes—a look of satisfaction that I might not be around so much.

It hadn't occurred to me that Belinda might be concerned for her inheritance, but something in her manner at that moment made me wonder if she'd thought I was after Aunt Beth's money. I'd believed Belinda was my friend, but if she and Hetty felt I had been scheming to get money that was rightfully theirs they couldn't think much of me. It hadn't crossed my mind before, but of course Aunt Beth was very comfortably off and had no one else to leave her money to, until I came along. Perhaps that was why they had become less friendly since their aunt showed her affection for me and my child.

'Well, if you are certain,' Aunt Beth said. 'But you must come to me until the wedding, my dear. I shall enjoy having you here, even if it is only for a few days.'

'Well...' I glanced at Belinda's face and something snapped in my head. Why did everyone always think the worst of me? I had sensed right from the start that Aunt Beth was lonely. If Belinda couldn't see that having my daughter around gave her aunt pleasure that was her hard luck. 'Yes, all right then. I shall tell Duncan tomorrow that he can buy a special licence so it will probably only be for a few days, but I will stay here until the wedding.'

I should never have said those things! I knew as soon as I'd spoken that I had made a mistake, but somehow it was too hard to take them back. Belinda was right. It would be best for Beth to have a father and I needed a husband. I wasn't the kind of woman who enjoyed living alone.

At the back of my mind a voice warned that this was wrong. I didn't love Duncan the way I'd loved Jack. I shut out the voices.

Jack had deserted me!

21

'Did you know that it is against the law to marry again if your husband is still alive and you aren't divorced?' Thomas looked at me as he put a plate of pie and chips in front me. 'Sorry, it isn't much of a meal, but I'm no cook.'

'I'll cook a meal for you later,' I promised. My eyes met his, challenging him. Of course I'd known but I'd done it anyway. 'Do you think I deserved to go in that river now, knowing what I did?'

'It wasn't a good thing to do, Maggie,' he said and looked serious. 'Didn't you think about what might happen, about people being hurt? That you could get into a lot of trouble?'

'I suppose I didn't think about how Duncan might feel if he ever discovered that we weren't truly wed,' I said and pushed the food away. 'I'm sorry but I can't eat. I feel sick when I think of what I did...'

'It was wrong,' Thomas agreed. 'You committed bigamy, Maggie. You could go to prison for that but somehow I think you have been punished enough. Why don't you tell me what happened? Didn't anyone ask you for a death certificate when the marriage was booked?'

'Duncan didn't tell the Registrar that I had been married before. We *used my birth certificate and I married him as Maggie Bailey.' It was the name Ma had given me, even though it wasn't mine.*

'And no one asked questions?

'No. Why should they? I wasn't known in Yarmouth. I don't think anyone thought it was odd. My friends were just so pleased that I was getting married and no one else knew me. None of Duncan's family came to the wedding. I don't think he told them.' I smothered a sob. 'Duncan was so happy that night, so sweet and gentle...'

* * *

Duncan looked at me as we stood together in his cottage. Aunt Beth had insisted that she would keep my little girl for the night.

'It is your wedding night, Maggie,' she told me. 'I want you to have one night alone with your husband, and you mustn't worry. Beth will be perfectly all right with me.'

'Yes, I know she will.' I kissed her cheek. 'Thank you for being so kind and for everything you've done for me, and the lovely sheets and pillowcases. I've been very lucky. Duncan's boss gave us a porcelain tea service and a linen tablecloth. Belinda and Hetty gave us a set of silver-plated spoons.'

She was silent for a moment, as if she wanted to say something, but somehow couldn't. Her hand moved towards me and then fell. I sensed she was hurting and I thought she was remembering the man she had loved and lost. The look in her eyes spoke of regret and pain and something more I didn't understand. She turned away to pour a glass of sweet sherry.

'The girls might have given you silver ones,' she said. 'But as long as you were pleased it doesn't matter. You can fetch little Beth tomorrow, but you are not to come in to work for at least three days. You can bring her with you as usual in the mornings, and you'll finish when luncheon has been served.'

'Will you be able to manage? You won't take on my hours your-self, will you?'

'I have advertised for a new girl,' she assured me. 'It won't hurt me to do my share until I find someone I like. I'm not really that old you know. My hair went grey prematurely because of an illness some years ago. I'm only in my late forties.' She hesitated, then. 'I shall miss you, Maggie. I can't pretend I don't wish you could work a full day, but Duncan doesn't want that, and you must do what he says now, my dear.'

'What are you thinking?' Duncan asked breaking into my thoughts. He must have seen something in my face, because he frowned, a flash of anger in his eyes. 'Are you thinking of him? You look sad.'

'No, I wasn't thinking of Jack. I'm your wife now, Duncan. I was thinking it was kind of Aunt Beth to look after Beth. I am not sure she is well enough to start working in the kitchen again.'

'It isn't your problem,' Duncan said and reached out to touch my hair. 'You are so lovely, Maggie. I've thought of you so often. You don't know how much I love you.'

His voice was hoarse with passion and I trembled as he bent his head to kiss me. Leaning in to him, my eyes closed as I melted into his body. Desire leapt inside me and I knew that I wanted him to take me upstairs to bed.

'I love you, Duncan. I am so glad we met that day.'

'You're mine now,' he said, his hold tightening about me. 'I don't want you thinking about Jack any more. He's gone and you belong to me.'

'Yes, of course. I told you, Jack isn't important.' It was a lie, of course, but by this time I had banished my conscience to a far corner of my mind.

Duncan groaned, crushing me against him. He swept me up in his arms and carried me upstairs. I wound my arms about his neck, holding on to him and laughing as he placed me gently amongst the sheets. I helped him take off my dress and he pulled it over my head, discarding it on the floor. Then my bodice and petticoat came off, and Duncan stared at me like a man dying of hunger. He spoke of love but when I think back it was more like an obsession. He tugged at his shirt, almost ripping it from his body in his haste to join me on the bed.

Our first coming together was hasty and over far too soon, but then Duncan began to kiss me slowly, trailing his lips and tongue over the sensitive parts of my body. I arched and whimpered as he brought me tenderly towards a climax, making me shriek and dig my nails into his shoulder as I writhed beneath him.

'Oh, that was so lovely,' I whispered burying my face against his shoulder, tasting the salt of his sweat. 'I am so glad we are married, Duncan.'

'Go to sleep,' he said in an odd voice. 'I love you, Maggie. Don't ever let me down.'

I promised I wouldn't, but I was drifting into sleep and I wasn't sure that he had heard me. I snuggled into the warmth of his body. It was so good not to have to sleep alone any more.

I murmured something as sleep claimed me. I did not know what I said, but when I woke just before dawn, I discovered that Duncan was not beside me. His side of the bed was cold and I sat up, looking for him. His clothes were gone from the chair where he'd laid them.

I got up and went downstairs. Duncan was making up the fire. He turned to look at me as I entered the kitchen.

'Did I wake you?'

'No, I don't think so. I woke up and found that you weren't there. Couldn't you sleep?'

'I'm used to getting up early. Besides, I need to leave for work in an hour. I was going to make breakfast and bring it up to you.'

'I can cook the breakfast,' I said and went to look in the larder. 'Would you like bacon, sausage and egg or just a boiled egg?'

'Bacon and egg,' he said. 'The sausages will do for dinner. I wasn't sure what to buy. You'll do the shopping in future. I'll give you some money every Friday night. You can keep what you earn for yourself and the child.'

'Thank you,' I said. 'I shall manage the money better, because I know how to make it stretch. I've had enough practice.'

'When you were married to Jack I suppose.' The glint in his eyes told me he was jealous. I hadn't realised until now how much he hated the fact that I had been married before.

'Even before that,' I replied. He'd always known about my marriage, why was he letting it bother him now? 'You know what my father was like—always drunk and short of money. I had to keep food on the table for us all: Ma, Robin and me...'

'Where is Robin? Is he with your sister?' Duncan's gaze narrowed. I saw suspicion and anger in his eyes.

We hadn't talked about Robin until now. 'Sadie gave him away. She knew I would give him a home when I married, but she signed him over to the church home and they wouldn't tell me where he was. I'm still trying to find him.'

'He is probably best where he is,' Duncan said. 'Besides, you've got enough to do with the house, your job, and the child.'

'Beth is never much trouble, unless she is ill. Do you like your egg cooked both sides or just one?'

Something dismissive in his tone when he spoke of Beth was disturbing. He had promised to love her because she was mine, but I was suddenly afraid that he would resent her; the way Pa had resented me. He had let Ma take me in, because, I suspected, they had received money at the time, but he had always resented the cuckoo in the nest. I did not want Beth to suffer as I had, and the first doubts began to creep in. I had married Duncan on impulse. I prayed that I had not made a mistake.

'Just one side with the yolk a bit runny.' His expression was cold and accusing. 'Did you know you spoke Jack's name just before you went to sleep? I thought it was him you wanted next to you not me.'

'Oh, Duncan!' I took the frying pan off the range, suddenly understanding this fit of jealousy. I went to him and put my arms about him. 'I'm sorry. I can't turn back time and not be married to Jack, but I would if I could. I wish you'd asked me to go with you when you left the lanes.'

'Do you really?' Duncan looked down at me, and I saw pain in his eyes. I forgave him his jealousy, because he couldn't help it. 'I couldn't help resenting that you'd been his, Maggie—had his child. Last night I wanted to be the first with you.'

'I wish you had been,' I said and reached up to kiss him on the mouth. At that moment I meant it, though in my heart I knew it was yet another lie and I shivered. My marriage was based on lies and I was beginning to understand what that might mean. Duncan pulled me towards him, gathering me into his arms and starting towards the stairs. 'What about breakfast? I thought you were hungry?'

'We'll eat later.'

'Don't you have to go to work?'

'I was going because I was angry,' he said. 'I thought you still wanted him, Maggie.'

'Don't be silly! It was good last night.'

'Do you mean that?' he asked.

'Yes, of course,' I said as he set me on my feet, his arms still about me. 'You are my husband and I love you. You have to believe me. I've forgotten about Jack. He means nothing to me now.'

I crossed my fingers behind my back as I lied. I did care for Duncan, but I knew that Jack would always hold a special place in my heart. How could I forget him when Beth had his eyes? Jack had been a charmer, always joking, making me laugh. Duncan was so intense. He loved me so much that I found it a little oppressive, almost frightening.

* * *

Duncan took me to see the boat yard later that day. He was very proud of his place of work and what he was doing. I had to inspect their latest project, a wherry that would be sailed up the Broads to Norwich when it was finished. It would be used for carrying goods like wood to the yards and for bringing back leather and other goods that would be loaded on to sea-going vessels at the Yarmouth docks.

Afterwards, we went for a walk along the front and then Duncan took me out for a fish and chip meal. He gave me some money and I did some shopping from a local shop. Their prices were expensive and I didn't buy much, because I knew I could do much better in Yarmouth. It was late afternoon when I went to fetch Beth.

Belinda looked at me angrily when I went into the kitchen.

'Where have you been?' she demanded. 'Aunt Beth expected you this morning.'

'I'm sorry. Duncan took me out and I thought it wouldn't matter if I was a little late.'

'Well, it did. My aunt had a little turn and she is in bed. I've had all the work to do and your child to look after. She has only had cake and milk, because I didn't have time to sit and feed her properly. She was crying and playing up because she wanted you.'

'She is usually so good with Aunt Beth,' I said. 'I'm sorry you've had it all to do, Belinda. Is there anything I can do before I pop up to see your aunt?'

'She is sleeping. The doctor gave her something to help her. He said she has been doing too much and ought to rest more.'

She meant it was my fault. Aunt Beth had been looking after my Beth all night and it was too much for her. Belinda had warned me that her aunt's health was not all it should be but I hadn't listened.

'I am very sorry. She suggested having Beth. I asked if she was sure.'

'You know she would never admit defeat,' Belinda said and looked worried. 'It isn't your fault. The doctor says it has been coming on for a while. It is her heart. If she doesn't take things easier, she could keel over and die at any time.'

'She must rest,' I said, feeling shocked. 'She told me not to come in for three days but I'll be here as usual tomorrow and I'll work for as long as I can, though I'll have to be home in time to get Duncan's tea.'

'What about Beth? My aunt can't look after her.'

'I'll ask Duncan if he knows anyone who would look after her while I'm at work or I'll put her in her cot in the annexe.'

'All right. I'm sorry I got on at you, but I think the world of her, Maggie. I don't want her to die. I'm not sure I could run this place alone. Hetty doesn't want to know. She has Tim to look after and Aunt Beth has always done the booking and talked to the customers. She was going to teach me but she never got round to it. If anything happened to her, we might have to sell.'

'You don't think she will die? She isn't as ill as that, is she? She should have said something. It was her idea to keep Beth last night.'

'She will die if she doesn't stop working and worrying over this place. I can carry on for a bit, but she ought to think of selling and buying herself a little cottage.'

'This place is her life,' I said. Didn't Belinda understand that the hotel had taken the place of the husband and children Aunt Beth had never had? She loved Beth, because it was the closest she had come to having her own. 'Couldn't you do the rest of it if I take over most of the cooking?'

'We're getting another cook,' Belinda reminded me. 'But I don't think I want to dedicate myself to the hotel the way my aunt did, Maggie. It has worn her out and it will do the same for me. If she sells up, I might get married sooner than I had planned.'

It was what she really wanted, a home of her own to keep nice and some children.

I went through to get Beth. Her face was dirty and she smelled of pee as I picked her up. Belinda hadn't put her on the pot and she was soaked through her knickers and her dress. I couldn't blame Belinda, because it was my fault. I had been making love with Duncan when I should have been fetching my daughter. It upset me because I had neglected her. Belinda couldn't look after her and cook all those breakfasts alone. Beth was my responsibility not hers.

'I am sorry, my darling,' I whispered. 'Mummy won't leave you so long again.'

* * *

Duncan didn't want me to go back to work so soon. He frowned when I came downstairs after settling Beth. She had grizzled a bit, perhaps because she was in a new place or because her bottom was a little sore after being wet for most of the day.

'I don't see why you have to go in tomorrow,' he grumbled. 'Miss Brown gave you another two days off and you will need to get used to the cottage.' He refused to call her aunt and seemed as if he wanted to set a distance between us. 'After all, she isn't really your relation, is she?' I shook my head but inside I felt closer to her than I did to him.

'I can tidy up a bit this evening. I promised Belinda I would do my old hours, just until the new girl arrives. It should only be for a few days. Aunt Beth has been really good to me. I can't let her down when she is ill.'

'I don't see why you should give up your days off. You're married now, Maggie. I don't want you wearing yourself out working at that place. You could probably get a few hours at the local shop here if you asked. I saw a notice asking for a part time worker this morning. You don't need to work as hard now.'

'I don't want to work in a shop, Duncan. I am a cook and I've got a certificate for cake making. It would be stupid to waste it and Aunt Beth has been good to me.'

'I don't know why you call her that. She is no relation of yours.'

'I know, but she asked me to, and it is nice to be on good terms. I've enjoyed my time at the hotel.'

'Well, I shan't forbid you, but I want you home in the afternoons as soon as that new girl starts. You're my wife and I would rather you gave up work than work yourself to death.' He came towards me, looking serious. 'You shouldn't let people use you, Maggie. You don't need them now you have me.'

I knew that he was jealous. Why should he be jealous of my employer? Was Duncan going to be jealous of everyone and everything in my life? Would he be jealous of Beth?

* * *

Aunt Beth stayed in bed for just over a week. I went up to visit her in her room a few times and she thanked me for coming in to help Belinda out until she was on her feet again.

'Did your husband mind?'

'No, of course not,' I lied. I'd discovered that it was easier to lie than to tell the truth.

'The new girl starts tomorrow,' she said and reached for my hand as I sat on the edge of her bed. She was wearing a pink nightdress and bed jacket, and she looked rested and younger than when her hair was pulled back in a severe knot at the back of her head. I thought that she must have been pretty when she was young, but grief, loneliness and hard work had aged her beyond her years. 'You will be on your new hours then and I'll be down soon to look after Beth. I've missed her so much.'

My fingers closed round hers. 'Didn't Belinda tell you? I've found someone to take care of her from tomorrow. I've managed with her here this week, but it has been very difficult. Her bottom got a bit sore the other day, because she was wet and it made her cry.'

'You will only be earning fifteen shillings,' Aunt Beth reminded me. 'Will it be worth your while, Maggie? I don't want to lose you too soon.'

I didn't answer her at once, because Duncan had said the same thing that morning before I left for work, and we'd had our first real quarrel.

'By the time you pay your bus fare it will be a waste of time. You could earn more at the shop and be home sooner. Just because that woman gave you a job when you first came here you don't have to stop there now. You should be glad to take it easier and look after your home and me.'

'But I owe her so much...' I sensed violence in him and it made me uneasy. *'Please try to understand, Duncan.'*

'Don't be so bloody daft, Maggie. She got her money's worth out of you, don't you worry.'

'That's a horrible thing to say. Aunt Beth has been so good to me.'

'She isn't your aunt! I'm your husband and I want you to give in your notice. I mean it, Maggie. If you stay there, she will have you working all hours and you won't get a penny extra.' His fists curled at his side and he was almost shouting. *'She takes advantage of you.'*

'*She isn't like that.*' *I was close to tears.* '*You don't know what you're asking.*'

'*I'm asking for you to act like a wife,*' *he said and slammed out of the house.*

'It won't leave me much when I've finished,' I told Aunt Beth reluctantly. 'But I should like to stay, at least until the new girl is settled and you are feeling better.'

She nodded, her eyes intent on my face. 'Duncan doesn't want you to work here, does he?'

'He says I could do a few hours nearer home and have more time to look after things.'

'He wants you waiting with his tea on the table,' she said and nodded. 'It is understandable, Maggie. You can't blame a man for wanting his wife to put him first.'

'That is the trouble. I can't always. I have to look after Beth when she needs it, and if she cries in the night I have to get up and settle her. Duncan doesn't think I should make so much fuss of her. He thinks I should leave her to cry but I can't...'

'It isn't easy to get used to a new way of life,' she said and squeezed my hand. 'You must learn how to balance the time you give to Duncan and the time you give to other things. Just remember that she isn't his child.'

'I'm not sure it would make a difference if she were.'

'What do you mean?'

'Duncan seems jealous of everyone and everything in my life. He wants all of me and there is no room for anything else.'

'I've heard that some men are like that. I expect it is because you are just married and he is anxious about how you feel. You were married before and that is bound to make him a little jealous. He will get over it in time, I'm sure.'

'I've told him that Jack isn't important,' I said. 'But I love Beth. She is my daughter. When she cries I want to comfort her.'

'That is natural, but you must take things slowly I am sure Duncan will become less intense when he is sure of you.'

'Yes, of course he will,' I agreed and leaned down to kiss her cheek again. 'You are not to worry about me. I shall come in tomorrow as usual and you must rest.'

I returned to the kitchen. Aunt Beth was always concerned for me, but she didn't understand what it was like to live with a man like Duncan. He was so intense about me, so passionate and angry when I did something he didn't approve of. When we made love, it was good. I was fond of him, but I had soon learned that I was not truly in love with him—the way I had been with Jack.

Jack had become a little moody when things started to go wrong for him, but most of the time he had been easy going and fun to be with. I had never felt he would hurt me, even when he was angry about something. I wasn't sure about Duncan. I sensed violence in him, a passion that he could not always control.

* * *

Duncan hit me three weeks to the day after our wedding. I was an hour late getting home. It was Aunt Beth's forty-sixth birthday and we had all had a glass of sherry after the lunches were served. I had bought her a small bottle of Yardley Lavender Water and she had been thrilled with it, kissing me and thanking me, even though Belinda and Hetty had bought her a beautiful silk scarf. It must have cost far more than my gift, but she merely glanced at it before closing the wrapping paper. She took my perfume from its wrappings, opened it and dabbed some on her hanky.

'You always know what I need, Maggie,' she said. 'Mine was almost finished and it helps me when I have a headache.'

'Do you often have headaches?' Don't forget the doctor says you should rest more.'

'He is an old woman. Drink your sherry then, Maggie. You had better go or you will miss your bus.'

I had been reluctant to leave her, because she looked so fragile and I sensed the loneliness in her so I delayed longer than I should. I arrived at the bus stop just as the bus was leaving. I waved my hand frantically but it didn't stop. I knew that I would have to wait for another hour for the next one so I decided to do a little shopping. Meat was cheaper at the butcher here than where we lived, and if I bought the cheaper cuts, I could make a nice casserole or stew that would last us nearly a week.

I collected Beth and hurried home, wanting to get the tea on before Duncan came home. The door was unlocked and as I rushed in, I saw that he was sitting at the table, drinking a glass of beer.

'Where have you been?' he asked suspicion in his eyes. 'You're late—an hour late.'

'It was Aunt Beth's birthday,' I replied. 'We had a sherry and I missed the bus so I did a bit of shopping. I bought a nice bit of scrag end. It will make a lovely stew.'

'I'm tired of bloody stews! I want a proper roast or a good chop.'

'You didn't say. I was trying to make the money last.'

'Are you saying I don't give you enough?' he demanded. I put Beth on the settee and she got down immediately, toddling towards Duncan. She pulled at his trouser leg the way she had with Aunt Beth's customers. Instead of picking her up or giving her a sweetie the way the hotel guests did, he kicked her off and she screamed in fright. 'Keep that damned kid off me...You haven't answered. Do I give you enough money?'

'Don't do that to her!' I cried, snatching Beth up and carrying her upstairs to her room. I soothed her and put her to bed. 'Mummy will bring some milk and cake soon. Don't cry, darling. Duncan didn't mean to hurt you.'

I didn't think Beth was badly hurt. Duncan had just shaken her off and she was startled, because everyone at the hotel had made such a fuss of her. She couldn't understand that he didn't want to pick her up.

The door slammed. When I ran downstairs Duncan had gone. I crossed to the window and looked out but didn't call him back. I made the stew because it was all I had, leaving it on the range to cook while I went upstairs to wash and feed Beth.

Duncan hadn't come home by nine-thirty so I banked up the fire and set the table for morning. I had never known him to stay out late like this and I was worried when I went to bed a few minutes before ten.

I looked in on Beth, who was sleeping soundly then undressed and got into bed. A crashing sound downstairs woke me. Someone was down there!

I got up cautiously and crept down the stairs in my nightgown. Duncan had lit the gas lamp, but a chair had been knocked over. He was standing by the table and it looked as if he were trying to pour himself some beer from the jug we kept in the cold pantry, but he was spilling it.

'Don't you think you've had enough already?'

Duncan whirled on me, his eyes wild. He reminded me of Pa and I took a step back instinctively. My mouth was dry and my heart thundered. I was remembering the way Pa had beaten Ma when he was drunk, eventually killing her. Duncan was just like him! The jealousy and passion churning inside him had turned to violence.

'Damn you, Maggie!' he roared and lashed out at me with his fist. He struck me in the face and I staggered back. 'Stop nagging me, woman! Can't a man have a drink in his own house now? Bloody babies and Aunts... drives a man to drink!'

As I watched, stunned and sickened, he staggered to the settee and flopped down. He attempted to drink what was in his glass and it tipped over his shirt. He swore and dropped it on the floor, the beer spilling out as he stretched out on the settee and closed his eyes.

'You disgust me!' As I said the words, I felt it was true. His behaviour was a mirror image of the man I'd believed to be my father for so many years and it sickened me. What had I done? How could I have been such a fool as to marry this man? The signs had been there if I'd thought about it more—the intensity, the jealousy, but hidden. I'd just rushed into it because I'd felt pressured to find a new home for us and Duncan had seemed the easy way out. It was thoughtless and selfish on my part and now I was reaping the harvest I'd sown.

I felt the sickness swirling inside and I made a rush for the sink, vomiting the bitter tasting bile. I was numb all over, unable to believe this was happening to me. The nights I had listened to Michael Bailey hitting Ma, listened to their rows and vowed it would never happen to me.

What a fool I'd been! I walked slowly upstairs, going into Beth's room and locking the door after me. I sat in the nursing chair I had bought recently, looking at her in the dim glow of the night-light. How could I have been so stupid as to marry a man I didn't know? I had seen the jealous intensity in Duncan's eyes when he looked at me, but I had mistaken it for love. He had promised to be good to me, but ever since that first night when I had unwittingly spoken Jack's name as I fell asleep, he had been feeding on his jealousy. It wasn't just because I had brought home cheap meat. He was jealous and angry because I had stayed a little later to celebrate Aunt Beth's birthday. He couldn't bear me to care about anyone else. He was obsessive about me, dangerously so.

I should never have married him! I had known in my heart it was wrong. I wasn't sure why I had done it. It was an impulsive act that I bitterly regretted. I had never regretted my brief marriage to

Jack, even though he'd run away and left me to look after his mother and our child. I wasn't sure if he had deserted me, or if something had prevented him coming home but I knew I missed him.

'Oh Jack, why did you leave me?'

I sat for a long time just looking at my child sleeping peacefully. How could I stay with a man who resented her? He might turn his violence on her. That thought terrified me. He could kill her in a drunken rage.

Michael Bailey had been a reasonable husband and father until he came back from the war, a man changed by the horrors he'd seen. I had been married to Duncan for three weeks and already he had struck me. He was worse than Pa had ever been.

I put my hand to my cheek. It felt tender and I knew there would be a bruise. I couldn't be bothered to bathe it in cold water. I wasn't going to try and hide the bruise the way Ma had when Pa hit her. Duncan could live with the results of his handiwork until I left him. It suddenly came to me that I should leave now. Why should I wait for him to do it again? He had lost all right to my respect by hitting me. He was drunk and he might not have realised what he had done, but in my eyes that did not excuse him.

I had a little money put by. Quite a bit more than I'd had when I came to Yarmouth. I could manage until I found a job and somewhere to live. I stood up and went to my own room. Lighting the lamp, I eased my wedding ring from my finger.

I searched through my things until I found Jack's ring. I had thought about selling it after I married Duncan, but now I was glad I hadn't. Jack was my real husband. Duncan and I had gone through a marriage ceremony but he wasn't my husband, because Jack might still be alive.

I was being hard not giving Duncan a chance to say sorry. If I hadn't had such bitter experiences with Pa, I might have accepted that it was just a mistake, a result of our stupid quarrel but the memories were burned into my mind. I believed that if I stayed Duncan would hit me again, and each time he would become more violent.

I wasn't going to live the way Ma had!

I packed my things, then lifted Beth into my arms as she slept. She protested a little but she didn't cry out. I slung one bag on my shoulder and carried the other. It was difficult but I only had to struggle up the road to the bus stop. 'That's a good girl,' I whispered as I crept back down the stairs. I had put my shoes into the bag. I would slip them on after I left the house.

Duncan was lying on the settee, still snoring. He must have had so much to drink to make him sleep this long! I felt disgusted, sick to my stomach. He didn't deserve a second chance. Ma had given Michael Bailey so many chances and he'd thrown them all away. In the end he had killed her.

Duncan stirred a bit as I opened the door. I froze, expecting him to wake and jump up. If he did, he would drag me back and hit me again, because I knew he would never let me leave him. He had made that plain in the first few hours of our marriage. Thankfully, he did not wake.

* * *

I was tempted to go to the hotel. I knew that Aunt Beth would take me in if I went to her for help but Duncan would come for me and cause trouble. I couldn't put her through all the stress and upset. I would write to her when I arrived at my destination, wherever that might be.

I was still wondering where I should go when I got to the railway station. I might have gone anywhere in the world, but the announcer was telling me that the next train was for London and somehow it seemed right.

Sitting on the train, I wrote a card to Aunt Beth. It was one of the humorous ones so beloved of the seaside visitor I'd bought at a booth on the station. I told her that Duncan had hit me and that I had left him. I put it in my pocket, reminding myself to post it when I got to London. I could almost see her face, hear her voice asking me if I were sure. She would probably tell me I should give him a chance to apologise.

I should never have married Duncan, never got involved with him in the first place. I had snatched at what I thought was a better life, but it had gone wrong so quickly.

Why had Duncan been so suspicious, so quick to feel jealous? He'd had no need to be. If he had treated me right, I would have done my best to make him a good wife, even though I'd known almost at once that I wasn't in love with him. Making love with him was good, and I thought that was perhaps because I had a passionate nature, and I needed the release of physical love, but he didn't make me happy in other ways, as Jack had. Perhaps I'd shown that in some way, even though I had tried to please him. Maybe he had sensed that things were not quite as they should be. I had whispered Jack's name that first night and perhaps in my heart I had wanted it to be Jack lying beside me.

My throat felt tight as I let myself think about Jack again. I had tried to shut him out of my mind and my heart for months, believing that it was the only way, but now I admitted that I still loved him. I might always love him.

I wasn't sure where I was going until I got off the train in London. Then I knew that I would ask Mrs Wayman to take me in for a while. She had offered me a bed if I ever needed it, and she would look after Beth while I searched for a job and a place to live.

* * *

When Mrs Wayman opened the door later that day she looked as if she might faint. She stared at me for several minutes.

'It's Maggie,' she said at last. 'Yer look so different... smart and your hair is different. You've had it cut in the new way.'

'Yes. I was working in a hotel kitchen and it was so hot. I had it cut and it is much cooler.'

'Who gave yer the bruise? I suppose it was a man; it always is.'

'Yes. I thought he cared about me, but he didn't. He is violent so I left him and came back to London.'

Her gaze fell on my bags. 'You've come to stay,' she said and nodded her head. 'Yer had better come in, lass. I'll put the kettle on and you can tell me all about it.'

'Are you sure I can stay? Charlie won't mind?'

'Charlie will do as I tell him. Did yer get the letter I sent last week? Is that why you've come?'

'I haven't had a letter. I'm sorry. Did you send it to the hotel?'

I hadn't written to tell her I was married, because I had been afraid that she might pass the news to others and Jack's family would find out that I had married again.

'To the address you sent me,' she said. 'When you first found somewhere to live, with the sister of that friend of yours.'

'I left Hetty's house a while back,' I said. 'She probably hasn't bothered to do anything with it yet. Why did you write to me?'

'Come into the kitchen and sit down, Maggie. I'll pop the kettle on. The little one has grown since I saw her but it must be well over a year.'

I took my coat off, glad to be able to get rid of the bags and let Beth free. I'd had to carry her most of the time, and it had been a struggle getting on and off the train and the tram that had brought me a part of the way here.

Mrs Wayman's kitchen was large and warm, but it looked shabby after the kitchen I was used to at the hotel. Regret swept over me but I pushed it away; that life was behind me.

Mrs Wayman made a pot of tea and poured it into thick, earthenware mugs, adding milk and a spoonful of sugar. She didn't speak until she placed mine in front of me and sat down at the opposite side of the scrubbed pine table.

'I don't know anything for certain, mind,' she said. 'But Sam Holmes came here asking if I knew where yer were.'

Jack's brother had come looking for me? Why? A tingle went down my spine as I stared at her.

'I'd sent Jack's brother a letter with Hetty's address but I hadn't told him when I moved out. Did he say what he wanted?'

'He said he might have a bit of news for yer, Maggie. That's all I know. I made out I didn't know where yer were, in case yer didn't want him to know but I wrote and told yer just in case.'

'Thank you, that was kind of you.' My heart missed a beat. 'I wonder what he had to tell me.'

'There's one way to find out. Go and ask him yerself.'

'Yes, I shall. Not for a day or two, though. If you wouldn't mind looking after Beth for me, I shall look for work and somewhere to live.'

'You can stay here for as long as you wish, Maggie. I've thought of taking a lodger in and I'd rather have you than anyone else.'

She was about the same age as Ma, but life had treated her better. Charlie was a good husband and she hadn't had to struggle quite as much as Ma. Plump and good-natured, she wore a blue dress that she'd made herself, and her dark hair was curled in a roll at the back of her head. I knew that her offer was genuine.

'Thank you,' I smiled at her gratefully. 'It depends where I find work. I may have to look further afield, because I want something decent. I've been earning proper wages and I'm not willing to settle for eight shillings at the bakery. I hope to find work as a cook. I should like to stay here until I find something suitable.'

'You're not thinking of leaving London again?'

'I don't know yet. I might if it is the right job for me.'

I couldn't tell her the whole truth. She would be terribly shocked and think less of me. The truth was that I was ashamed of myself for what I had done. Duncan had hit me because he was drunk, but I had married him because he could give Beth and me a home, knowing that I didn't truly love him, and that my husband might still be alive. And now I'd left him without telling him why. I had brought this trouble on myself, and I hadn't been fair to Duncan. He shouldn't have hit me, but if I'd been honest at the start, it would never have happened.

'You must do as you think best,' she said and looked thoughtful. 'It's just that... have you considered that Jack might be trying ter find yer?'

'You don't think that's why Sam came looking for me?' My heart slammed against my ribs, my mouth suddenly dry.

'Sam was a bit odd in his manner. He wouldn't tell me anything.' She took a sip of the hot, strong tea. 'If Jack was worried about something, the law for instance, well, he would go to his Ma's house first and find Sam living there. If he is in a bit of bother, he couldn't go searching for yer himself, could he?'

I could hear the mantle clock ticking and children playing in the lane, but for me the world suddenly stood still.

'I hadn't thought about it,' I said, my nails turned into the palms of my hands. 'No, he wouldn't know where to look, if Sam couldn't find the letter I sent.'

'He said it was mislaid, but to my way of thinking he threw it straight on the fire.'

'I dare say he did.'

Sam had pushed me into a hasty decision, but it was my own

fault that I had run headlong into the worst mistake of my life. I should have come here to live when I left the cottage and stayed in London. By running away, I had made it impossible for Jack to find me if he came looking, and I had betrayed him by going through a bigamous marriage with another man.

I felt shivery. Mrs Wayman pushed the mug of tea towards me and I drank it, feeling the hot tea scald my throat as I gulped it down. My hand was shaking and I had to hold the mug with both hands.

'Put yer head between your knees,' Mrs Wayman told me. 'I'm sorry, lass. I didn't mean to upset yer like that.'

I took a deep breath and the world steadied. 'It isn't your fault. I thought he must be dead because it has been so long.'

'Well, you never know with men,' she said. 'Your Jack isn't a bad man. You mustn't hold it against him if he comes looking fer yer, lass. We all of us 'ave our burdens to bear, and by the look of yer it ain't been too bad fer yer recently.'

'I was lucky...' I'd had things easy, working for Aunt Beth at the hotel. If I hadn't married, I would still be there. What had possessed me to say I would marry Duncan? Jack had been missing less than two years! What would he think if he discovered that I had married someone else?

22

I stood looking out at the dirty street, watching rain trickle down the windows and felt trapped by the memories. It was like seeing a film in my head, violent scenes between Ma and Pa — and the funeral. I heard Sadie screaming at me, felt the shock as Ben slammed the door in my face. I saw Jack's guilty eyes as he told me Robin was gone. Ann had spat in my face, blaming me for Katie's illness and then Molly had died, leaving me alone.

I had tried so hard to find a new life, to make things right for Beth and me but then Duncan had hit me because he said I nagged him. Once a man started to hit you, he didn't stop. Michael Bailey had killed Ma. I wouldn't live with a violent man.

A siren sounded out on the river. The fog was starting to come down now that the rain had finally stopped, stealing in from the river and cloaking the sounds of the city. Everything seemed far away as my mind tried to make sense of what had happened to me.

Jack might still be alive! The thought filled me with hope and yet following on the hope came despair.

Jack would be disgusted if I told him the truth. He would never want to see me again once he knew what I'd done. It seemed to me that I had only one choice. I must disappear again, and this time it would be for good. I couldn't tell anyone where I was going, because if either Duncan or Jack found me, I would be in trouble.

Disappearing would be the sensible thing to do, but in a tiny corner of my mind a little voice kept telling me that I still loved Jack and I wanted to be with him. Supposing I didn't tell him about Duncan? Supposing we just went away somewhere that no one knew us? If he had been hiding from the police he wouldn't want to be seen where he was known. We could leave London. We might even go abroad somewhere. The church home had told me that Robin might be in Canada or Australia. Those countries wanted people from Britain to go and live there. I'd read somewhere that you could get some of your fare paid for you if you wanted to emigrate.

I was beginning to think more clearly now. I had to calm down and work this through. Duncan might wait for a while to see if I came home. He might not realise for a few days that I had left him.

I needed to know if Jack was still alive. Whatever happened in the future I would always be haunted unless I had the answer to that question. So I would go to see Sam in the morning. If Jack was alive, I would go to him wherever he was staying. I knew I ought to tell him the truth at once and take my chances, but if I did that I might lose him. I was confused, uncertain what to do for the best. Once again, I had to make a choice, and I'd made so many bad ones.

* * *

In the morning I put on one of my better dresses. A pale green in colour with a dropped waist and a white collar, it was something I had made myself from material Aunt Beth had given me and good quality. I had a string of beads I had found somewhere on a market stall and Jack's wedding ring on my hand. My shoes were white, bought for my wedding to Duncan.

'You look very smart,' Mrs Wayman said when she saw me. 'Quite the modern young lady. Are you going to look for work?'

'I shall go to Sam's house first. I expect he will be at work, but his wife may know something. If she doesn't, Sam can come this evening after he's had his supper and tell me whatever it is that he thinks I need to know.'

'That's right, Maggie,' she said and looked pleased. 'You acted a bit strange last night, but it was such a shock for yer. I dare say you're feelin' better this mornin'?'

'Yes, much better,' I said. 'I had accepted that Jack was dead, but if he is alive...'

'Yer mustn't set yer 'eart on it, Maggie. It were only my way of thinkin'. I don't know fer sure.'

'Of course not. I shan't be long. Beth shouldn't be much trouble. She'll use the potty if you sit her on it and she eats anything. I may look for work after I've been round to Sam's house, but I'll only be a couple of hours or so.'

'She could never be a trouble to me, Maggie. She is a little darling, a real charmer.'

'Yes, she gets that from Jack,' I said and smiled. 'Wish me luck?'

'For a job or news about Jack?'

'I'm not sure.' I crossed my fingers. 'Perhaps both.'

'You'll be all right lass. You're strong. You'll pull through it whatever the news.'

I left her house and walked the two streets to Sam's cottage. Why had I let him talk me into leaving it? If I'd thought things through, I might still have been living there. I would have had to take in lodgers, but I wished with all my heart that I'd taken the option.

I knocked at the door. No one came immediately and I was about to turn away as it opened.

'Yes, can I help you?'

'I wanted to see Sam. He came asking for me.'

'Maggie?' Jane stared at me in shock. 'Is it really you? You look so different... posh.' She was wearing a washed-out blue dress and her hair was scraped back untidily. From behind her a child's voice called to her and the bump beneath her dress was evidence of another baby on the way. It was hardly surprising she looked tired. This must be her fourth!

'It's my hair,' I said. 'I had it cut properly and I made the dress myself.'

'It suits you,' Sam's wife said, a slightly envious expression in her eyes. 'You must have done well fer yerself, Maggie.'

'I had a good job but I had to leave.'

'Sam is at work. I know he wants to see you for somethin' but I don't know why.' A dog had started to bark inside the cottage and the child was crying. She glanced over her shoulder as a little girl tugged at her skirt. 'Be quiet, Mary! Kids, they drive you mad!'

'Will you tell Sam I am staying with Mrs Wayman for the time being, though I may move on soon. I am looking for work, and it may not be round here.'

'You're not goin' back to the bakery then?'

'They don't pay enough. I want a decent place to live and someone to look after Beth when I'm at work.'

'I could do that fer a few bob,' she offered. 'I would have said before but you seemed set on leaving.'

'I thought I could make a new start somewhere else, but it didn't work out. I decided to come back here until I find another job that suits me.'

Jane looked over her shoulder as the child screamed again. 'Do you want to come in?'

'I'm going to see what jobs are going. I thought I would try up West; they pay better money in some of those restaurants than I could earn round here.'

'They will employ you when you look like that,' she said and chuckled. 'Sam says you're a real good cook, better than me.'

'Sam and Jack's mother taught me a lot of it,' I said. Jane could have learned from her mother-in-law the way I had, but she hadn't bothered. 'I've always loved to cook and make nice things. I'll come for a cup of tea another day.'

'It's a shame we didn't get to know each other better,' she said. 'Good luck, Maggie. I hope you find what you are looking for.'

23

I left the teashop later that morning feeling slightly stunned. I had just been offered more money than I'd ever expected to earn and a place to live. They were looking for someone who liked making special cakes, and the rooms over the top were available for rent. I could pay my rent and still have a pound a week. All I needed was someone to look after Beth for me.

I would need to pay for Beth's care and if I had Mrs Wayman looking after her the tram fares would cost me several shillings, but we would have a home of our own. I would be able to feed us cheaply from food that I used for the teashop, though it wouldn't leave much for emergencies. It was the chance I had been looking for but dare I take it?

However, if I took Beth to Mrs Wayman every day, people would grow used to seeing me. Duncan could find me easily if he wanted —and so could Jack. My cautious side told me that it would be safer to go right away.

The job was so tempting that I had wanted to take it there and then, but something had made me hold back. I'd told the owner that I needed to discuss it with the friend who looked after my daughter first and she'd agreed to hold the job provided I let her know the following day.

I wished so much that I had never gone for that first walk with Duncan. If I had told him the truth then I would be free to do as I wished.

The work at the teashop was exactly what I had longed for when I took the course in cake making. I wanted to start, but the fear that Duncan might find me nagged at the back of my mind. I knew that if he found me, he would try to drag me back with him.

As I left the tram and walked down the lane towards Mrs Wayman's house, I was turning it all over in my mind, wondering if I dared to take the risk. I didn't know yet what Sam would have to say when he came that evening. If Jack was alive, it could change everything.

I opened the front door and went in. 'It's only me, Mrs Wayman.'

'Maggie...' She came to the kitchen door and looked at me. Her face was wreathed in smiles.

My heart pounded madly as I walked towards her. 'What is it? Have you heard about Jack?'

'He's...' she began and then someone walked past her into the front parlour. For a moment I was turned to stone, and then my heart skidded and I could hardly breathe.

'Jack.' I took a step towards him as the floor came up to meet me. He caught me in his arms before I hit the ground and carried me to the sofa. I opened my eyes, tears blurring my vision. 'Is it really you?'

'I'm sorry, Maggie. Oh, God! Are you all right? I didn't mean to upset you.'

'Where have you been? I thought you were dead.' My head was clearing. I noticed the way his skin looked tanned, as if he had been in the sun a lot. He looked so healthy and so handsome that my first reaction was joy. Then I remembered. He had no right to look so sure of himself! Anger erupted inside me. 'You took those things and the money and you went off without a word. I thought you must be dead. How could you, Jack? How could you desert us?

'I'm sorry, Maggie. I took the silver because it was stolen and I didn't want the coppers coming to search the house. You and Ma might have been in trouble. The clock and the rest of the stuff was all right so I left them. I thought you would manage.'

You could have told me! I would have understood. Even if you were on the run from the police, you could have sent us a letter or something!

'I was on the run from Eddie not the police,' Jack said. 'I tipped the coppers off about that stolen lorry and I told them where to find Eddie's warehouses. He would have killed me if he found out I was the one who shopped him to the law. I had to lie low for a while. And I didn't want them coming after you. If you'd known what was going on they would have got it out of you somehow.'

'Damn you, Jack! Didn't you think about how it would look to us? Molly broke her heart over you. I think it was worrying over what had happened to you that made her ill.'

'Please don't blame me for that,' Jack said and a little nerve twitched at his temple. 'I did send you a post card when I got to the States but maybe you never got it. I couldn't sign my name to it but I thought you would know it was from me.'

'When you got to America? What the hell made you go there?'

'I needed to get away fast. I signed on a ship that I thought was going to Ireland with a cargo. I didn't realise that it was going on to America from there. I might have jumped ship in Ireland if I could but I think the captain was doubtful about me, and he kept me busy below decks. It wasn't easy, Maggie. I've never worked so hard in my life and I had a problem getting a passage back here. I found work over there and living in America is better than here by a mile. I thought about asking you to come out there, then I decided I would come back and fetch you.'

'I never got your card. Molly died and I went away.'

'Sam told me. The rotten devil! He practically forced you to let him have the house. I knew he always wanted it. He didn't pay you enough for the things you left. I made him give me another ten pounds. We shall need it for our fares. We'll have a cabin, Maggie. We shan't have to work our passage this time.'

'Go to America...' His expression seemed to implore me, begging for forgiveness. I felt close to tears as the anger drained away. Whatever he'd done he was my Jack and I loved him. 'Oh, Jack, I am so glad you're not dead.'

Salty tears trickled down my cheeks as he reached out and drew me closer. I lifted my face, welcoming his kiss, pressing into his body. He felt lean and fit, a strong, healthy man. The past long months had changed him. He was different, more confident, more of a man and less the cocky lad he'd been when we first met.

Jack gazed down at me with love. 'I've never stopped thinking about you, Maggie, loving you. I always meant to come back for you and Beth. I didn't know she was called Beth, but I've seen her. She is so beautiful! Will you forgive me for leaving you? I am sorry for all the things you went through, and for the way I was before I left. I was in debt to Eddie for the van I was trying to buy and working all hours. I didn't know what he was doing for a long time but one night when we were clearing a house the people came home unexpectedly and we had to make a run for it.'

'What did you say to him?'

'I demanded the truth. He told me I was in it up to my eyes and that if he went down, I would go with him and then they stole that lorry and the cigarettes.'

'The police knew about that; they told us when they came looking for you.'

'I couldn't get away from the others at first. As soon as my chance came, I went to the police and told them where to find the lorry and all the other stuff and then I hid until it was dark. I knew I had to get out quick before Eddie realised what I'd done.'

'You should have left us a note!'

'I was in too much of a state. I knew Eddie would kill me if he caught me and you couldn't tell him what you didn't know. If he'd thought you were in the know he might have hurt you and Ma. As long as you didn't know anything, you were safe.' Jack touched my hair. 'You've cut you lovely hair. It was so beautiful, Maggie.'

'I was working in a hotel kitchen and it was very hot.' I put a hand up to my hair. 'Do you hate it? I suppose it will grow again.'

'It suits you, but I loved it long when you let it down at night.'

'I'll grow it again.'

'Will you come to America with me?'

'Yes, if you want,' I said. 'You do know that Eddie is in prison?'

'He had a lot of friends. You aren't popular if you grass to the coppers, Maggie. Eddie isn't around, but I'm watching my back. One of his friends might decide to stick a knife in me if I get careless.'

'Jack! Please don't,' I begged. 'How soon can we leave?'

I was glad I hadn't taken the job in the teashop. It had been exactly what I needed if I were on my own, but Jack was here in my arms and he wanted to take me with him to America.

Duncan would never think of looking for me in America. We would be safe there, far away from Eddie and his criminal friends. Far away from anyone who knew that I had gone through a ceremony of marriage with another man.

'It will take a few days to get papers for you. I didn't have any when I left England. It was one of the reasons it has taken me so long to get back here to you, Maggie. I had to buy some and they were not cheap. I came home under a false name, but now I have proper documents. I just need to have your name and Beth's added to them and then we can book a passage and leave.'

'How long will that take?' I was impatient to be away, to be safe!

'A couple of weeks, perhaps a bit longer. I know I said I was watching my back, but I'll be all right, Maggie love. I promise no one is going to spoil things for us this time.'

'Jack...' Guilt was making me fearful. 'Do we have to stay in London? Couldn't we have the papers sent on to us?'

'I have a reason for staying here a bit longer,' Jack said and brushed his thumb over my lower lip. There was a teasing light in his eyes. He was the charmer I had married, but older and stronger, and I fell in love with him all over again. 'I can't tell you yet, Maggie, but I shall soon.'

'You're not involved in anything illegal again?'

'I'm not that stupid,' Jack said. 'Believe me, this is important, Maggie. I will tell you all about it just as soon as I can.'

I wanted to leave now, this minute! Just take Beth and run as far and as fast as we could, but how could I tell Jack why we should go?

The regrets tumbled in my mind. Why did I let Duncan believe I was a widow? Why did I marry him when in my heart I'd known that Jack might still be alive? It was Jack I loved, not Duncan. Duncan had sensed it and that is why his jealousy had made him violent. I'd done everything wrong! I'd made mistakes and I regretted them but surely, I was entitled to another chance?

Something was warning me to leave now. I should have told Jack the whole truth then and there, but I was trapped in a web of deceit. Jack was looking at me oddly, as if he sensed something was wrong.

'You don't hate me, Maggie?'

'Oh Jack! Maybe I should but I can't.'

'That's all right then.' He grinned confidently. 'Mrs Wayman says I can stay here with you and Beth until we're ready to leave. If you put Beth to bed she will look after her for us and we can go out somewhere. You look so smart, Maggie. Have you got another nice dress that you could wear to go dancing? I've always wanted to take you dancing. We'll go to the Pally this time, but once you're sure of yourself I'll take you somewhere decent.'

This was a new Jack, a Jack with money in his pocket. He was offering me the kind of life he had talked about before we got married. As he talked, I realised that he had found a good life in America. He had a job and a place for us to live when we got there. Nothing had been left to chance. It was a golden future and I could see it glittering before me. Just a few steps away.

* * *

'I love you so much,' Jack said as he held me to him that night. I snuggled into the warmth of his body, feeling happy and loved. 'I missed you every second I was away. Did you miss me?'

'You know I did,' I said, pressing myself closer. 'You broke my heart, Jack. I thought you would come back at first, but then I made myself accept that you must be dead.'

Jack's hands stroked my hair, then down the arch of my back. His touch sent shivers running through me. I moaned softly with wanting. I wanted to stay like this forever, to block out the thoughts that were casting a shadow over my happiness.

How could I be happy when it was all based on lies? But I was afraid to be honest. Afraid of losing him again.

As Jack began to stroke and caress me again, bringing me slowly but surely to a climax, I pushed the fears away, giving myself to him completely. I cried his name as my nails scored his shoulder and I shuddered convulsively as the pleasure broke over me in waves.

I prayed that nothing would happen. Please let Duncan stay away until we were on a ship heading for America. Please don't let anything go wrong this time. My prayers were frantic and selfish, but surely, I was entitled to some happiness?

'I love you...I love you...' I whispered as Jack held me. 'Whatever happens to us, Jack. Never forget that I always loved you.'

* * *

Jack went out early the next morning. He had things to do, business and our papers to sort out. He told me to take things easy and buy some new clothes for Beth and myself to ship with us to America. He gave me a crisp white five-pound note.

'I don't need all this, Jack. I've got several dresses I like and Beth grows out of things so quickly. It is a waste of money to buy too many at a time.'

'Well buy something you like and keep the rest for when you need it. I want you to have nice things, Maggie. I've got a good job over there and we'll live twice as well as we could here.'

'I think I'll take Beth and visit Jane this morning. I saw someone about a job yesterday, but I shan't need it now so I'd better go there first, and then to Jane's.'

'You do what you want, love,' Jack said. 'I shall see you this evening.' His fingers stroked my cheek. 'Don't look so worried, Maggie. I know things haven't worked out in the past, but that is all over. I am going to look after you from now on. You might even get that teashop.'

He was offering me too much; it was as if all the things I had ever wanted were there for the taking. I was terrified that something would happen and it would all disappear into the mist.

'You know it is what I want,' I said but I was too tense to smile. 'If I could have that as well as you and my children it would be perfect.'

'You think we shall have more?' he teased.

'After last night I should say it was inevitable it will happen one of these days, if it hasn't already.'

Jack chuckled and set off whistling, well pleased with himself. I took Beth and caught the tram heading up West. I got off when I saw the teashop and went in to tell the owner that I wouldn't be able to take the job. She wasn't too pleased with me, but accepted my decision.

'I have other applicants. Perhaps in the future you may change your mind?'

'I don't think so. My husband is taking me to America.'

'I thought you were a widow. I must have been mistaken.'

I smiled but left without answering. The streets of London were teaming with people hurrying through the gloom of a damp morning; grime coated the facades of public buildings and historic landmarks alike. London was a city of contrasts: huge, important buildings, ancient palaces, pleasant parks and the mean streets of the slums. It had been home to me once, but as the tram rattled its way back to the docklands, I knew that it no longer held anything for me.

24

Jane welcomed me to her home, looking anxiously at my face. It didn't smell as sweet as when Molly and I had lived there and there was an air of neglect, the horse brasses dull from lack of polishing.

'Is everything all right, Maggie?'

'Yes,' I lied to her. 'Everything is perfect. You knew about Jack when I came yesterday, didn't you?'

'Sam did tell me, but he made me promise not to tell anyone. I wanted to, Maggie, but I knew that Jack would come round to you once Sam told him. So I went to his work as soon as you'd gone.'

'Jack was there when I got home in the afternoon. He has explained everything. It was Eddie he was in trouble with not the police.'

'Sam told me. He would still have helped him even if it had been the police, but he was relieved it wasn't.'

'Yes, I know what you mean. Sam couldn't afford to break the law. He has his family to take care of and he wouldn't want to put you in jeopardy.'

'No, he wouldn't. Jack made him pay extra for the stuff he had off yer. If I'd known it was worth so much, I would have told him before yer left.'

'It doesn't matter,' I said. 'I hope it hasn't made you short of money?'

'We can manage. Sam works hard and he doesn't drink. We save a bit for a rainy day, but I may take in a lodger or some washin' if we need extra.'

I opened my purse and took out ten shillings. 'Jack gave me some money to spend. I haven't spent anything yet. Put this in your purse and don't tell either of them.'

'You shouldn't give me your money, Maggie.' Jane hesitated, but then put the money in her pocket as I shoved it in her hand.

'I know what it is like to be short.'

'I know you've had it hard,' she said and smiled. 'But it's going to be wine and roses for you in future from what I hear.'

When I left Jane's house, I called in at the post office and bought a postcard. I would write a note to Aunt Beth and tell her I was fine and thinking of going abroad to live. I'd been fond of her and wondered if she was well and happy but of course she had her nieces to care for her. I thought she'd been genuinely fond of Beth and me too, perhaps, but she would soon forget me now that she had a new girl working for her at the hotel. She'd been kind to me and I wouldn't forget her but I had to put that time behind me and forget.

* * *

This should have been a happy time for me with all the promise of a bright new future, but the shadow of fear hung over me. My guilt was eating at me, reminding me that I didn't deserve my good fortune.

I was apprehensive as I walked back to Mrs Wayman's house.

A couple of women were on their doorsteps gossiping. I felt their eyes on me as I passed. They had stopped talking and I saw hostility in their eyes. I didn't belong here any more.

When I went inside Jack was waiting for me.

'We're going out this evening. Mrs Wayman will look after Beth. I thought you could do with a treat, Maggie.'

'You are spoiling me, Jack. It frightens me a little.'

He reached out to take my hand. 'You're afraid it is too good to be true, aren't you? I swear I shan't let you down this time, Maggie. I'm working in a timber yard. I've been the foreman but when I get back, I shall be the manager and we'll live in the manager's house. It will be long hours but I've never minded hard work.'

'What happened to your ideas of running your own business?'

'I'd rather stick to a good job. Besides, we'll have a business. The way you cook, Maggie, we shall soon have all the customers we want. I don't care about being rich. It's being happy with the people that you love that counts. Life isn't worth sixpence without love.'

'Oh, Jack...'

Tears misted my eyes. He was so loving and my guilt was like a knife in my breast. He deserved the truth but I couldn't bear to tell him.

* * *

Jack paid for the best seats and treated me to some chocolate toffees. We sat in the back row, his arm about me as we watched the program. The big feature film was a romance with Fred Astaire and his sister Adele, but the second feature was a Keystone Cops and we laughed and laughed, hugging and kissing each other.

'That was such fun,' I said as we left the cinema and walked home through the darkened streets. 'I enjoyed myself so much, Jack. Thank you for taking me, and for coming back for me.'

'Have you forgiven me?' Jack asked.

Of course I had! Would he forgive me if he knew the truth?

'I love you, Jack—it is enough.'

We paused outside Mrs Wayman's house to kiss before we went in. Jack drew back, gazing down into my face.

'I was afraid you might have found someone else, Maggie. Afraid you would say I didn't deserve you.'

'Oh, Jack...'

My heart ached. I wanted to tell him that I was the one who didn't deserve him but even as Jack looked for the key Mrs Wayman had given him, a shadow loomed up out of the darkness.

'You bloody bitch, Maggie!'

Duncan's voice startled me. His face looked pale, yellowish in the light of the gas lamps. I moved away from Jack, shaking my head and holding out my hands to ward him off. His expression was murderous.

'No, Duncan, don't...please don't.'

'I've been going out of my mind wondering where you had gone,' Duncan yelled loud enough for the whole street to hear. You cheating slut! Why did you leave me without a word, Maggie?'

For a moment I could not speak. Jack hadn't spoken. I couldn't look at him for fear of what I might see. He would hate me.

Anger took over as I faced Duncan.

'You were drunk and you hit me. Michael Bailey hit Ma nearly every night and then he killed her. I vowed that no man would ever do that to me.'

'I didn't mean to do it,' Duncan said. 'You're a cold bitch! Married a few weeks and you run off then I find you with another man.'

'The other man is Jack Holmes, my husband. I thought he was dead when I said I would marry you, Duncan, but he wasn't and now he's come back. He is my husband, my true husband, and the man I love. I married you so that I had a home for myself and my daughter. I didn't love you. I never loved you.'

The words were meant for Jack. I wanted him to understand, but I didn't realise how cruel I sounded. Duncan's face went a deathly shade. He flinched as if I had struck him with a whip. For a few seconds he just stared at me, and then he flung himself at me. His hands reached for my throat. He grabbed me, squeezing hard, a queer blind look in his eyes as he attempted to strangle me. In another moment, Jack had him by the scruff of his neck. He hauled him off me and gave him an almighty push so that he stumbled and fell.

'Take your filthy hands off her,' Jack snarled. 'Maggie is my wife and if you ever attempt to...'

Duncan snarled and threw himself at Jack. They started wrestling, throwing punches, kicking and yelling abuse at each other. It was horrible to witness. I screamed at them to stop but they weren't listening. Doors opened along the street. Men came out to watch what was going on, their wives behind them, some were in their nightwear, as if they had heard us while upstairs and come down to investigate.

'Stop it, please stop it,' I begged. 'It's my fault. I'm sorry...so sorry. Please don't fight over me. I'm not worth it.'

Neither of them took any notice. They just kept hitting each other over and over again, intent it seemed on killing one another, and then, suddenly, I saw something flash silver and I realised that it was a knife. It was in Duncan's hand. He had been losing the fight, because Jack was fitter and stronger, but now he had a weapon. He drew his arm back and then thrust it forward violently, plunging it deep into Jack's stomach. He screamed in agony as the blood spurted.

'No!' I cried and ran towards them. 'Kill me. Not Jack…Please, not my Jack.'

Duncan stepped back. Jack stumbled. I caught him in my arms as he fell and we sank to the ground together, me holding him. The blood was pouring out of the open wound where Duncan had pulled the knife back. I pressed frantic hands to the wound, trying to hold back the crimson tide, trying to stop it gushing out of him. It wouldn't stop. My hands were covered with Jack's blood.

'Jack…Jack, my darling,' I sobbed as I bent over him. 'Oh, my God! Forgive me. I lied and it was wrong. I thought you were dead but it was too soon…too soon. Forgive me. I am so sorry. I love you… love you so much…I never loved anyone but you…please believe me. You have to believe me. Don't leave me. Don't die.'

'Maggie…' It was an effort for him to speak. I could see the life fading as he lifted his hand trying to touch my face. 'I love you…always…'

'Don't leave me,' I begged as I pressed his hand to my cheek. 'I can't bear it if I lose you. I never loved him, Jack. It was always you. Forgive me…forgive me.'

'Maggie, your pa…'

'Shush.' I bent my head to kiss his lips. I tasted blood. As I drew back, I saw that blood was trickling from the side of his mouth and his eyes were staring at me but not seeing me. He was dead. My beautiful, charming husband was truly dead this time. 'I know, Jack. I know, my darling. I've always known. I love you so much.'

I looked up as I became aware of Duncan standing there, the knife still in his hands. 'Kill me then,' I said bitterly. 'Why don't you finish what you started? I might as well be dead now that he is.'

Duncan's eyes were filled with horror. He threw the knife down and turned. He walked away without speaking. More people were out on the street now.

'Murderer!' I heard the cry from several voices but no one followed him.

I looked down at Jack. I kissed his mouth again and then I closed his eyes. I held him, deep, silent tears falling on to his face. I felt cold inside, numbed with shock. My darling Jack was dead and I wished that Duncan had killed me too.

Duncan's hand had held the knife that killed Jack, but it was my fault. I should never have lied to Duncan. When I'd turned on him in my anger, I'd pushed him too far. I was Jack's murderer.

'Come away in, Maggie love.' I felt a hand on my shoulder but I didn't turn my head to look at Mrs Wayman. I just sat with Jack's body in my arms staring into space.

I sat there for a long time until the police came and took him from me. Even then I screamed and clung to him, trying to hold him but they tore me from him and Mrs Wayman took me inside, away from the eyes that were still watching.

Everyone in the street knew my shame now. Women would spit at me when they saw me and men would think I was a whore. I was ruined, finished—my life was over. None of that mattered because I no longer wished to live.

25

There was silence as I finished speaking. I felt as if I had run for miles and I was exhausted, wrung out with emotion, drained. After a few moments I raised enough energy to look at Thomas. He was sitting in the chair at the opposite side of the fireplace and he was frowning, clearly disturbed by my story.

'Are you thinking that you should have left me to jump in the river now that you know it all?'

'I've known it all from the start,' he said. 'From the moment you told me your name, Maggie. I let you talk, because it was what you needed. It is the only way sometimes. You've bottled it up inside you, blaming yourself for everything that happened, torturing yourself.'

'Don't you think I deserve some punishment after what I did? Duncan killed Jack and then he walked into a police station and gave himself up. He didn't wait for them to try him and find him guilty. The night you found me by the river, that was the day they found him hanging in his cell.'

'Yes, I know. It was in all the newspapers. He knew what he'd done, Maggie. He couldn't live with himself, because he wasn't really an evil man.'

'I wanted him to die,' I said. 'I've hated him so much. The bitterness is still inside me. He took everything I had.' In the past days since Jack's death, I'd lived like a ghost, lost in my misery, leaving my beloved daughter to another's care. Now, I was suddenly back in the present, hurting desperately but aware of others and thinking once more.

'And he paid for it,' Thomas said. 'It was a moment of desperation, because he knew he'd lost you. Afterwards, he must have regretted his action so much. You have to forgive him, and you must forgive yourself, Maggie.'

'I'm not sure I can.'

'But you must. You have a child to care for and...' he hesitated, then, 'I am not certain but I think I know where Robin is, if you still care?'

'Of course I care!' I jumped to my feet, a surge of excitement rushing through me. Excitement and a sense of disbelief. 'How do you know? I don't understand. You've hardly left the house since you brought me here.'

'It isn't certain yet,' he said. 'And it isn't me you have to thank. Jack made all the arrangements. He convinced the authorities that you were Robin's sister and that he would be given a proper home and a good future.'

Why hadn't Jack told me? He'd wanted to surprise me once it was certain. Oh Jack, my darling, Jack. Tears rose to my eyes once more.

'How do you know all this?'

'Because Jack came to us. I was working on the case with him.' Thomas smiled. 'Did you think it was just chance that I found you that night? I went to your friend's house to talk to you. She told me that you spent a lot of time walking by the river so I came looking for you. I asked people if they had seen you, and I found you just in time.'

'Yes...' I stared at him for several minutes and I knew he was right. 'I would have killed myself, but I was being selfish as usual, just as Ma always said. I should have thought of Beth.'

'You were grieving,' he said and pulled on his coat. 'I have to go, Maggie. I have work to do at the Sally Army's home. You are not the only *desperate woman or man. We give homes to quite a few of them and sometimes we can give them peace too.' He smiled at me. 'We need a cook. Any chance of you standing in for a while? We don't pay much, but it would cover your keep and a few bob for the child.'.*

'Maybe for a while,' I said. 'I owe you more than I can ever repay— especially if you really have found Robin. Do you think they will still let me have him back after what happened?'

'I'll do my best for you,' he said. 'No promises but I see no reason why you shouldn't get him. You didn't kill Jack, that was Duncan.'

'Because of what I did.'

'We all make our own choices, Maggie. Duncan made his.'

* * *

I was working at the Sally Army. Cooking and serving tea to those that came in needing a moment's warmth out of the chilling cold of a bitter day in late February.

'Shall we see you in the morning, Maggie?' I stopped as the young woman approached me. She was carrying a small child. Her name was Ellen, at least that was the name she gave, and she was another of Life's casualties. Thomas had brought her here when she was pregnant and near to starvation. She stayed at the home after her child was born, because she had nowhere else to go.

'Yes, I expect so,' I said and looked at her son. 'He is lovely, Ellen. He reminds me of Robin when he was a baby.'

'You haven't heard anything yet?'

'No...' It was nearly three months since the night I had stood by the river and considered throwing myself into that patch of water where the moonlight made a golden pool. 'Thomas is trying to convince them that I am capable of looking after him as well as my daughter. Sometimes I think they will never let him come back to me.'

'Can you afford to keep him on the wages you earn here?'

'It won't be easy, but I'm only here for a while. Thomas knows I can't stay forever. I shall have to look for something better soon but I wanted to help if I could.'

I was thoughtful as I left the hostel and started to walk home. Mrs Wayman had braved the gossip to keep me with her, despite hostility from her neighbours. She looked after Beth while I was at work and I was grateful to her, but I knew her husband thought she was mad to let us stay. Some people thought I should go to prison for what I'd done, but even though they disliked me no one had told the police what they had heard, and Duncan had not told them why he killed Jack. He had taken my secret to the grave, and I think that was his way of telling me he was sorry.

The grief was as sharp as ever, but I had learned to control it, to hide it. Beth was all that mattered now. My child deserved the best I could give her. I was determined that she should have a better life than mine.

I thought I might go away somewhere. Everyone knew me in the lanes and heads turned every time I passed the women gossiping outside the corner shop. They stared but did not speak. Some of them spat as I passed and one or two called me filthy names.

What did I care?

The ache inside me was still so raw that nothing anyone else said or did could hurt me.

Mrs Wayman alone had been kind. She hadn't said one word of condemnation, perhaps because she knew that I was punishing myself already. No one could blame me more than I blamed myself.

I knew that Jack's death was my fault, and Duncan's too. Hanging was a cruel end for a man whose sin had been to love too much. He had put me on a pedestal and I wasn't worthy of such devotion. He had been wracked with jealousy. I believe now that he had always known the truth, known that Jack had disappeared, but he had believed like me that he would never return. He had hit me once when he was drunk. Perhaps it might never have happened again, but I hadn't given him a chance.

Maybe I deserved the looks I got from my neighbours, but I didn't want Beth to grow up as the daughter of that woman who married two men and drove one to murder the other. I would have to move on soon.

'Ah, there you are Maggie,' Mrs Wayman said as I went in. 'Beth has been as good as gold today. She calls me Gan. I don't know where that came from but I think she means Granny.'

'I am sure she does. I've been teaching her to say it.' I reached into the playpen and picked up my beautiful daughter. What would have happened to her if Thomas hadn't stopped me throwing myself into the river.

'Was it a hard day, Maggie?'

'Yes and no. One of the residents died. She was forty-five and she looked nearer sixty. She had been ill for a long time. It was a happy release, but that kind of thing throws a shadow.'

'Yes, it must do,' she said. 'Oh, there is a package for you on the table. It has a postmark from Eastbourne.'

'Eastbourne? I think Ma's cousin lives there.'

I put Beth down and picked up the brown paper package. It was quite bulky. Inside were two sealed letters and a small bundle of white five-pound notes.

'There's some money,' I said. 'Who would send me something like this?'

One of the envelopes looked official because it had the name of a firm of lawyers printed at the top. The other one was an untidy scrawl that had something familiar about it. I opened the first and gave a little cry of surprise.

'It is a firm of lawyers in Eastbourne. They say my mother has left me something.' My throat tightened. 'That means she must be dead. I never knew her and she is dead.'

'What else does it say?'

'The lawyer wants me to go and see him. He says that there is a property in Eastbourne and some money. He has sent me twenty pounds in case I can't afford the fare.'

'That was thoughtful of him,' Mrs Wayman said. 'You must certainly go, Maggie. It sounds as if it is the best bit of news you've had in a long time.'

'I was thinking I would soon need to move on.'

'You don't have to. I like having you here.'

'I know what you've had to put up with because of me. Charlie doesn't really want us here, and some of the neighbours have sent you to Coventry because of me—haven't they?'

'Good riddance to 'em!' she said stoutly. 'You've a home with me for as long as you wish, Maggie, but you may not need it now. Sounds as if you've 'ad a bit of luck at last.'

'I shan't forget you,' I said and opened the second letter. 'Oh no...'

She looked at me in concern. 'Somethin' wrong?'

'This letter is from my mother,' I said. 'She starts by asking me to forgive her. She says that when I was on the way she had to hide it because it would shame her family. Her lover was dead and she couldn't marry...'

'There's a good many more like that,' Mrs Wayman said with a snort. 'It doesn't excuse her not getting in touch all them years.'

'She says that she did ask if I could go and stay with her but not until a short time before Ma died...' I broke off as I read the next line. 'No! How could she? How could she do that to us.'

'What is it, Maggie?' I offered her the letter and she took it, shaking her head because she didn't understand what had upset me. 'What does this bit mean? *"I wanted to tell you so many times,*

Maggie. When I held Beth in my arms. When you stayed with me at the hotel and we were alone." Good gracious! She never was....'

'Miss Brown. Aunt Beth.' I said feeling prickles all over my body as my nerves jangled. 'The name she put on my birth certificate was her proper name—Elspeth, not Elizabeth as everyone thought—and my father's name, Grange. She gave me the name I would have had if she had married my father.'

'Maggie, she's the woman you worked for in Yarmouth.' Mrs Wayman frowned as she handed the letter back. 'If you're her daughter, why didn't she leave you the hotel?'

'Because she had promised it to her sister's children,' I said. I read a little further. She begs me to keep her secret. Even though she is dead, she still doesn't want anyone to know she had a child. She can't bear the thought of the shame even in death.'

I got up, reaching for the coat I had thrown over a chair. 'Where are you going, Maggie? Don't go off like this! You're upset.'

'For a walk. I have to think about this.'

'Don't let it hurt you, love,' Mrs Wayman called. 'She isn't worth fretting over, Maggie. If she couldn't even tell you she was your mother, she wasn't much to write home about.'

I didn't answer. I couldn't. It was too much to take in. I had often wondered why Miss Brown had taken me on just like that, why she'd told me to call her Aunt Beth, the genuine delight she had shown in caring for Beth, the affection she had given me. I had thought it the kindness of a stranger, but Belinda had sensed something more. It was the reason she had been jealous. She hadn't guessed the truth but she had felt something and she hadn't liked it. She had thought Aunt Beth might leave me a part of the hotel, but according to my mother's letter no one in Yarmouth knew about the property in Eastbourne.

She was my mother, and she had never told me. Yet there were times when I had known she was hiding something, when I'd sensed she wanted to speak. She must have been so shocked when I turned up at her hotel. Perhaps she'd thought I knew but was keeping it to myself.

When she first saw me, she must have wondered if I had come to shame her. She had soon realised I had no idea who she was, and then she had fallen in love with her granddaughter. Even then she had kept her secret. What must it have cost her to keep silent all those years? I had sensed her loneliness but it was her own fault, her own stubborn pride.

We were very much alike.

Tears stung my eyes and my throat was tight. I walked with my head up, my emotions jumbled up inside me, thoughts tumbling in confusion. I had seen my mother every day for more than eighteen months, spoken to her, laughed with her, done the meanest of work in her hotel for a few shillings a week—and she had never spoken. She had never given me the faintest hint that I was her daughter. Yes, she had told me that I was a good worker; she had said I was honest and that she liked having me work for her but she'd never told me I was her child. She had never put her arms round me and told me that she loved me.

I believed she had loved Beth. Perhaps she had spent too many years shutting out her feelings for me. She had given me away as a baby because she couldn't bear the shame of having a bastard child, but it wasn't so easy to shut out the memories. I knew that only too well. I realised that I felt sorry for her, because she had missed so much—all the love that might have been between us. Now I understood what had tugged at my heartstrings as I saw her with Beth. I had never realised but they were a little alike—grandmother and granddaughter. It was too sad for words.

I could be proud and stubborn just like her. I had tried to forget Jack, made myself believe he was dead, because it was easier like that and instinctively I knew that my mother had been the same.

She'd put me out of her mind. We were very much the same, proud, stubborn women who did what they wanted with their lives and didn't think of all the heartbreak it could bring.

Jane and Michael Bailey had brought me up. They had done their best by me while I was a child, but later the resentment and rejection had crept in. I wasn't their child and they felt that they should have been given more for taking on the burden. I wondered how much Beth Brown had sent for my keep. I certainly had never seen much of it.

For a moment I was filled with bitterness. My mother had rejected me at birth. She had given me away to people who had never loved me. Everything—all the pain and the mistakes, the grief and heartaches—they had all come from that one act of my mother's. They say the sins of the father are visited on the son, but perhaps this time it was the sins of my mother. How different my life might have been if she had acknowledged me from the start.

She had written to Ma, asking Robin and me to stay with her, perhaps at her property at Eastbourne so that she could keep her secret. Had she ever intended to tell me the truth? I didn't think so. She would simply have lied, told me she was Ma's cousin, though she might have given me something.

She had left me a property and some money. Blood money! I thought angrily. She was buying off her sins because she couldn't die with me on her conscience.

My walk had brought me to the edge of the river. I stood looking down at the oily waters, watching the debris swirl in a current as the tide turned. It was dirty and cold. There was no moonlight to tempt me into a golden pool, only the stark reality. If I drowned in that filthy water the rats would come and feed on my flesh. A fitting end perhaps but not one I wanted. I laughed mirthlessly and turned away, the anger building inside me.

'Damn you, Beth Brown!' I said aloud, causing a passer-by to stare. 'Why couldn't you have told me while you were alive? I would have kept your secret.' I could have loved her so much if she'd had the courage to tell me. I would never have married Duncan. I would have stayed with her, nursed her, cared for her until she died.

Tears blinded me but I dashed them away. I wasn't aware of anyone about me as I fought the wave of grief.

'I could have loved you.' I said. 'You were my mother...Beth's granny.'

Beth called Mrs Wayman granny, but she had known her real one. It was so unfair! Why hadn't we been told? Why did I have to find out now when it was too late?

'Maggie...' I heard someone call my voice and looked round. Thomas was striding towards me through the gathering gloom. I was suddenly aware of how cold I felt. 'Are you all right? Mrs Wayman said you'd had some bad news?'

'I've had good news and bad news,' I told him blinking away my tears. 'My mother left me some money and property, which means she has died.'

'Maggie, I am so sorry.' He looked at me in concern. I had no secrets from Thomas. I had poured my heart out to him, and he knew what that meant to me. 'Why did she never get in touch with you?'

'Pride,' I said. 'She was too proud to let anyone know that she had an illegitimate child. She kept it a secret, even though I worked for her for more than eighteen months. Her name was Elspeth Brown, Beth for short, and Grange was my father's name.'

'Beth Brown...Aunt Beth?'

'Yes.' I lifted my head, tears hovering. 'She could have told me. I would have kept her secret. She could have told me!'

He reached out, holding me to his chest, soothing me, and patting my back in his own awkward way. 'It's about time you cried. You carry it all inside, Maggie. She must have cared for you. You told me how good she was to you and Beth. She has left you what she can, that's love of a kind.'

'I would have preferred a hug, a few words of love.'

Thomas stood back, his expression grave. 'How many of us do just as we ought, Maggie? We lie to people we care about, we hide things we don't want them to know, and we bottle up our feelings. Beth had kept hers inside for so many years. She was young and frightened when she had you. She must already have been running that hotel. Perhaps your father was one of the guests. He might even have been married. She had an affair and she was ashamed. She hid her shame from her family and friends...went away somewhere to have her child.'

'Eastbourne,' I said. 'She has left me the property there. She couldn't take the hotel away from her nieces because they wouldn't have understood, and she didn't want them to know her secret.'

'So she lived a lie for years, hiding her sorrow and her shame. She must have longed for you so often but she could never hold you in her arms. I think she is more to be pitied than hated, Maggie.'

'I don't hate her. I love her,' I said. 'She was so good to me. I wish that she had told me so that I could have told her that I love her.' I brushed the tears from my face. 'I was angry at first. It seemed such a waste when we might have had these last weeks together. She was ill but she hid it from us all, and now she has gone. It's too late for everything.' For months I'd lived near my mother and I'd been happy. I knew she'd cared for me and loved her granddaughter. She hadn't been able to tell me, because of the shame she felt still after so many years, but she had done all she could for me, and in my way I'd loved her.

'Not quite,' Thomas said. 'You have Beth. She is a part of your mother too, Maggie. She carries her blood just as you do.'

'Yes, I know,' I smothered the sob in my throat. 'I wish I had pictures to show her as she grows up. She was too young to remember how lucky we were to find a refuge with...my mother. I can't call her Ma. Jane Bailey was Ma, and in her way she was my mother. She had a hard life and she didn't deserve to be killed by her brute of a husband.'

'A lot of people don't deserve what happens to them in this life, Maggie. I see it and hear it every day.'

'You are a good man, Thomas. One of the quiet brigade that never gets recognised but does a lot of good for others.'

His cheeks turned pink. 'I do what I can to help. I'm only one man, but I serve as I'm called to do where I'm needed.'

'You were there when I needed you. I shall never forget you, Thomas.'

'You will be going away soon. I knew you wouldn't stay long. I offered you the job because you needed time to heal, but I think it is happening. Isn't it, Maggie?'

'Little by little,' I said. 'I shall get there.'

'I know you will, because you are strong.' He smiled at me. 'I have a surprise for you.'

'A surprise?' There was a prickling sensation at the nape of my neck. 'Robin...they will let me have him? He is coming back to me?'

'He is waiting for you at Mrs Wayman's house.' Thomas put out a cautionary hand. 'Don't get your hopes up too high, Maggie. He is a bit nervous of seeing you.'

'He doesn't know how much I love him. He thinks I knew that Sadie gave him away.'

'I have told him that you didn't. He knows that you have been searching for him all this time,' Thomas said. 'I'm not sure what they did to him in that home, but I don't think it was the good home they made out. Some of those places...well, they aren't fit to take care of kids that's all I can say.'

'Oh no...'

'I'm sorry, Maggie. He needs you, but he also needs time.'

'I have to see him!'

I walked swiftly until Mrs Wayman's house was in sight, and then I ran, leaving Thomas to follow at his own pace. I rushed in at the door and then stopped as I saw my brother standing near Beth's large, high barred cot. He leaned down to stroke her face.

'Robin...' He jumped startled, turning to me with fear in his face.

'I wasn't doing anything wrong. I wouldn't hurt her...Maggie' His eyes were dark with apprehension, as if expecting to be punished. 'You won't send me back there because I touched her.'

'Oh my darling.' I went to him, kneeling down to put my arms about him. He wasn't as thin as he used to be, but the way he tensed made me fear for him. What had they done to him at that place? 'You are Beth's big uncle and it's your right to love her and look after her. We are all going to live together in a place called Eastbourne. Sometimes I shall be working, perhaps after you come back from school, and then you can look after her for me, can't you?' He nodded, looking solemn. 'You will look after her when she starts to go to school and you will love her—we shall all love each other. I do love you so very much, Robin.'

His eyes were accusing. 'You didn't fetch me from Sadie's. She was so cross and then she gave me away. She said you didn't want me either.'

'She was wrong to say that, Robin. I've always loved you. I think Sadie was spiteful because she knew I loved you more than I loved her. I've looked for you all these months, Robin. I wrote letters and begged them to let me have you back but it was Thomas who made them let me have you.'

'Will I live with you always, Maggie?' He was staring at me, uncertain, cautious, unable to believe that I meant it.

'Forever, and ever.' I put my arms about him. His arms remained at his side, his body not flinching this time but not responding. 'I am so sorry for what Sadie did, for what other people have done, Robin. I love you and from now on it will be just us. We shall have someone to help us look after Beth when we can't, my love, because I shall have to work but there won't be anyone else in our family.' He was nearly eleven now, still a child, and he was hurting, but I would find a way to heal him with my love.

'Jack isn't coming with us? I liked Jack.'

'I liked him too,' I said. 'He can't come, Robin. He would if he could but he is with the angels now—like Ma and Pa.'

Robin looked anxious. 'You won't die, will you?'

'Not until I'm an old lady and you are grown up with a family of your own.'

'I only want you and Beth,' Robin said. 'No one else. Other people hurt you. Pa hurt Ma and he hit me. He tried to burn your face with the iron, Maggie.'

'But you didn't let him,' I said. 'You were so brave, Robin. You were looking after me that day and you saved me.'

'I'll always look after you and Beth,' Robin vowed. He looked so solemn, so intense. 'I'll never let anyone hurt you. Other people are bad but you and Beth are good. I shan't let them hurt you.'

I looked across at Thomas. He gave a little shake of his head. I wondered who these other people were and what they had done to my brother. Perhaps he would tell me one day but I would not ask. I would give him all the love I had to give—him and Beth. There would be none left over for anyone else.

'We shall look after each other.' I kissed the top of his head. 'The bad people won't hurt us again, my darling. I promise you. The bad people are gone now and I'm here.'

I gave Robin a glass of the orange juice I bought for Beth and a piece of my sponge cake. He ate every scrap and licked his fingers.

'You're the best sister in the world, Maggie.'

'And you're the best brother.'

He looked at me uncertainly and my heart caught. Robin had been hurt. We had both been hurt, but that was over. I was determined to put the past behind us and move on.

'You are safe now,' I told him. 'You're with me and friends now, Robin. Things will be right from now on. I promise you.'

He looked at me for a long moment, and then he nodded. It would be a while before he smiled and learned to trust again, but one day it would happen, because I would make it all right.

* * *

'He will be all right in time,' Thomas told me when Robin and Beth were in bed. We had walked down to the river together so that we could talk without being overheard. The fog had lifted and it was a clear night. The river looked dark and mysterious apart from a patch of reflected moonlight. 'I'm not sure what they did to him, Maggie, but I shall try to find out. Some of these homes...some people...abuse children. I believe Robin has been abused. I don't know who or what, but I shall try to discover the truth and if I do, I shall expose it. There are other boys who are still suffering.'

I sensed the anger he held inside, the need to do something about the ills of the world. 'You are a good man, Thomas. A good friend. I shall miss you.'

'I shall visit sometimes,' he promised. 'I shan't forget you, Maggie. You are one of my successes. I am counting on you to make the most of your life.'

'I am going to try. I shall see what this property is like. If it isn't suitable, I shall sell it and try to rent or buy a property I can turn into a teashop with rooms over the top.'

'You may not have to work.'

'I need to work. It is what I have always done, what I want to do.'

'What about Beth?'

'I shall employ a girl to help with her and the house. I'll need someone to live in if I can find the right person.'

'Would you do me a favour?'

'Yes, of course, if I can.'

'Will you take Ellen with you? Give her a chance. She can look after Beth or help serve in your teashop. I know it is a lot to ask but...'

'No, it is a small thing compared with all you do,' I told him. 'I like Ellen and I think she likes me. Yes, I will take her, if she wants to come.'

'Thank you.' Thomas smiled. 'You think of yourself as a bad person, Maggie, but if you're not careful you could be in danger of becoming a good one.'

'Thomas!'

I stared at him for a moment and then I started to laugh. He joined in and we clutched at each other in delight. Passers-by turned to look at us but we ignored them.

'If I wasn't dedicated to the Sally Army I'd marry you, Maggie.'

'If I didn't have Robin, Beth and a teashop to run I might marry you,' I replied, though I thought he was teasing. He must be in his forties and I still wasn't twenty. 'We would probably end up hating each other so it is a good thing we are just friends.'

'True friendship is a rare thing. I'd rather have a good friend than a dozen wives.'

'I should think so too,' I said and started to laugh again. Now I had started I quite liked the feeling.

26

The lawyer handed me the key to the property we were standing outside. It was or had been a small shop and, he told me, there were several rooms over the top.

'It would sell easily,' he suggested. 'I believe Miss Brown did intend to sell once the last tenant left, but she changed her mind about a year or so ago.'

I unlocked the door and we went in. The whole place was dusty and needed decorating, but it was a perfect size. There was room for ten tables in here and a glass counter with my cakes and sweets. I walked through to the back, discovering a kitchen and a little sitting room. Again, it needed some work, but it would look better for a clean.

'It's perfect! Just what I've always wanted. I shall turn it into a teashop and I shall sell cakes, toasted teacakes and cucumber sandwiches.'

'You do know that you also have two hundred pounds? Sensibly invested you would not need to work. You could sell this commercial property and buy a small cottage. The extra money it brought would provide you with an income.'

'I can earn what I need here. I shall spend some of the money getting it just how I want it, and I shall live over the top with my children and my friend. It may be a bit of a squeeze, but we shall manage.'

'You have three bedrooms, a dining room and a parlour, also a box room that you might have made into a bathroom for a few pounds.'

'A bathroom? Yes, that would be nice,' I agreed. 'I noticed that there is some electricity. I rather like cooking on gas or a range, but it is good for other things. I shall have to have the wiring checked and make sure it is safe.' His expression was doubtful. He thought I was too young for so much responsibility. 'Please do not look so concerned, Mr Simpkins. This is exactly what I need.'

'Well, if you are sure. I had a buyer for it, but I shall tell him it is not for sale.'

'It is definitely not for sale,' I said. 'Thank you so much for bringing me here. I shall be in touch about the money. Perhaps you could put it into my Post Office account?'

'I can certainly give you a cheque, but you could have an account at the bank now that you are a property owner, Mrs Holmes.'

'Thank you, but I like the Post Office,' I said. 'They were happy to take my shillings when that was all I had. I think I shall stay with them.' Jack had had a few pounds due to him when he died, which had been handed to me grudgingly by his brother Sam. I'd given most of it to the Sally Army, because I didn't feel comfortable with keeping it, even though it was mine in law.

The lawyer was making notes and nodding. 'Just as you please. You can collect your cheque from the office whenever you choose.'

'I shall come tomorrow.'

Suddenly I was impatient for him to leave so that I could be alone in my wonderful shop. My mind was busy with plans for buying the tables and chairs I would need. I would have blue table-cloths and blue and white china. I needed to find out where to buy everything, but no doubt my lawyer could help me. It was all so new and exciting. And it was all due to my mother—the woman I'd known as Belinda's Aunt Beth.

'Thank you, Aunt Beth,' I whispered. 'It is wonderful. Just what I wanted and needed.'

I had a new life to look forward to now and I would try not to make a mess of things this time.

I would come tomorrow and start scrubbing the floors and the windows. But first of all, I should look upstairs at the accommodation. We were stopping at a guesthouse for now but it was a waste of money when we could be living in our own home. Even though I had more money than I could properly contemplate, I wasn't prepared to waste it.

'Oh, Jack,' I whispered. 'It is what I've always wanted...' Before I'd left London I had stood by his grave, placed flowers there and said a little prayer. I'd felt then that he was with me, that he understood and didn't blame me for the things I'd done wrong.

'*Be happy, Maggie. I love you...*'

I could hear his voice as clearly as if he were with me. I spun round looking for him but I was alone. I knew he could never come back to me and yet of late I had felt that he was with me more and more.

'*I'll always be here, Maggie...*'

I felt a breath of air on my face, almost like a kiss. Jack wasn't really here with me, but somehow, I felt that wherever he was he had forgiven me for all my sins. I knew without a shadow of a doubt that Jack had loved me and I would carry that knowledge to my grave. I had known real love. I would not need to look for it again. My brother and Beth were all I needed, and Ellen, who had a sad tale and was now my friend.

'I love you,' I said. 'I wish you were here with us to share it all, Jack, but you aren't and you can't be. I have to do this right. I wanted to be with you, to fall into the moonlight and dissolve into that golden pool. I wanted the forgiveness of death but that isn't possible. I have Beth and Robin to look after, and there's Ellen too. You don't know her, but she's had a hard life—a lot worse than mine, believe me. I've got a chance now and I'm going to take it. I'm going to make a good life for all of us.'

'That's my girl...'

Tears caught at my throat because I could almost feel Jack with me in the room. I knew the voice came from my mind, from my memories of the happy times with him. We'd had such a short time together, but the memories were sweet now that I had forgiven myself. I could remember without guilt. It was enough.

'I love you, Jack, but I can't look back. I have to move on.'

I left the shop, locking the door carefully. My mind was filled with ideas for my teashop. The future had a golden glow and this time I wouldn't let go...

MORE FROM ROSIE CLARKE

We hope you enjoyed reading *A Mother's Shame*. If you did, please leave a review.

If you'd like to gift a copy, this book is also available as an ebook, digital audio download and audiobook CD.

Sign up to Rosie Clarke's mailing list for news, competitions and updates on future books.

http://bit.ly/RosieClarkeNewsletter

Why not explore the *Welcome to Harpers Emporium* series, another bestselling series from Rosie Clarke!

ABOUT THE AUTHOR

Rosie Clarke is a #1 bestselling saga writer whose most recent books include *The Shop Girls of Harpers* and *The Mulberry Lane* series. She has written over 100 novels under different pseudonyms and is a RNA Award winner. She lives in Cambridgeshire.

Visit Rosie Clarke's website: http://www.rosieclarke.co.uk

Follow Rosie on social media:

        twitter.com/AnneHerries
        bookbub.com/authors/rosie-clarke
        facebook.com/Rosie-clarke-119457351778432

Sixpence Stories

Introducing Sixpence Stories!

Discover page-turning historical novels from your favourite authors, meet new friends and be transported back in time.

Join our book club Facebook group

https://bit.ly/SixpenceGroup

Sign up to our newsletter

https://bit.ly/SixpenceNews

Boldwood

Boldwood Books is an award-winning fiction publishing company seeking out the best stories from around the world.

Find out more at www.boldwoodbooks.com

Join our reader community for brilliant books, competitions and offers!

Follow us
@BoldwoodBooks
@BookandTonic

Sign up to our weekly deals newsletter

https://bit.ly/BoldwoodBNewsletter